SHELF MONKEY

COREY REDEKOP

ECW Press

Published by ECW PRESS
2120 Queen Street East, Suite 200, Toronto, Ontario, Canada M4E IE2

LIBRARY AND ARCHIVES CANADA CATALOGUING IN PUBLICATION

Redekop, Corey
Shelf monkey / Corey Redekop.

ISBN-13: 978-1-55022-766-6
ISBN-10: 1-55022-766-1

I. Title.

PS8635.E338S54 2007   c813'.6   C2006-906797-X

Editor: Jennifer Hale
Cover Design: David Gee
Text Design: Tania Craan
Production: Mary Bowness
Printing: Transcontinental

The publication of *Shelf Monkey* has been generously supported by the Canada
Council, the Ontario Arts Council, and the Government
of Canada through the Book Publishing Industry
Development Program.

DISTRIBUTION
CANADA: Jaguar Book Group, 100 Armstrong Ave., Georgetown, ON L7G 5S4

PRINTED AND BOUND IN CANADA

ECW PRESS
ecwpress.com

For Cathy,
who never left.

For Nikki,
who left too soon.

For the Monkeys,
who won't leave me alone.

Acknowledgements

Writing a book is a solitary experience. Getting it suitable for public consumption requires a great deal of outside help.

So with that in mind, I would like to extend my thanks:

To Cathy Cotter, who always believes in me, especially when I don't;

To Miriam Toews, the first person to read the novel as a whole, and whose encouragement and excitement went far beyond the call of duty;

To my parents Marilyn and Ted, and my siblings Lisa, Nikki, and Teddy — a warm, loving, and understanding family who cannot in any way be blamed for the way I turned out;

To Morley Walker, for giving me a job at my lowest point, and actually paying me to read;

To Jen Hale, for being an exceptionally patient and understanding editor, and the rest of the ECW staff;

To Oprah;

To the publishers and staff of the 3-Day Novel Contest, whose seventy-two hours of caffeine-fuelled literary mayhem gave birth to the kernel of what *Shelf Monkey* turned out to be;

To the authors of every book I've ever read;

And to all my friends who suggested that I some day write a book. If you must blame someone, blame them.

Beware the man of only one book
— Chinese proverb

From Associated Press

SURPRISE DEBUT AT NUMBER ONE

AP — Despite not having been reviewed in any major newspaper, a small, unheralded novel has debuted at the number 1 position on practically every bestseller list in North America.

My Baby, My Love, a novel by neophyte author Agnes Coleman, was released last week to little fanfare, the inaugural publication of television host Munroe Purvis's new imprint, MuPu Inc. Purvis trumpeted Coleman's novel last month on his talk show *The Munroe Purvis Show*, yet industry analysts held out little hope of the novel making any sort of impact in what has so far been a dismal publishing season.

"This is a phenomenon; I've never seen anything like it," Coleman's agent Harold Kura crowed in an interview with Associated Press. "These are Harry Potter numbers we are seeing here. It bodes very well for Agnes, as well as MuPu."

In a press release, Munroe admits no surprise at the novel's sudden success.

"For too long, people have been told what to like, what to read, what to think. I see this novel as proof that critics are out of touch with their audiences. Miss Coleman's novel is one of great warmth and wisdom, and the only surprise I see is that people are surprised by its success."

Scrambling to catch up to its popularity, late reviews of *My Baby, My Love* have begun to surface. Most are intensely negative, with many critics labelling the book as awful or worse. A *New York Times* review called the book "facile," "borderline insulting in its banality," and "almost staggeringly idiotic."

Riding the unexpected wave of popularity, MuPu has announced that its upcoming second release, *Milk and Hugs*, will be released substantially sooner than anticipated, with its initial print run raised to 500,000 copies.

FILE # 09978

DOCUMENT INSERT: Journal entry of Thomas Friesen.
From patient files of Dr. Lyle Newhire

Tommy? Tommy-boy? Hey, Tommy! TOOOMMMMMMYYYYY?

Well, Doc, there it is. That's the voice that haunts my dreams. At the movies, during work, having dinner, enjoying infrequent sexual relations. Weeks, months pass with complete silence, life has resumed its normality, and then — ah, there you are, you little parasite, howling from your cave in the memory receptacles of my brain, sending shivers of dread down and up my spinal column, causing instantaneous paralysis and near-pants-wetting anguish.

I don't know if this is what you want, asking me to do homework on whatever strikes me as being important. Christ, are you so lazy I can't talk about this in group? I have to waste my free time writing papers to satisfy some half-baked psychiatric theory? Write it down, just put down whatever springs to mind, hey, it'll be a reverse literary Rorschach. What do you see, Doc? Repressed memories of patriarchal abuse? Childhood sexual favours with strangers in exchange for a Skor bar? A game of touch football with schoolyard chums that got a bit too, oh, shall we say, chummy? If you want to know what's bothering me, Doc, ask me, don't pussy around with this 'what I did during my summer vacation' bullshit. Write about how I feel. You've got, what, twelve years of medical training, and you've got the professional range of a substitute teacher. There's money well spent.

I wouldn't be so sensitive about this if you weren't so insistent that I not censor myself. I'm not normally so obstinate, calling you "Doc" with a snide overtone of contempt, not like me at all. Maybe something snapped loose on impact. The ganglia that monitored social interactivity severed, useless, sputtering sparks of cerebrospinal fluid all over my braincase. But hey, that's the point, right? Get all the anger out, let the ink do the shouting, then we can talk about what's really bugging Thomas lately, why he decided to not look both ways, why he just doesn't seem to be so happy anymore. Talk out the depression, diagnose, and then drug his cares away. Eradicate, then medicate. Know what? I don't feel like writing about it just this second. I'm not running from my problems, I'm postponing the inevitable. I'll face up to it when I'm ready. My dementia, my schedule.

anger issues — sees me as surrogate enemy? — could result in violent behaviour — would hospital stay be appropriate?

Tommy-boy! Hey, asshole!

Boy, he's insistent, isn't he? Much as I'd like to just scrap this whole thing, tell you to fuck off (wait, does that count as telling you to fuck off? If so, good, if not, fuck off), you lucked out and got one of those rare people who simply cannot *not* do their homework. Always on time, always typed, title page and plastic binder, that's me.

Do you know what depression is, Doc? Not your textbook definition, do you know what it really is? Depression is a nasty little boy sitting behind you in math class, flicking boogers at your head. It's standing blindfolded before the firing squad, praying that you don't shit your pants when they execute you. It's realizing that you're not you anymore, this isn't your world, you're Holden Caulfield now, lost and lonely in New York, and you hate absolutely everything and everyone for being such phonies and don't even care to figure out why. It's waking up every four minutes, insomnia grating away the world until it's a jagged smudge of motion that holds no relevance to you anymore. It's a malignant boulder in the throat that you cannot talk around. If you can squeeze a word past the granite, and oh God it's agony to speak, even a little is like a drink of scalding oil, the words are accompanied by a rush of tears that you just cannot stop! So you're quiet all the time, because you can't possibly make conversation in such a state. Can't even go to a Timmy Ho's for a coffee. Can't order a double double without freaking out and scaring the server, and once it starts, only exhaustion stems the flow.

Well, back to it, shall we? Got to hand this in, get my gold star.

Thomas, Tom, Tommy!

No one calls me that anymore, I am insistent on that. Thomas, thank you ever so much, or Mr. Friesen, if you fancy

3

the more formal address, but I prefer not to stand on ceremony. If you're one of those psychologists who strives to uncover the one defining moment in a person's life that ends up ruining that person forever, writing your doctoral thesis on the after-effects of the detritus you can fish out of one poor soul's past, well Doc, congratulations, mission accomplished, high-fives all round.

The voice even has a name, lest you conclude this is one of those anonymous bogeymen content to reside themselves in childhood closets and under bunk beds. Vikram Mansur. One of those kids everyone just knew was going to turn out juuuussst fine. Smart, composed, and oh so smooth as to be frictionless. Even by grade 5, he had already perfected the smile that wins over teachers, parents, students. The grin, slightly crooked, teeth gleaming yet not too gleaming. Open and inviting, with just a hint of veiled violence to balance the equation. An iconic smile. A smile to gain trust, cajole enemies, weaken knees, spread thighs, and ultimately save mankind. The smile of a leader, captain of the softball team, BMOC, head of the Conservative Party, CEO of one of those planet-destroying multi-conglomerates that everybody loves, like Wal-Mart or Old Navy. The menacing smirk of a bully, although only a few of us ever fully understood how bottomless the well of his cruelty really was.

TOOOOOMMMMMMMYYYYYYYY!

There's no denying it, I was a nerd, full-bore and classic. Homework done on time, conscientious and hard-working to a fault, uncomprehending that being singled out for praise by Mr. Waldmo was tantamount to joyfully pissing on the heads of my classmates. "Attention, everyone, Thomas has just written the most remarkable essay on what he did last summer at band camp. Thomas, do come up to the front, will you? Come, recite your magnum opus for the class, and be sure to speak slowly, so that your fellow students will have ample time in which to plot your death. It helps build character!" Why do teachers do that? Do they take some PTA-approved mind-altering drug during their education degrees that effectively erases all memories of elementary school? Only a few remarkable children in this universe can take such praise from an adult without paying for it later.

Oh, the myriad ways it comes back at you, Doc.

Sniggering and name-calling. Nice essay, dickwad.

Thrown erasers at the back of the head.

An "accidental" shove into a wall of lockers.

A full-bore ass-thumping on the way home after class, caught in the back alleys where you hoped you wouldn't be seen but knew that you would. My nose is still slightly bent from one of those encounters; not Vikram, Douglas Benderchuk that time. Cunt. It's minor, really, a ding, a flaw among many, an irregularly shaped pebble in a sandbox, but every photograph magnifies the curve into something approaching the sharp 90-degree turn of a surprise off-ramp.

Fuck.

But that was grade 4. By grade 5, largely due to the steep learning curve of my proper place in the universe, I had almost perfected the art of being unseen. Muted colours were my forte; old jeans, brown sweaters, nothing new, nothing remotely threatening to others. I was invisible, the shadow of a student, absent in all but the merest hint of pale saggy flesh. A vague outline dressed in corduroy. A black-belt sensei of early teen-years camouflage. My shoulders and back had devolved, forming the omnipresent turtle-shell hump of the eternally picked-on. Eye contact was taboo. Silence was compulsory. Even my odour was practically nonexistent, a delicate musk of stale air and faint terror, easily eclipsed by the bathtubs of eau de toilette the girls washed themselves in. Jocks looked right through me. I was smoke, irritating their eyes until they could focus on a target for their mindless wrath, by which time I would be long gone and some poor luckless dupe had taken my place. If it weren't for morning roll call, I would have eventually forgotten I had the power of speech.

Present!

Vikram, though, Vikram saw me. He *saw* me. In a life already devoid of everything but cool waters and smooth sailing, I was that one hidden reef he kept bumping up against. Vikram's personal mote, that's what I became — the eyelash lodged firmly in his iris, fine sand that scoured his lens and blurred his vision until he went lunatic with anguish. He couldn't sleep until I had been excised from his life. My being allowed to exist was

5

offensive to his sense of self. Why? Who knows? Go look him up if you're so interested. Maybe he was sexually abused or something. Is it wrong of me to hope that this was the case?

Yo, Tommy, you motherfucker, look up!

I can't remember how we all ended up in the school library. Someone was sick maybe, or it was raining outside, so we all had to spend recess indoors. The library was always my sanctuary. No one of importance ever hung around there, or if they did, there were enough aisles and shelves to conceal myself behind until they had gone. It was home away from home. Better than home. Warmer. A home free of worry, of the incessant probing of parents, poking into every facet of my day, well-meaning but clueless as to the factual horror life had become. My house was where I slept, where society dictated I must consume evening meals, bathe, and make small talk. The library was my home. I was not judged by the stories I read; I judged them. I was the father, scolding the novels that let me down, contemptuous of my sons Joe and Frank for solving a mystery in one hundred pages when I had figured it out in thirty, admonishing them, "Go play with that Drew girl down the street, take Encyclopedia Brown while you're at it, stop wasting my time, I've got a Roald Dahl I'm trying to get through here!" By the end of eighth grade, I had read the fiction section in its entirety. Miss White, the head librarian, would just hand new books directly to me as they arrived, a little gleam of recognition in her eyes.

mother figure?

I knew a kindred soul even then, and Miss White and I were on the same page. She had that look of uncertain fear when some of the older students wandered through, asking her stunningly obtuse research questions for their papers that seemed obvious to illiterates, so stupid these gorillas were. "Yeah, uh, where's the, you know, cyclopedias? I need somethin on rocks." Then they'd snort back a monstrous amount of snot, swallowing it with a loud glug.

classic inferiority complex

She could have destroyed these plankton. She wanted to; I could sense her desire to impart the wrong information, to give them bad grades, to fail them into early marriages and low-income housing and gas jockeydom. She never did, and I never summoned up the courage to ask why. We were both losers. She

6

had reconciled herself to this. I, however, would listen closely from behind the kindergarten section, grimacing as she spelled out the exact title and author and location in the library so these worms could find their books. Then, quickly and quietly, taking such pain to remain invisible, to keep myself vague, I crept to the shelves they were looking for, and took the books away. I like to think that there exist a few Fs and Incompletes on someone's transcript as a result of my mock-heroics. Helps me believe school wasn't a complete waste of my time. Some people may split atoms, cure cancer, or fight terrorism, but me? I got Gord Folbert to repeat the eighth grade. Good times.

You ever get lost in a book, Dr. Newhire? I mean, so into the pages, into the ink and the words and the metaphors and symbolism, just so into the story, that there is nothing else? You and the book, that's all that exist anymore. People have commented that I'm too obsessed with books, a pack rat of literature. Of course, these are the same people who come in their pants when heavily armoured figure skaters manage to flick a lump of rubber into a goal with a piece of wood. Others get themselves addicted to live-feed Internet sites, watching someone else's life unfold via digital camera and blog as they ignore the tragedy that is their own. So, who's right, in the end?

The philosophers are absolutely correct, we create our own realities, and right at that moment, in those pages, your reality is *Vanity Fair*, or *Charlie and the Chocolate Factory*, or *Less than Zero*, or *I Am the Cheese*, whatever floats your goat. These novels do not belong to the author anymore, they've been incorporated into the collective unconscious. They have become my realities, my experiences, my lives. I am T.S. Garp. I am? I was, rather. I've changed my mind, the philosophers are dead wrong, I do not create my reality. Didn't even have a hand in it. Vikram is the creator. He is the Supreme Being, he is God, and no matter what Nietzsche would have us believe, the asshole still exists. And from the POV of an eleven-year-old book geek — acne already setting up base camp for a stay of upward of a decade until they decide to retreat, leaving only residual forces behind to keep the villagers in line — for that boy, Vikram was a tyrant, a God of wrath and maliciousness.

TOMMY! TOMMYTOMMYTOMMYTOMMYTOMMY!

How could I ignore it? He sat there, two desks behind, with his coterie of greasy-haired flunkies and over-eyeshadowed prebimbos.

Hey, I'm talking to you.

I know you can hear me.

Flicking paperclips at my head. Lounging about like this was his world to rule. It was mine! My terrain! Where was Miss White? I should have fought him for it, should have stood up to him, taken the beating, done SOMETHING! I watch the scene unfold now, this paper in front of me, and I scream at my younger self, FIGHT! DON'T COWER! YOU FUCKING WUSS! But Thomas the loser just shrinks into his chair, his hair now barely visible over its moulded plastic back. *I Am the Cheese*, that wonderful novel, it is now the only refuge Thomas has, it's too small to cower behind, it's only a cheap Scholastic paperback edition, even a boy as slight as Thomas can't hide behind it, but it doesn't deter him, he won't budge, won't move, won't acknowledge the taunting, now multiplied by many, a chorus of high-pitched voices, all yelling,

Tommy!

Tommy!

TOMMY!

Thomas is beginning to crack. Thick globules of sweat slide down his back: the itch is maddening. He understands that this will never stop without action. Elementary physics, equal and opposite reaction, all that stuff. The playmates of Vikram now expect blood, and Vikram has never shied away from a challenge. Already, Thomas can hear the chair legs squeak as Vikram begins to rise.

Tommy.

Just the one word, one last time. Flat delivery. Lies dead on the floor. Scariest thing young Thomas has ever heard. He knows this is it. No acknowledgement equals pain.

He turns his head slightly, just enough to place Vikram in his peripheral vision. His eyes are already swamped with tears. He curses himself silently. "Yes?" he asks, swallowing down the vibrato that threatens to overwhelm the word.

"Hey, Tommy!" says Vikram, and his smile now beams at full-wattage, a loving smile. How could you not but melt at the sight of it? "Hey, hey, Tommy," he says, nudging the nearest cohort. Here it comes. "Hey, Tommy-boy. I. Am. THE. CHEESE." And the murder of children collapses in paroxysms of vicious glee.

Fuck.

What can you say to that? It's perfect. The complete and final destruction of the last refuge poor Thomas ever had. And there's no comeback, other than maybe "Good for you," and even *that* took me fifteen years to think of. And all little Thomas could do was pack up his books and walk away, the laughter following him as he slinked past Miss White to the hallway, burning through his clothes, searing his skin with shame. Thomas would never forgive Miss White after that. The way she stood there, the adult with all the power, yet as meek and afraid of Vikram as Thomas.

I talked to Vikram last week. He walked into Java Central, every inch a vanity-spewing Tom Wolfe Master of the Universe. He's in banking now, he tells me, which I presume means he *is* banking. Upper echelon in money lending, processing, withholding, and coveting. He's rich, married, with two kids and likely a side-harem of moist and willing banklets. The definition of fulfilled promise. We talked, and joked, and reminisced about the old times he deluded himself into believing we both shared. He teased, we laughed, and I fantasized thrusting a coffee scoop deep into his eye socket, removing his frontal lobe through the gaping wound two tablespoons at a time. But I satisfied myself by inconspicuously spitting in his cappuccino. A big snot-laden horker. Actually, I felt bad about that, so I pretended to trip and spilled the drink on his Brooks Brothers coat. He was very good about it, and the store will pay for the dry cleaning, so no harm done.

Fuck, am I a wimp.

TRANSCRIPT
The Munroe Purvis Show — Episode 725 (excerpt)

Announcer: It's three o'clock, and who is it time
    for?
Audience: Munroe!
ROLL CREDITS
Announcer: That's right, Munroe! Munroe's guests
    this afternoon include the young girl from
    Alabama who fell down a well, twice! Felicity
    Kay! The host of the new reality series
    Desperation, Neil Wesberg! And the author of
    My Baby, My Love, Agnes Coleman! And now, put
    your hands together, it's time for Munroe!
ENTER MUNROE PURVIS
Munroe: Good afternoon, everyone, how's every
    little thing?
APPLAUSE
Munroe: We have a packed show today, I can't
    wait to tell you all about it. This is a show
    that means a lot to me, today, we are . . .
Audience mem: I love you, Munroe!
LAUGHTER
Munroe: Wow, thank you very much, that's great.
    What a wonderful, wonderful thing to say. Can
    we get a mike over to her? Jim, can we . . .
    Thank you, Jim. What's your name, Miss?
Audience mem: Janice. Janice Reid.
Munroe: Janice, what a lovely name, thank you,
    Janice. Janice, I'd like to ask you a question
    if I may. Janice, do you like to read?
Audience mem: What? I'm sorry?
Munroe: That's fine, dear, take your time.
LAUGHTER
Munroe: Do you like to read, Janice?
Audience mem: I guess so. I mean, I can read, if
    that's what you mean.
Munroe: I am so sorry, I didn't mean to imply
    that, my apologies, Janice. Forgive me?

10

Audience mem: Oh, I'd forgive you anything, Munroe! I love you!

Munroe: And I love you, too, Janice. I love everyone here, what a great audience you are, give yourselves a hand! Come on!

APPLAUSE

Munroe: My question for Janice is actually for everyone. Do we like to read? Well, duh! Of course we don't! Reading is boring. I mean, who here has actually read anything by William Shakespeare? Hands up if you have. One? I applaud you, Miss, you have far more patience than I. Give her a big round of applause, everyone, she has suffered greatly.

LAUGHTER

Munroe: Let's face it, folks, most of us here have better things to do than sitting around the house, trying to push our way through a book just because someone tells us it's supposed to be good for us. Am I right?

APPLAUSE

Munroe: Well, I'll take that as a big yes. Wow. Well, sorry, folks, played a little trick on you there, but I am wrong, everyone, plain and simple. Reading doesn't have to be boring. Reading can be, dare I say it, fun! And I'm going to prove it to you, right here, today, on this show! I am very excited about this. Today, I am beginning what will become a monthly staple on this program. I am pleased to announce that today is the first official meeting of the Munroe Purvis Book Club!

APPLAUSE

Munroe: Now, I pledge to you, this isn't going to be one of those scary book clubs you've all heard of, where people sip tea and eat crumpets, and discuss the metaphor on page 172. I mean, what does that even mean? What the heck's a crumpet anyway? I promise that this is going to be about books people actually read! Faulkner? Who? Forget it. Steinbeck? Steinblech, am I right? Wolfe, Russo, Pinter? Forget those Toms, Dicks, and Harrys! Who here has ever read *Moby Dick*? Who wants to? It's not a book, I'll tell you what it is, it's broccoli, that's what, something you're supposed to eat because it's good for you, not because you like it. Well, I hate broccoli, I won't eat it, I'm a grown-up now, I can do whatever I want. I'll eat what I want, I'll read what I want, and I'll be gosh-darned if some highfalutin professor with bad posture is going to make me feel bad about it. I'll choose my own books, thank you very much.

APPLAUSE

Munroe: Books about me, about us, you and me here, normal folk with normal problems. Good people. Decent people. People like Janice here. People who work for a living, who pay their taxes on time, who go to church every Sunday. What do the problems of some dead Dutch prince who can't make up his mind whether or not to kill himself have to do with the likes of folks like us, am I right?

APPLAUSE

Munroe: So in this vein, my first guest this afternoon is a wonderful author who has just published her first novel. In fact, I couldn't help myself, when I read it, I started up my own publishing company, MuPu Incorporated, to print and distribute this wonderful story.

APPLAUSE

Munroe: It's about a woman who is faced with a terrible choice, whether to sacrifice the life of her husband for her child! I tell you, I cried buckets when I read this story.

Audience mem: Marry me, Munroe!

Munroe: I'm afraid Janice may have first dibs,

Miss, but if things don't work out, well, I'll
keep you in mind.

LAUGHTER

Munroe: I'm so excited, I can't wait, let's
bring the author out right now, give her a big
hand, Agnes Coleman, everybody!

APPLAUSE

ENTER AGNES COLEMAN

Munroe: Agnes, thank you for coming out here
today.

Agnes: Oh, like I could ever resist you, Munroe.
I owe you everything.

Munroe: How so?

Agnes: Your show kept me sane, through my
divorce, my child custody lawsuit, and the
writing of this book!

Munroe: You've had a difficult life up until
now, haven't you?

Agnes: Oh, Munroe, I . . . oh, God . . .

Munroe: It's all right, Agnes. Here, take my
handkerchief. Better?

Agnes: Yes, thank you. I'm sorry, I promised
myself I wouldn't . . . it's just that, I
don't know, it was so hard for so long . . .

Munroe: That's just fine, dear. You take your
time. After all, if it weren't for your pain,
you wouldn't be here today, would you?

Agnes: No. I just felt I had something to say,
and through the years of therapy and writing
and soul-searching and prayer, I was able to
survive.

Munroe: And thank God you did, am I right,
people?

APPLAUSE

Munroe: Now, I don't want to give anything away,
but in your book, *My Baby, My Love*, your
central character, uh —

Agnes: Margaret?

Munroe: Margaret, yes, thank you, Margaret faces

a difficult decision.

Agnes: Yes, that's correct, Munroe. Margaret's only daughter Amber is dying, and Margaret's husband Peter is the only possible donor, but the operation will kill him.

Munroe: Fascinating. But Peter, now, he doesn't want to die, does he?

Agnes: Oh, no, if it were up to that (expletive deleted)

Munroe: Please, Agnes, your language. This isn't HBO.

LAUGHTER

Agnes: Oh, I'm sorry, Munroe. I get so worked up when I talk about Margaret. Peter treat . . . he treated her so badly. I'm sorry, I . . .

Munroe: I understand completely. I hated him too. In fact, the entire audience will. If you'll check under your seats, you will each find a copy of Agnes Coleman's wonderful novel *My Baby, My Love*, plus a complimentary Munroe Purvis tote bag.

APPLAUSE

Munroe: We have to go to commercial, but when we return, Agnes will let us in on how she wrote such a remarkable book. And so short! You can read it in an hour, I promise!

CUT TO COMMERCIAL

TO: ermccorm@yahoo.ca
FROM: iamashelfmonkey@gmail.com
SUBJECT: A fan of The Dutch Wife

Dear Mr. McCormack,

If you are reading this, then I've succeeded in convincing you to throw caution to the wind and open this attachment. Let me assure you, this is not a hoax. I am not a deposed Nigerian prince begging you to help retrieve the vast millions I have stocked away in a Swiss bank account by supplying me with your credit card numbers. Nor is this a virus waiting for your gullibility to overcome common sense, patiently awaiting its destructive release onto your hard drive. I wouldn't know where the fuck to even look for a virus, let alone how to send one along. Nor am I willing to help you with the length of your penis, get you instant financing for a fourth mortgage (provided you're a Christian), or Get.U.Horny.With.BlackChicks.

I promise you, I am that Thomas Friesen. The Thomas Friesen with his mug plastered on the front page of every newspaper and rag on the continent. The subject of RCMP manhunts and G-Man profiling. My very own *America's Most Wanted* special. Cursed by millions of house-wives and television personalities. Hiding out with Elvis, Gandhi, and Sasquatch, if *The Weekly World News* is to be believed. I wonder if Bat Boy is here. Salman Rushdie ain't got nothing on my *fatwa*; at least he had the British government to keep him warm at night. I even managed to push a suspected al-Qaeda operative off the FBI's Ten Most Wanted list. A little overboard, don't you think? It's not like I'm out there strapping dynamite to my chest and striding naked through The Gap or anything.

You may not remember, I'm hoping you do, but we met once. You were travelling cross-country on a book tour promoting your novel, *The Dutch Wife*. I was in the Winnipeg audience at McNally Robinson Booksellers, eagerly clutching my copies of *Paradise Motel* and *The Mysterium*, listening as your Scottish burr rolled over passages from your work.

Actually, audience is an overstatement; only myself and one other were in attendance purely for your reading. The others were there pretty much for the food, noisily munching on arugula salad and provolone-laden sandwiches, blissfully ensconced in an orgy of culinary blandness, doing their substantial best to drown out your voice.

You, on the other hand, manfully contended with crunchy cauliflower and muted whispers, bravely ploughing on when it was apparent people were more concerned with attaining yet another cup of imported Mocha Java. By the end, when the diners had fled, only the two of us remained, offering up what meagre applause we could.

You took it in stride, however, signing my copies (now in the clutches of the RCMP or CSIS, no doubt) and surprising both my fellow listener and I by sitting down and talking to us personally. We shared a glass of red wine, discussed books we both enjoyed, and you promised to send me a copy of *The Dutch Wife*, which I thought was astoundingly generous of you, thank you. Loved it, by the way.

You also mentioned something, really an off-the-cuff remark, but something that is the impetus for my risking the time to write to you now. I was railing against the works of some author or other, Dean Koontz maybe, ugh, when you drew me up short. You leaned over the table, staring at me as if I had just clubbed a baby harp seal to death and offered its remains to you as a gift. "Thomas," you said. "Thomas, every author deserves respect. Many of them spend years of their lives to bring you their work, their thoughts, their beliefs. You may not like what they have to say, or the manner in which they say it. It may be the worst thing you have ever seen put to paper. But they spent a lot of time and energy on it, and that deserves your respect, regardless of the quality. Be critical, yes, by all means, but be kind."

I've thought about that a lot lately, obviously. Does the effort count? Does the time spent in invention nullify the trouble it may take a person to finish a novel? Should I admire *The Bridges of Madison County* simply because Robert James Waller took three years to write it? Should that count, even when the result is a steaming heap of utter crapola?

With all due respect, sir, no. Not at all.

What's my point? you ask, no doubt reaching for the phone to call the police. Please don't. I have scant energy left, and I'm afraid of what might happen if I can't keep my spirits up. Being on the run is no picnic, despite the allure of the open road. Kerouac was given a choice. I have none. My options ran out months ago, the money soon after, and I'm rapidly running out of places to hide. As I write this, the television in the corner (I'm at a café, that's all I'll tell you), the television is broadcasting my face into every home, every bar, every trailer park. Vegas odds on my capture are rising. Oprah has taken on extra security as a precaution. Phil Donahue has gone on Larry King to call for my execution. Geraldo has organized televised manhunts. The world of syndication is becoming a police state, thanks in no small part to my efforts. I'm keeping my head down, but it's only a matter of time now.

I'm writing to you to plead my case. I do not seek absolution. Bless me, author, for I have sinned, am continuing to sin, and see no end to my sinning. I do not ask for sanctuary. Ladies and gentlemen of the jury, I am guilty, no question. There may be a case for a lesser charge due to mental defect, I could exploit that, but I admit, I knew what I, what we did, was wrong. Evil. Deluded and insane. Even though it felt really, really, oh so good, so unbelievably right at the time.

All I want is to apply a level of context to it all. A reason for the hoopla. Without context, terrorists are simply disgruntled psychos with bad hair days. I'm not disgruntled, Mr. McCormack. Never been. If anything, I'm gruntled to the extreme, an exemplary instance of maximum gruntlitude. I crave the context, I need to define the purpose behind my actions, the motivation for a complete disregard for all things good and moral. I've spent a great deal of energy on self-reflection lately, and I cannot simply up and disappear. It was all for nothing, otherwise.

You are an author, Mr. McCormack. A good one. You were short-listed for the Governor General's Award, you're no stiff. Words and phrases are your instruments, you understand the process, both of writing and reading. You write of lives. You study and present the human dilemma with skill and empathy. You might understand why I did it. You might even sympathize.

Also, you are a disinterested third party. It's been said the act of confession is easier when it involves someone one has no chance of ever running into. There's simply no one else whom I can risk contacting, anyway. My family has disowned me. Mom and Dad, I could never risk it. They've suffered enough anyway. The way they've been publicly reviled, you'd think they'd given birth to the unholy cloned mélange of Manson, Hitler, and Michael Jackson. I understand they've uprooted themselves several times to escape my infamy, and good for them. The farther away from me, the better.

My friends — well, the few relations that I had in school, anyhow, friends mainly because the desk map dictated we sit together in math class — they can simply not be trusted. They've been doing the talk show circuit, milking every last drop of money and airtime they can from their past association with the psychosis that is I.

If you are interested, write back at this e-mail address. I'll check it when I can. I don't know how fast an e-mail can be traced to its place of origin, or even if that's possible, but I'll have to take the chance.

Yours truly,

Thomas Friesen

TRANSCRIPT

The Munroe Purvis Show — Episode 1056 (excerpt)

Announcer: It's three o'clock, and who is it time for?

Audience: Munroe!

ROLL CREDITS

Announcer: That's right, Munroe! This afternoon on Munroe, it's the seventeenth meeting of the Munroe Purvis Book Club. Joining Munroe today will be author Gerry Ewes, discussing his new novel, *Diamonds out of Diapers*. And now, put your hands together, everyone, it's time for Munroe!

ENTER MUNROE PURVIS

Munroe: Good afternoon, everyone, how's every little thing?

APPLAUSE

Munroe: We have a terrific show today, as I'm sure you are all aware. Today is the latest meeting of my fabulous Munroe Purvis Book Club!

APPLAUSE

Munroe: Thank you, thank you, please, if you applaud all day, we'll never get to the book!

LAUGHTER

Munroe: If you'll all look beneath your seats, you'll find a copy of this month's book, so that you can follow along. It's an absolute pearl of a novel, it's called *Diamonds out of Diapers*, and you are going to love it, guaranteed, if you haven't already read it. I don't see how you couldn't have, it's been number one for what, three weeks now? Still, there may be one of you out there who never got around to reading it. 'Fess up, did someone here not do their homework? Don't be afraid, raise your hands.

LAUGHTER

Munroe: Everyone? Everyone here read it? Well, that is just . . . wait a moment, I do see a hand up there. Mark, can we get that gentleman a mike? What's your name, Sir?

Audience Mem: Carl.

Munroe: Well, Carl, what's your excuse? It better be a good one, we're holding up the show for you.

LAUGHTER

Audience Mem: The bookstore was out of copies.

LAUGHTER

Munroe: Perfect answer, A plus, Sir, well done. Well, I'm sure you'll catch up if you pay attention.

Audience Mem: I promise, I'll get the next one.

Munroe: That's all I ask. In fact, so you'll have no excuses, I'm giving you a copy of next month's book right now, how about that, folks?

APPLAUSE

Munroe: You know, I'm feeling generous today. Maybe it's just because I'm so excited about today's book, but everyone gets a copy of my next book when you leave today!

APPLAUSE

Munroe: I'll tell you all about it at the end of the show, but in case anyone watching today has to leave early, it's called *Touring Depression*, by a wonderful, fabulous writer I've discovered named Carole Immen, who I am positive you will be reading great things about very soon.

APPLAUSE

Munroe: But before we get started and bring today's author out, I'd like to start on a serious note, if I may. My book club is proving to be astoundingly popular, thanks to good people like yourselves, and I couldn't be happier.

APPLAUSE

Munroe: Yes, go ahead, you deserve to applaud
   yourselves. Thank you. But. When something
   becomes popular, there are some who
   automatically strive to tear it down. The club
   is so popular that the naysayers, well,
   they've been crawling out like lice. There has
   been a lot of talk in so-called serious
   newspapers about the supposed quality of the
   books I have personally published for your
   enjoyment. These quote unquote critics have
   attacked my choices, they have attacked me,
   and yes, I am afraid, sadly, they have
   attacked you. Attacks on myself, I can abide.
   It is part of the price of being famous and
   successful in this troubled world of ours. But
   to extend the attacks to you, my viewers,
   that, I'm sorry, that is unforgivable. Words
   such as vile, banal, poor, tragic, and
   nauseating have been bandied about in the
   press. "Lacking in any sort of artistic merit
   whatsoever, lowering the IQ of anyone within
   eyesight, leaving the reader just that much
   dumber as a result." That's a direct quote
   from the "New York Times Review of Books," by
   the way. J.M. Coetzee, I believe the
   reviewer's name is. Exactly, who's that, some
   nobody with nothing better to do than
   complain! These insufferable literati, they
   are sitting in their ivory towers, sipping
   champagne, and spitting it out from on high
   onto the heads of regular folks like me and
   you, and they expect us to lap it all up and
   ask for seconds! I am furious! The gall of
   these people! To suggest that you have somehow
   been lessened as a person by reading my picks,
   that is disgusting. This really gets my goat.
   Something must be done to curb these malicious
   assaults. I am sending out a plea to all my

viewers, please, do not purchase these publications. Boycott these magazines. Do not watch these television programs. If they recommend a book, shun it! Ignore their rants on supposed good taste and quality. What do they know, am I right? They are just mean, petty little men and women who couldn't get dates in high school!

APPLAUSE

Munroe: Thank you. I knew I could count on you, the real people, the best people in this country, in this world.

APPLAUSE

Munroe: Now that that's out of the way, let's bring out today's author, what do you say?

APPLAUSE

Munroe: He has written a simply marvellous novel about the perils of single fatherhood, after the mother of his child has selfishly left the family to join a lesbian feminist commune. Please welcome, everybody, Gerry Ewes!

APPLAUSE

ENTER GERRY EWES

Munroe: Thank you for being here, Gerry.

Gerry: No, thank you, Munroe. It's because of you I'm here.

Munroe: How so, Gerry?

Gerry: Before your book club started, I don't think I'd ever read a complete book in my life. I honestly had trouble reading more than a chapter of the Bible a day, and even that was a pain. Oh gosh, I'm sorry, I didn't mean —

Munroe: That's fine, Gerry. I don't think I'll get in too much trouble if I say that even the Bible could have used a good editor at times.

LAUGHTER

Gerry: Good book, though.

Munroe: The best.

Gerry: So, anyway, on your advice, I picked up a copy of *Trading Blankets* at Wal-Mart —

Munroe: One of my picks, for those of you who don't remember, by Eric Brun, I think.

Gerry: Yes, that's the one. So I bought a copy, and I couldn't believe it, not only did I finish it, I realized, hey, I could write a book as well. It didn't look that hard.

Munroe: Fabulous! You see, this is what I was talking about, people. Regular folk! We've got to break for a commercial, but when we return, we'll be talking more to author Gerry Ewes about his astounding novel. Stay tuned.

APPLAUSE

CUT TO COMMERCIAL

TO: ermccorm@yahoo.ca
FROM: iamashelfmonkey@gmail.com
SUBJECT: A very grateful Shelf Monkey

Dear Mr. McCormack,

Thank you. Thank you, thank you, thank you.

Now, where to begin? This isn't going to be easy. I'm accustomed to pencil and pad, the classic tools of the trade, but that's not an option. I can't take the chance of that pesky postmark pinpointing my hiding place. My handwriting is illegible, anyway.

Writing on a computer is frustrating, isn't it? There is a pleasing physicality to writing by hand, something so supremely gratifying about watching the paper pile up on the corner of your desk as you complete page after page. Computers mute the satisfaction. They have annihilated the earthiness of the process, even as they placate you with toolbars replete with handy thesaurus and dictionary (lexicon! vocabulary! wordbook!), symbols, automatic tab and margin functions, spellcheck, layout, and **your** choice of font. But it's all just magic, shards of Dumbledore wizardry forming sentences on glass, transitory, impermanent. Sure, we don't have to suffer the stigma of writer's callus anymore, and thank God for that, I never thought I'd live to see WC go the way of polio, but are you telling me all this typing doesn't cause some physical ailment? And forget the carpal, I mean 21st century writer's callus; big ugly warts sitting atop the tip of each finger, deadening tactile sensation until our hands ultimately evolve into clumsy, fleshy oven mitts. Besides all that, computers are vulnerable in a way that paper never was. There is something infinitely demoralizing at the prospect of having one's work at the mercy of a decorative fridge magnet. Plus, I get screen sick after twenty minutes or thereabouts.

I don't have the luxury of complete isolation. My computer has no wi-fi, so I must endanger myself with public appearances, saving this correspondence to my USB and using a public terminal to send it to you. The internet waiter (waiternet? Internet service personnel? waitress of the Web?) keeps bothering me, asking if I want more black sludge that is somehow but not quite completely unlike coffee. And this terminal costs seven dollars per. And that ain't prorated per minute, that's seven bucks whether I use it for the entire hour, or the three minutes it takes me to upload this as an attachment and send it to you. It's not like I have a lot of money right now. I don't suppose you could Western Express me some running-from-the-law money? No, I suppose not.

I am not cut out for this life. Not at all. I'm weak. Book reading has left me soft.

I was a lawyer, did you know that?

Of course you do, who doesn't? FALLEN LAWYER, that's what the headlines say. Sells more papers that way. Everyone loves to see lawyers taken down a peg, even when they're invaluable. People would rather lose a case than win, if it meant their lawyer looked bad as a result. Sure, I got fucked over in the divorce, but my lawyer'll never work again. Boo-yah!

It's an overstatement anyway. I never passed the bar. I articled a few months, then quit. Or had unemployment of a medical nature thrust upon on me. Whichever you prefer.

You know what? Fuck it all anyway. I don't want to talk about it. Don't *need* to talk about it. After all, Newhire's been whoring himself out to the public airwaves, waving my psychiatric assessments about to anyone who'll listen. Playing up the suicide attempt like it actually means something. Oh, hell, maybe it does. If it weren't for the "cry for help," I'd never have ended up like this, but that's more of a direct linear line of progression through time, not the Newhire-approved psychological cause-and-effect relationship. I hear he's working on a book deal, the definitive exposé into the sordid world of the Purvis conspiracy. So much for doctor/patient privilege, but hey, who am I to complain?

But, let that lie for now. Peruse his article in *Psychiatry Weekly* if you're interested, or *People* if you just want the bullet points. For me, I lived it, it's the past.

But every story must start somewhere, and as I am the narrator of my life, it's my prerogative to start my tale immediately afterward. No reason why, except a stone has to start rolling downhill somewhere.

"Now, Thomas, no one thinks you're crazy."

Is it just me, or should a psychiatrist never use the word "crazy," even in a positive context?

It floated there before me. Crazy. *Crazy.* I watched the letters gather strength in his mouth, roll about the tongue, before finally escaping on the back of an exhalation. They bobbled in front of me, swaying slightly in the oscillating breeze of the office fan.

It had been three weeks since I had forcibly acquainted myself with the bumper of a 1992 Chevrolet Cavalier. Dr. Newhire sat in his leather swivel chair, making notes on an official-looking yellow pad. A bit premature, I thought, as I hadn't yet made a sound. My jaw was still wired, the only part of me truly damaged from the "accident." While coherent speech *was* possible, the harmonizing throbbing ache kept me mute to answering all but the most pertinent questions. "Do you have to use the bedpan?" and "More morphine?" were about the only queries I deemed deserving of a response. Perhaps conversation wasn't required, Dr. Newhire's pad displaying a list of preset syndromes from which he could choose a diagnosis.

Newhire, as I'm sure you're aware, Mr. McCormack, from all the free publicity he's milked from our relationship, has teeth the colour of old urinals, and a beard consisting of five pockets of sparse fur separated by four vast empty acne-scarred plains. I kept myself busy as he prattled on by counting his moustache hairs.

"I want to assure you, Thomas, you don't have anything to worry about," he said.

"I don't?" It came out through the wirework, *Uh don?*

"No, depression is a fairly common condition. You're perfectly normal."

"I am?" *Uh eh?*

"Yes. It's simply a medical condition, an imbalance of chemicals that helped shape your response to workplace stress. Many people in your profession suffer from the same condition. Mind you, not all of them take matters to such, uh, extremes, but still, you're alive and safe, that's what counts now."

"Great." *Grut.*

"How do you feel?"

"Grut."

"Good, that's good." He jotted something down on the pad, no doubt an incisive exploration into my psyche based upon the combined total of six unintelligible words I had said. I only saw him for a few months, and he's parading about on daytime television, charging a five-figure fee for speaking engagements and making a mockery of the doctor/patient relationship. Pill-pushing asshole.

On Newhire's recommendation, I started feasting on anti-depressants, morning and evening doses, enhanced by emergency pill snacks to quell the shakes and crying jags. I went through them very quickly. Crying became second nature. I cried all night. I bawled all day. I sobbed on the phone to my parents. I wept to Newhire. I blubbered to my boss as I quit. I swore off anything that reminded me of law. *Law & Order* left me weak and dehydrated. Reruns of *Perry Mason* made me vomit. I cried for two weeks. Then off and on for what seems like forever. I sat in my little apartment for months, permanent ass dents forming in the couch, gorging myself on video games and nachos. I lost all interest in anything beyond my next serving of anti-depressants and the tribulations of Victor Newman on *Y & R.*

I didn't mind the drugs, truth be told. I had a momentary spasm of horror, yes, worried that such medication was sure to bring about the loss of identity on a par with Finney's pod people. Am I still me, or am I now a more passive, society-adjusted, Paxil-approximated replicant?

But the after-me seemed to enjoy itself, particularly as the lovely little pharmaceuticals cautiously adapted themselves to my biorhythms and began altering my DNA at a sub-nucleic level. The world recycled itself anew as I watched, becoming both a deep placid lake and its wavering reflection of the earth above as my brain-split strived to mend its synapses. It's not that I couldn't tell that the world was real and solid; it was more like I became intensely focused on the minutiae of life, as if there were a mirrorverse behind every action that I could observe if only I concentrated hard enough.

It suited me, this almost reality. It fit in with the pattern of my life, almost being something. I was *almost* a lawyer. *Almost* successful. *Almost* deceased. As I lay in bed each day — as I did almost constantly, a side-effect of the exquisitely crafted bliss capsules being lethargy of a near-incapacitating nature — I could see that being almost was what I was destined to be. In school, almost invisible. In law school, almost on the dean's list. By girlfriends, almost loved. I was almost. Winnipeg was the perfect location for me. Almost the longitudinal centre of the country. Almost big. Almost important. Almost more than a punchline on *The Simpsons*. And Manitoba, almost a power. Almost a real province. Almost a place to stop on your way from Alberta to

Ontario, but you were almost there, so why bother? Almost something. (More than Saskatchewan, though.) Was it because of me, this almost state of being? Had I caused the almost, was I doomed to spread almost about the world as I travelled, infecting the innocent with lethal doses, leaving them bereft and always wondering why they were almost something themselves?

After eleven weeks of such musings, my savings now a fraction of their former numeral, my rent due and bills piled high, I took stock of myself.

Face

- Lumpy. Unshaved. Slovenly. Nice eyes, and a captivatingly off-kilter smile when I could manage it. Not without promise, but a definite fixer-upper.

Body

- Oh good Christ that's horrible. Move on.

Beard

- Jesus. Where did *that* come from? Kind of scraggly and patchy, yet modestly decorative in a brooding bohemian poet sort of way. Perhaps a beret would be in order?

Belongings

- One laptop computer, old but serviceable.
- Various legal textbooks and treatises, soon to be put in the recycling bin, a final fuck you to the law and all who practise its arcane rites.
- Clothes, unwashed but not beyond repair.
- One television, thirteen inches, an enviable size for a man to have, but not in his choice of entertainment centre.
- One DVD player.
- Several DVDs, all widescreen format. Have you ever watched *Lawrence of Arabia* in widescreen format on a thirteen-inch television screen? It loses its grandeur somehow.
- Shelves and shelves, and shelves, and shelves, and under the bed, and above the fridge, and behind the couch, and on the couch, and next to the table, and correcting the wobble in the kitchen table, of books.

Clearly, something had to change. Not wanting to modify my lifestyle so much that I'd have to physically leave the apartment, I began to look into more innovative approaches to fill my life.

Aromatherapy filled three days of Internet research into the healing power of smells. I began to *feng shui* my furniture to improve my chi, or some such bullshit. Boy, I really feel like slitting my wrists. Perhaps if I move the couch thusly . . . ah, now life is worth living again!

Obviously, I wasn't in a tremendously clear mindset.

"What should I do now?" I asked Newhire.

"Get a job."

"Thanks."

"Don't mention it. Do you have my cheque?"

"Here."

"Thanks."

So easy, the concept: find employment. People do it all the time, you hear about such cases on the streets. "Why, my uncle had a job once!" Problem was, law school had taken its toll. I had three years of arcane legal memoranda and legislative trivia brainwashed into me, effectively tearing down the soft-shelled ordinary citizen and replacing it with the Armani-armoured warrior. The "real" world was alien, obscure, something to be discussed with similarly attired workmates and adversaries over triple espressos, only referred to in obscure Latin phraseology so as to emphasize the vast difference between our world and 'the other.' I couldn't function in a society where people actually talked to each other. Where words spoken mirrored emotions felt.

In other words, I was feral. And broke.

So my options were now open to other employment endeavours. A little fudging on the ol' résumé, some patchwork and glue on the cv, and I'm all set. No need to mention the breakdown, just say the law was not for me. Happens all the time, career changes. No shame to want something else. Just need to choose. Medicine? Education? *Physical* Education? Theatre?

Job one.

Java Central. Polo Park Mall. Coffee jerk at minimum wage plus meagre tips. Thought I'd aim low, get my feet wet. Not as bad as I'd feared.

"Excuse me?" I caught up to him just as he was leaving. "Excuse me, Sir? Sir?"

"Yeah?"

"You just came out of the washroom there."

"Yeah?"

"Well, I was just in there before you, cleaning up, and I went in again just after you, so . . ."

"So?"

"So." So? So so so so so. So. "I couldn't help but notice that, after I had cleaned the washroom thoroughly, you know, top to bottom, not a stain left, that sort of thing, I couldn't help but observe that you made a little bit of a mess in there."

"Yeah, so?" Christ, this guy only knows two words!

"So, well, the thing is . . . the thing, you see, uh, well . . ." Aw, fuck it all anyway. "So, did you not see the toilet? You don't have a white cane and a black lab retriever, or even glasses, so I surmise that your vision is near 20–20. So what's the deal? That python between your legs too much for you to handle, is that it? You lack the wrist strength to control it, so you just let it go where it pleases? I can see where that'd be bothersome, but I'd expect you to still take some responsibility for its actions. Because that isn't simply a mess you left back there, it's the mother of all messes. You have splashed urine everywhere except, it seems, the actual porcelain receptacle designed to receive your piss. What, you think that the bowl is only a suggested target for urination? What the Christ is wrong with you? Maybe if you took off your goddamn sunglasses when indoors, maybe then you'd get a fucking clue!"

"THOMAS!"

End of job one.

Not my finest moment, but instructive. Anyway, the thrill of the job ended the moment I had mastered the ancient art of latte preparation, about two days in. Pop some pills, move on, scratch the job from the cv. Red flag the service industry for future employment.

Job two.

Temporary gig, but money is money.

"All right, people, listen up, attention! My name is Nick, and I am your handler today. If you have any questions, please direct them to me and me alone. Do not talk to the actors. Do not talk to the director. You are extras, which means you are furniture, as far as everyone else is concerned. If you talk to the actors or director you will be fired. Do as you are told. Stand and move when directed to. Understand? Good. Now, the first shot, we need only one. Um, you."

"Me?"

30

"Yes, I need you to stand here, thank you. Put your arm here, lean against the wall. The actors will be having a conversation. You listen, but don't say anything. You are background. Got it?

"Yes. Stand here, listen, look interested."

"Perfect. All right, we ready? Good. Actors on set, please!"

Okay, focus. Look interested. Pay attention. Don't look at the camera, pay attention to the actors, be attentive, be . . . "Hey, aren't you J Lo? Cool, I'm in a scene with J Lo! Could I get an autograph, quick, before they start filming? Oh, hey, Richard Gere! Plea— hey that hurts! My arm!"

Job two finito.

Job three.

Depression starts to sink in.

"What do you want out of life? Do you want to be rich, or work at McDonald's? Do you want to golf on public courses, or own your own? Do you lease your car? How many kilometres are on the odometer? Does this make you happy? Would you rather own your own Lexus? Can you do anything to dig yourself out of debt, or are you going to just waste away, barely earning enough to stave off homelessness? Are you really going to live like this? Are you going to let yourself down? Are you? Are you?"

Never! Oh, God, help me!

"Are you going to live up to your potential?"

Yes!

"Do you want more?"

Oh, yes!

"DO YOU DESERVE MORE?"

OH, YES!

"Then welcome to the wonderful world of Primerica Financial Planning! After our intensive one-week program, you will be fully licensed and qualified to assist and advise people just like yourself in mapping out their financial futures. And of course, in addition to the fees you will charge for this advice, you will also earn large cash bonuses based on the number of members you personally recruit to the Primerica family."

Aw, shit. I'm depressed, but not *this* depressed.

End of job three.

*

I love books. The shape of them, the smell of them, their weight, their ideas. The possibilities and secrets that are inked into their pages. Their appearance on a shelf, unread, undefiled. Open on a coffee table, spine cracked and shedding. Stuffed in a backpack. A copy of *Henderson the Rain King* as you trek through Africa. *The Shining* on the bus. *The Beach* on the beach. *The Satanic Verses* in the back pews. Reading is more than mental exercise or entertainment for the others and me. It is our escape from our tormentors. It is our vacation. It is our religion. The act of reading can be as sacred as a visit to the confessional. *And Farley Mowat did look down from on high, and saw that it was good.*

I once read that less than two percent of people read more than one book a year. Don't you find that depressing? Whose slack am I taking up? Sure, *Desperate Housewives* is entertaining, even informative in a "gee I wish I looked that good why can't we all be that funny" sort of way. And an hour later, you've experienced a week of someone else's life, and then you can return to your own existence, if you can stand how shabby, how utterly ordinary it all is. Christ.

But a book, now, that's a *life*. So much more than the sum of its parts. Paper and ink, symbols and patterns, the alchemical foundation of existence itself. There's a crumb of Mary Shelley in every author, a particle of God, raising the dead from equal parts wood, pulp, and Times New Roman font, shaping Adam and Eve from clay and bones.

There is no better feeling in the world than entering a space filled with books. It doesn't matter how the space is defined, how it's decorated, what flagrantly rotten Top 40 lite-pop aural slush spills out from ceiling speakers. It's the books, eagerly awaiting your perusal, lined up like prostitutes on the street, c'mon honey, whatchoo want, I'll make you happy, you lookin' for a good time? Virginal spines on newly dusted shelves, the aroma of fresh ink and glue in the air, coquettishly tempting you to open me, read me, run your fingers along my lines, trace my upraised title, take off my jacket, READ ME, DO IT, YOU KNOW YOU WANT TO! Or libraries, brothels of literature, old hags showing their stretch marks and cigarette burns, promising you a good time, sailor, I've got some tricks left, don't let the appearance fool you, just because some yahoo scribbled in my margins doesn't mean I can't pretend it's the first time with you, baby, just don't treat me too rough, or there'll be trouble, I've got friends, see, friends with power, they cut up your card like *that*, baby. Old age homes, pet shops, and orphanages (read: second-hand bookstores) promise new friends for a reasonable price and a good home, you'll just have to dig through the pile, oops, not that one, he's balancing my table leg, here, I've got a Craig Nova, light on the mileage, who's looking for someone just like you. Not your type? That's all right, he is an acquired taste. How about a Richard Ford, only one previous owner, practically a steal, only read once by a little old lady who fell for the John Irving blurb.

READ, on the other side of the equation, READ is a space designed by de Sade and Dante, the first circle of Hell, literary limbo, a publisher's wet dream, the author's nightmare. A vacuous, arid, vile product of bottom-line economics. Sales are everything, creativity is nothing. Art never enters the equation. At READ, the book is pure product; whatever sells in great quantities is kept, whatever does not is bargain binned into oblivion. Formerly a Depression-era warehouse for police-seized booty, it has been redesigned and packaged as a vast fluorescent shadowless void, a bleak terrain of Kubrickian emptiness. Three floors of monolithic black shelving that would give Cicero pause. At the end of each aisle stands a mirror, polished and angled to allow for the maximum illusion of endless space. In the right spot looking into the mirror, infinite yous are trapped by infinite metal shelving, a nightmare of spatial ambiguity so endless, so unfathomable, Burgess Meredith would have ground his glasses underfoot himself in that old *Twilight Zone* episode rather than be cursed with perfect eyesight. Customers wander the aisles like Romero's living dead, dragging baskets of books, occasionally latching onto the hapless employee unlucky enough to stroll into their eye-line. "M. Scott Peck! Robert Warren! Deepak Chopra!" they moan, seeking the Self Help/Divinity/Philosophy/Christianity/Other Religions acres of the store. The walls are tattooed with semi-humorous quotations of the famous:

> "Outside of a dog, a book is a man's best friend. Inside of a dog, it's too dark to read."
> — Groucho Marx
> "Every book is the wreck of a perfect idea."
> — Iris Murdoch

A laboured attempt at feigned cheerfulness in the dreary vacuity of the dead zone. Even the name of the store adds to the authoritarian overtones. **READ**. It's not a name, it's a bold font command from Big Brother, bellowed out through oversized megaphones at the hapless Winston Smith. **READ!** Enter the bookstore, and **READ!** And inside this nightmare are stacks of books, each with an identical snow-white cover stamped with the title in bold black font — **BOOK**. The pages in this brave new world offer no stories anymore, no ideas, no themes. In the ultimate example of the loss of individualism, there is just one word, repeated over and over — **CONTENTS**. Add to this the confusion over the actual pronunciation of the store's name — Is it reed? Red? Read, or read? — and you have the perfect example of Orwellian doublespeak. Why have one name, when two will do, each correct yet imprecise? Is it present tense when you enter, past tense as you leave? The effect as a whole is a pervasive yet unconscious malevolence that keeps the customer eternally off-balance, perhaps not on the level of Stephen King's Overlook Hotel, but certainly akin to his story "1408." To move through the automatic doors, feeling the sudden shove of sterilized air against your face is to feel your soul escaping, screaming upward as it flees to Heaven, where it is berated and stomped on by Hemingway for being such a fucking pussy.

READ is pure evil. No doubt about it.

However, it does offer its employees a fine dental and health benefits package, as well as Christmas and Easter bonuses, and who was I to argue with financial stability? So, pride in one hand and ego squished like a used tissue in my back pocket, I entered **READ**, and destroyed my life.

I'll have to stop there for now. Need to organize my thoughts. My fingers are tired, and my hands are shaking from seven caffeine refills.

Yours truly,
Thomas

AUTHOR STRIKES UP CORRESPONDENCE
WITH FUGITIVE

WATERLOO — Canadian author Eric McCormack contacted RCMP yesterday, saying that he was in possible contact with Thomas Friesen, one of several missing suspects in the ongoing Munroe Purvis investigation.

McCormack, a past nominee for the Governor General's Award for Fiction for his novel *First Blast of the Trumpet Against the Monstrous Regiment of Women*, reports he has been contacted by Friesen, who "seems desperate to tell his story."

"Friesen is living off borrowed time, and he knows it," said Detective Amanda Daimler, a criminal profiler with the FBI who has been assisting the RCMP. "I believe his mania is forcing him to try to build himself up some good will, a myth to sustain him. He sees himself as a glamorous criminal, like Bonnie and Clyde."

FBI and RCMP are currently working to determine how best to use the information McCormack has pro-vided them. Detective Daimler admits, "For now, the investigation has slowed considerably. We need to examine this new information, see where it takes us."

When reached for comment, Dr. Lyle Newhire, a psychiatrist and former therapist of Friesen who has been working closely with the RCMP, told Canadian Press, "I don't understand for sure why Thomas has contacted Mr. McCormack, other than he apparently feels there exists some sort of kinship between them. Thomas suffers from a deeply ingrained sense of inferiority, coupled with near-paralysing bouts of manic depression. I think he fancies himself to be misunderstood, in the vein of the classic antiheroes of fiction. I only hope that this can all be resolved soon."

Dr. Newhire is currently preparing an account of his time with Friesen, to be published by Knopf some time next year.

TO: ermccorm@yahoo.ca
FROM: iamashelfmonkey@gmail.com
SUBJECT: First Blast of the Traitor Against the Monstrous Regiment
of Shelf Monkeys

Dear Eric,

I'm tempted to leave a simple "Go fuck yourself," but the ingrained conscientious objectors of a hundred generations of Mennonites tell me to be more polite. How about "Suck it!" as an alternative? Too pithy? Well, I am a lapsed Mennonite. Let's leave it at "Fuck you."

You don't mind if I call you Eric, do you? I mean, we've gone through so much together already, you and I. I'm chagrined to discover that you've opted for police involvement so early in our relationship. What, you think I don't read? The papers print a very favourable portrait of you, playing you as a Clarice Starling to my Hannibal Lecter. Don't fret, I'm not going to go all Tom Harris on you. No taunting. No riddles. No mysterious clues as to my where-abouts as I continue to wreak havoc, sending ticking packages wrapped in brown paper to Montel Williams and Regis Philbin. None of that James Patterson shit. I just wanted to tell my story. I'm a little hurt, that's all.

I suppose I should send out hellos to everyone else, as this is now presumably a mass e-mail. Hello, all! Hi, Detective Daimler. Look behind you!

Just kidding. I'm a little stressed. As I'm sure you've learned from acquaintances and co-workers, I have a tendency to make jokes under duress. Seriously, Detective, you may want to look into your staff for a possible leak. I don't think you'd have voluntarily tipped your hand to the press so soon.

I just Googled myself. You know how many hits I found? Three hundred seventy-one, omitting multiple search results. Just for fun, I ran Descartes for comparison purposes. I won, if not in complete matches, at least in terms of actual Web sites devoted to either of us. I exist on the Web, therefore I am. What I am precisely, I don't rightly know just yet. I have sites devoted to my capture, tracking my every move through newspaper headlines, television updates, and just plain old rumour and innuendo. My name pops up regularly in association with Bin Laden, Arafat, Hitler, Kazinsky, Dahmer, George W., and others of that ilk. In other words, scum of the basest order. You'd think I'd firebombed a school bus full of pregnant war widows or something. Of them all, www.thomas-friesen-must-be-drawn-and-quartered.com is my favourite. Agnes Coleman is a regular contributor.

There's more out there, and I think maybe that's what got people scared. Hell, I'm scared myself. The idea that a subsect exists that seeks to emulate me gives me hope. And fear. And a niggling sense of nausea.

I suppose I should just stop and disappear, but where's the fun in that? I don't know how much longer I can stay underground anyway. Contrary to reports, I do not find this at all glamorous or exciting. Being a fugitive is hard work. I wish I were being paid for this.

READ, as I'm sure you all know by now, is the newest mega-box-hyper-super-huge bookstore, a massive expanse of novels, textbooks, music, DVDs, and book-related paraphernalia. Fields of fiction. Whole square kilometres of history. Leagues of health, science, pets, gay issues, religion, politics, gay politics, movies, sports, women's studies, and more. A nirvanic potpourri of the "eloquent," "fast-paced," "unforgettable," "breathless," "thought-provoking," "rib-tickling," "heart-stopping," "eye-popping," "hair-raising," "award-winning," "expertly crafted," "Kafkaesque," "Bosch-like," "Hemingwayian," "delightful," "sensational," "menacing," "gripping," "inspirational," "emotionally engaging," "astoundingly beautiful," "immensely readable," and "stuff nightmares are made of" —

Oh, God, it's Heaven.

— "bitter," "wise," "exhilarating," "poetic," "stylistic," "probing," "authentic," "dazzling," "supercharged," "explosive," "brutal," "brutally funny," "incendiary," "sensational," "magnificent," "tart," "eerie," "perfect," "near-perfect," "passionate," —

I'm drowning, going to asphyxiate from accolades.

— written by "a storyteller in the grand tradition," "a star on the rise," "a grand master," "an old pro," "one of his/her generation's most gifted authors," "a superb stylist," "a terrifying visionary," "a sensitive poet," "an undiscovered treasure," "a hitmaker extraordinaire," "a consummate satirist," "the winner of the Pulitzer/Pen-Faulkner/Booker/Hugo/Nebula/Giller/Orange/ Nobel Prize"—

Throw me a life preserver.

— with the monikers Austen, Naipal, Davies, Findley, Shakespeare, Munro, Huxley, Capote, Hunter, Kinsella, Jin, Ishiguro, Vidal, *et al*, all for your reading pleasure, and many at forty percent off the regular cover price.

People flock to it by the thousands, astonished by low, low prices and wide variety. There is one copy of everything, and if they don't have it, they'll get it for you, no sweat. That **READ** has all the architectural charisma of a wedge of rancid feta makes no difference. It's heartening in its way, that so many people would herd themselves into a bookstore. It's verifiable proof that books fill some rudimentary need, even if it's only the latest *Garfield* collection or *Chicken Soup for the Crack-Addicted Abused Mothers of Disenfranchised Teenaged Runaway Hitchhikers' Soul*. I will admit, I myself was not immune to its wholesale charms.

There were worse places to work, I was sure. I'd always wanted to work in a bookstore, free reading material at my disposal. And I couldn't afford to be particular; my savings had now dried up into government-issued dust, and bill collectors were threatening to make themselves known on a face-to-face basis with me. While I don't as a rule use my thumbs *every* day, I have grown rather fond of the opposable little guys.

There was no way I was going to mess up this interview. In the bag. Slam-dunk. This is what I told myself as I stood in the cold outside **READ**'s front doors, fighting to subdue a rising tide of panic. I had a shelf of pills organized by dosage and side-effect lined up in my medicine cabinet for just such occasions, medical marvels designed to relieve anxiety and stress at the moment of conception. One is enough for an average-sized man, two would give a raging bull elephant pause, and three pills could remodel King Kong's New York rampage into a scholarly debate between man and giant ape on the dietary merits of a banana-rich diet.

I took three, figuring Kong had nothing on me. Dry-swallowing the pills, relishing the chalky aftertaste, I took a deep breath, then another, and walked confidently through the doors.

An enormous head attacked me the moment I entered.

I wish that were a metaphor for something.

Massive teeth pinned me to the doorframe, wedging me between a trash can and an incisor the size of a four-slice toaster. Pale bloodless lips pressed up against my chest in an obscene parody of a kiss. Moustache bristles the width of pencils scraped against my neck, exfoliating me against my will. I screamed, lashing out wildly, my fists connecting with flesh, one entering a nostril, the other plunging into a fleshy cheekbone, feeling for all the world like I had thrust my arms into a barrel of slugs. Sucking sounds joined the chorus as I extricated one hand, hollering with revulsion. The head shifted, slid down, giving me a glimpse of enormous eyes, dead yet sparkling with maliciousness. I began to hyperventilate, my breath shallow with panic. The world darkened. My knees buckled, the head pushing me down with its weight, my arms hugging it to my face, clutching as if it was a life preserver. Fireworks suffused my vision, the behemoth smothering me into unconsciousness, no doubt as a prelude to devouring me, a no-longer-squirming tidbit, a noontime snack.

At least I didn't bathe this morning, I thought as a pitch-black hollowness beckoned.

Choke on me, motherfucker.

"You okay, friend?" The head was trying to converse with me

"Man that looks weird." These are the last words I'll ever hear?

Then, blinding light, as the face was pulled off mine with a loud *schtlup!* My pupils constricted in fear, and I staggered about blindly, feeling hands grab my shoulders as I walked into a wall.

"Head," I said, looking about, colours and shapes congealing before me. "Big head. Big."

Voice to the left of me. "Yeah, that's one big head, my brother, I'll give you that." The speaker turned me around to face him, filling my vision with a broad blur. "Sorry 'bout that, friend, it got away from us."

"Wha?" That's all I could say. I thought I'd made my point. My hands began frantically shaking, trying to rid themselves of what I was positive were boogers the size of biscuits. "Away? Head?"

"Shit, he's really out of it. Warren, help me get him into the back." Fuzzy angels took hold of my arms, leading me through a maze of corridors and swinging doors, finally plopping me down on a leather sofa.

I moaned in terror as fingers rudely snapped themselves before my eyes. "C'mon, friend, focus. Back to reality." The blur gradually began to coalesce itself into a solid mass of definable shape. What that shape was, was still a mystery.

"Do you have an angry octopus on your head?" I asked it.

Laughter from behind it. "He's fine, Aubrey. And an acute observer."

The Aubrey-blur grunted, shifted, came into focus. "Christ!" I blurted.

"That's a new one, he thinks you're Jesus."

The blur was a thin young man, darkly intense, sporting what I at first took to be a member of the mollusc family but was in fact a prodigious amount of dirty blood-red dreadlocks. "Jesus never had hair like this, I reckon," he said, grinning down at me. "Try again, dude."

I hazarded a guess. "Great Cthulhu?"

A look of pleased astonishment arose on his face. "A Lovecraft reference?" he asked. "And here we just met. You and me, we're going to be good friends, brother."

"Wow," I said, held in thrall by the hairy squid atop his head. It must have taken him decades to achieve such an ungainly mass. "Damn, that's some hair."

"You know, I get that a lot," he said, helping me to my feet. "You've got quite a bump there, you remember anything?"

I replied the only way I could. "Big head."

He laughed, echoed by the large man I could now see standing behind him. "Yes, big head. Very, very big head."

"I didn't imagine it?"

"Nope, no sir." he said. The dreads shook with his laughter. He walked past me, absently brushing his shoulders. "C'mon, let's go see what almost killed you, if you're up to it." I followed him toward the front doors, meekly rubbing my scalp.

"What the hell is that thing?" I exclaimed. It lay where it had fallen, a lopsided leviathan with a deranged rictus grin. The hollows where I had pummelled it had magically filled themselves in.

"What, you don't recognize him? Warren, give me a hand here, willya?" Aubrey and the large man I surmised to be Warren lifted the head off the ground, balancing it on its chin. I fearfully took a few steps back, disguising my trepidation as the need to gain perspective. From a distance, and without the elements of surprise and horror, it was easily identifiable.

"Munroe Purvis, right?"

"On the nose, very good," said Aubrey. "We're putting him up on the wall to the left there. He's just a little slippery." Warren grabbed the face by its nose, lifting it easily over his head, and set it flush against the wall above a set of display shelves. It rebounded slightly with a meaty thump.

I took a closer assessment while Aubrey and Warren finished with the hanging. The visage was composed of a polymer of some kind, squishy yet firm, layered in disturbingly lifelike hair. I experimentally poked the cheek, watching my finger sink effortlessly into the flesh. The feeling of rampant slugs on my skin returned and I withdrew the finger hastily, quivering. The *schlepping!* noise of boots stuck in mud arose as the hole slowly filled itself in.

"It's grotesque," I said finally. "It's like something out of *The Wizard of Oz.*"

Aubrey chuckled. "Yeah, it's pretty repugnant. But realistic. More real than the real thing, you ask me." He hugged himself. "Gives me the willies just thinking 'bout it."

"You're just letting your personal feelings get in the way," said the big man. "Ignore who it is, and admire what it is. Myself, I'm in thrall to it. I feel its spirit about us. Aubrey, can you feel it? He's here, right now. Munroe is watching us through his plasticine representative. He'll show us what to do." Warren prostrated in front of it, salaaming shamelessly. "Oh, great Purv, you are so wise! Show us what to read! Tell us how to think!" He rolled over onto his back, convulsing and dribbling spit onto the floor. "I feel the spirit, it's in me! I am the Purv, and he is I!" He then began babbling in tongues, shivering violently.

It may have been a delayed reaction to the attack, or perhaps it was the near-lethal amounts of anti-depressants coursing their way throughout my anatomy, but either way, I couldn't control myself. I laughed helplessly.

Aubrey made a show of solemnity, placing his palms carefully on Warren's head. "I feel it within you, my son. It is an evil presence, foul and black."

"Save me, father! Save me!" Warren yelled.

"Unclean demon, I cast thee OUT!" Aubrey's hands flew upward, pushing Munroe's spirit to the skies. "BEGONE! THE POWER OF CHRIST COMPELS YOU!" he wailed, before collapsing into giggles beside Warren. I tried valiantly to get my laughter under control, before giving in completely, leaning against a bookshelf for support. The three of us stayed there, clutching our stomachs and cackling for no reason we could understand other than we had hit a nerve with each other. Customers wandered by, unperturbed by both the gibbering idiots and the great head of the beast.

Gradually, we managed to sober up and silence ourselves, except the occasional exhausted giggle. Aubrey rose unsteadily to his feet. "Dude, get up," he said, offering Warren a hand. "C'mon, seriously, before Page sees us."

"Ah, whatever," said Warren, remaining prone on the floor and breaking into a fresh spasm of giggles. "You own her, dude."

"Now, you know that's not true. And even if it was, you certainly do not own her, so get up before you get yourself fired."

"All right, all right. Buzzkiller."

"So, what's it for?" I asked. "The head."

"Promotion," said Aubrey. "The Purv here's got the world's most powerful book club. This graven image is going to sit above a display of the books."

I'd heard of the book club, of course. Ever since Oprah had lent superstar status to the book industry, clubs were big news. Just mentioning her name in the same breath as a novel shot it up the charts. I took a take-it-or-leave-it approach to most of her selections, but I admit she picked some winners. Ann-Marie MacDonald, of course, and Franzen, even though he eschewed the honour. Toni Morrison, for everything she ever wrote or thought of writing. Anyone who convinced people to read Rohinton Mistry was okay by me, even if a lot of them couldn't understand it.

Then Oprah stopped, and the world stopped with her. Sales

sank. Publishers panicked. Audiences mourned the loss of someone to tell him or her what to read. She eventually started up again, but the damage was done. Attempts were made to fill the void with little success. No one cared what Joan Lunden thought of a book. Ditto the ladies of *The View.* One book club even succeeded in *raising* the illiteracy level of America; an author, despondent that Kelly Ripa recommended his novel, tore out his own eyes rather than face the shame.

Munroe Purvis, though, he operated on an entirely new plane of televised existence. Curly headed, overly plump, and oozing sincerity from his pores like so much sweat, he made Dr. Phil look like a paedophile, and Maury Povich look like . . . well, like an even greasier Maury Povich, if such a thing is possible. Women loved him, in a completely asexual "want to take him home to meet mom and dad but would never sleep with him it just wouldn't be right" sort of way. Donahue meets the Beaver, but softer. An oversized couch-cushion of a man. He was the biggest thing to hit the publishing industry in years.

The thing that rankled, the thing that prodded your open sores with a vinegar-dipped poker, the thing was, his book club publications were, to a one, vile. Literary merit held no meaning for him. Style, originality, composition, character, these were terms anathema to his authors. Purvis was the ultimate in indiscriminating consumerism, happy if he could read a book in less than a day, and ecstatic if the binder's glue held the pages together. His choices were obscene in their banality. Nora Roberts was too edgy. Movie novelizations were too long. Reader's Digest Condensed editions? Too dense by half. God help him if a novel's content challenged his sense of self beyond the rigours demanded by the weekly edition of *TV Guide.* In a Munroe novel, B followed A, C followed B, the end. B would never take a detour to R to catch a flick or engage in a little stimulating subtext.

Munroe's personal appraisals of his choices were nonsensical, devoid of any hint of valid criticism beyond liked it, loved it, or a combination of the two. His print reviews, carried by all major newspapers, were almost poetic haikus of hot air, faultless examples of how to distil any topic into seven words or less, preferably never more than two syllables each.

Munroe Purvis was ghastly. Abominable. Atrocious. His book club choices sold in the millions, and his audience clamoured for more.

"But why the head?"

"Simple," replied Aubrey. "It's the next generation of the life-sized cardboard cut-out, a synthesis of modern technology and old-fashioned hucksterism. Purvis sells books. Therefore, duh, a giant head in the likeness of Purvis will point people toward what he commands they buy. Therefore, whatever is placed underneath the head will also sell."

"His choices, you mean."

"Well, yes. Amongst others." Aubrey pointed to Warren, busily stacking the display shelves from a set of boxes along the wall. "Most of those boxes contain his latest picks. But one box, you will note, contains several copies of Chip Kidd's *Cheese Monkeys*." He removed a copy of Kidd's novel from a box, and slapped a gold sticker embossed with the words MUNROE RECOMMENDS THIS! on its cover.

"Purvis recommends *Cheese Monkeys?*" I was impressed.

A vicious grin lit up Aubrey's face. "Yeah, that'll happen." He happily put the novel on a shelf, obscuring several copies of Munroe's latest release, Laureen Hoper's *Lightbulbs and Dreams*. "I'm just tryin' to help a brother out, y'know? Boost the sales of someone who deserves the recognition. By placing Kidd's novel in with the dreck, it guarantees that someone will buy them, maybe even read them."

"And this works?"

"You tell me. Last month, we sold twelve copies of Will Self's *Great Apes* before anyone complained. Hey, *caveat emptor,* right?"

"Yeah, fuck 'em if they can't take a joke," Warren chimed in, cheerfully putting MUNROE stickers on copies of William S. Burroughs' *The Soft Machine* and chuckling all the while. "This oughta send a few customers into therapy."

"You want to try?" Aubrey asked me.

"What, you serious?"

"Almost never." He held a page of stickers out to me. "Go grab something you like, I'll put it out here."

The notion that I should not do such a thing — that it would be tantamount to quitting the job before I had a chance to honestly screw it up — made a brief appearance in my thoughts, but the ten RECOMMENDS stickers, reflecting fluorescent light on my face, taunted me into action. I looked about eagerly. What would tick a Munroe-ite off? Something sacrilegious, yet seemingly inoffensive. Nersian's *The Fuck-Up* popped itself into my head, but the title was too off-putting for anyone to believe Munroe had ever even cracked its spine. Ditto Burrough's *Queer*. The lightbulb clicked on and I took off, hoping against hope until I laid my eyes upon it. Seizing my pick, I hightailed it back, chuckling giddily as I proudly held out my choice to the two shelvers: *George Bush, Dark Prince of Love*, by Lydia Millet. Warren applauded as I stuck a gold star proudly on the cover.

"Very nice choice," Aubrey said.

"I figured the title might fool some into thinking it's a biography," I said, flushed. Aubrey placed the novel dead centre on the display. Man, it was such a rush.

"I know, it's strange," said Warren as if I'd just spoken this aloud. "I've had almost every narcotic known to man, but I never feel as good as when I perform this little act of sabotage. Well, almost never."

"Wait, how did you know I'm not like a secret shopper?" I asked. "I could get you guys fired for this." Aubrey brought his hands to shoulder-height, palms up to indicate *what's life without risk?* It's fair to say, I admired Aubrey from the moment I met him. "I'm Thomas," I said, extending a hand.

He shook it cordially. "Aubrey. And the immense man there is Warren." The giant arched an eyebrow in acknowledgment. "You here for a job, Thomas?"

"How'd you know?"

"You've got the glazed, nervous aura of the hoping-to-be-hired about you," he said. "I also know that we're looking for people at the moment." Aubrey pointed down one of the endless aisles. "You want Page's office, the end of Aisle 9, right next to Food, Vegetarian."

"Thanks." I walked toward the mouth of the aisle.

"Oh, and Thomas?" Aubrey called after me. I turned around. "You remember Great Cthulhu?" I nodded. "Well, Page isn't that bad, all things considered, but it's a close thing."

"Thanks for the warning."

"Just watch out for the shoggoths, and you'll do fine. Oh, and don't make eye contact, she might think you're flirting."

"And that's a bad thing?"

"Very bad." Aubrey said. Behind him, Warren shuddered.

Click, click.

"So, why would you like to work for **READ?**" She pronounced it *red*, which I supposed ended the argument. Her pen clicked in her fingers. Open and closed. In and out. *Click, click.*

"Well," I began, bracing myself for the onslaught. *Click, click.* "I've always been a big reader. I mean, huge. Ten, eleven books a month, easy."

"Really." She uncrossed and recrossed her legs. Idly, remembering Aubrey's flirtation warning, I imagined myself having sex with Page and immediately regretted it, the image of my penis flattened in a laundry mangle imprinting itself onto my soul. I covered up my wince with a cough. Page Adler is not the sort of woman men dream about. There is something unsettlingly severe and Dickensian about her pinched features; Miss Havisham without the whimsy. You could say she just missed being pretty, but that would be a level of benevolence on par with Gandhi. There is a disquieting incompleteness to her features. Perhaps it was due to her hair, done back in a severe bun and stretching her skin so tightly the plates of her skull were rearranging themselves to accommodate the stress, her facial pores now tiny mouths yelping for mercy. The parts all worked separately (two eyes, one nose, various other cavities and fissures), but taken as a whole, she looked like a child's jigsaw puzzle. Several puzzles, thrown into a box, then randomly put back together by children with severe visual impairments.

Click, click.

"Ten or eleven books. Impressive."

Click, click.

"Nowhere near what Aubrey reads, but impressive."

Click, click.

I found myself entranced by her hair, amazed that she could

even blink with it so tightly wrapped behind her head. My eyes began twitching involuntarily, expecting the snap of the hair band at any moment.

"Why do you think that might be an asset here at **READ**?" She pronounced it *reed* this time, a tiny smile twitching at the edges of her mouth as I soundlessly processed the discrepancy. Would I have the gonads to mention it? *Click, click.* She enjoyed the confusion this caused.

"Well, in all honesty, I've been in a lot of bookstores where the employees couldn't tell you one word about a book. Any book. In fact, I came to this very store some time ago, and the employee helping me was unable to find me a copy of *Interpreter of Maladies* by Jhumpa Lahiri. He had never even heard of it! I mean, it only won the Pulitzer a few years ago!"

Nothing. *Click, click.* Keep going.

"Not only do I read voraciously," *Good word!* "but I also study book reviews in major newspapers, and try to keep abreast of new publications." *Click, click.* "In this way, I hope that my knowledge of books will not only help a person find the book they're looking for, but perhaps help them discover something new."

Page arched her eyebrow; she only had the one, an elongated tract of hair in desperate need of harvest. Raising one side in what I supposed was meant as a look of wry scepticism resulted in the effect of a bushy brown caterpillar raising its head for a look-see. "And why would that be an asset at **REED**?"

"Because . . ." It's a trap, be careful. Don't mention the store's name. ". . . it will increase sales?"

What passed for a grin flitted across her face as she made a checkmark on her clipboard. The smile didn't help soften her features. The image of Roy Scheider shovelling chum into the mouth of a mechanical shark swam through my mind.

She looked me in the eyes. I bit back a scream. "Why did you quit your last job?" *Click, click.*

"It just wasn't for me." Be honest, but not too honest. "I was very aware of how unhappy it made me, and I feel that a miserable" miserable? Hah! Fingers blubbering the lips crazy, more like . . . "lawyer is not an effective lawyer. There are enough poor lawyers out there without me muddying up the pool." Good. Solid answer.

No crying or anything.

"What's it like, being a lawyer?"

What's it like being a bitch? "It had its moments."

"Moments?"

"Moments. Brief periods of satisfaction."

"But not enough?"

"No, not nearly."

"Good pay, I'll bet."

"Meh." I shrugged and waggled my fingers in the international signal for *comme ci, comme ça*. "Legal Aid."

"Ah."

Click, click.

"Well, I'll be honest with you, Thomas. I need someone, and I need someone now. I've had a few people quit on me recently, and I'm short-staffed." She leaned forward. I congratulated myself on not recoiling in fright. "But," she said. Why is there always a but? "But I've had bad luck with people like you in the past."

"People like me?" Lawyers? Lapsed Mennonites?

"Readers. Bibliophiles. People who erroneously believe that the printed word is worth more than printed money. I've fired them before, and I hold no compunctions about doing so again. That's why I have an opening right now. I will not stand for anything less than complete commitment to the achievement of each month's projected sales quota. This is a business, it's about making a profit, and if I run it like a car dealership, then that's the way it is, clear?"

Click, click.

"And frankly, Thomas, if I may speak frankly, the fact that you quit the law does not impress me. It appears to me you might be a quitter." She leaned back and regarded me, recrossing her legs. A torrent of sweat gathered in my armpits/crotch. "Are you a quitter, Thomas? Should we end this interview right now? Am I wasting my time with you?"

"No." Did I just piss myself?

"Good. I need people who will sell books, not read them. Reading is secondary to sales. I understand you may believe that the artist is more important than the consumer, but that belief stops the moment you punch in for work. I expect knowledge of the product, of course, but the customer is always right. *Always.*

Clear?"

"Crystal."

"Good. Do what I say, make the sales, and we'll get along fine. You start on Monday, we open at ten o'clock, be here by nine-thirty, dress appropriately, no nose rings, eyebrow rings, or anything of that sort. Conservative dress, nothing flashy, no nods to your unique individuality. Long-sleeve shirt, one colour, pants, one colour, shoes, one colour. No labels. You may take any hardcover home you would like to read, provided you return it in pristine condition. Otherwise, it comes out of your pay. You get forty percent off all purchases, including clearance items. Paycheques are every second Friday."

Click, click.

She stood up, extending a talon toward me. "Welcome to **RED**, Thomas."

I grasped her claw, shook it firmly. "Thank you, Ms. Adler."

"Page."

"Page."

I managed to leave the building without collapsing, swearing, or assaulting someone. The fresh breeze slapped me around for a bit as I gulped down oxygen by the lungful.

"Whooo. Friend, you look terrible." Aubrey was slouched up against the wall, rolling a cigarette with his fingers. "She's a type-A peach, ain't she?"

I nodded, my head clearing. "She's a piece of work. She's what Shakespeare would call one seriously scary lady."

"That she is, that she is," he said, sealing the smoke with his tongue. "You smoke up?"

"Only when I'm depressed. Gimme." He tossed me the cigarette along with his lighter and began rolling another for himself. Cupping my hand against the wind, applying flame to paper, I inhaled deeply, getting instantly dizzy in that good pre-cancerous way. The soothing smog worked its way down my windpipe, telling my lungs to relax, it'll only be this one time. Too late, the sharp-sour tang of unwashed feet hit my smell receptors, informing me that, by the way, I was not inhaling tobacco/nicotine/arsenic/toejam smoke, but was in reality now smoking a highly illegal and fairly potent spliff. I held the smoke down, musing on the possible side effects of marijuana when combined with a sizable dose of anti-depressants, then gave up the thought for being too depressing. Besides, is there such a thing as being too relaxed? And is that a bad thing?

"Don't let her scare you, dude," Aubrey said, taking the lighter back and igniting his own, savouring the taste with a heavy sigh.

"Too late," I gasped, releasing the breath and enveloping my head in a cloud of happiness.

"She may appear vicious, but when you get to know her . . . ah, forget it. She's Satan incarnate."

"How do you put up with her?" I asked, another lungful of goodness massaging my nerves. Again, I was mesmerized by his hair, the tentacles swaying in the wind, a sea anemone gathering snacks. "She doesn't come across as a people person."

He shrugged, holding a weed cloud in his lungs for a few moments. "Page and people, no, not a good mix," he said, exhaling. "She'd be happy if there was some way she could manage the store and keep people out of the equation, but you can't sell without salespeople. Can't sell without people to sell to. Page is all about the money. I'm all about the books. She hates me, hell, she detests people in general, but I can move the product, in her parlance, so she tolerates my existence. She rarely comes out on the floor anyhow. Just stay out of her way, and you'll be fine."

"She's more afraid of us than we are of her?"

"Hardly. She'll gut you in a second and use your steaming entrails as casserole filling, if she thinks you're not living up to your earning potential."

"What if I play dead?"

"Since when has that ever deterred a carrion-eater?"

"Charming." I stubbed the embers out against the wall, putting the roach in my jacket pocket for future consumption. "I guess I'll see you Monday."

"Monday it shall be then. How's your head, by the way?"

I massaged my forehead. "I'll be fine," I said, sheepish in my embarrassment. "I just hope that wasn't an omen."

"Hey, brother, you just had your hand up the nose of a well-known television personality, then went toe-to-toe with the high priestess of the damned. I would guess that there's nowhere to go but up."

Good place to stop for a rest.
Yours,
Thomas

From Variety

Munroe Biopic Announced

LOS ANGELES — With the Munroe Purvis investigation still ongoing, Fox Television has announced they have reached a deal with MuPu Incorporated to bring the life and times of Munroe Purvis to the screen.

Margaret Compar, head of Program Development at Fox, says in a press release, "Mr. Purvis's life has been one of immense hardship and struggle, a truly inspirational story that we hope will provide a valuable glimpse into the inner workings of this most remarkable and influential man."

When reached for comment, Ms. Compar's press secretary Marcel Oxford told *Variety*, "The recent unfortunate and tragic developments in Mr. Purvis's life will be covered in some detail, of course, but we are working hard to ensure this will not be simply a tasteless exposé into a grotesque and horrific occurrence. We have been working hand-in-hand with Munroe's company to develop Mr. Purvis's life into a biography format for some time now. He has had a significant impact on our culture, and the recent events of his life notwithstanding, his story of struggle and redemption is a classic American tale that everyone involved with the production is very proud of. That's why we are now raising the reward for any information that may help solve this horrendous crime."

Fox Television has pledged one hundred thousand dollars for information leading to the capture of any of the remaining fugitives in the Munroe Purvis case. "An arrest would provide a fine ending to the movie, we admit," says Oxford. "But far more important to us is that a ruthless criminal be brought to justice."

As of this writing, insiders have pegged occasional *Family Feud* host and former *Home Improvement* co-star Richard Karn as the likely frontrunner to portray Mr. Purvis.

TO: ermccorm@yahoo.ca
FROM: iamashelfmonkey@gmail.com
SUBJECT: The descent into the mouth of Hell

Dear Eric, Amanda, tabloid journalists, and entertainment lawyers;

If there is to be a bidding war for my story, please go as high as possible. Take them for all they'll cough up. Ewan MacGregor must portray me in the movie, understand? I will not accept a lesser actor to properly breathe life into the anguish I feel the part demands. No sitcom second bananas, no *Full House* refugees or *21 Jump Street* has-beens. No, I need someone with the gravitas of Obi-Wan Kenobi and the insouciance of an Irvine Welsh junkie. I demand one hundred thousand dollars up front, plus two percent of the gross if I am innocent in a court of law, not the court of popular opinion. A real judge, not Judge Judy. If MacGregor isn't available, I'm flexible. Jake Gyllenhaal, Tobey Maguire, Jude Law, or Topher Grace will be adequate. All right, that *Dawson's Creek* dude with the crescent-shaped head, but that's as far as I am willing to go.

On second thought, maybe forget the *Jump Street* thing, get Johnny Depp.

The First Day

What you might call my spiritual awakening.

I tell you, Eric, some people don't deserve the privilege of literacy.

I'm dressed for the occasion. Comfortable Hush Puppies. Eddie Bauer shirt and slacks. Clean socks and underwear. Hair stylishly mussed. Unsightly yet mandatory employees-only vest with Hello My Name is Thomas May I Help You badge on the pocket. Handful of happy pills dancing with fried eggs and toast in my stomach. Lookin' sharp! So sharp, I arrived ten minutes late.

Every morning, Page held a quick employee meeting before opening the doors to the masses. Usually these were perfunctory events — customers good, browsers bad, sales important, push Munroe's latest discovery, blah, blah. Luckily I managed to slink in undetected and take a place directly behind Warren. Hopefully my years of camouflage training in high school would allow me to suddenly appear on everybody's radar, yet be dismissed as having already been present since the beginning and simply hidden behind the living landmass.

"Now, this week's club," Page was saying. "Warren, it's your turn to lead the group." Warren jerked reflexively, and was about to protest when Page stopped him short. "Don't bother to argue, I'm not in the mood. You know the schedule, everyone has to lead the book club at some point, and it's your turn. I've got a copy of this week's choice, *The Love Market*, in my office. It's the new Munroe, and it will sell like gangbusters, so I want to promote it to the hilt. Pick it up before you leave today, and I expect you to have read it thoroughly before Wednesday night."

"Could I switch with Heather?" Warren swung his chin toward a woman standing nearer the front. "She's much better at that sort of thing. Besides, I don't know anything about talking to those people."

"I don't mind, Page," Heather chimed, clearly delighted at the prospect. "I *adore* the elderly."

"Hey, it's not old people that bother me, it's . . ." Warren stopped himself.

Page drummed her fingers, clearly angered. "It's what, Warren? It's your turn, and I might add that I do not appreciate being argued with in front of the staff. But since you brought it up, what bothers you?" All heads turned toward us. I ducked a little more, smiling uneasily at nearby employees suddenly aware of my existence.

Warren sighed, a low, drawn-out gust. "It's the books. You never have any books I want to talk about, you just have the latest Munroe."

"Ah. And that's a problem, is it?"

"Well —"

"You have a problem with having to do your job, and read what your customers are reading?" Page's breath came out in plumes of frost. "Do you think you are somehow entitled to not fulfil the requirements of the job that everyone in the room abides by, including myself? If you don't enjoy your time here, Mr. Krall, I suggest . . ."

"If I could just jump in here a minute," interjected a voice. All heads swivelled left. I could just make out the red octopus of Aubrey's hair across the room. "I think what Warren is trying to say is that the store's book club has appeared lately to concentrate solely on Munroe Purvis selections."

Page audibly gritted her teeth. "I'm still waiting to hear the problem with that."

"Well, *Page*," said Aubrey, emphasizing her name in an exasperated drawl, "surely you haven't forgotten that the point of the bookstore is to sell books." A few snickers went up around the group, quickly transformed into coughs as Page shot them a look so cold it could sterilize. "Now, I'm just thinking out loud here, but it seems to me that using the book club to persuade people to purchase books that they are going to buy anyway might just be a lost opportunity."

"The book club is a way to allow the community to meet and form a closer bond, both with each other and this store, Aubrey."

"I get that, but shouldn't we try to sell them something new as well?" Aubrey's rational tone was akin to speaking to a child who couldn't understand why the sky was blue. "What's the point of inviting these people in, having them avail themselves of the free coffee and muffins, not to mention the employee man-hours that we put in, if not to sell them something? And it only makes solid economic sense to sell them something that they weren't going to purchase anyway. In this way, you see, we may double our sales. It's only obvious."

"Yes, but we also want to keep our customers happy, Mr. Fehr." You could almost see the thought-balloon above Page's head, filled with scenes of unimaginable carnage. It was like watching a particularly gruesome fight, one of those cable television specials that are only available on pay-per-view because of the intense amount of bloodshed that was sure to occur. You couldn't believe that it was happening, and that you were still watching. My first day, and already a public firing? I didn't see how Aubrey could come through this altercation unscathed. "What makes our customers happy is Munroe publications. They want to discuss the books as if they're on the show with him. In this way, they have the vicarious thrill of reading something recommended by someone they admire, and they feel closer to him. They are then contented, and thus more likely to see **RED** as a place they can be comfortable in. I have made my decision, and you and Mr. Krall have not given me any reason to change my mind." Page looked to her clipboard. "Now, last on the agenda . . ."

"If we could just for once push a book they haven't had shoved down their throats by a corporate logo." Aubrey wouldn't let it go. "Kazuo Ishiguro has a new release, it's not too threatening, and I'm sure if we just try, we might just expand our customer's minds beyond the usual pap."

Back to Page. Her back was if anything even straighter, as if her vertebrae were being fused together from the blazing heat of her anger. No one dared breathe, lest the slightest breeze upset the tension.

"This can wait until later, Mr. Fehr," she said finally, in a tone of utter reason so unexpected the audience reeled as if slapped. "Meet me in my office?"

"Of course, Page." Aubrey gave a slightest of apologetic nods. "I didn't mean to overstep my boundaries."

"No apology necessary." Page's spine relaxed, and my knees almost buckled with relief. "Now, I think that's everything." She glanced at her clipboard. "Oops, I forgot, Thomas. Thomas Friesen, are you here?" She looked over the room. "Mr. Friesen?"

I timidly raised my hand above Warren's shoulder. "Here, Ms. Adler," I said, instantly back in kindergarten.

"Ah, there you are. Everyone, one last thing, we have new employee starting today. This is Thomas. He'll be taking over for Emily." A chilly ripple of resentment threads itself through the group. At me? "Thomas is a former *lawyer*"

FUCK! FUCKING FUCK FUCK FUCK!

"who I am quite positive will be a terrific asset to our store's little team. Thomas, I'll leave it to you to get acquainted with the staff. Danae, look after him, will you?" The group broke up, employees dispersing them-selves through the store.

"Hey, sorry, didn't see you down there, guy," Warren apologized. "Been there long?"

"Uh, long enough."

"Oh, you saw that, huh? You enjoy the floorshow? Hope it

didn't turn you off working for our happy little family here."

"Yeah, what was *that* about?"

"They're always like that. I've never understood it, but the way I figure, if you can sell like Aubrey, you can pretty much act how you please."

"Well, I guess, but *still . . .*" The explanation didn't sit well with me. Aubrey's behaviour was a bit too forward to be ever tolerated by an employer. "You don't think they're . . ." I let the sentence hang in the air, hoping that my insinuation was strong enough that I wouldn't need to utter the words.

"What?"

"They're . . ." I thrust my hips back and forth a few times.

Warren made a face. "Hey, there's no call for that kind of imagery, dude; this is a family bookstore." He wobbled on his feet as the distasteful notion cemented itself in his mind. "No, it's nothing like that. I don't get their relationship either, but it's not that. It's like, like . . . well, I don't know what it's like exactly, similes fail me. But if there is something that it's like, something you never get used to, then that's what it is." He checked his watch. "Gotta go, dude, the doors are about to open and I've got a wicked whiz coming on. I've got a lunch hour at about one, see you in the break room?"

"I have no idea. I haven't even filled out a form yet."

"I'll help you with that." I felt a light tapping on my shoulder, which I took as an indication that I should swivel around. Turned thusly, I stood looking at a woman dressed entirely in what I can only describe as librarian chic. A woman who finally fit my image of what the term *zaftig* was supposed to mean. The kind of woman *I* dream about. Round in all the best places. Black hair bound in a ponytail, with a loose strand or two dangling fetchingly loose. Dark plastic rims outlining eyes of an almost black brown. Freckles abounded before me, highlighting cheekbones and nose in such a way that I became acutely aware of such things. She knew she was good-looking, but saw no need to flaunt it. A sweetish perfume tickled my nose hairs. I inhaled deeply.

"Thomas?" she asked. Did I detect a note of lust in her voice, or was I just desperately lonely?

"Yes?"

"Do you always flare your nostrils like that?"

I stopped sniffing. "No, sorry, uh, allergies." I sniffed again to demonstrate how plugged up I was. "Too much smog in the air, or something."

Warren snickered. "Yes, something in the air." He pushed an enormous elbow through my ribs. "So much *something*. Really hard to breathe in here, right, Thomas? Could it be love?"

The woman took pity on me, unmistakably annoyed at Warren's teasing of the new boy with the hopeless schoolboy crush. "I'm Danae," she said, extending a lovely hand toward me. Perspiration filled my palm. I willed the appendage to dry and manfully gripped her hand tightly, not too tightly, just enough to show that I was indeed all man, but still had a sensitive side that could permit me to cry at sentimental movies and funerals, and if she'd only give me a chance, I could in all probability be the one for her, the soulmate, the yin to her yang, the other side of her coin. By the end of the handshake, I was exhausted.

Danae wiped her palm off on the seat of her pants. Dammit. She looked to the big man beside me. "Warren, don't you have a Munroe to get from Page?"

He nodded solemnly in a playful show of obsequiousness. "Oh, yes ma'am. Can't wait to crack it open. Just wanted to make sure my new mate here was well taken care of."

"Well, leave that to me, won't you?" She swept Warren away with her hands. "Off you go, little boy. There's literature to sell." Warren snapped together a jaunty salute and lumbered off to his grazing grounds, grinning at me all the while and throwing me a wink that could be seen from space.

If she saw the wink, Danae took no mind. "I'll be your tour guide today. If you'll follow me?"

"Lead on, Bwana."

Danae escorted me through the jumble of aisles to her workstation. "Do I get an employee map?" I asked as we rounded the fifth corner on our trek. "You know, in case I get lost and you're not available."

"You'll get used to it. Just remember, moss grows on the north side of a bookshelf."

"I'll keep that in mind."

"In an emergency, the binding glue of most books, if sucked out of the spine, contains essential nutrients that can be used to sustain life almost indefinitely." We reached an antique desk hidden behind Asian-American Studies. She perched herself behind an enormous flat screen and motioned for me to have a seat on the metal folding chair to the side. "Have a seat here, and I'll get you entered into the computer." She began typing on the keyboard.

"So, what's your position here?" I asked as I sat with a sexy slouch, trying for an air of Cary Grant nonchalance, but instead settling for what I hoped was a stuttering Hugh Grantesque effacement.

"I'm the assistant manager." I straightened up in my seat. "And before you ask, no, I don't date employees."

"I quit."

"Funny. How do you spell Friesen, E I or I E?"

"I E. You assume I'll want to date you?"

"You wouldn't be the first, sport."

"Could I be the last?"

"Cute. Social Insurance number?"

I gave her my card. "Hey, we just met, next thing you'll be asking me for my telephone number."

"Telephone number?"

"Uh . . . I'll let you know."

"Don't be coy, now."

"No, I'm just . . . temporarily between phones at the moment." My telephone had been disconnected the week previous for massive funds owing. "Besides, I hate them. Phones. Don't you just hate its air of despotism? It's this tiny little man who sits in your corner and demands your attention at any time it sees fit. No matter where you are, what you're doing, you leap to attention when it calls for you. And cell phones, don't get me started. We'd all be better off without them, you ask me."

She stopped typing. Her brown eyes considered me. "What an intensely charming little rant, if only it meant something. You must have practised in front of a mirror for hours." Busted. "And if someone gets sick and I need a replacement? How do I call you, what do I do?"

"Tell them to walk it off? I'll give you a number when I've

received my paycheque, promise."

She sighed. "I'll put my number in for now. Just don't let me forget."

"Does this mean we're dating?"

"I assume you have an address, or should I just put down 'beneath Osborne Street Bridge' or something?"

"Apt. 27, 182 Furby Street. Just south of Broadway."

"The bridge would be nicer."

"Hey, once you get past the constant threat of drive-by stabbings, it's not so bad."

She placed her hands in her lap. "Done. Just please try to get a phone soon, before Page finds out what I've done."

"You're scared of her, too?"

"I've met nicer rabid dogs." We shared a smile of mutual terror. "Are you always so flirty?" she asked.

"Opening night jitters," I said. "I kind of ramble on when I'm nervous."

"What comes after Q?"

"R?"

"You'll do fine." She stood up. "Follow me, Thomas, and I'll give you the grand tour. Or do you prefer Tom, or Tommy?"

"Thomas," I said, a little too forcefully. "I, um . . . I've never liked the name Tommy, that's all." She took a pause, looking at me with a distinct tilt to her head, the tilt that says you're hiding something, and you're doing a shitty job of it, but I'll let it slide, just be aware that *I'm* aware, you dig?

"Okay, Thomas it is," she said. We strode off in a westerly direction. "Now, the biggest part of your job will be handling customer requests. Page doesn't approve of lengthy discussions as to the literary merits of any particular book, so keep your answers short."

"What *does* Page approve of?"

"Sales. Volume, not discourse, is the lifeblood of this store. Did she give you her used car analogy?" I nodded. We walked in silence for several hundred metres before reaching what appeared to be the Fiction acre. Danae stopped and blew an errant strand of hair from her face while she thought about something. "Listen, Thomas, I don't mean to freak you out, what with this being your first day and all, but you heard what happened to Emily, right?"

"What, the previous me? No."

Danae took a breath. "Look, you seem relatively stable. But this place, it can have an effect on you."

"You're scaring me."

"I mean to. Emily was like a lot of us here, she loved books. I mean, why else would sane people work here, right? But this place, it isn't about the books, it's about the sale of books. Got me?"

"With you so far."

"Emily, well, got a little frustrated with Page and the whole money thing. She began to berate the customers for their ignorance. Eventually, Page got wind of it, and . . ." Danae made a motion with her hands, wiping invisible crumbs away. "Page got rid of her. One day here, next day, poof."

"Why are you telling me this?" I asked.

She sighed, revolving her eyes ceilingward. "Because I egged Emily on. We all did. The place'll affect you, you know, in a Hill House sort of way. We can all get that way, and as it turned out, she was the one to take the bullet for the team." She noticed the oblique terror in my eyes, and put her hand on my arm. "Don't mean to frighten, sorry. Aubrey says you'll do well, I just want to make sure."

"He said that? I've known him like four minutes."

"He's a good judge of character. That and books. Never wrong about books." Danae peeked at her watch. "Sorry, gotta go. Page and I have a meeting about sales figures or some bullshit thing. I'll find you at lunchtime, see how you're making out."

"What should I do?"

She pulled out a degrading TRAINEE tag and pinned it to my vest. "Just stay in this general area, answer questions, and if anything gets too complicated, find another employee, or direct them to the front of the store."

"And where's that?"

"Just say, by the big head. You know the one I mean?"

"Intimately."

"Remember, women account for eighty percent of all hardcover sales, so push the big books on the females. Weird, but true." She walked off, waving goodbye over her shoulder.

As instructional training goes, I've had better.

I take a linebacker stance in Fiction, my designated area, thank Christ.

An intercom click, husky voice on loudspeakers. "The store is now open."

"Music" fills the aisles, vanilla pudding for the ears.

Ah, Gino Vanelli. Perfect.

"Hello, may I help you with anything?"
"No, thank you, I've found what I was looking for."
"All right." That wasn't so hard.

When you get caught between — Hey, wasn't this the theme from Arthur?

"Hi, can I help you find anything?"
"Yes, my son is a science-fiction fan. I'd like to buy him something for his birthday."
"I see. Well, we have a wide variety of choices. Does he like the work of Asimov, or are you looking for something a little older, say Bester or Sturgeon? Maybe a Zelazny?"
"Well . . ."
"You cannot go wrong with Philip K. Dick. He's one of the old grand masters of the genre. *Ubik*, that's his finest, I'm sure I could find you a copy around here somewhere, or maybe *Do Androids Dream of Electric Sheep?*"
"That's a weird title."
"Well, it was made into a movie, *Blade Runner,* years ago, but the book is much better. Very dark. Very philosophical."
"I don't know . . ."
"Trust me, your son will thank you."
"I'll think about it. I know he likes video games. Aren't there any books based on video games?"
Sigh. "Yes, just over this way, I think."
"Thank you. Oh, *Brute Force*, this is perfect. Oh, and *Star Trek*, too. Why didn't you just point me over here?"
"Sorry."

Bette Midler warbles about the air underneath her armpits. Great, that'll be stuck in my head all fucking day.

"Hi, can I help you?"

"Yes, why don't you have a legal fiction section?"

"I'm sorry?"

"Every week I'm here, every time I have to go through every goddamn aisle looking at every goddamn title. Why don't you have a section on just legal thrillers?"

"Well, I could mention it to . . ."

"Every goddamn week. No one does anything. Every goddamn week! That's all I want, why don't you guys ever listen?"

"Sir . . ."

"You got your science fiction section, you got your horror all over there, you got your westerns, why no legal thrillers, huh? You think I like having to go through all this crap?"

Barbara Streisand? Who the freaking hell listens to Streisand anymore?

"Can I help you find anything, Miss?"

"Yes, where's the newest book, I heard it on the radio?"

"Uh . . ."

"They were talking about it this morning, did you hear it?"

"No, I'm afraid I didn't listen to the radio this morning."

"Huh. It's about this guy who's afraid? Of something? I think it was in Africa, or Italy. No, Kansas. It sounded really good, it just came out, I'm sure you must have it."

You gotta be kidding me. "I'm afraid I need more information, miss."

"Oh, what good are you? Why don't they ever hire people who understand books?"

Céline Dion screams the theme from Titanic. *Should have seen this one coming.*

"Hi, how are you today?"

"I don't know, where do you keep the John Grisham?"

"Under G, just over there."

"Oh, you file books alphabetically. That's handy."

"Isn't it?"

"Do all stores do it this way?"

"No, we're the first."

REO Speedwagon? Oh, come on, who the hell even remembers them anymore?

"Hi, can I . . ."

"Where's the latest Munroe book?"

"Under the giant head, next to the cash registers."

Peter Cetera. Wow, I was honestly just in the mood for the theme from The Karate Kid II.

"Excuse me, where's the head?"

"By the front door, can't miss it."

More Streisand, now with Kris Kristofferson for added emotional impact. Even Streisand doesn't listen to this much Streisand.

"Yes?"

"Yeah, where's the head, I couldn't find it?"

"By the front doors, right to the . . . wait, you mean the Big Head? Or the washroom?"

"The can."

"Sorry, uh, I have no idea. First day."

Wow. Anne Murray. Is she even still alive?

"Hello."

"Yes, hi, have you ever read this?"

Oh, thank God. "Yes, that's *Slaughterhouse-Five*, it's a classic."

"Looks interesting, do you think my son might like it? He's just starting college."

"He'll love it, guaranteed. It blew my mind when I read it in high school. It's about a man flipping through time, going from

World War II to a future where he's caged by aliens."

"What?"

"I know, it sounds strange, it is strange, but trust me, Vonnegut is a genius."

"Well, maybe I'll get him something else. I don't like that title anyway. Where's the latest Munroe . . ."

"Giant head, cash register." Fuck.

Chris DeBurgh. Now I know I'm being punished for something.

"Hello."

"Yes, I want to return this book."

"OK, you just go down that . . . *A Confederacy of Dunces?* Why?"

"It's stupid, it's too long, it's boring."

"But . . . it won the Pulitzer. It's a classic."

"Who cares, it's dumb, I don't want it."

Who are you people?

Elton John, you Hakuna Matata—singing motherfucker, get out of my head!

Clan of the Cave Bear? Follow me. The *Prodigal Project* series? Right this way, under Religious Fiction. *Slow Waltz in Cedar Bend?* Over here. *The Celestine Prophecy?* Around the corner. *Buffy the Vampire Slayer?* In Children's Books. *The Bear and the Dragon?* Under C for Clancy. Sean Hannity? You seriously want to buy a book by Sean Hannity? What the hell is wrong with you? Why don't you just stamp "ignorant dumbfuck" on your forehead and get it over with! Stop. Breathe, breathe. Happy place, find your happy place.

Cher, sans Sonny. Don't hum it, don't hum it. Damn.

Lunch.

Aubrey sat at the table as I walked into the employee lounge, his head buried in a copy of David Foster Wallace's *Infinite Jest* while absent-mindedly consuming a suspicious concoction of eggplant, tomato, and some spice undoubtedly never meant for human consumption. After a solid minute of being ignored, unconsciously whistling some Beyoncé tune, I *ahemed* for attention. Aubrey slowly lifted his head from the Wallace, his head seemingly weighed down with thick prose, and smiled in acknowledgement as he took me in. "Hey, brotherman, how goes the good fight?"

"Ignorance is winning, Vegas odds seven to two against common sense and good taste."

He chortled, sprinkling his food with hair dust. "There are some horrible books out there, no question."

"It's not the fact that bad books exist," I said. "That I can deal with. But there's so much good out there, it breaks your heart when they just sit there on the shelf, all lonely and unwanted."

Aubrey nodded as he scooped another suspicious morsel into his mouth. "Yeah, and meanwhile, you manage to sell three *Star Wars* novels and two Karen Robards. It'd be funny if it weren't so goddamn tragic."

"You think you got it bad, you have no idea," said Warren, walking in behind me. He sat next to Aubrey, hoisting his size fifteens to rest on the tabletop. "Take a look at this." He tossed a glossy paperback onto the table. *The Love Market*, written by Edward Miller, published under the imprint of Munroe Purvis himself. Aubrey gave a cry and shielded his Wallace from the unholy taint this book was sure to imbue on any literature within its strike zone. "I know, I've already finished the first fifty pages on my washroom break. Better than Pepto, two pages in and the shit just flowed out of me." I daintily picked the book up by a corner and read the back cover, taking care to to touch as little of it as possible.

> *Once again, Munroe Purvis brings you a story guaranteed to tug at the heartstrings, a gut-wrenching tale of love gone awry, of beliefs displaced, and of the unbreakable bonds of family.*
>
> *Freddy Conrad thought he married the woman of his dreams, when he one day awakes to the ugly truth of who his wife really is. Despite being pregnant with twin boys, Edith has turned away from Freddy and taken up a volunteer position with an abortion clinic. Torn between the woman he loves and the*

need to shield his unborn children from her insanity,
Freddy takes a step that may lose him his wife, but
may save his soul.

"Edward Miller's The Love Market *made me*
realize who I truly am, and I hope his extraordinary
novel affects you as strongly as it has me." — Munroe
Purvis

I laid the object back down. "Wow, it just screams quality, doesn't it?"

"Yes indeed, and it reads even worse, and now *I*," announced Warren as he brusquely slid the book off the table, "*I* have to lead an evening seminar on the merits of this bestseller. I mean, what could I possibly say? What does Freddy represent? Does the novel function as both a story and as propaganda? Aubrey, you've done this before, got any pointers?"

"Cram their gullets with cake, and they'll be satisfied. Believe me, they have no desire to talk of themes or subtext, they all just want to gush over how wonderful Munroe is for opening this world to them. Keep the coffee flowing, try to keep your nausea down, and you'll be fine."

"Is it always like this?" I asked the pair. My first day, and the despair over my choice of lifepath was already building.

"Well, you've kind of entered the store in a transition phase," Aubrey said. "Page recently let someone go, and we're all a bit upset over it. I think you'll feel resentment from some around here, but it'll pass. It's not your fault, after all." I nodded, remembering the blast of frosted air I received from others during the morning meeting when Emily's name was mentioned. "You getting on all right, otherwise?" asked Aubrey.

I walked to the vending machine, opting for the least unhealthy chocolate bar and bag of chips available. "Otherwise, I've been lost all morning. This place is gargantuan. I don't think I've seen one other employee since we've opened."

"Oh, we exist, you just have to know where to look," Warren said. "God, am I hot." He began to take off his vest, which sat atop a sizable bulky black sweater.

"I'm not surprised," I remarked as he pulled the sweater over his head. "Why are you wearing DEAR JESUS GOD WHAT THE HELL HAPPENED TO YOUR ARMS?"

I should say at this point, Eric *et al*, that I am not normally the sort of person who points out another person's deformities in a deafening and ignorant fashion. Like most people, I downplay the physical limitations of others, taking pains to treat a person as an individual, composed of the same emotions and needs as the rest of humanity.

However, what Warren suffered from was so clearly not natural, not typical, not in any way a standard deviation from the norm that I blurted out my exclamation before realizing the possible offensiveness of its content. Nevertheless, I stand by my startled little-girlish scream. Warren was a freak. His sizable arms, now bare to the fluorescent lights, revealed an array of colours and ridges never conceived by the human body. The hands and wrists were pink and healthy, untouched; beyond the wrists, gangrenous green meshed with sickly black, while veins of red pulsed around scaly patches of scarlet. It all melded into a shade I shall charitably describe as ochre, until disappearing beneath his undershirt.

Aubrey looked stumped, but composed. "Jeez, dude, what was it this time?"

"A mixture of natural and artificial ingredients, including the distilled venom of the queen bee," Warren said. He pirouetted his right arm in the air admiringly. How he kept from shrieking in pain is beyond me.

"You're allergic to bees, aren't you?" Aubrey asked. Warren drooped his head timidly, letting his arm dangle loosely beside him. "Jesus, bro. You could have been killed, idiot. Didn't you think to ask beforehand?"

"Rent was due," he said. "Besides, it's not as bad as it looks."

Aubrey's eyes bulged. "Should it be so . . . bluish?"

"You should have seen it two days ago; it looked like an over-stuffed kielbasa. Black, too. But the hallucinations have subsided, that's something."

Aubrey turned to the corner of the room where I had busied myself with cowering in terror. "Mr. Krall here, you see, earns extra money offering up his body for science. I have offered counsel to him in this regard, even offered him a place to stay should eviction become imminent, but as you can plainly see . . ." He motioned toward Warren, who was now gaily waving his arms in my direction, visibly enjoying my discomfort.

I swallowed down my gorge. "I don't mean to pass judgement, Warren, live and let live and all that, but good Christ that can't be healthy."

A mild shriek rose from the lounge doorway. "God, put those away before Page sees them!" said Danae as she entered, tut-tutting disapprovingly. Warren acquiesced, donning his sweater while muttering about the heat. "Well, you should have thought of that before you came to work, numb-nuts," she scolded, retrieving a bag lunch from the fridge and plopping down next to Aubrey.

"Well, I'm sorry, Danae, but these things show through anything lighter than a parka," Warren said, a wide grin on his mug. "They glow in the dark, too. But, good news, the company paid out to keep it quiet, so I'm set for a while." His sweater on, he appeared more or less normal, for a seven-foot-tall giant.

Danae pulled a yogurt carton from her lunchbag. "What does this make, now, eight?"

"Nine," Warren bragged. "I have been injected, swabbed, lathered, scrubbed, boiled, rubbed, and rolled in nine yet-to-be-released beauty and medicinal products."

Aubrey rolled his eyes to the ceiling. "I thought you had sworn off your crusade after your testicles retreated."

"They dropped back out a few weeks later," he groused. Warren's gaze latched onto my potato chips, which I had all but ignored in the excitement. "You gonna eat all those, Thomas?"

I tossed the bag aloft. "Enjoy. I'm not as hungry as I thought." Warren snagged it with one lengthy arm, shovelling its contents into his mouth with alarming speed and precision.

"Nice manners, buddy," said Danae. "Oh, hey, let me ask you guys something. Is it more depressing that Britney Spears can get a book published, or that people actually want to read the damn thing?"

"Uch, don't get me started," said Aubrey. "Thomas, you have an opinion?"

"Well, much as I hate the fact that a person who has never read a book thinks she can write one, there's no way she wrote it by herself, so I'm not so much depressed as annoyed by that. But someone wanting to shell out thirty-five bucks plus tax for such drivel, well, *that* makes me weep for our species."

"Fuckin' A, dude," said Warren.

"Nail on the head," agreed Aubrey. "Oh, I got one. Who's got it worse, Jane Austen for being shelved next to Jean Auel, or Steinbeck for having to share shelf space with Danielle Steel?"

"Steinbeck," Danae said. "Not because Steel's any worse than Auel, although that's arguable, but because Steel's fan base is so much larger. Both are popular, but Steel's more prolific, so on average more people visit Steel's area, and so there are that many more opportunities to see and ignore Steinbeck than Austen."

"Steinbeck was selling pretty about a year ago," Aubrey reminded us. "Oprah."

"Well yeah, but until that, you couldn't force people to read it. If Steinbeck were water, they would have died of thirst rather than take a sip, at least until Oprah came down from on high and ordered the acolytes to drink."

"See, this is what I think," I ventured, wanting to get in on the conversation and impress them with my insights. "You ever been inoculated?" All three nodded. "Okay, so what is an inoculation anyway? It's a tiny virus. You're intentionally making your body sick in order so that you can fight sickness later."

"This isn't going to be a government conspiracy thing, is it, Thomas?" Aubrey wondered. "Not that I have anything against that sort of obsession, I'm just wondering how we got on this topic."

"No, follow me on this. This is why people cannot summon up the gumption to challenge themselves in their reading habits. Literature is a virus, see. For whatever reason, parental insistence, an attractive school librarian, no TV, whatever, we were inoculated at a young age against literature. Sure, it made us all cry at first, having to concentrate our fragile minds, but after a while the body adapted. My mom made me read *Hop on Pop*, and now I can read Pynchon without flinching. Others, however, the inoculation didn't take, or they never got the shot and now they're too old to survive the initial needle, and consequently they've remained allergic to literature, they have no built-up immunity. Sure, they can still take the low-grade fever viruses okay, they can survive a Mary Higgins Clark with no serious after-effects, and maybe they even like the thrill of pushing their tolerance by reading a Crichton or a Dan Brown, something that makes them feel like they're smart. But dare to put a Pynchon or a Helprin or your Foster Wallace there under their noses and *wham!* Anaphylactic shock. The nervous system can't take it and shuts down, and the victim is paralyzed, and must now suffer a *Who's the Boss?* marathon on TBS to recharge their batteries." I broke off my rant as the others seriously considered this.

"So that's why the customers run from us," Danae said. "It's not from annoyance at our hyper selling techniques and eagerness to please, it's a visceral, instinctual reaction to what we represent. We're carriers of the plague."

"I like it," Warren said. "Makes perfect sense. Typhoid Warren, that's me."

"While it may make some sense logically," Aubrey offered, "the analogy may serve to turn people off the art form further. 'Literature is a virus' is hardly the slogan you'd want to promote too actively, it might ensure that parents never introduce their children to the written word. Think of how it would look on a T-shirt, it'd be a relations disaster. We can't change the world, much as we'd like to. All we can do is try and keep the good books out of the sales racks, try to keep the authors afloat."

"It makes me cry, seeing good books get remaindered," Danae said. "Kind of like watching a friend fail miserably at something."

We looked at one another across the expanse of the table, a vague unhappiness permeating the spaces between us. I felt the sudden urge to link hands, form a circle, start chanting to ward off the encroaching darkness. Instinctively, I fingered the meds in my pocket.

Danae broke the silence. "Oh, since we're on the subject, guys, I've got a perfect montag for the next meeting."

"Oh, yeah, me too," gushed Warren, suddenly perked up. "It's a sweet 'tag, when's the next meet?"

"Shut up, the both of you," whispered Aubrey viciously.

"Oh, man, sorry," said Warren, glancing at me. "Wasn't thinking."

"Sorry, I forgot, sorry," Danae said. She blushed as Aubrey

scowled at her, lowering her head, a red stain appearing from her neck to hairline. A good colour on her. The three of them busied themselves with their food.

"What?" I asked. I was on the receiving end of a very cold front. "What's up?"

"Nothing, friend," said Aubrey. "Nothing at all. Just . . . stuff between us, that's all. Right, guys?" Warren grunted into the chip bag. Danae pensively contemplated her yogurt cup.

"What stuff?" I asked, trying to keep my voice light. Aubrey studied a particularly vexing paragraph. Danae fished Patrick Ness's *The Crash of Hennington* from her purse. Warren continued inhaling my bag of Old Dutch Bar-B-Q. I waited under an oppressive passive-aggressive umbrella of silence, feeling left out. "Well," I started. Danae jumped at the noise. "Much as I'd love to continue this atmosphere of rejection, I guess I'll go check the shelves, see if anything strikes my fancy."

"What do you read, friend?" asked Aubrey, his face submerged in Wallace's prose.

"Whatever strikes a nerve," I said testily. I was ridiculously offended, somehow, that these strangers had secrets they didn't want to share with me. "I'll read whatever I choose. If, of course, that's all right with the three of you." I stalked out, immersing myself in the territory of words outside.

After work ended for the day, having been instructed by Danae on how to search for unavailable books and deal with difficult customers, i.e. keep agreeing with them until they've worn themselves out, and exhausted from the unending barrage of best-forgotten consumer questions (a highlight: "Where are the books where animals solve crimes?") I fled into the night, an Auster wedged under my arm. I passed Aubrey on the way out, saw him nodding approvingly at my reading material, and decided to play the small-minded victim and snub him.

I walked home, curled up in my papasan, cracked open *The Book of Illusions*, and did my best to forget the day, forget the past, forget that this was undoubtedly the first day of the rest of a very long, dull, disappointing life. I should have quit then, but the lure of more free books brought me back the next day.

I think I'll leave on a cliffhanger. My fingers are tired, and

Detective Daimler is undoubtedly itching to get this letter to the shrinks down at Quantico to glean some fresh insights into my psychosis.

Yours truly,
Thomas

DOCUMENT INSERT: Verbatim FBI tape recorder
transcript. Speaking: FBI Detective Amanda
Daimler (primary), RCMP Detective Mel George,
Doctor Barbara Carella, Munroe Purvis.

DAIMLER: Mr. Purvis, can you hear me? Can he
 hear me?
CARELLA: I'm sorry, he comes and goes, I told
 you.
DAIMLER: Can you give him something? Wake him
 up?
CARELLA: I'm afraid he's very critical at the
 moment. I couldn't risk it. I think you should
 come back. I'll call if there's any change in
 his condition.
DAIMLER: Yes, I guess — wait, his eyes are open.
 Mr. Purvis, can you hear me? Nod if you can
 hear me. Mr. Purvis, my name is Detective
 Daimler, I'm an agent with the FBI. Detective
 George with the RCMP is also present. We'd
 like to ask you a few questions, if you're up
 to it.
PURVIS: Hurts.
DAIMLER: Doc?
CARELLA: I'm sorry, Mr. Purvis, I cannot
 increase the dosage. This is a bad idea,
 Detective, he's in no condition —
DAIMLER: No, we need to do this now. Mr. Purvis,
 can you answer a few questions?
PURVIS: Yes.
DAIMLER: Good. We'll go slow, okay? Can you tell
 me anything about what happened to you?
PURVIS: Where am I?
DAIMLER: You're in Winnipeg, sir, St. Boniface
 General Hospital.
PURVIS: What happened?
DAIMLER: Has no one told him anything?
CARELLA: No, I thought it best you tell him.
 I've had my hands full with the press.

DAIMLER: Right, keep them out of here, all
   right? We're going to put an officer outside
   to keep people out. Can you do that, Mel?
GEORGE: No problem.
DAIMLER: Mr. Purvis, you've been in a coma for
   two weeks, do you remember anything?
PURVIS: Weeks?
DAIMLER: Yes, two weeks. After your program,
   your show in Winnipeg, do you remember what
   happened?
PURVIS: Yes.
DAIMLER: Afterward, your bodyguard, Mr., uh,
   Daly, he said he took you straight to your
   hotel room. Is this correct?
PURVIS: Yes.
DAIMLER: You were last seen going into your room
   at approximately eleven-twenty or thereabouts.
   Is this accurate?
PURVIS: Yes.
DAIMLER: Mr. Daly says you were gone from the
   room when he checked in on you the next
   morning. Where were you, Sir?
PURVIS: Where?
DAIMLER: Mr. Purvis, you were discovered on the
   sidewalk in front of this hospital at
   approximately eight o'clock in the morning,
   the day after your show. We're checking to see
   if there are tapes, can you tell us what
   happened?
PURVIS: Hospital?
DAILMER: Yes, sir, the hospital. Can you tell me
   where you were? Who did this to you?
PURVIS: Oh, that bitch.
DAILMER: What bitch, Sir? Sir? Mr. Munroe, who
   is the bitch? Sir? Doc?
CARELLA: He's out again. I'm sorry, I should
   never have allowed this. He needs to be kept
   stable, please, I need you to leave now.
DAIMLER: Damn it, we need —

CARELLA: This man is in tremendous pain, Detective. He needs rest. I'm sorry, but you need to go. I will call you when he's able.
DAIMLER: No need, I'm not leaving. I'll be sitting in the corner until he wakes up.

TO: ermccorm@yahoo.ca
FROM: iamashelfmonkey@gmail.com
SUBJECT: Oh, figure it out

Dear Eric (and all others, hello to you as well),

Well, if I wasn't before, I am now officially screwed. Had to hock the computer for survival money. No more popping out of hiding for brief moments to see my shadow. I weighed the options, and food seemed slightly more important than my laptop, now gathering dust on some pawnbroker's shelf. I did my best to delete its contents, but hey, who knows? Could be some useful tidbits left on the hard drive. No doubt I've neglected to delete a folder detailing my exact whereabouts, or worse, my weird predilection for Italian horror cinema. If you find it, fellas, more power to you. The hunt is on!

The television networks say it's only a matter of time until my inevitable capture. I gather that officials now know my location, and even now, federalés are surrounding the building (I'm at a public terminal, in full view — no spiderholes for me), slowly advancing on my position. I can feel the dot of heat from the laser sighting on the back of my neck.

Well, I guess I should just turn around and surrender. Oops, just my imagination. Still got some time left.

You never appreciate how time is a factor in your life until you're faced with the end of it.

Luckily, most Internet cafés are equipped with fairly dim lighting schemes, the better to play *Everquest* with. Add in the sickening aquamarine glow from the LCD screen, and my features are effectively masked from any gamer who might accidentally raise his head up from the personal adventures of Man_Slayer592 to take an MMORPG breather. Not that that ever happens. Those dudes are focused!

The weeks passed relatively quickly at **READ**, my psyche expeditiously adapting to the meagre requirements of indiscriminating patrons. The layout of the store became second nature, and I rapidly unearthed the hiding spots every employee took full advantage of. The travel section behind the maps. Language arts.

Philosophy. Computers. Actually, the computer section was invariably full, but these customers were so well-versed in their choice of books they tended to completely ignore store workers, as you'd ignore a lamp or unsightly damp spot on the rug of a neighbour's home.

The mystifying rift between my co-workers and myself was now somewhat patched, although they were still guarded in their conversation. Other employees, less discerning in their choice of friends and more willing to freely chat, passed along rumours of Aubrey's unholy command of all things printed.

"I swear," said Marcus, a pimply twenty-something currently completing his Masters in folklore and mythology, "I swear, the guy's on a whole other planet. I once asked him, 'What's the name of that book with the guy in the red jacket?' He gave me three different books in less than a minute. I think he's the Matrix."

The only way I can think of to adequately describe Aubrey Fehr is by example. Have you ever watched a nature documentary? One of those National Geographic *cinema verité* things. There is always, sandwiched between an imposing baritone voice and a tremendously stirring soundtrack, that inevitable moment when whatever subject it is the filmmakers have chosen — lion, hyena, tiger shark, tiger prawn, tsetse fly — that subject reveals and unleashes its inner nature, revising the drama from G-rated filmstrip infotainment into PG-13–approved bloodletting: the moment of pure animal instinct, where claws are revealed, teeth bared, poison unleashed, and unholy carnage ensues, all the while the narrator intoning, "The kill is quick and merciless. The circle of life is complete. The harp seal cub has learned a valuable lesson; in this bleak, unforgiving world, it is survival of the fittest."

Wait, that's wrong, scratch that. I'm describing Aubrey like a wild animal, ready to go off at any minute. I'm sure that's the portion of this narrative that will be highlighted and studied for years to come. Academics will point to this vague description and say ah, so that's how it was. Aubrey was a savage beast, the violence was inevitable to his nature. Criminal psychologists will add this to their list of behavioural indicators. Dr. Newhire, your thoughts? Well, Dr. Phil . . .

What I mean is, in those documentaries, amidst the blood and gore on display solely for ratings purposes, rarely if ever does anyone question the motives of the subject. The lion does what comes naturally, hyenas scavenge because they are scavengers, and sharks kill bathers because they look like seals, not because of some reflexive critical response to Spielberg. Motivation doesn't exist. They are because they are. Aubrey, to a tee.

Aubrey is the only person I've ever met who was because he was, who acted because that is who he was. You'd never look at him and think, there's a guy who's trying too hard, or, who does he think he is, looking that way? Aubrey was authentic. I could describe his manner as Zen-like, but that would presuppose some expertise on Zen beliefs and teachings that I simply don't have. Descartes would have loved him. Aubrey was beyond the concept of proving existence through thought. Yes, Aubrey thought, therefore, Aubrey was, but he took it further — Aubrey was; therefore, Aubrey was. He read; therefore, he read. He existed; therefore, he existed. He was pure.

Aubrey wasn't a vegetarian, which was probably the most surprising thing about him. A thirty-something dreadlocked Caucasian earth-loving tree-hugging Birkenstock-wearing string-bean who eats meat? Odd. But rest assured, if Aubrey were a vegetarian, no one would question him on it. There'd be none of that apologetic sense of guilt, no vague assertions of a belief in animal rights or loathing of plant life. If Aubrey were a vegetarian, it would be because he *was* a vegetarian. You'd never consider the possibility that he could ever be something else.

As the weeks passed, I subtly tried to penetrate the shady triumvirate. We'd go to movies, sometimes just Warren and I, sometimes Aubrey, sometimes both plus Danae. Those were my favourites. Coffee dates were planned and executed, nothing fancy, just friends talking; trying to show the world how trustworthy I am. No go. It was grade 3 dodgeball again, last picked to play. Aubrey became completely closed off and unresponsive when I refused to take the hint and flat out ask what a tag was, why is it secret, can I play along? Warren was continuing medical testing that rabbits were not only unsuited to, but violently refused to participate in because there're just some things even a rabbit won't agree to. His arms had returned to their former pallor, but now he'd lost most of the feeling in his legs because of an unfortunate reaction to an as-yet-unreleased antiperspirant, lending him a Herman Munster–type lurch to his walk. When I asked him about the tags, he would grab me in an affectionate headlock and noogie me until I passed out. Danae, more generous than the others, sat and talked with me during breaks, ever-so-gently rebuffing all my attempts to solicit information. And dates. "It's nothing," she would say, "And stop asking me out." She'd oftentimes touch my arm sympathetically when I appeared frustrated. I tried to appear frustrated a lot.

I slowly gathered the less-than-significant importance of my position. I became attuned to the unconscious cringe of the consumer as I or another of my ilk approached with one of our over-friendly Hi Can I Help Yous at the ready. No thank you, I'm just looking, please, if I need help, I'll ask for it, hey, back off! They didn't want my help, didn't yearn for the pleasure of my company, and even worse, had no interest in anything I might recommend as book counsel. Embittered, I began to experiment, urging customers to purchase all things Munroe. I took kind of a performance-artist pleasure in my sadly successful attempts to lay bare the ignorance of the shopper, simultaneously destroying any credibility they may have once possessed while separating them from their money. But part of any good performance art piece is an appreciative audience, and the more it became apparent that my audience just didn't get it, the more depressed I became, and the more pills I ingested. Win or lose, I was only feeding the Purvis empire, so rebelling against it, even with no chance of winning, became my only option.

To pass the time, I occupied myself with my Employee Recommends shelf, trying to find the right balance between established classics and deserving yet unsung newcomers. The outside world really cannot understand how stressful the shelf is. The shelf, while ostensibly an unobtrusive sales method, holds a far greater meaning to those who organize it. To those lucky few, the shelf is an extension of the self. (You can't spell shelf without self. Coincidence? Also, you can't spell fugitive without F U.) Sure, you can gussy it up, disguise it in places, let the world believe that you like nothing more on a rainy day than to curl up with Aristotle's *Poetics*;

maybe you'll even grow to believe it yourself. But lying alone in the dark after the last late-night comic has called it quits, when the covers are pulled up and the inhibitions are lowered, you can't deny that Clive Cussler rocks your world. The shelf is your Rorschach test, your subconscious, your id, and what sits upon it determines not only what people think of you, but also what you ultimately think of yourself. It's quite the balancing act, one that I'm positive has sent more than one philosophy major up and down the poorly carpeted aisles of their mind in dismay.

I was determined to be as truthful as I could, baring my soul and allowing the world (and Danae) to get a glimpse of the tortured, brooding, yet sensitive poet who lay beneath the skin. *The World According to Garp* was high on my list, as was *Cryptonomicon* and James Ellroy's latest, but what else? There was only room for five, maybe six choices, depending on size. Should I opt for Jim Dodge and his *Stone Junction*, or promote something newer yet equally ignored, say, Stephen Fry's *The Stars' Tennis Balls?* Push newer authors, or old reliables? Or go the other direction, go old, classical, try to intimidate the customer with my vast reservoir of accumulated knowledge. Seamus Heaney's translation of *Beowulf,* or Pinsky's *Inferno?*

Other employee shelves were no good as inspiration. Most were a mixture of recent bestsellers and highly promoted/suspect new releases. Page's space, predictably, was a scientifically determined sampling of guaranteed bestsellers, comprised solely of Munroe Purvis paraphernalia, the omnipresent MUNROE RECOMMENDS THIS! sticker on each cover. The latest Clancys, Grishams, Turows, Kings, and Rices were all well represented, along with arguably lesser yet popular fantasy luminaries such as Terry Brooks, Robert Jordan, David Eddings, and Ed Greenwood. Some finer choices hid between the garbage, and on rare occasions a genuinely wondrous surprise presented itself. (A tiny woebegone wallflower named Maxine had nestled amidst the disappointingly standard set of Nora Roberts and Barbara Taylor Bradford a copy of Carson McCullers's *The Ballad of the Sad Café.* When I questioned her on it in the lounge, she mumbled incoherently, fled the room, and quit the next day.) On balance, however, the dreck and dross outnumbered the exemplary by a wide margin.

Danae's shelf was far more interesting in content. Ayn Rand was present, leaning on Plato's *Republic* for support. Close by were Orwell, Graham Greene, and Joseph Heller. Warren's shelf was centred on the fantastic, tendering selections by China Mieville and William Gibson, alongside *Dhalgren, Looking Backward, The Steampunk Trilogy,* and *The Hollow Chocolate Bunnies of the Apocalypse.*

Aubrey's shelf was in constant flux, perpetually altering in form and substance. On any given day, Austen mingled with Zelazny, Tolstoy traipsed with Tolkien. Aldous Huxley battled for space with Roch Carrier. Martin Amis wielded supreme executive power one day, only to be usurped by the combined forces of Iain M. Banks and Theodore Sturgeon the next.

I ultimately settled on all-Canadian content. First, Findley, *Not Wanted on the Voyage.* Then, a dollop of Atwood, *The Handmaid's Tale* let's say. No, too obvious. *Cat's Eye.* Throw in a local hero, *Republic of Love* by Shields, and top it off with a few newer talents, a Vanderhaeghe, a Kenneth J. Harvey, Winter's *This All Happened,* and, of course, an Eric McCormack, your very own *Inspecting the Vaults.* It felt good to put those books on the shelf, good to see the THOMAS'S PICKS sign hanging over the front edge, great when I saw someone intently peering at the display, and ecstatic when I caught a glimpse of Aubrey himself poring over the titles at the close of the day. If only someone had actually used my advice, but by day's end, not one copy had even been nudged out of place.

Sorry, Eric. I tried.

That evening, Aubrey stopped me in the parking lot as I began to make my way home. "Need a lift, Thomas?"

I did, actually. The temperature was nearing twenty above, hinting at the intensely uncomfortable mix of heat and humidity that Winnipeg routinely offers up as alternative to the nad-numbing cold of its winters. I wouldn't give him the satisfaction, however. Earlier, he had flat-out refused to talk to me when I asked him once again what the big mystery was, and deep down in the root cellar of my soul, I am just that petty. "Actually, I think I prefer to walk today," I said with a touch of smugness. "Could use the exercise." I inhaled deeply, indicating that I found the moist night air a refreshing change of pace.

He called my bluff. "Good, I don't have a car, I'll walk too." He grinned. I snorted back a retort and set off, sure that my sudden rage would raise my body temperature, leading to heat stroke in less than twenty minutes.

We trod in silence toward downtown. I kept my head down, eyes on the ground, walking determinedly forward, not turning to see if Aubrey was keeping up. After some time had elapsed, having trudged blindly into a forest of coniferous fir trees, I was forced to shift my eyes front and admit that I was completely off course.

"You feel like a coffee?" I asked.

"Why not?" We shuffled off toward Old Market Square.

It was open poetry night at the Mondragon, a cozy hippie-commune-vegan-anti-everything-that-was-bad-in-the-world-and-it-was-all-the-Conservative-Party's-fault sort of place. Nice. Nestled in the corner by the fireplace, a trio of what appeared to be Cuban lesbian revolutionaries were ooh-ahh-oohing into a microphone while a fourth admirer of Eddie Bauer flannel worked on keeping a beat with her bongo.

We sat down at the table farthest from the floor show and read the blackboard above the espresso machine for the day's specials. The caffeine flavour of the week was "unfair trade" coffee. "Savour the Guilt" was its slogan. The message, I gather, was that they couldn't afford fair trade coffee, only the coffee of oppressed workers who didn't make a living wage, so while economics were forcing them to sell the hideous brew, they were going to make damn sure you didn't enjoy it.

A man with magenta hair and more metal than skin cells in his face approached us. "Geb yug anydin?" he mumbled over countless tongue studs.

"Two coffees, black," said Aubrey. "You're looking good, Teddy."

"Tangks, Augrey."

"Is that a new piercing?"

"Widge one?"

"Left ear, third from the top."

The waiter absently fingered the earring, the skin underneath still raw and crusty. "Yeh, Allison dib it. Thot I shoub eben oud both sides. You lieg it?"

"Very striking. Do you like it, Thomas?"

I nodded. "Very much. Metal is definitely your thing."

Aubrey snapped his fingers. "Oh, Teddy, I got you something." He dug into his bag for a moment, retrieving the latest edition of Edward Abbey's *The Monkey Wrench Gang*. "Here, you'll like this."

Teddy took the book and read the back. "Thangs, Augrey," he sputtered, obviously pleased.

"No sweat."

Teddy left to get our coffees. I looked at Aubrey. "Did you know we were coming here?"

"I wanted to talk, and I think you do too."

"So talk."

"Coffee first."

Teddy eventually returned with two enormous mugs in one hand, his nose already in the Abbey. I sipped the coffee hesitantly and let the liquid warm my stomach, trying not to taste the sweat of the browbeaten migrant farmers that undoubtedly coated every bean.

I finally broached the subject as calmly as I was able. "What the hell is going on? You've been giving me the runaround for weeks."

Aubrey regarded me mutely, stirring his coffee for a good length of time. "Sorry 'bout that, brother. Precautions have to be taken."

"Bush bites the bag!" flannel sister number two yelped.

"Precautions?" What the fuck was this? "What the fuck is this?"

"Well, friend . . ."

"And stop calling me friend, I hate that. *Nothing* you've done lately constitutes friendship."

Aubrey stopped stirring. He stopped everything. His hair stood still. "I know, I've been an asshole. I'm sorry."

"Calling yourself an asshole and then apologizing does not redeem yourself for your assholishness."

"My uterus, my freedom!" shouted flannel number three.

"Thomas," he began again, "what do you read?"

"You know what I read. You've seen my shelf, I know."

He rocked back in his chair, balancing himself on the back legs. I felt like an exotic species of insect he was testing the reactions of. "What makes a good writer, in your opinion?" he said finally.

"Style. Characters. Plot. And the ability to abandon all three when necessary."

"And what makes a bad writer?"

"Same thing." He nodded, as if what I said made sense. I was getting too pissed off to care. "Look, I don't know what makes bad writing, I just know what I like. Maybe it's like pornography, hard to define, but you know it when you see it."

"Interesting," he mused.

"Fuck you, it's not interesting, it's boring." I stood up. "You know what? *You're* boring. Why I should care about whatever the hell we're talking about is beyond me, but I'm done. You can have your little clique, makes you feel important. See ya." I grabbed my bag and headed for the exit.

"I'm having a get-together tomorrow at my place, sort of a personal book club," he called after me. "You should come."

"Fuck your get-together, and fuck you," I loudly replied across the several tables. No one so much as looked up at me. It seemed outbursts and spats were a common occurrence on the property. "Life's too short for these elliptical questions and Yoda answers. What is going on that's so important? Tell me, or I walk."

He laughed, a short bark. "It's not important, not at all. But I can't tell you what it is, it won't make sense unless you're there."

"What's the book?"

"Well, it all depends."

"On?"

"A variety of factors."

"Example."

"It's hard to explain, easier if you just show up."

"You're planning to hunt me for sport, aren't you?"

"Come and find out."

"Screw you."

"Danae is coming."

"I'll bring chips." Hey, I'm only human.

The next night, I arrived an hour early. I figured if this was some sort of ambush, an hour should be enough time to scope the place out and alert the authorities. Just who those authorities might be, I couldn't tell you. I'd been reading a lot of Spillane at the time, using Vachss as a chaser, which had bolstered my courage, if not my common sense.

Aubrey's house was a slightly dilapidated split-level directly alongside the Winnipeg western perimeter. He maintained that his parents had willed it to him, and I saw no reason to question him on it at the time. It lurked innocently at the end of its street, a full two or three housing plots away from its nearest neighbour. It was one of those branches on a map that appears to simply vanish into the ether rather than come to an end, as if the city planner had begun sketching out his plans for the latest suburb, had gotten sidetracked when he was attacked by the munchies and fled the office for a satisfying cruller/coffee combo, and in the temporary javasucrose high had subsequently forgotten about the whole thing, leaving the construction crews to scratch their heads, wonder when the rest will be built, and write it off as no-man's land. Here there be tygers.

I rang the doorbell. The door opened, revealing Aubrey in jeans and T-shirt. "Thomas, you're early! Well, come on in!" He was playing it cool, no question. He sped himself to the kitchen while I looked for a place to hang my jacket. "I'm just getting some nachos ready, have a look around!"

The house was a dream, Heaven in two stories and three bedrooms. Books lined the walls floor to ceiling, so closely packed an observer could be forgiven to think that the walls of the house were the books, a weird architectural attempt to recycle unwanted novels. Piles filled each corner, each book seemingly haphazardly placed, but on closer inspection revealed a great amount of care in their location. Many were scuffed, marred, bent, and dog-earred, but it was the natural erosion of good living and good reading, not mistreatment. These books were *loved*. Charlie Mingus cooed softly from corner speakers placed throughout the house, melting into a selection from the Lounge Lizards, giving the entire place the aura of a homey yet palatial used bookstore. I drooled in envy.

"You like?" Aubrey asked from behind me.

"I love. Tell me, is this a load-bearing stack of books?"

"I know, I know, I have a problem." He handed me a Two Rivers in exchange for my coat. "I had one of those early-in-life moments when I had to choose an addiction, and heroin seemed so played out, y'know?" He led me to the living room, the one room that stood out for its lack of order. Unlike the fondly kept stacks of other rooms, here the books lay everywhere. "Forgive the mess, brother," he said, sweeping his arm around to indicate the house in its entirety. "You've caught me mid-bedlam. I've been reorganizing the collection."

"How?" I could discern no pattern to the madness.

Aubrey lobbed my coat onto a pile of books by the couch. "Well, this room here is mostly just old books that have no real value to me, so I just throw them anywhere. Watch your step. But the other rooms, and against the walls here, I was bored with alphabetical, publisher wasn't working, and size and colour never satisfied, too many variables. Drove me nuts. You see here the mid-point of my latest attempt, organization by font."

"You're kidding." I walked out to the nearest room, his bedroom. I opened a few books at random from the nearest pile, then another one. Sure enough: Ehrhardt.

"My basement is mostly Cheltenham and variations. The kitchen is currently Arial and Bembo, the guest bedroom Bodoni. It's not easy, a lot of fonts look alike."

"No shit." This was literary insanity beyond the par. Jealousy shivered through me.

The doorbell rang. "Man, everyone's early tonight. Have a seat." I made myself comfortable on his chequered sofa while he answered the door, the Lounge Lizards now being replaced by a jaunty Django Reinhardt. I was inspecting the books on the shelves behind me for font (Helvetica?), when I felt someone sit next to me, shifting the couch cushions. I glanced over, hoping it was Danae.

"Hey, handsome, come here often?" Yes!

"Almost never. Yourself?"

"Oh, only when I'm bored. I'm bored a lot." She looked looser than she did at work, more free. Black jeans and loose hair was a terrific look for her. I wedged myself into the corner of the couch for a better vantage point. "Hey, Aubrey!" she shouted, "I love what you haven't done with the place."

"Thanks," he yelled back from the kitchen. "Beer?"

"Lovely. Where's Margarita?" Danae started looking about the room. "Have you seen her, Thomas?" I confessed ignorance, trying to figure out why she was looking for a cocktail among the cushions and novels. "Is she here, Aubrey?"

He walked in, beers in each hand. "She's somewhere around, she can't go far, she was . . ." Aubrey stared intently at my lap. "Shit, Thomas, you're sitting on her."

"What?" I looked down and yelped, seeing a pair of furry legs sticking out from between my shirt and the arm of the couch. I leapt to my feet, revealing to light the ugliest thing I have ever seen crammed into the fabric. "Jesus, what is it?"

"Ubf!" it replied.

Danae leaned over and pried it loose from its fabric prison. Freed, it began to pant wildly, lying limply in her lap. "Ubf!" it said again.

"Oh, God, I killed it!"

Aubrey took the organism from Danae and began inspecting it for damage, casually flipping it over and over in his hands like pizza dough. "It's okay, friend, she's fine, happens all the time." He righted the thing in his arms and scratched it absently, its hair slowly puffing out to reveal an extremely hairy Pomeranian. "She's paralysed, can't move her back legs, but she's got a good sense of humour. Don't you, girl?"

"Ubf!" Margarita said happily, squirming wildly in his arms, rapidly transmogrifying his black T-shirt into a camelhair sweater. "Ubf! Ubf! Ubf!"

I took a closer look. She seemed content, no ill effects suffered after close contact with my ass. With her fur and lack of mobility, I had inattentively assumed her to be a throw pillow. "Sorry, Margarita," I said, scratching her where I approximated her ears might be. "So you're the Master, I take it? Or are you a raging alcoholic?"

"Very good, most people don't get the reference."

"Ubf!"

I retook my seat on the couch next to Danae. Aubrey handed Margarita to her, whereupon Margarita commenced burrowing her nose into Danae's thighs. I envied the dog. "So," I began, then stopped, staring at Danae and Aubrey. I took a confident swig from my beer to gather my thoughts, and started again. "So."

Danae giggled. "So." She touched my arm in amusement. "I think you'd better fill him in, Aub. The suspense is killing him."

Aubrey sipped his beer, gathering his thoughts. "From the beginning then?" he asked me.

"Worked for Shakespeare."

"Have you ever read Bradbury, Thomas?"

"Of course I have," I replied, more than mildly offended. *Martian Chronicles, October Country, Something Wicked.* I'd be a pretty poor person if I hadn't."

"What about *Fahrenheit 451*?"

"Oh gosh, uh, duh?" Now I was definitely insulted. Ray Bradbury's science-fiction classic of intolerance and insanity, where books are illegal and burned on sight. How could I *not* have read it?

Danae snorted. "Stop treating him like an idiot. You know he's smarter than that."

Aubrey dropped his head, the Gorgonian hair-snakes drooping in self-reproach. "You're right, sorry. Just like to hear myself talk, I guess."

"You guess?" Danae chided.

"Fine, I get it, consider me chastised," he said, flustered. "I'm just feeling him out, Danae, is that all right with you?"

"Just get on with it, the others will be here soon."

"Others?" I asked. "From the store?"

"Something like that." Aubrey filched some rolling papers and a baggie from under the couch and began rolling a thick, lovely joint. "Thomas, what was Bradbury's main point in *Fahrenheit*?"

I thought this over. "That books are more than ideas, more than paper and ink. That they are, in their way, people themselves, individuals. They affect you in the same way that a living person does. Our lives are emptier without such beings. Kill a book, kill a person, that sort of thing. That's what I got out of it, anyway. I haven't read it in a while."

"Exactly, destroy a book, take a life." Aubrey looked unreasonably proud of my answer. "That's precisely how Danae and I, and a few others, that's how we feel, right?" Danae nodded, also pleased with my answer, and shifted closer to me. I blushed despite myself.

"Now," Aubrey continued, "if we take as a starting point our belief that books are more or less people, then it must follow, as with people, that there are both good books and bad books. Correct?"

"Er, sure, correct," I acceded. I hoped this what was Danae wanted to hear.

"And, all things being equal, there are, let's face it, some people this world could do without."

"Right again."

"So it is with books. Hate a person, hate a book. Evil book, evil person. Put it to death, no one cares, the world is better off without it. Take Charles Manson. Didn't he forfeit his right to belong in society? Or *My Baby, My Love*. Trash, utter garbage. What's the difference, really, between the two?"

"Absolutely. Wait, no, what?" I suddenly clued to in what Aubrey might be advocating. "Wait. No. Books are not people."

"Not what you just said."

"Hey, Manson harmed a lot of people."

"So has Agnes Coleman."

"Well, okay, yeah, but not in the same way, not physically. Manson had followers —"

"So does *My Baby, My Love*. People have —"

"It's not the same thing."

"You said it yourself, Thomas, kill a book, kill a person. You believe this, I know it."

"Yeah, but only in Bradbury's context, not real life. There is a difference."

"There is no difference!" Aubrey shouted, standing at attention, his crimson tentacles lashing the air in anger. I shrank back, instantly ashamed of my cowardice in front of Danae. "Some books are simply a waste of paper, a waste of effort both to write and to read. These books are evil, and must be stopped!" He paused, panting slightly.

Danae placed her hand on my shoulder. Gooseflesh had prickled up my arms. "Jesus, Aubrey, calm down!" she ordered. "You're freaking him out." Aubrey nodded, his shoulders slumping. He dropped himself into his chair, a baleful look in his eyes. "Thomas," Danae said, taking my hand. "Thomas, look at me." I turned my attention from Aubrey, allowing Danae's face to fill my vision. Damn, she was gorgeous. "Don't mind him, Aubrey's just passionate is all. Look, all we're doing is having some fun. Every few weeks, a group of us gather together, like we'll do later on tonight. We light a bonfire, chant, sing, and have fun. Then, we burn a 'tag or two."

"What?"

"It's from *Fahrenheit*," Aubrey said. "Warren's idea. We call our choices montags, after Bradbury's protagonist. We meet, we debate, we burn. It's therapy, really. An incendiary biblioclasm of soul-soothing proportions."

"You . . . wait. Oh my God, you burn books?"

"Uh huh."

"You're kidding me, right?"

"Nope."

"For serious?"

"For real."

"You guys are freaks."

Danae put her hand to my mouth to shush me. I pretended to talk, trying to muffle out some words between her fingers, hoping she'd keep them on my lips. "No, it's not like that, Thomas. We don't burn based on content or ideas, like some crazed right-wing nutjobs. Well, not usually, anyway. Nobody's perfect. I mean, it's not like we're burning *Huckleberry Finn* because we don't appreciate the use of the word nigger, or *Harry Potter* because we're afraid it promotes Satanism to our children, ignorant shit like that. We're not like those southern senators wanting to ban Capote and *Heather Has Two Mommies*, anything with the slightest hint of homosexual content because it makes their loins tingle unpleasantly and they might go all *Queer as Folk* on their good ol' redneck buddies. What we do is, we each bring one or two books that we feel the world is arguably better off without, a book lacking in style, originality, or artistic merit, a book with no purpose but profit, or just something that's really, really bad. I brought a new Candace Bushnell tonight, God I hate her! She's so fake, so facile. I know that's what she's trying to show, her characters are facile, but does her writing of them have to be as well? Hemingway wrote about the shallow and disenfranchised too, but he made them real, he made you care. Aubrey, what's yours?"

"Well, I initially was going to bring a Bentley Little, but Brian Lumley just published another *Necroscope* novel that is so wearisome in its slavish worship of Lovecraft I just couldn't resist.

I don't know if I dislike him more for his lack of talent or his unabashed thievery of H.P.'s themes and characters. Either way, it's a very bad thing indeed."

My head was swimming, and not only because I could taste the delicate saltiness of her fingers. I grabbed her hand away and started shaking my head to clear it. "Look, this seems wrong, somehow. Book burning, it's so . . . it's just plain wrong! It's sacrilegious somehow. Nazis burn books, fundamentalist morons burn books, not us. The Taliban burns books! The, the, the parents in *Footloose* burn books!"

"It's just for fun, Thomas," Aubrey jumped back in. "We're not out to change the world here. There's no grand ulterior motive, no wanton destruction of whatever pisses someone off. Checks and balances are in place. Everyone brings a book, and makes a case for its destruction. If anyone disagrees, we put it back, no arguments. Consider us a secret sect, if you like, like the Illuminati or the Freemasons, only far less influential."

I sat there, letting this sink in. Of course, there were books I despised, and people associated with them. Assembly line cookie-cutter novels. The ridiculous stories written by religious extremists, fearful that the godforsaken combination of homosexuality, women's rights, and common sense would somehow eradicate mankind. The diarrhea that was Bill O'Reilly.

"But everyone hates *something*," I insisted. "Someone will always hate Charles Frazier, someone always loves Sydney Sheldon. What's the cut-off? I mean, everyone writes for profit, in the end. They're all trying to make a living. Some are just better than others."

Aubrey clapped me on the shoulder. "Checks and balances, brother. It's all in place, a system of rules we've pledged to honour. We keep each other honest, you'll see."

"It's all symbolic anyway," Danae said. "It's a game. Some people bowl, some poke voodoo dolls, we burn. A game's a game."

The doorbell rang, interrupting my confusion. A moment later, Warren entered, noticeably limping. I guessed the feeling must be returning to his legs. "Hey, Tommy-gun, welcome to the club, man!" He looked at Aubrey elatedly. "Didn't I tell you? I told you he was one of us. Hey, what'd you bring?" He waved a paperback at me. "Look at this, a Robert Ludlum, see, only it's not, he's dead, it's written by some hack and released under his name. He was never very good anyway, but this? Pure money grab. Let the dead R.I.P., am I right?" He hunkered down in front of me, wincing at the effort. "So, what'd you bring, huh? What you got?"

"Thomas is still thinking it over," said Aubrey.

"What's to think about?" Warren gracefully shoved me over and loaded himself on the sofa, squeezing Danae and I together in a heavenly mash. "Dude, it's just like summer camp. It's a campfire sing-along, but with the cultish overtones of Jonestown. We just do it for fun, like exercise for our souls, dude."

"Cultish?"

He winked at me. "You'll see, dude." He looked back at Aubrey. "He's in. He's in, if I have to carry him there myself."

"Like you could," I said, half-jokingly. "Looks like you can barely keep yourself urk!" Warren had placed me in another excruciating headlock, and was laughing wildly as he smothered my face against his armpit.

"I reckon I could still carry three of you, buddy, lame as I am." I gagged in assent. "Say uncle?" Another gag. "Good enough." He tossed me limply back against Danae. "Now, are you coming?"

"Why is that always your response to anything I say?" I wheezed.

"Works, doesn't it? Now, once more, are you coming outside, or would you prefer heating up my other armpit?"

"Gee, what a choice." Danae hugged me. That was it. I was going.

That's it for today, Eric. My paranoia is acting up again. I've been sitting in public too long.

Yours truly,
Thomas

From The National Post

TALK-SHOW HOST TO VISIT CANADA

TORONTO — American talk-show personality Munroe Purvis has announced that he is taking his popular television program out of New York, and on the road to Canada.

"It has been obvious for some time that a large number of my viewers live north of the American border," Purvis said in a release, "and it behooves me to thank them for their continued viewership and support."

Purvis's planned route is at yet unannounced, but he promises that all major markets will be visited in turn.

"Canadians have given American culture so much over the years," Purvis says, "it's about time one of us gives something back to our friendly neighbours to the north. That's why I plan an intensive all-Canadian agenda in my book club while I'm visiting; to enhance the northern civilization through the promotion of their own tragically ignored homegrown talent. I'll be doing the same when I visit Mexico. For English books, of course."

Purvis has already begun choosing novels for the tour. *I'm All Out of Tea*, by Saskatchewan author Nicholas Rapley, has been selected as Purvis's first Canadian recommendation.

"Mr. Rapley's story made my heart weep," remarked Purvis. "It's a remarkable story, one man's quest for personal redemption in the heart of sheer prairie desolation."

"I'm utterly overwhelmed," Rapley told the *Post*. "To have earned such an honour, at a time when I can really use the cash."

TO: ermccorm@yahoo.ca
FROM: iamashelfmonkey@gmail.com
SUBJECT: Still running

Dear Eric,

I wonder if all this publicity will boost sales of your novels. I guess some good can come out of this after all.

Well, more good, anyway.

I'm all set here. I've found a surprisingly secluded corner of a library, with large dividers and low traffic flow. Perfect. No refills on my coffee, but you can't have everything.

This is where my tale goes a touch Palahniuk.

The four of us walked into the field behind Aubrey's house. Five, if you count Margarita, safely tucked into Aubrey's backpack, contentedly drooling and ubfing. Aubrey led the way, his flashlight bopping along the ground. I remained silent, walking behind the others, unable to shake the belief that this night would end with my death.

Eventually, we came to an ancient, blackened oil drum half hidden by grass and weeds. I kicked at a dark pile at its base. Ashes scattered up into the wind. A torn cover page stuck out of the pile, a V.C. Andrews opus, I think.

Warren set about starting a fire with a terrifying amount of lighter fluid and some prefab Safeway logs while Aubrey put his backpack down, digging out Margarita and a faded blanket she could curl up in. "Ubf!" she said, ecstatic to be outside. I wished I were so satisfied.

Warren had done this before. Soon a pleasing blaze warmed us, or maybe it was just Danae pressing up against me. "Excited?" she asked.

"That's not the word," I replied, trying to appear cool. "Frightened beyond comprehension is closer."

She tightened her arms around my chest. I melted. "It'll be fine, Thomas. Just go with the flow, you'll get into it." She laid her hand on my cheek, turning my face to hers. "I promise," she said. I believed her.

We weren't alone for long. Faces appeared in the darkness,

following their own dancing beams of light. Men and women nodded to one another as they joined, huddling around the fire. There seemed to be no need for talking. I didn't recognize any of the new arrivals, but two or three looked familiar.

"Who are all these people?" I whispered in Danae's ear.

"People like us. Bookstore employees. Assistant librarians. English teachers. Second-hand bookstore managers. Burt over there reviews books for the *Free Press*. Bookworms and bibliobibuli, to use Aubrey's terms. People who believe in the sanctity of the written word, and despise those who would abuse the privilege."

"You've put a lot of thought into this," I muttered. "How long has this been going on?"

"A year or so." Danae stretched her face upward, settling her lips on mine. "Now shush," she sighed into my mouth. I could think of no argument to this, and settled on putting any qualms I may have still held into the kiss.

"Does this mean we're, y'know, a couple or something?" I asked, my grin fighting with my groin for largest physical example of my happiness. "Because I am totally behind it."

Danae took a step back and floored me with a leer of pity. "Take it for what it is, Thomas."

"And what is that, exactly?"

"A sign of friendship."

"Just friends."

"Just friends."

"Friends is good." I forced the grin to remain as my penis screamed with frustration and flatlined. "I can't get enough of friends." I turned away, facing the fire, my skin burning. "Friends are — just great. Friends who french each other are even better." The strangers began to pull books from their backpacks. Such was my confusion over Danae that I never even questioned what was going on.

"I'm a complex person, Thomas," she said behind me.

"Why is it the crazy ones always claim to be 'complex?' They can never admit to the craziness."

Her arms came around my hips, clasping hands around my belly. "Your being here means a lot, Thomas. Maybe I got carried away in the moment."

"We had a moment?"

"We're about to." A crescent moon of booknerds had formed itself around the can, the people staring into the flames. "You'll understand soon," Danae breathed, taking my left hand, while a rotund young man in a red jacket and Tilley fedora grasped my right. "I promise."

"What's happening?"

"Just go with the flow, Thomas. You'll get the hang of it."

Aubrey stepped forward, pulling his jacket hood over his head, Grand Exalted Master of the Canadian Inquisition. "Are we all assembled?" he asked the group.

"We are," they intoned on cue. I peered about, looking for any sign that this evening might end with my evisceration atop an altar, my entrails strung out like festive crêpe paper while the coven drank ecstatically from a silver chalice of congealing Friesen blood.

Aubrey raised his face to the clear night sky. "I now call this gathering of the Shelf Monkeys to order."

"Shelf Monkeys?" I hissed to Danae. "What's a Shelf Monkey?"

"You are, dummy. We all are." She squeezed my hand, indicating I should shut the hell up for a while.

"Brothers and sisters." Aubrey began to hold forth, taking on the tone of a Baptist preacher about to unleash fire and brimstone upon the unworthy. "We meet tonight to right the wrongs of society. Tonight, we shed our pasts. We are no longer who others believe us to be. Tonight, we are free. Tonight, we reveal our essence. Tonight, we truly become ourselves." Aubrey placed his hand atop his heart. "From this moment forward, I am Don Quixote."

He pointed at Danae. "From this moment forward," she recited, "I am Offred."

The man to her left spoke up. "From this moment forward, I am Queequeg."

And so on, around the circle. Strangers, identifying themselves through fictional characters, finding meaning through role-play.

"From this moment forward, I am Scout Finch."

With every sentence, coming closer.

"From this moment forward, I am Gandalf."

Well, I saw *that* one coming. There's one in every crowd.

"From this moment forward, I am Hagar Shipley."

"From this moment forward, I am Lyra Silvertongue."

What was that one from again? Pullman? Shit, what was I going to do? I began exploring my memories, trying to find a character to call my own. Presumably, there had to be some connection, some common theme. Or was the criteria simply a personal favourite, with no necessarily shared personality traits?

"From this moment forward, I am Lady Fuchsia Groan."

Fuck, hurry up! Choose!

Warren's turn. "From this moment forward, I am Kilgore Trout."

Gandalf! No, already taken. Samwise Gamgee! No, forget Tolkien. Holden Caulfield. Ouch, too obvious. What means something to you? T.S. Garp? Chili Palmer? Winston Smith? Ford Prefect?

"From this moment forward, I am Ford Prefect."

You bastard! Think! Quolye, no. Tintin, no. Jerry Cornelius, Gideon Clarke, Screwtape, Dirk Gently, no, no, no, no.

"From this moment forward, I am Ignatius J. Reilly."

"From this moment forward, I am Raoul Duke."

Wait, is that even fiction? I can't remember.

"From this moment forward, I am Valentine Michael Smith."

Dammit! That's a good one! Oh, God, I'm next. Think.

Think

"From this moment forward,

Think.

I am

THINK!

known as

Got it.

Yossarian."

Bingo.

The circle murmured its assent. Danae crushed my hand in joy. Aubrey opened his arms, turning slowly. "We welcome a new member to our coven tonight. The Shelf Monkeys welcome Yossarian to our ranks. Welcome, Yossarian."

"Welcome, Yossarian," the circle groaned. I clenched Danae's hand, stifling the overwhelming urge to step forward and proclaim myself an alcoholic.

Aubrey walked around the oil drum. He faced his congregation, the flames lighting his face from below, lending him caverns for eyes. "Do we have any montags for the pyre this evening?"

The gentleman known as Ignatius held up his hand. "Uh, I have one, everyone."

Aubrey faced him. "State your case, Ignatius."

Ignatius pulled a large hardcover from his backpack. "Well, this," he said, showing the book to the group, "is a new one from Terry Pratchett." A collective gasp shot out. Not Pratchett! "Hey, hey," he sputtered apologetically, noticing a visibly angered Warren. "I love the guy, too, but he's just stretching out this Disc-world crap too far. It just came out, called *Monstrous Regiment*. I think he must have written it in his sleep or something, it's really thin. He's relying on his name to sell the thing. The nerds'll gobble it up. I'd like to nominate it, please."

"Has anyone else read the accused?" Aubrey asked. The Monkeys looked at each other expectantly. No one volunteered. "All right then. May I have a volunteer to read it?"

"Aw, Aubrey," said Ignatius. "I never get to burn anything, c'mon!"

"The rules, Ignatius, must be obeyed. No montag unless read and seconded. Anyone? Kilgore? Scout?"

"Hey, don't look at me!" exclaimed a slight woman, Scout. She mimed spitting something bitter onto the ground. "I like Pratchett and everything, but I'm still trying to get the taste of that Andrew Greeley out of my mouth from a month ago."

"Oh, yeah, that was a nice one," mused Raoul Duke. "Good flames, nice heat, a real log of shit."

Warren raised his hand. "I'll do it."

"Very well, Kilgore, we shall rely on you to throw yourself on Ignatius' grenade. Thank you."

"Thank you, Kilgore," the circle intoned. Cameron handed the book over. Warren accepted it, clearly annoyed at him. "Nominate a Pratchett!" he said. "Dickwad. We'll just see who nominates Pratchett."

Valentine Michael Smith stepped up. "I have a montag, Don Quixote."

Aubrey bowed his head. "Make your case, Valentine."

William held aloft his offering, a small paperback. "I present the offender, Anne Rice's *Ramses the Damned*." The circle muttered excitedly. "Anne Rice has committed the most heinous of sins. She has traded on her reputation, hoping that her status as bestselling novelist and highly regarded author of gothic horror will blind readers to the fact that Ramses is a cheap, thinly disguised bodice-ripper of the basest sort. Where she once possessed subtlety, she now wields a hammer. Her characters are thin. Her descriptions are ludicrous. She has soiled the prestige that *Interview with the Vampire* once afforded her. I ask you now, judge her as I have judged. Burn the heretic!"

The circle swayed and moaned. We had all read *Ramses*, no question. We *were* booknerds, don't forget, and if such as we could ever claim a queen, Madame Rice would surely be in the running.

"Are there objections?" Aubrey asked. The circle remained silent. "What about you, Yossarian?" he asked, pivoting toward me. An arm unfolded, pointing a finger. "Do you object to Valentine's argument?"

I stood still, bewildered. Danae pushed me from behind, sending me into the middle. The half-moon closed ranks behind me. Margarita began to bark.

"Ubf! Ubf! Ubf!"

"Well," I began. "You are right, uh, Valentine, *Ramses* is a bad novel, not up to Rice's best work by far. But, I'm sorry, I don't know how you all work this, but doesn't an author's past work count, shouldn't it count for something?" I was sweating underneath my shirt.

"Ubf! Ubf! Ubf!"

I plunged on, unsure. "I mean, she wrote *Vampire*. She gave us Louis, and Lestat, and Armand. Simply because her later work lacks the originality and verve of her best, should that be enough to condemn *Ramses* to the flames? Sure, she's kind of gone off the deep end lately, but there are certainly worse books out there, and —"

"Enough!" Aubrey shouted. "Yes or no, Yossarian. To burn or not to burn?"

Good question. "Oh, well, uh . . . no," I replied as firmly as I could. Why should I make this easy on them?

"Yossarian has spoken. The verdict is clear. *Ramses* shall be spared."

"Goddammit!" Valentine shouted. "C'mon, Aubrey, the thing just reeks. Let's burn it, please?"

Aubrey turned away to him, giving me a reassuring wink. "Yossarian has spoken, Valentine."

Valentine Michael Smith retreated into the circle, head held low. "But it sucked," he whispered to Raoul Duke, who nudged him to keep quiet.

"Me next!" Hagar Shipley stepped toward the fire. "I submit Tibor Fischer's *Voyage to the End of the Room*!" She waved the offender above her head. "Mr. Fischer has committed a grave offence against us, against those who seek to challenge the rest of the world through provocative ideas and a canny grasp of language."

"Oh, here we go again," jeered Danae.

Hagar shot her a dark look. "Tibor has single-handedly sought to destroy the reputation of one of our finest living authors," she continued. "His oblique, vile criticisms of literary icon Martin Amis and his *Yellow Dog* must not go unpunished. He is a sad, sad man, whose sole purpose in life is seeking to raise his profile by destroying the careers of others!"

"Aw, *Yellow Dog* wasn't that good, Emily," said Lady Fuchsia.

"Emily?" I whispered to Danae as the rant continued. "What, *the* Emily?"

She nodded, the firelight catching a wetness in her eyes. "She's just so — *committed*," she said. "There but for the grace, Thomas."

"Her name is Hagar, Lady Fuschia," Aubrey sternly corrected.

"His actions must be corrected!" Emily/Hagar screeched at Lady Fuchsia, who looked ready to launch a tactical nuke in retaliation. "Calling *Yellow Dog* as obscene a thing as seeing your uncle masturbate is abusive and disgusting! He even uses his newfound infamy to his advantage, bragging about how clever he is! Tibor cannot go scot-free, he must be held accountable! Justice for the unjust!"

"Jesus, Hagar, have you even read the fucking thing?" asked Warren.

"NEVER!"

Aubrey held up his hand, shushing Emily's rant. "Brother Kilgore raises an excellent point, Hagar. We cannot destroy that which we have not suffered through personally. It would be a repudiation of our principles. If allowed, we would become that which we abhor. We cannot allow this to pass."

"But, come on! *Amis!*" Emily said, her eyes pleading for support. "We can't put down Amis! It's wrong, it's just wrong, it's like calling Mozart overrated." She looked out at us. "Isn't it?"

"It's not like Amis is suffering for recognition," said Raoul Duke. "Now, who's this Tibor guy, that's what I want to know."

"It's just one guy's opinion, Em . . . er, Hagar," said Ford Prefect. "How is that different from us?"

Danae walked up and hugged her. "It's okay, Hagar. We all get frustrated, it's okay. Look, we'll read it together, all right? You and me. And next time, if it's awful, you can try again. All right?" Emily nodded miserably, breaking the embrace to return to her place in the assembly.

It continued on into the night, members offering example after example of books they deemed unsuitable for general consumption. Lesser novels by Norman Mailer and John Irving were put on the chopping block by Ford and summarily rejected. Cheaply bound romance novels with titles like *The Kilted Lover* and *A Thrill to Remember* were quickly considered and just as quickly ignored, as no one wanted to waste their time reading them anyway. Queequeg polarized the group arguing that while Hemingway's *The Old Man and the Sea* was unarguably a sacred, untouchable text, should a *Reader's Digest Condensed Version* also be considered thus? Danae managed to get Bushnell on the pile, while Aubrey lost his *Necroscope* battle when Raoul Duke revealed himself to be a closet Lumley fan. (Well, somebody has to be, I guess.) Feeling obligated as a first-timer, I found myself reluctantly agreeing to read a Jayne Ann Krentz opus of a solitary woman torn between love and employment, or some bullshit like that. Hazing the new guy, that sort of thing. The ambiguous merits of Ann Coulter's polemic *Slander* were fiercely debated, Lyra quite convincingly arguing that her liberal-bashing screeds were so unbelievably biased that they thereby could qualify as satire, thus crossing the line into fictional diatribes. Gandalf pleaded angrily to get Margaret Laurence's *The Stone Angel* incinerated, but was shouted down by Emily/Hagar Shipley, for obvious reasons. I gathered it was rather poor form to elect a novel that contained another Shelf Monkey's alter ego.

"He's been trying to burn that book for *weeks*," Danae mumbled in my ear. "He just doesn't like it, it's stuck in his craw for some reason, even since he was forced to read it in high school. He'll never get it past Emily, but if she ever misses a meeting, she's screwed. I won't give him the satisfaction, though. I mean, c'mon, Laurence wrote *The Diviners*, for Pete's sake."

"Good for you," I said, weirdly touched by her determination. I didn't care for *The Stone Angel* all that much either (the old lady was a real hag of a main character), but that didn't mean it was flame-worthy.

Eventually, the offerings dried up, a pile of books lying meekly at Aubrey's feet. Michael Crichton's *Airframe. Crucible* by Mel Odom. Naomi Campbell's *Swan*. Paulo Coelho's *Eleven Minutes*, a montag I couldn't wait to immolate. Something called *Angry Housewives Eating Bon Bons*. Danae's offering, Bushnell's *4 Blondes*, a 'tag seconded by Hagar, thirded by Lady Fuchsia.

"The Shelf Monkeys have chosen," Aubrey sang out, "and it is good." He poked the embers of the fire with a stick. A throng of tiny combustibles leapt into the wind. Gathering the novels in his arms, he turned to us, the wind pulling back his hood, letting his hair lash about, flagellating his face with flaming whips.

"We are in agreement, then?"

"We are."

"Ubf!"

"The evil must be destroyed?" Aubrey's voice had risen, becoming a ghostly shriek on the wind. He was in his element, the dreadlocks standing at attention, a mixture of Christ and Pilate, demanding sacrifice in the name of the greater good.

"YES!" the monkeys shouted back.

"Was Montag right?"

"YES!"

"Ubf!"

"Is it a pleasure to burn?"

"YES!"

He pitched the books into the pyre, sending flames and fireflies rocketing into orbit. Ink swiftly altered its chemical composition, melting down the pages, becoming molecules of gas. Inexpensive paper curled, changed colours, settled on black. Glue popped and boiled. Ideas evaporated. Characters died in agony. Leaves of sin filled the sky, joining the stars.

What do you know? Montag was right. It *was* a pleasure to burn.

Exhausted, exhilarated, purified, we set out for home. Danae sidled up next to me as I strode homeward, sliding her cool fingers into mine and whispering into my ear. "Do you get it now?" she teased. I nodded. Unquestionably, I got it. When the pages had caught fire, I had a woody the likes of which I hadn't possessed since going on the meds. The kiss, the flirting, the physical lust, all made sense now; it was foreplay to the main event. We had shared an experience that brought us closer than sex ever could. We began to walk. Danae linked her arm through mine and rested her head on my shoulder. A crisp breeze bit through our clothes, nipped at our souls, reminding us of the glory of the world. We said nothing. We were beyond the power of words; we had proved it that night. Outside Danae's apartment, we held each other close for a few seconds, an undemanding hug that far surpassed any post-coital clinches I had enjoyed in the past. Animals were never meant to be alone, I know that now. The simple act of embracing someone, feeling your dual heartbeats slowly synchronize, that's all it takes to achieve true happiness. We muttered some non-committal pleasantries, promised to see each other later, and I walked homeward, not a thought in my head. Once home, I immediately went for my bookshelves, grabbed my battered paperback copy of *Catch-22*, collapsed on the sofa, held the Heller to my heart, and fell blissfully asleep.

I'd never felt better in my life.

It was an opiate, more satisfying than tobacco, more addictive than heroin. At the end of the day, wrung out from inane questions, unruly kids — "Why do you keep the graphic novels behind the Special Orders desk? I'll buy one, I promise this time! No one's looking, c'mon, just one Manga, please? Asshole!" — and the malignant chunky cranium of Munroe Purvis wordlessly mocking our efforts from open to close, burning books was the ultimate in stress release. There were rules, of course. You could not steal from a library, that was the first. Libraries are the holy sanctuaries of Shelf Monkeys, and their purity must not be corrupted by our peccadilloes. Neither could we take advantage of the small independent bookstores, or sellers of used books. No, the books must be purloined from the biggies, which gave me Chapters and **READ** to choose from. At first, I shamefacedly purchased my montags, fearing the wrath of Page should my bibliokleptomania be discovered. Bargain bins were a treasure trove of the accursed, and with my employee discount, practically a steal unto itself. Aubrey shamed and emboldened me with his fortitude, smuggling books out within the tangles of his hair, sometimes wearing a rainbow Rastafarian hat to hide the edges of the covers. Legerdemain, that's what Aubrey called it. Misdirection and subterfuge. Always carry a bag, that's the standard ruse. During frequent employee searches (probably forbidden under the Charter, but I was in no position to complain), Page and her associates would always search a suspicious bag to the exclusion of everything else; say, unusually baggy khakis with multiple deep pockets.

As reverent as we were toward the booksellers who were eking out a living against the superstorification of the world, the authors we treated far less kindly. I had asked, rather meekly, whether the independent author should be respected as well, the author who struggles to get the book published, using small presses and likely never seeing a dime. Couldn't we, *shouldn't* we show some leniency in this instance? Was the well-meaning hack not worthy of some extra consideration?

"I understand your concern," Aubrey said when I broached the subject. "It's too easy. It's like punching a child."

"Exactly. Sure, torch the big sellers, or the authors from Knopf and Penguin. They got something out of it. But isn't there something, well, unseemly about taking pot shots at someone's labour of love? Authors like that don't write for profit, they write for the love of it."

"If you feel like arguing this point in front of the others, be my guest. But don't be surprised if you're shouted down. A poor self-published novel wastes as much of your life as a poor *Globe & Mail* top ten selection." He could see I wasn't convinced. "Try this, Thomas. Knowing now what you do, if you had the chance, would you kill Hitler, or Hussein, or Milosevic, before they came to power? Wouldn't you have the responsibility to do everything you possibly could to stop these monsters?" I agreed it was possible I might. "Now, again with the benefit of hindsight, if you could have stopped Jackie Collins before she had a chance to destroy a whole generation of bored housewives, well, wouldn't you have at least tried to convince her of the merits of a life devoted to something more appropriate to her talents? Like a travel agent?" I humbly agreed that I would, ashamed of my timidity in the face of such wickedness. If the loss of the royalties on one book could be enough to curb the next Fern Michaels, I didn't see as I had a choice.

As the weeks went on, my courage bolstered by our hidden rebellion, I smuggled out more and more 'tags from **READ**. The oil drum was an abattoir. We charred our enemies by the armful. Emily eventually granted Mr. Fischer a stay of execution for being too talented to warrant inclusion on the pyre of the damned, settling for a more worthy Wilbur Smith tome that was begging for the purification only the glory of fire could provide. Michael Slade provided enough warmth to heat my apartment for a month. Steve Alten dazzled us with his prose-laden pyrotechnics. Tim LaHaye and his repugnant little *Left Behind* bestsellers? Ahh, that feels good. Richard Marcinko? Toss another on the barbie! Pat Robertson? Man, does that warm my going-to-Hell little heart. Bill O'Reilly? Did you know he actually had the gall to write fiction, and actually admit that it was such? The flames burned extra bright that night. Oh, it was all so sweet and tasty, it just had to be fattening. And if it turned out that our nominations did indeed display a slight political bent to them, c'est la vie, and who the fuck cares? All in good, clean, biased fun.

"Why Offred?" I asked Danae one day. I had cornered her at her desk with yet another blatant attempt at taking our relationship to another level. I said that the burnings were better than sex, and I stand by that statement; however, just because you like Space Mountain doesn't mean you don't want to try the Log Ride.

"Why what?" she asked, her head buried in some sales reports.

"Why Offred?"

"Well, why Yossarian?"

I shrugged. "I didn't have a lot of time to choose, and it popped into my head. Accidental."

"Nothing is accidental, Thomas; we all went through the same thing." She put the file down and leaned back in her chair, propping her feet up on the desk in a relaxed yet businesslike gesture that I found disturbingly erotic. "When Aubrey first came up with the idea, it was just a bullshitting session one night at his house. The three of us, we were, well, high, and Aubrey started going off as he does on the ineffectiveness of our lives, the poor quality of writing, the unfairness that people would rather waste their money on trash than challenge themselves. I remember this, he actually threw a book into his fireplace, it was *The Celestine Prophecy*, why we had a copy I don't know, and the three of us, we just sat there forever, watching it burn. It was like getting a glimpse of Heaven, although that might have been the pot talking.

"Anyway, that's where it started, the whole 'secret society' thing. It was Warren's idea to dress it up like a cult, he had been rereading *Cat's Cradle*, I think it was a Bokonism thing. We agreed on the basics, but the thing just seemed, I don't know, *forbidden*. We needed the names to take some of the pressure off. We decided to take a name of a character, but it had to be an immediate choice. Something about the subconscious mind culling forth the character we most identify with. Again, we were high. Aubrey came up with Don Quixote, no surprises there."

"Windmills?" I asked.

"Big-time tilting at them. Warren took Kilgore, I guess with the idea that he's an unappreciated genius who ignores society and believes in secret cults and societies, or something. You ask me, I think he just likes the idea of behaving like a drunken reprobate."

"And Offred?"

Danae ducked her head in embarrassment. "I know, the whole feminazi patriarchal slave-to-males thing, right? Maybe there's something to that. I don't feel particularly oppressed, but I do like the idea of taking control of myself. I guess the world is overwhelming, and she fought back. All I know is, Offred was the only name I could think of. Make of it what you will. The others, I'm sure they have their own explanations. I don't see much of Hagar Shipley in Emily, and August is as far as you could get from

Valentine Michael Smith. Weirdly, Burt is Gandalf, but I couldn't tell you why." She levelled a finger at me. "Now, the question becomes, why Yossarian, Thomas? Do you identify with him, or was it simply the last book you had read?"

I rubbed my forehead for a minute. "You know, I have no idea," I admitted. "Being surrounded by insanity, maybe, or being powerless."

Danae smiled. "It'll come to you."

"Do you like the name?"

"I think it suits you. Again, don't ask me why."

"Do you think it's sexy?"

She bit her bottom lip, shaking her head in exasperation. "Thomas, it's —"

"— not you, it's me," I finished. "I think I'll get that tattooed on my arm."

"Ooh, tattoos are sexy."

"Really?"

"No."

I tried to quit Danae, look elsewhere for sexual release, but the pickings were slim at **READ**, and aside from the job and the meetings, there was nowhere else I ever went. I wandered the stacks, my eyes glazed over with lust as I imagined Danae and I performing acts that would cripple the cast of Cirque du Soleil. **READ** became my own intimate gargantuan love nest. I added literary themes to our lovemaking; whichever book I laid eyes on was used for sexual inspiration. Tom Clancy sex was mechanical, very technical, dry and republican, heavily reliant on manuals. Fucking by Dashiell Hammett, we traded quips and witticisms along with our spit. Orwellian sex was clinical yet desperate, alongside a picnic of fresh jam and coffee. Jane Austen was a letdown; I had to tempt Danae, take my time, be a gentleman, woo her with flowers and courtly conduct, and in the end, no sex was forthcoming. Those were the rules. We popped pills with William S. Burroughs, drank scotch and rum with Hemingway, and just plain fucked each other raw with Henry Miller. You can't even imagine what we did in front of Bukowski. We named our body parts. I'd start in on the Brontë sisters while Danae fondled my Balzac, then I'd move my attentions south toward her Anaïs Nin, and she'd reciprocate by stroking my Dickens.

And at the end of every session of congress, we would respectfully remove the visage of Munroe Purvis from its perch, and violate it in indescribable ways.

I tried to keep such lovely fantasies to a minimum, as the sizable maypole I erected during each daydream was threatening to become a constant feature of my physical makeup. That, and Danae once questioned me as to why I was blushing as I stacked new Anaïs Nin editions on the shelves. I hurriedly squeaked out an excuse, occurrence of the flu, perhaps I was feverish, or maybe the store's heating system was on the fritz, all the time imagining Danae straddled over my bookcart.

Good times. I wonder if we wo

MUNROE PURVIS FUGITIVE IDENTIFIED

SAN FRANCISCO — Thomas Friesen, missing fugitive in the ongoing Munroe Purvis case, was recognized yesterday at the Golden Gate Valley library in San Francisco, California.

"I knew it was him," Head Reference Librarian Hanley Jones told Associated Press. "He was crouched over the computer for hours. Never looked up once, which kind of looked suspicious. We unfortunately get a lot of homeless men in here looking up pornography on the Internet, and he seemed the type.

"Then, just as it was coming to me, he gathered up his stuff and left. Well, when it hit me who he was, I immediately called the police."

Police have confirmed, through the library's video surveillance recordings of the lobby, that Friesen was indeed in the building.

Representatives of the Munroe Purvis estate, along with donations from Fox Television and the 700 Club, have increased the offered reward for information leading to the apprehension of Friesen to one million dollars.

"I don't even want the money," said Mr. Jones. "I just want Munroe to get well, and for Mr. Friesen to get the punishment he deserves."

Detective Amanda Daimler, an FBI agent who is heading up the investigation, admits confusion as to Friesen's whereabouts.

"Until now, we had been operating under the assumption that Mr. Friesen had remained in Canada, perhaps still in his hometown of Winnipeg. It appears that he is far more resourceful than we had anticipated."

Police are advising local citizenry to be on the lookout for a young man, Caucasian, bearded, possibly brown hair, wearing a Niner's baseball cap.

TO: ermccorm@yahoo.ca
FROM: iamashelfmonkey@gmail.com
SUBJECT: Missed me

Dear Eric,

Sorry that last e-mail cut off like that. An hour after I fled the library (oh, and how galling is that? A librarian, turning me in! You'd think if *anyone* was going to sympathize . . .) federal agents had sealed off the building. I watched from across the street, it was very impressive in its thoroughness. I've seen my face on every television and newspaper lately, flyers are on every lamppost, there's a one-million-dollar bounty on my head for my capture or, failing that, death.

I'd ask for the money in cash.

The weeks passed. Books were sold. Montags were captured, tortured for information, and destroyed. The four of us began congregating at Aubrey's every few nights after work, discussing books, music, the news, whatever. When Rex Murphy held one of his biannual radio programs on the year in books, we treated the day as some would treat the Stanley Cup playoffs, chowing down on nachos and giving rousing cheers whenever Rex would verbally gut a caller. "I apologize, caller, I must have misheard you, did you just have the utter temerity to wax eloquent on the literary treacle that is Mitch Albom?" We cheered as if Gretzky himself had come out of retirement, or, in our sphere of knowledge, J.D. Salinger.

It became routine, but there was joy in it; there was never the fear that it could become boring. Some nights we'd read silently to ourselves, content to simply be in the others' company. Other nights, we would challenge ourselves with the kinds of games only nerds can enjoy. I would mention a title, Aubrey supplied the author, Danae and Warren would try and keep up.

"Books and authors, Thomas," Aubrey would start. "Go."

"The Jonah Kit." I challenged.

"Ian Watson. *Six Easy Pieces.*"

"Oh, uh . . . Walter Mosley. *The Unlimited Dream Company?*"

"Come on, give me a hard one. J.G. Ballard. *Shroud.*"

"Oh, that's . . . I know this one, John Banville, ha!"

"Okay, brother, give me a hard one now."

"A Werewolf Problem in Central Russia."

"Victor Pelevin."

"No way," Warren said. "No way you knew that, Aubrey, no way!"

"He's right," I admitted. Aubrey bowed to the applause, and the game would continue.

Warren disappeared for days at a time, reappearing with new ailments: his legs had healed, but as a trade-off, he was now completely bald. "A bold new choice of hairstyle," he called it. Sadly, in contrast to the sculpted symmetrical bulk of his body, his head was a lumpy mess, lending him less the air of a cool Bruce Willis/action hero–type, and more the charisma of a mental patient out on a day pass. Danae and I continued our playful banter, but I felt I was making progress. With every weekly meeting of the Shelf Monkeys, she became more and more enamoured of me, barely containing her excitement as I argued against and burned to cinders page after page of Larry Bond and Janette Oke and Elizabeth Lowell. Myself, I would have done anything for her by that time. I was starting to feel whole again, myself again, a sensation I hadn't recognized in months, maybe years.

Munroe rapidly elevated himself in our ranks to the top of our hit list. By assent, the meetings now began in Aubrey's house, where a pre-taped copy of the latest Munroe Book Club was screened to whip us into a righteous froth of vengeance. We'd launch spitballs and bottlecaps at the screen as Munroe read portions of whatever offal he was pimping that week, his baritone wavering tremulously as he choked back his tears. Heartily incensed, we'd run out into the night, burning the books, igniting Munroe himself in symbolic effigy, again, and again, and again.

I phoned Danae one evening. "Hey, do you think we're snobs?"

"What's that, sexy?" she asked. She had lately taken to calling me by a series of pet names, a turn of events I chose to take as heartening rather than condescending. It was our thing. She never made the names sound like she was demeaning me, never went, "Ooh, whatsamatta, schweetie? You depressed? Who's a good boy?

Whoshagoodboy?" Not that I wouldn't have rolled over for a tummy scratch now and then.

"Are we snobs? Burning books, making fun of others?" It had been bothering me lately. Two meetings previous, the Monkeys had unanimously agreed to begin a Master List of the Condemned; authors whose total output was so hopelessly inept and useless that discussing the quality of their books in singular fashion was deemed a meaningless exercise and a waste of a good bonfire. Frank Peretti. Nicholas Sparks. Eric Van Lustbader. Books spun off from television shows and video games. Any series based on a trading card game. Anything from Bethany House Publications. They were all just too easy. At the time, I voted yes wholeheartedly, gratified that my earlier promise to William/Valentine Michael Smith to peruse a Beverly Lewis was now moot. Now, I wasn't so sure.

On the other end of the line, Danae sipped from her coffee cup, transmitting the smutty noise of liquid slurping across shivering electric wiring directly into my brain. Wow. I *was* whipped. "I don't get you, Thomas, what's up?"

"We get together, all of us, and all we do is cut down authors we hate. At work, we laugh at people who spend their money on evangelical fiction and vanity biographies. I mean, we're not hurting anyone or anything like that. We just think we're so much smarter than everyone else."

"I'm not seeing the problem here, hon," she said, boredom threatening at the edges of her voice. "What, this bothers you?"

"Look, just because someone wants to willingly read a Pat Robertson or a Jerry Jenkins, it doesn't necessarily make them a bad person."

"Doesn't help."

"I mean, in the end, all the authors are doing is trying to make a buck, same as us. Doesn't matter if it's awful. If someone wants to read it, if it fills a need, who are we to criticize? Aren't we just mad because these people make more money than us? That they wrote a book, while we still make minimum wage?"

"What, you want to write a book?" she asked, suddenly excited. "That's a great idea, you should do that! I've often told Aubrey to —"

"No, you're not getting it, I don't want to —"

"What would it be about?"

"What?"

"Your book. What's the plot? Could I be in it? I always fancied myself a literary heroine. Someone sexy, strong, yet feminine and graceful. Could you give me bigger boobs?"

"Oh. Uh." I was losing my momentum. "Look, don't change the subject, I'm trying to be serious. I don't want to write a book, I'm saying that maybe we're no better than the people we hate. Or not much better. Why do I have an animosity toward Richard Paul Evans? Sure, he blows chunks, but he donates some of his profits to charities. Or he says he does, I don't know. I mean, do I despise him because he's a horrible writer, or because he makes me feel inadequate?"

"Oh, probably a bit of both," Danae said. "How about a mystery?"

"What?"

"Your book. Or a coming-of-age story? You'd be good at that, all those life lessons you've learned."

"I'm not writing a book. I don't like writing cheques, for Christ's sake. What makes you think I could write a book?"

"Hey, if Fiona Sigler can do it . . ." She made a gagging sound.

"Who?"

"Oh, Munroe's latest. Comes out next month, we got an advance copy. Page made me read it. Called *Freedom Fries and War Widows*."

"Sounds awful."

"It doesn't disappoint on that front." She let out a deep, throaty, sexy sigh that threatened to resurrect Charles Dickens from the dead to pen another novel. "Look, hon, if you're having a crisis of conscience or something, look at it like this. What we're doing is, we're performing a public service."

"We are?"

"Most certainly. For every book we destroy, we save someone from the peril inherent in reading it."

I was intrigued. We didn't simply burn books. No, that would be crazy. We were protectors of the weak and powerless. Liberators. "Well I must admit, that sounds wholly reasonable."

"When we weed a lesser author from the stacks, we make room

for a stronger, more capable author to take its place."

"I never thought of it like that. Kind of like pruning dead branches from a tree or something."

"Yes, only that's not strong enough." Danae was getting revved up. Her voice quickened in excitement. "It's Darwinian, Thomas, that's what it is. Only the strong survive. We're hyenas."

"We're thinning the herd."

"We're right, they're wrong."

"You're either with us or against us."

"We're saving mankind."

"We're superheroes?"

"We *are* superheroes, that's right!" I could hear her jumping in her chair. "This is awesome! I'll be Libraria, Mistress of the Dewey Decimal System!" She cackled in euphoria. "I'll shoot classification numbers from my fingertips! Freeze, or I'll catalogue you!"

"And I'll be . . ." Who could I be? I was already Yossarian, I can't be expected to keep all my aliases straight. "By day, I'm Thomas Friesen, mild-mannered bookstore employee. But by night, under the cover of darkness, I become . . . *Captain ISBN!*"

"Just captain?"

"Well, I hope to work my way up to General, but I'm new at this."

"What's your power?"

"I can proofread one thousand words per minute."

"Impressive."

"Can I wear a cape?"

Danae whooped in delight.

I tried again with Warren, figuring the possible yet unlikely use of his sexual wiles on me would be less effective. We had spent the day at Assiniboine River Books, a store devoted, whether by accident, design, or sheer laziness (Bingo!), to displaying its wares in no discernible manner. A holistic approach is the only method one could use that would assure success, as you could never hope to find a specific book you were interested in. The guy behind the counter was of no help, immersed, as he was, in one of the less-than-classic whack mags the store also offered by the barrelful. If, however, you allowed yourself the pleasure of a daylong browse through the books heaped throughout in intimidating mountains, you would be guaranteed to find something far more interesting than you had planned.

After an hour, discovering a passable copy of *What's Bred in the Bone* concealed under kilograms of bloated water-damaged trade paperbacks, I asked Warren, "Hey, uh, are we snobs?"

"Definitely, dude," he said, sitting on the floor, nose buried in a tattered copy of Dick's *The Man in the High Castle*. "We are so much better than everyone else. We are the top of the food chain."

"No, seriously, put down the book, I'm serious," I said. Warren closed the novel, exaggerating a sigh of reluctance. "Warren, we're snobs, aren't we? Burning books, making fun of others. What makes us any better than them?"

Warren scratched his cheek, smiling in amusement. "Thomas, look at me, all right? What do you see?"

"Seven feet of well-buffed man muscle."

He feigned shyness. "I didn't think you'd noticed. No, seriously, what I am is the wet dream of every college and university sports team. I can dunk, I can spike, I can run the ball up the middle, all that load. It would be so easy for me to make good money at it, if I do say so myself."

"And yet, here you are."

"Exactly. Because, despite my enormous size and gifted athleticism, I'd rather sit here with you reading books than show off my skills to a fawning public. I figured out a long time ago what I was, Thomas, and I've worked very hard to make peace with it."

"Your parents must be very proud."

"My parents don't talk to me much anymore." Warren stuck his hand into the nearest pile, pulling out a random book and reading its cover. "Hey, *The Bear Went Over the Mountain*! I love this place." He sighed. "No, the parents, when they saw me shoot out the birth canal, they had dollar signs in their eyes. NFL fullback, NBA centre, NHL goon, they didn't care, I was their ticket out of lower-middle class. I don't blame them, but Dad never really forgave me for getting straight As in English and Cs in gym. I could have done better, but I never saw the point, y'know? It's like when those Doogie Howsers get Fs, even though they could write the textbooks they're so smart. It was all too easy, and boring besides." I nodded. "Anyway, to return to the question, yes, Thomas, we are snobs. High quality snobs, of course, but snobs, definitely. But then, so are my parents. To them, sports are more important than other considerations. Myself, I'll take Doug Adams over Doug Flutie. We're all snobs, Thomas, some of us just hide it better."

"But all we do is make fun of others for something we can't do ourselves." I shoved my hand into another lump of books and pulled one out. "Look," I said, holding it up. "Nora Roberts. I mean, the lady writes books faster than I can blink, for Pete's sake. Aren't we just being petty and jealous? So what if she gets published, at least people are reading. All most people want in the end is comfort, they don't want a challenge. That's not always a bad thing."

"Comfort," Warren mused. He thought it over for a second. "Huh. Right, look at it like this. You like fast food, Thomas?"

"Uh, sure, I guess."

"Me too. Sometimes, all you want is slop on Styrofoam. But, now, could you actually live and thrive on fast food? We all go to McDonald's once in a while; you get that sickening craving for a Quarter Pounder, even though you know in your heart it's equal parts sawdust and cow scrapings, and you have no choice but to slap down your three bucks and devour a pathetic meat-like substance that the fryboy probably pissed on. A fine meal of homemade lasagna dripping with mozzarella and marinara would be equally filling, plus you wouldn't feel so cheap and greasy. Yet which is better?"

"Well, the lasagna. But now, that's only my opinion."

"Yes, there's always going to be room for personal preference. Face it, you like fast food. I *like* fast food. But we don't eat it all the time, right?"

"No."

"No, because you'd eventually die from liver failure. Here, same thing. Roberts is fast food."

"Filling, but not very good for you."

"Exactly, nothing wrong with it once in a while, but it's all empty calories. There's no real nourishment, and you end up feeling kind of queasy afterward. You'll also be hungry again in an hour. You could live on Nora Roberts, sure, have her for breakfast, LaVyrle Spencer for lunch, and Dan Brown for dinner, but you'll end up bloated and groggy. It was quick, it was tasty, it was easy, it hit all the right spots, but *fuck* if you don't actually feel sick after a while. In the end, it's just not healthy. There're doctors all over who'll say a diet of fast food is no good, and it'll eventually kill you. Same thing with us."

"So we're not snobs. We're dieticians."

"Exactly."

"You hungry?"

"I wasn't when I came in here, but now that you mention it."

"Once in a great while, an author comes along who single-handedly transforms the literary world. An author whose altogether unique perspective and talent effortlessly redefine our notions of storytelling. An author who speaks for those who cannot speak for themselves. An author who reinvents the wheel, so to speak."

Harold Kura took a sip from his water bottle, using the moment, allowing the pause to add to the effect, letting his words sink through the many layers of the human cranium, waiting until absolute comprehension had been achieved. An instant vacuum was created as his audience held its collective breath. Behind Kura, Page leaned forward anxiously from her chair, her hands on her knees, her eyes glued to the back of his coif in anticipation. What could he be waiting for?

His teeth revealed themselves in a bleached smile, dazzling in their ivory purity. His fingers strummed the podium. "Agnes Coleman, God bless her, is just such an author." A rush of exhaled air filled the store, followed closely by applause of the volume one would normally associate with the Second Coming. Kura's grin stretched wider. He knew his audience, and would wring every last ounce of adulation from their sweaty palms by the time he was through with them.

Agnes Coleman. Did ever such a wretch of a writer deserve comeuppance, Eric? I ask you.

Aubrey, Warren, and I reclined in the back row, the applause rising about us like steam. Coleman's second novel, *Baby, I Was*

Nothing Before You (written and published with a speed that makes Nora Roberts look like Pynchon), had been controlling the charts since its release, and her appearance had been hyped for weeks. Page had been praised in the *Winnipeg Sun* as scoring a coup no less miraculous than the reanimation of Edgar Allan Poe's corpse. Coleman had previously said she would not visit Canada on her book tour. ("Too cold for me, thank you very much," she quipped on a *Tonight Show* appearance. "I have no intention whatsoever of visiting a country where polar bears wander the streets." Leno's jaw promptly dislodged from convulsions of laughter.) Page had been persistent in her appeals for a visit to the point of fanaticism, however, inundating Coleman and her agent with verbal and written pleas until they had no choice but to visit Winnipeg, lest Page immolate herself on Coleman's doorstep in a final, tragic dénouement.

It had all been worth it, from Page's point of view. **READ** was full to bursting, fire code be damned. Munroe acolytes lined the aisles, sat atop bookshelves, crowded the stage, swarming about until all semblance of order was ignored and it was all you could do to find enough space to breathe. The line-up for seating had begun to grow before the store had opened that morning, and now, at 7 p.m., it seemed there wasn't one free square foot of space left in the entire store. Throughout the day, the three of us had each taken shifts to ensure we would have a seat, and now we sat mutely among the hoi polloi, ensconced in a near-religious zeal that would have been funny had it not been so palpably scary. People of all sorts were in attendance on this beautiful September evening. Little old ladies, holding copies of Coleman's newest as they would clasp a rosary: ten Hail Marys for every disparaging thought on the quality of the book. Intellectual poseurs. Businessmen. Mothers, nursing their babies. Fathers, balancing Coleman novels in one hand while frantically holding on to their children's arms, fearful of a random trampling. Aubrey leaned over to me, and whispered one word. "Altamont." I nodded my agreement, chilled. It would take only the slightest extra push to send this group into a rage that would make a gang of unruly hockey dads seem mild-mannered by comparison. For a moment, I envied Danae's prescient decision to stay at home that evening, not wanting her attendance at the reading to been misconstrued as admiration. But to see a MUNROE RECOMMENDS THIS! in the flesh, in person, to be just that one iota closer to Munroe himself? This was a chance I would never pass up.

Thanks to Munroe, Coleman's name was now bandied about libraries, bookstores, and Internet chat-rooms with the same fervour that once accompanied the rerelease of the *Star Wars* films or the next Harry Potter. After all, Agnes was the first, the most successful of all Munroe novelists, the proof that absolutely anyone can become a sensation. The public is helpless against such a publicity onslaught. You have as much a chance of halting a tsunami with a child's sand pail as you have trying to convince a Munroe fan as to the non-existent merits of Coleman's published vomit. If attacking Munroe as an odious slime was akin to heresy, attacking a MUNROE RECOMMENDS THIS! author was at least worthy of a stoning. I wouldn't have put it past the crowd. If Coleman came out and ordered them all to prostrate themselves before her, writhing in frenzied orgasm, before drinking the grape Kool-Aid, there'd be one hell of a mass suicide to report the next morning.

Making matters worse was Warren's constant shifting in his chair. A casual observer might mistake his jittering for nervous anticipation, but truth was, Warren was in near-crippling pain. An unforeseen yet hardly surprising result of a still-in-the-testing-phase men's impotence cure, Warren was the at first proud then anxious and now quite fed up with owner of a truly monstrous episode of priapism. Having an eternal pillar of fertility between one's legs would be most men's definition of Heaven, but after two weeks of hauling around the CN Tower, the glory and glamour of possessing the world's longest freestanding woody was taking its toll. Warren had taken matters into his own hand — his left, then his right, then alternating — until his arms were sore with repetitive strain disorder, but all the sperm-releasing orgasms he could muster had not quelled his prick's mahogany strength one iota. Loose pants, while comfortable, were out of the question; the pup tent he displayed could double as a coat rack. Consequently, he wore tight pants and underwear, trying to disguise his discomfort by keeping his chubby as close as possible to his body. While the technique, when combined with overly lengthy sweaters that hung to mid-thigh, served to effectively mask the elongation from public view, the resulting awkward limp would do John Cleese proud, a shambling gait that looked exactly like what it was, a series of hops and slides that could never be interpreted as anything but the futile efforts of a man trying to manoeuvre his legs around one absolutely leviathan (and severely chafed) erection. Compared to this, Portnoy had absolutely nothing to complain about.

"And so," Kura said, wrapping up his inordinately long introduction, "it is my privilege, my honour, and my good fortune to introduce to you now, a lady of grace and elegance, a major talent by any standard," my eyes were now insisting on rolling themselves upward, "I present to you, Winnipeg, Miss Agnes Marie Coleman." Page bounded to her feet. The noise of the largest herd of buffalo ever to gallop the open plains erupted, as hands slapped hands until blood blisters formed, a sonic blast of love urging Agnes to leave the safe confines of the break room, come forth, bless us, love us, blow us kisses, blow us. It swept her up in aural waves of mania, carrying her to the stage. I swear, she floated; her feet never touched the ground. The sermon from the bookstore was about to begin.

"Thank you, oh thank you so much!" she squealed as Kura took her hand to help her up the stairs, then hugged her in welcome. Page offered her hand in greeting, and instead found herself ambushed and struggling in an emotional three-way full-body squeeze play with Agnes and Harold. Even when star-struck, Page simply did not like to be touched. She controlled the impulse to shove Agnes off the stage, slowly extricating herself from the fleshy sandwich. Agnes faced the crowd. "I love you all, oh this is too much, please!" She held a hand to her chest, a show of humility, all for me, you shouldn't have, oh, stop. The crowd lapped it up.

In person, Agnes is just about the least dynamic person you could ever hope to see. A combination of ultra-expensive silks and pastels adorned her squat frame. It was the wardrobe of the recently insanely rich, a mixture of decadent fabrics that people born to wealth would never be caught in public in. She dressed the way she *thought* rich people dressed, highlighting how out of place her money was to her upbringing. The sort of awful taste only significant financial backing can achieve. Hopefully, she'd wise up and hire an image consultant to berate her into style. Without access to the camera filters and Vaseline fogging provided by Purvis personnel on his program, her overabundance of patchwork makeup was clearly visible. Still, she appeared content, which I could never say for myself, so who knows? Maybe the application of dense blankets of pancake about the face and neck leads to happiness. I made a mental note to stop at a drugstore on my way home.

"Gosh, oh gosh, thank you," she panted as the applause subsided. "This makes it all worthwhile, this is why I came. To be here, meeting real people, kind people, good, good people." She emphasized the *good*, a likely attempt to downplay her disastrous appearance at Book Expo America the previous week. Kura had somehow convinced the Expo producers to squeeze Agnes into a panel discussion on "The Purpose of Fiction After 9/11." She wound up sitting between Alice Sebold and Rick Moody, alone and ignored. After an hour of disoriented silence on her part, Agnes had been roundly booed by all in the room after she said she had not only never read anything by any of the eleven panel members, but never read anything not recommended by Munroe Purvis, period. John Irving and Tom Wolfe postponed their feud to jointly release a statement of condemnation. Maya Angelou herself called Agnes an abomination and an insult to her craft. It was an extraordinarily beautiful moment, an exquisite case of *schaden-freude* for all involved. Needless to say, Aubrey had immediately procured a videotaped copy of the event, which played in a near-constant loop on his television, Agnes's vacant stare a classic of silent Keatonesque comedy. She would have gnawed off her leg if it might have allowed her to flee the room any sooner.

She cracked open the book that lay before her on the podium. "I thought I'd start with a small reading from my latest novel, *Baby I Was Nothing Before You*, before taking some questions. That is, if you don't mind," she tittered, as yet another blast of frenzied clapping filled the air. "This is from Chapter 7, where my heroine Marjorie is telling her son Quinn about his life-threatening illness." She cleared her throat. A muffled series of squeaks arose as the acolytes leaned forward in their chairs, a few hurriedly rifling through pages of their copies in order to follow along.

Marjorie played with her left ear-bob, knowing that the moment had finally come. "You see Quinn, my precious, oh-so-precious love Quinn," Marjorie explained to her beautiful son, her heart aching with sad sorrow, "sometimes, when your stomach hurts, it's not because you're hungry."

"It's not?" Quinn asked, his trusting eyes watching Marjorie with love.

"No, honeypie. Sometimes, you see, God has a different plan for some of us . . ."

Sighing, I tuned her nasal droning out, busying myself by mentally rehearsing the questions I had prepared for the occasion. Aubrey and Warren were similarly occupied. We had spent the better part of a week preparing our dream questions for Miss Coleman, bandying possibilities back and forth across Aubrey's living room. We weren't just your average book readers, we told ourselves. We were not just people who couldn't abide her books. No, we were warriors for justice, balancing the scales for every struggling artist who couldn't find an agent. Books were our armour, arcane knowledge and esoteric definitions our weapons of choice. It was cruel to be sure, but then, war always is. The illiterate gorillas who stomped my books into papier mâché fodder were about to receive the holy retribution of an avenging angel.

In a roundabout way.

"So I'm not going to be alive for Christmas?" Quinn sobbed. "I won't get to see Granny again, or Uncle Martin?"

Marjorie wept with heart-rending grief. "No, sweetie-pookins, no." She grabbed Quinn and held him with all the love a strong and loving mother can provide. "No, you won't make it, but we'll have Christmas early, ok? With Granny and Uncle Marty and all your cousins, they'll all come to see you before...before..." Marjorie wailed.

"Mommy?" Quinn wiped at his eyes. "Mommy, why does God hate me?"

Members of the audience were openly weeping by this point in

Agnes's narrative. The room filled itself with the distinctive yet indescribable sound of snot forced out of hairy narrow tubes and damply colliding with thin sheets of tissue. Christ, I had a lump in my throat. It was mob mentality of the Big Brother hate rallies and Oprah Winfrey screamfests; if one of us screamed, we all screamed. If one cried, we all broke down into quivering masses of emotionally needy jelly. Agnes's face looked to be succumbing to natural erosion, the saltwater from her ducts digging canyons through her makeup, joining forces with liner and blush to congeal under her eyes, lending her the air of a very effeminate football player, a place-kicker, say. Harold Kura leaned forward, holding his face in his hands, his elbows atop his knees. He was audibly bawling.

> *"And when you meet God, Quinn, when you stand next to him at the Pearly Gates, you tell him that you understand, that you know his love is all-encompassing, all-compassionate, and that you are happy to be in his loving glory."*
>
> *"I will, Mommy," Quinn said. "I'll make you so proud of me, Mommy."*

She shut the book, her eyes closed. "Thank you," she said, her voice hoarse. There was nary a dry eye or non-runny nose in the building, save Aubrey and Warren. I silently cursed the medications, sure that they were to blame for the slight mistiness of my tear ducts.

Kura stood up and embraced Agnes in his arms. "No, thank you, Agnes," he said.

And the crowd went wild. People hugged each other. Strangers hugged strangers. Terrorists laid down their arms. Nations united. A new order of peace and goodwill was at hand.

All right, that never happened. But I guarantee you, the United Nations never had an audience as emotional as Agnes Coleman had that night.

"Miss Coleman will now field some questions, and then we'll have a signing," Kura announced. That was our cue. Our arms immediately shot into the air, only preceded by the six hundred or so arms of everyone else. Clearly, it was going to be difficult to win this arms race. "Yes, you," said Kura, singling out one appendage from many. A small elderly woman rose to her feet, as the sea of arms reluctantly dropped.

"Yes, Miss Coleman," she said. "I just wanted to tell you how much your novels have meant to me."

Agnes clapped her hands together. "Oh, gosh, thank you *so* much!" she squealed. "I'm so happy, you don't know how important it is to me for my words to touch someone! Thank you!"

"Thank you, Miss Coleman," said the woman, tears flowing down an already damp face. "I love your books. I love you!"

"I love you, too!" Agnes tweeted. The crowd applauded as the woman sat back down, her shoulders heaving with emotion.

Warren nudged my side. "I don't know about you, but her book left me feeling a bit touched too. I threw up all night."

"Miss Coleman! Miss Coleman!" Aubrey was yelling as the arms began to rise again. "Miss Coleman! Agnes!" But Agnes had already moved on to the next obvious questioner, an equally aged woman who could barely contain herself. "Fuck," Aubrey whispered. He jittered in his seat. "C'mon, c'mon." As soon as the woman finished her list of platitudes, he shot back up. "AGNES!"

Kura motioned toward Aubrey. "Yes, the excitable gentleman with the hair, yes." The crowd chuckled appreciatively along with Kura as Aubrey composed himself, affording the audience a full view of his mane. On stage, Page visibly stiffened, her lips pursing themselves into a bloodless white scar.

"My goodness!" Agnes said. "Sir, I have got to introduce you to my stylist." More guffaws ensued.

Aubrey waited out the laughter. "Miss Coleman," he said, "I just wanted you to know just how deeply, deeply your book affected me. I can honestly say, I have never read a book quite as . . . moving."

"Moved him all the way to the toilet," Warren muttered.

"Where do you come up with such ideas?"

"Why, God bless you, young man!" said Agnes. "I'm just so overjoyed my novels can speak to people of your persuasion." *Persuasion?* "My ideas, oh, they just come to me. Like magic. Very good question."

"Uh . . . thanks," Aubrey said. Arms began to rise about him as

Kura scanned the room for another potential softball. "Uh, I do have a follow-up question as well, Miss Coleman," Aubrey called out.

"Oh. Yes?"

Aubrey cleared his throat, glancing at the index card he held in his hand. "Yes, Miss Coleman, I was just wondering, in your novel, when Marjorie finally convinces Uncle Martin to abandon his atheistic beliefs and come for Quinn's early Christmas, was this, if I'm not wholly mistaken, your subtle commentary on the state of world politics today, *vis-à-vis* Marjorie's persona being in fact a crafty representation of the American military complex, and likewise Uncle Martin the embodiment of the Iraqi government, in particular the dictatorship of Saddam Hussein?"

It was Christmas Eve. Not a creature was stirring. The question hung in the air between Aubrey and Agnes like the Hindenburg preparing to incinerate itself. All it needed was a spark. I could feel the waves of heat from Page's gathering rage as she mentally commenced Aubrey's disembowelment.

"I'm sorry," Agnes said, "I'm afraid I . . . I don't understand the question."

"I apologize, Miss Coleman, I'll try to be clearer. I'm not good with words, I'm not a novelist such as yourself. But the thematic subtext of Marjorie and Martin's relationship, what with Marjorie's duplicity in convincing Martin of Quinn's desire to make sure his uncle had a place in Heaven when what Marjorie really desired all along was to impose her religious viewpoint onto Martin's in order to make herself feel like she was truly accomplishing something in what would otherwise be a drab and uneventful life, this would, I believe, appear to indicate a desire on your part to present a *roman à clef* of George Bush's religious hypocrisy in his declaring Iraq to be an evil empire, disguising his true motives of enhancing his power base through the control of the flow of oil."

" . . . "

"Or have I read too much into it? Are you perhaps simply demonstrating the inherent possibilities of narrative as a satire unto itself, a self-parody, a post-modern metafiction on the level of David Foster Wallace?"

Agnes's eyes took on the empty look of a rabbit caught in the headlights of an onrushing bus. "I'm sorry . . . I . . . I've always supported our troops, of course —"

"I don't mean to call your patriotism into question, Miss Coleman. If anything, I want to praise your resourcefulness in camouflaging your contempt of Bush's policies underneath the facile nonsense that is your work. I applaud you." Aubrey began to slam his hands together, the lonely sound swallowed up by the befuddlement his question had evoked from the crowd. "Good for you!" he yelled. "Bravo! Come on, everyone! Give her a hand!" Warren and I clapped along enthusiastically. A few other people nearby half-heartedly joined in, confused as to whether their applause was in praise or derision. Agnes flinched at every CLAP! Her eyes beseeched someone to come to her aid.

Kura stepped up to the mike. "All right, I think that's enough. Let's —"

"Miss Coleman!" I yelled, leaping up to prevent Kura's slick evasion of Aubrey's nonsense. "Agnes, there are certain ongoing themes in your novels thus far regarding the intrusion of church into state politics. Do you envision yourself completing a third novel along the same themes, perhaps creating a trilogy forming an ongoing series of *bildungsromans* showcasing the political machinations of religious fundamentalists?"

"What?" Agnes's shoulders twitched with suppressed sobs. "Roman buildings?"

"Are you making a sublime criticism through Martin's pig-headedness of those among us who would seek to prevent the possible medical advances available through stem cell research?" Aubrey asked, raising his voice over the chorus of discontentment growing throughout the room.

"Are you pro-choice?" I called out.

"Do you support the euthanasia movement?"

"Where do you stand on mercy killings?"

"What's your take on the Patriot Act?"

"That is enough!" Kura hollered, drenching the first row with spit. Agnes tottered beside him, while Page handed her tissues from her purse. "I don't know what you think Miss Coleman has done to deserve such treatment, but —"

"You're FIRED, Aubrey!" Page screamed.

"Yo, Agnes!" Warren called out as he stood up awkwardly, and in some pain, his voice nonetheless effortlessly drowning out everyone else. "The pages, ouch, the pages of your novel are of such rich fibre, Ms. Coleman, I have to know, they are so soft and absorbent, did you foresee the eventual use of your novel to wipe my ass?"

That was the straw. The camel lay broken and dying on stage, while the three of us hastily barrelled ourselves through a suddenly violent throng of dowagers and housewives. Aubrey and I cowered behind Warren's limping bulk as he bolted for the exit, enduring a processional of slaps and punches and the occasional thrown hardcover. We made the safety of the front doors, and as we tore out of the building, laughing into the night, we could hear Agnes wailing over the ruckus, and as shameful as it sounds now, it was the sweetest thing I'd ever heard.

"YOU PRICK!"

I winced. If you think what we did was shocking, hearing Page burst into obscenities is a million times worse.

"Thomas?" Warren murmured.

"Yeah?" I whispered back.

"I think that did the trick."

"What?"

"My erection's gone."

"Well, that's something at least."

Warren and I sat outside Page's office, fretfully awaiting our respective turns in the chamber of discipline. We had been treated like heroes by many of the staff upon our arrival at that morning's meeting, shocked that we dared to show up for work at all. Even I was impressed by the size of my balls that morning. I originally opted to stay home and assume my unemployment was a given, but Aubrey bolstered our self-assurance with assertions that we must go forth boldly and face the music, lest we be labelled as being ashamed of our actions and cowards to the cause. Our status as near-mythic deities was short-lived, however; as soon as Page charged in, a curt "Everyone get to work!" replacing her standard pre-opening spiel, the adoring eyes of my workmates rapidly averted their gaze to the floor. Page thrust out her hand, three fingers extended, one for each of us. "You three. My office. Now!" Recognizing well ahead of time that our deeds would never go unpunished did little to alleviate my dread. No one really enjoys a chewing out, deserved or not, but it's the anticipation that kills you. I had fully prepared myself for a pink slip and forcible ejection from the premises the moment we began plotting the surprisingly easy downfall of Agnes. The way I saw it, the previous night's entertainment would function both as valuable personal therapy and as an effective form of social anti-depressant, a quick-fix mood elevator that had the added bonus of pissing off so many people I didn't care for. I wasn't worried about myself, and Warren and Aubrey could certainly look after themselves. The lack of news cameras at the actual event softened the impact of our protest, but only just. Page somehow had managed to keep our names from publication, the *Free Press* instead labelling us "unknown agitators" and describing Aubrey as "a bushy-haired employee"; to my mind, a much preferable interpretation to our actions than the *Winnipeg Sun's* glaring giant-font front-page headline TASTELESS PUNKS MAKE AUTHOR CRY.

"Do you have any idea how much damage your stunt has caused this store?" Page yelled. Her voice came through the thin door clearly, adding to our discomfort. Why couldn't she just fire us calmly? Honestly, some people just look for excuses to be irrational.

"Oh, chill out, Page, Jeez!" Aubrey shot back. He was giving as good as he got. "You think we'd set the woman on fire! We just let off some steam. All we did was correct an error."

"What in God's name are you talking about? What error? You, you verbally assaulted an invited guest! Not to mention the near riot you caused! Did you know she actually fainted from the stress you caused her? God, we'll be lucky if no one sues. There are major slander issues here."

"Stop blowing it out of proportion," he retorted. "Nothing we said remotely counts as slander. Thomas says so. Insulting, yes, which was the point, but not slander, so you're safe." I beamed. My law degree had finally come in handy.

"In fact," Aubrey continued, "the entire event could be viewed as a performance art piece, a prolonged example of literary satire.

Maybe we could do it all the time, it'll become an honour for invited guests to be dragged across the coals by the **READ** threesome, authors will line up and beg for it. We can sell tickets. Tell you what, I'll draft up a proposal, see if we can get an arts grant."

"You three are gone! You are banned, you hear me? I'll have the police drag you out if you stay, I don't care if you own —"

"Just try it," said Aubrey, his voice suddenly lowered. "You just try it, Page. I dare you." It was deathly quiet on the other side of the door. Something very odd had just occurred, but I couldn't think of what. Murmurs, indistinct, wormed their way back outside the office. I looked at Warren, who shrugged in shared confusion, and the two of us leaned our heads toward the door, striving to hear more.

"— can't do that," Page was saying.

"Watch me," Aubrey said. "You want to make this ugly, I'll match you step for step. Lawyers, trials, the works. I'll close this place down before I let you win."

"Why?" said Page. She sounded scared. "You'd destroy what we've built, for what? Just so you can get your kicks?"

"We've had a good run, Page. We've each made some money, more than I ever believed we could. I'm sure you'll do fine on your own. Besides, I've been unhappy lately, you know that. It's about time I stretched my wings and flew off for a bit."

"Please, we worked so hard. Why can't you just leave me be, take your money and just go."

"Nope. I gave you Emily, but this is more important. Those two out there, with their ears against the door, they're friends of mine. I talked them into it. I'm responsible for them, and I will not have them lose their jobs. You leave us alone, and everything will go along just as it always has."

There was a troubling minute of complete silence. I pressed my ear up against the wood. I could just make out Page's voice, a violent whisper. "If you ever do this again, I'll call your bluff. I'll put everyone out of work. You, Danae, those idiots outside, everyone. I won't stand for this anymore."

"Just so we understand each other," Aubrey said. I jerked my head back at the sound of his footsteps approaching. Aubrey opened the door and stepped out, closing it slowly enough that Page's angry breathing was audible. His skin was a morass of oils, his dreadlocks wilting with sweat. He slid a hand down over his face, saw us sitting there, forced a smile to the surface. "Cheer up, brothers, we live to fight another day!"

"What, that's it?" asked Warren, deeply flummoxed. "We're good? Just like that?"

"We're good to go, Warren," Aubrey said. "Everything's, uh, copacetic. You just have to know how to talk to her. She's a pussycat, really."

Warren and I exchanged a look. "You know, we could hear everything in there," I said.

"Yeah, c'mon, Aubrey," said Warren. "You better buy us dinner first, you gonna fuck us like this."

I nodded my confusion. "What's going on, Aubrey? 'Fess up. We should be on the street begging for spare change by now."

"You got pictures of her or something, that it?" Warren asked.

"Yeah, there's no way she'd just let it drop, Aubrey," I said. "We knew that going in. I was already prepping my résumé."

"Look, it's not something I want to talk about," Aubrey said. He walked quickly away, Warren and me in hot pursuit.

"C'mon, dude, what's going on?" Warren asked as we took a left at Gay/Lesbian fiction. We were now running. Our footfalls echoed through the aisles. "Aubrey, what gives?" Warren yelled, his knees rising to my chest. I was taking two steps for every one of Warren's. Aubrey faked a left at Hockey, went right instead down Football/Soccer, then cut across Golf, and broke into a full sprint, giving us the slip at Travel.

"Where'd he go?" I wheezed to Warren. He craned his neck over the shelves, then grabbed my collar. "This way! Canadian History!" We dashed forward, Warren in the lead, effortlessly weaving his bulk through several families as he followed the red bobbing locks through Children's Fiction, catching sight of Aubrey near the U.S. History/Performing Arts Criticism cloverleaf, and finally breathing down his neck as Aubrey began to lose steam at the Spirituality/Self-Help junction.

Aubrey whirled back at us, sending me careening left into the bookshelves as I swerved to avoid a collision, books flying as I drove my arms into the shelves to catch my balance. Warren, being the greater in mass, ran past Aubrey by several metres before he could bring his velocity to a halt. The three of us stood there warily for a moment, scrutinizing each other, punctuating the silence with deep ragged breaths, scads of Gilbert Morris and Karen Kingsbury scattered about our feet.

Warren broke the peace. "You're going to tell us what's going on here, buddy."

"Let it alone, guys," Aubrey begged softly. He crouched and started to gather the books in his arms. "Please don't ask me again. Please."

"I don't think that's an option anymore," I said.

Warren loomed over Aubrey. A strange look had come into his eyes. "I swear to God, Aubrey, if you don't spill —"

"Drop it, all right?" Aubrey practically shouted this at us, his voice pushing us away into the stacks. I was stunned. Even Warren looked fearful. "You both still got your jobs, everything's taken care of, so just fucking let it go already! Jesus Christ, I thought you ingrates'd be happy!" He stalked away, fuming, throwing his armload of Janette Oke to the carpet. "Leave me the fuck alone for a while! Jesus, can't you guys do anything without me?"

Warren and I stood there for a time, quietly dazed as we stared after him. "Now, what do you think —" I began to ask, stopping short when I looked up.

Warren's large eyes swam in water. "What the . . . the . . . what the hell was that about?" he whined. Being yelled at by Page was one thing, but this was something else altogether. The contrast of Warren's massive frame with his face, screwed up in sadness, was appallingly pathetic. "Thomas, what's going on?" he asked again, his baleful eyes lending him the look of an enormous basset hound. He started to hiccup. "I mean . . . Aubrey . . . he . . ."

I shook my head weakly. "We'll find out, big man," I assured him. "You, me, Danae. We'll corner him at home or something, make him confess. We'll go after work, okay?" Warren's bottom lip fluttered. The dam was full to bursting. "Warren, come on, pull it together. You want Page to see you like this?"

"Yeah, but . . . *man*." Warren wiped a tear away before it could escape his eye. "I mean, man, I . . . why'd he have to *yell*, dude?"

Awkward is nowhere near a strong enough word for how I felt at that moment. Should I hug him? Pat him on the back? The seven-foot monster is going to cry, the Hooded Fang needs a hug. What's the appropriate manly response to such an event? Doc Newhire would tell him to let it out, but come on, we're in the middle of a fucking bookstore here.

I opted for tough love. "Hey, soldier! Buck up!" I punched him on the arm. "Suck it up, buttercup!"

Well, it got his attention. His eyes cleared. He grinned. "Did you just say 'suck it up, buttercup'?"

"You heard me!" I went into *Full Metal Jacket* mode. "You think you've got it tough, well, go home and cry to mama, you want a hug, you pussy! We're here to work, motherfucker!"

Warren smiled, then snapped to attention. "*Jawohl*, Sergeant Schultz."

"I was really going for the R. Lee Ermey thing."

"Hey, you're lucky you got Schultz. Threatening you are *not*, bud." He punched me back on the arm, lightly. I was sore for days. "Thanks, bro."

"No prob."

"That was weird, huh?'

"One word for it."

"It's just." He thought for a second. "It's like when your parents yell at you or something when you're young, you don't know why, but man, you feel it deep." He took a deep breath. He wasn't happy, but neither was he a blubbering fool.

"Uh, don't tell anyone, okay? About this?"

"You think anyone'd believe me?"

That evening, having corralled Danae into joining up, the three of us split cab fare to Aubrey's place. Warren was sullen and quiet, still working to rein in his emotions. He took a moment to build up his game face after we arrived. This game face, I noted with not a small degree of fear, was a face that truly belonged on someone of Warren's stature, fearsome and warrior-like, a face to be carved into the side of mountains to inspire and intimidate further generations. I opted for a simpler yet no less effective look of sustained confusion.

An unsurprised Aubrey responded to our knock. "Come on in,

guys," he said. "Beer's in the fridge, pizza's on the way, and . . . Warren, you look awful, have you been crying?"

"Almost." The warrior in Warren decided to loosen up a bit. "C'mere, dude." Warren grabbed Aubrey in a crushing bearhug. Aubrey gasped for breath, but I held Danae back from helping to free him from Warren's squeeze. Aubrey had this coming.

Later, Warren's sentimental nature quelled under a mountain of cheese and pepperoni, the four of us quietly drinking and smoking our ways to oblivion. I hazily recalled why we had come.

"So what the fuck, Aubrey?"

"Aw, brother," he began. "You don't need —"

"No, no, you don't leave us hanging now," Warren said. "I'm about wiped out from all this, but I swear to God I will kick your ass through the wall if you don't 'fess up."

"Brotherman, that's uncalled for."

"I think it's definitely called for, brother."

"Second!" I seconded.

"Aubrey," Danae said, inhaling a large fogbank from the communal joint, "I think it's about time."

"Danae, it's not that simple. You know that."

"These two deserve the truth now," she insisted. "After last night, you owe them that."

"They're big boys. I owe them nothing."

"Hello, what's going on?" I asked, sliding away from Danae. She looked at me with a pained expression. "You know something here, you didn't tell me?"

She glanced at Aubrey. "I'll tell them, Aubrey. Say the word."

Aubrey stuck his fingers in his hair. "Aw, Danae," he complained.

"Hey, we put our asses on the line with Agnes!" Warren yelled. He jumped up and grabbed Aubrey by the collar, swinging him around with the ease of a dog playing with its favourite chewtoy. "Thomas and I should have been fired, you too! We were prepared for this, but you have to have your little secrets!" He dropped Aubrey, cocked an arm, and shoved Aubrey's head into a monstrously painful-looking headlock. "The truth, now, or this comes off."

"Brother," Aubrey squawked. Warren increased his squeezing. Aubrey's eyes bulged.

"I'll pop it off, buddy, I mean it! Thomas, give me a count-down!"

I held up my right hand, fingers extended. "Five," I said peacefully.

"Warren, let him go, he can't breathe," Danae said.

"HHUNGH!" Aubrey agreed, turning blue.

"It's coming off at one, brother!"

"Four." I folded the thumb in. I nonchalantly took a bite of pizza.

"HURG!" Lilac now.

"Warren!" I held Danae's arm.

"Three," I said, chewing. Pinkie in.

"Hwawk!" Violet.

"Time's running out!"

"Warren! Let him go!"

"Two."

"Hnuu." Deep purple.

"You're killing him! Thomas, stop him!"

"You think I could?"

"Phlugh."

"One." Index finger left.

"Off with his head!"

"I own the store."

"Zer — what?"

"What?"

"   . . .   "

"Did you catch that?"

"Warren, let him go, man!"

Warren unclenched his bicep. Aubrey collapsed in an asphyxiated heap.

"I didn't just hear that, did I?" Warren asked me. He bent down to Aubrey's level. "Did you say what I heard, buddy? Tell me you didn't."

Massaging his throat, Aubrey bobbed his head feebly.

"You own the store?" I asked. "You own **READ**? How is this possible? And *you*," I turned to Danae, wild, "*you* knew about this?"

"I promised I wouldn't say anything," she said quietly. "Don't hate me, 'kay?"

"Don't blame her," Aubrey gasped. "I asked her to keep a secret."

Warren clenched his fists reflexively. "You own the store. You *own* the *store*? How is this possible, we've known each other, what, two years now, you don't think to ever mention to me that you're my boss?"

"Well, technically, I'm your boss, too," said Danae.

"That's not the same thing, you know it," I said sharply. "You never lied about yourself. We always knew who you were. We accepted it. This, this is different."

"Damn right, different," Warren said. "This here is betrayal." He advanced on Aubrey, who skittered pitifully away, coughing weakly.

Danae jumped up and positioned herself in Warren's path. "Okay, everyone calm down," said Danae, putting a tiny palm against Warren's chest. "Warren, we'll explain everything, just back off, all right? Go get Aubrey something to drink, will you?" Warren glared at her for a moment, and then lumbered off to the kitchen, swearing under his breath. He returned with a glass of water, spilling a fair deal on the floor as he shoved it in Aubrey's direction.

"I don't get this, not at all," I said, watching Aubrey greedily slurp down the water. "How can this be, you hate **READ** more than any of us."

"In league with the devil, pal," muttered Warren.

"Look, guys, I'm sorry," Aubrey said, wiping his mouth with the back of his arm. "I never wanted anyone to get hurt."

"Aubrey and Page are equal partners," said Danae. "They own the place fifty-fifty."

"I hired Danae, that's how come she knows." Aubrey pulled himself up from the floor and plopped himself dejectedly on the couch. He lowered his eyes and studied the rug. "Page and I, we met at business school."

"Business school, that's rich," Warren snorted.

"It was years ago, I went to make my parents happy. Hell, I was McJobbing myself to death, anyway. I had nothing else to do, and it seemed to them like I had decided to do something, so they were all for it. I hated the stuff; have no head for any of it. Barely passed."

"That's where Page was," Danae said. "They were in the same year together. They, well." Danae paused. "They hung out."

"So?" I asked.

Danae's cheeks flushed. "You're not getting it, they *hung out.*"

I mulled her emphasis over in my head for a second, then felt nauseous. "You and Page, you hung out?" I asked. "Like, hanging out? *Biblically* hanging out?"

Aubrey nodded, shamefaced. "Oh my *God!*" Warren said. "This just gets worse and worse."

"Hey, Page was different then," Aubrey protested. "I'm no great catch either in the looks area, y'know? It was just convenience. Fuck-buddies. She really was way more likeable before she got all money-conscious."

"Amen," said Danae.

"Page wanted to make money. I know books. I had this idea, thought we could hold our own against the big stores. I convinced Page to help, she wrote up a business plan, we got some financing, bought the place together, and things just went from there. We hired a few people," Aubrey waved at Danae, "and we built the place up. We agreed up front, she handles the money, I do the ordering. She runs the place, and I just hang back and enjoy myself. It was terrific there for a while. I'd set up displays and readings for local authors. Worked with independent publishers. Had open mike poetry nights. Made the place homey."

"But people weren't coming in," Danae said sadly. "Not enough to keep the place going."

"No, and Page was desperate. She wanted to buy me out, completely gut and transform the place. She was right, too, but I couldn't do it." He lifted his eyes, meeting mine. "It was mine, too. You understand? I couldn't go back to unemployment. This was the only thing I'd ever really accomplished. So I . . . compromised."

"Sold out, more like," Warren sniped.

"I started ordering more copies of the books that sold, the for-sure profit earners. Page had been studying the trades. She could see what I thought, just a few at first, just enough to keep us fluid. I mean, just because it sells, it doesn't mean it's worthless, right? Atwood sells, Munro sells. These are good things. Then, okay, Oprah books, sure, they had some quality. They weren't all Wally

Lambs. I convinced myself I was still true to my ideals. I mean, ideals are great, but they only buy so much food. But now suddenly, more money was coming in. I bought the house here, told myself it was an investment. But as soon as I bought it, I needed more. So, more compromises. More Harlequins, less non-profit publishers. Soon, it became all about the money."

Feeding the machine, I thought. Like I didn't buy lotto tickets every week.

"It's not that bad, hon," Danae said, rubbing Aubrey's shoulder. *Hon?* "We all want money, it's not necessarily a bad thing."

"Oh the fuck it isn't!" Warren said. "Don't let him off 'cuz he's all hang-dog now! How much you worth anyway, *brother?* You let me destroy my body for cash, you can't even help me out?"

"Hey, I offered!"

"Sure, you offered!" Warren spit on the floor. "Everybody offers! I didn't think you actually *had* money! It's an idle offer, none of us are *supposed* to have any money! That's the way we are!" Warren stamped petulantly about the room. "I mean, the lies, dude. *The lies!* 'Oh, Warren, the house was a gift from my parents.'"

He knocked a shelf of books off the wall.

"Let me get the beer, Warren, I have a little extra this week."

He kicked over a floor lamp, the bulb exploding.

"Don't worry about the ganja, I know this guy, gets me a *really great deal.*"

He attacked the fireplace with a poker, hacking at the logs.

"Knock it off, Warren," I said. He was quickly whittling his way through the room. I didn't want to be around when he ran out of inanimate objects to abuse. "Leave the room alone, it can't defend itself. You can get the beer next time, it makes you feel better, okay?"

Warren took a mid-rampage break, holding a potted fern over his head. He looked at Aubrey, bellowed with frustration, and flung the plant against the wall. "How could you do it, man?" he asked, scanning the room for something fragile to toss, his shoulders shrinking in despair. "Why didn't you just tell us?"

"I didn't want to be like Page, brother, I wanted to be like us," said Aubrey. "This is all I ever wanted. The four of us, together. Food, conversation, the occasional burning. That's why I, hey, not my music!" I ducked as a pressed-wood CD case flew above my head, accompanied by another Warren-yowl. "That's why I hired Danae, it's why I told Page to hire you two! I couldn't come out and tell you I was your boss, it'd ruin the whole group dynamic."

"Hey, wait, you let Emily go!" Warren exclaimed. "Why'd you do that, you could have kept her on, she was one of us."

"You think I didn't try?" Aubrey stood up. "I like Emily fine, but she was off her rocker! She was yelling at the customers! It was business, man! I tried to keep her on, but she never stopped!"

"And what was last night?" Warren yelled. The two of them were now almost nose-to-nose, or considering Warren's dimensions, nose to chest. "Seems last night, what we did, that makes Emily look pretty damn normal. Why'd we do it, huh?"

"Because I had to!" Aubrey yelled back. "I sold out, you're right! The place is destroying me, I had to fight back! I couldn't let the fuckers win anymore! Every day, I got Munroe leering down at me. I got sane, intelligent people asking me when the next Munroe book comes out! I have kids looking for his approved comic books! He's destroying a whole generation, guys! He's killing us! I can't back down, I can't let Page win, I cannot do this anymore!" He stepped back from Warren, breathing heavily. "I can't do it. I can't fight anymore. Page wins. I quit."

"Whoa, let's not be hasty now," I said, jumping in. "Look, quitting is not the answer, for any of us. I, for one, need the money, and the only thing worse than having a job is looking for one. I'm not quitting, no one here is quitting." I looked to Warren. "You wanna quit?"

"Wouldn't give that bitch the satisfaction."

"Danae, you quitting?"

"No way."

"And no way I quit. And if you quit, brother, Page fires Warren and me without hesitation. So you're not quitting. *Capisce?*"

Aubrey heaved out a phlegmy breath. "Fine, brother, whatever. I'll stay. We'll all stay, it'll be one big happy love-in."

"It's not that simple," said Danae. We all turned to her. "You have to tell everyone, Aubrey. The Monkeys, if not the other employees. They need to know the truth."

"They'll hate me," Aubrey said.

"Yeah, maybe, but they deserve the truth. We look up to you, Aubrey, we love you, but they need to know the score. Emily needs to know. This has gone on too long."

"She's right, brother," Warren said. He took a step toward Aubrey, and buried him in his arms. "We love you, brother. It'll be okay. Right, Thomas?"

"Uh, yeah, absolutely. But no more lies, okay? From either of you," I said evenly.

"Lies are done with, brother," Aubrey said, his voice muffled from his continuing forcible cuddle with Warren's chest.

"No more," said Danae. "No more lies, sweetie. From any of us."

The next morning, Aubrey came clean to the staff. "I'd like to apologize to those of you offended by my subterfuge. It was never my intention to act as spy, and I want to assure you that nothing you have said or done in my presence has ever been taken by me at more than face value." The employees look at one another in confusion. Page stood to the side, barely suppressing her glee at Aubrey's disclosure. "You are all wonderful people," he continued, "and it is my hope that we can maintain both our relationships as employer and employees, and our friendships." Aubrey stood proud before the group as he said this, but his fingers twitched nervously. The tentacles wiggled in self-reproach. A moment of intensely awkward silence passed.

"Well, thank you very much," Page said primly. She looked sympathetically at Aubrey. "I know that must have been difficult, and I'm sure no one here holds you any ill will for your deception. Now." Page turned to the assemblage. "Does anyone have any questions for Aubrey?" Feet shuffled in embarrassment. "Anyone? A question? Nothing? Yes, Waylon?"

A small, weaselly man stepped forward. I didn't recognize him. Did I not know anyone else in this place? "So, Miss Adler, will Aubrey be our boss from now on?"

"Well, he always has been your boss, Waylon. Isn't that right, Aubrey?"

"Yes, that's right," Aubrey replied quietly.

"So we have, I have to do what he says?" asked the weasel.

"Please, Waylon, Aubrey is right next to me. You may address him personally, he won't bite," she tittered.

Waylon cleared his throat. "Well, Aubrey, so we have to do what you say now?"

"Well, technically, I guess that's true," Aubrey said. "But the day-to-day running of the store will still be entirely up to Page."

"But, you *are* the boss now," Waylon said. "We *have* to do whatever you say."

"But I won't be giving any orders."

"But still, you're the boss."

Aubrey shook his head in annoyance. "No, Waylon, I'm not the boss, Page is the boss, I'm just co-owner. Page is in charge here, not me." He looked helplessly out at the employees, some of whom were exchanging heated whispers.

"But, you *could* fire me, if you felt like it," Waylon continued. "You could fire any of us, right?"

Aubrey thrust his hands into his mane and began to scratch. "I, I, I don't want to fire you, Waylon."

"But you *could*."

A rotund little woman stepped forward. She worked in Self-Help, I think. "Did you fire Emily?" she asked.

"No, Page and I discussed Emily, and *together* —"

"You fired Emily?" another woman asked. The whispers were growing angrier.

"No, no, Emily had personal problems, I never wanted to fire Emily. I —"

"What Aubrey and I decided," Page interrupted, "was that Emily was emotionally unsuited for the workload we asked of her. Emily brought her problems upon herself, and while Aubrey and I gave her ample opportunity to improve, in the end, we jointly, and I stress *jointly* concluded that Emily would be happier elsewhere. Now, I expect this to be the last we hear on this subject." Page rubbed her hands together. "We have gotten off topic. If I may say so, I believe Aubrey has taken a brave step here in his acknowledgement of his position, an acknowledgement long overdue." Page let a sly smile play at the corners of her mouth. "I would also like to apologize for my own part in Aubrey's secret little fantasy." Page darted a look of sublime grace toward Aubrey, a humble admission of her own fault that somehow managed to convey an air of utter moral superiority in the matter. "Aubrey, or should I say Mr. Fehr and I both ask your forgiveness in this charade, and I only hope you do not look upon us too harshly. In fact, Mr. Fehr deserves a round of applause for his courage." Page began to clap, her vindictiveness coming through in every collision of her hands. "Come on, everyone! A hand for Mr. Fehr! Bravo!" Aubrey reddened and walked away, the back of his neck an iridescent ruby. He faded into the books. I hung back behind the group, blind with anger, as Page continued to applaud long after Aubrey had disappeared. I quickly dry-swallowed two emergency pills, willing my hands to stop shaking.

"Now," Page said, Aubrey's humiliation complete. "To business, everyone."

*Phil Collins, post-Genesis, pre-*Tarzan. *Yeah, that'll motivate us to sell.*

"You own **READ**?" asked Burt/Gandalf. "Holy shit!"

"I can't believe this," William/Valentine Michael Smith said. "What, all this time, you never thought to mention that?"

The Monkeys weren't taking the news well, either. To soften the blow of Aubrey's confession, Danae had brought marshmallows to roast beforehand. Tasty lumps of blackened sugar on a stick had only heightened everyone's energy, unfortunately. They were keyed up and ready to burn. Emily/Hagar clutched an overpriced Britney Spears novella. Burt/Gandalf carried *Digital Fortress* under his arm. I made a mental note to prepare my outraged defence of Edward Bunker, his name poking itself out of Tracey/Lyra Silvertongue's parka pocket, mocking me.

Muriel/Lady Fuchsia Groan was staggered. "Do you know how many books I have stolen for this? How many times I could have lost my job? This was your idea, and you were never in any danger?"

"Hey, yeah, he owns the books!" Gavin/Ford Prefect said.

Cameron/Ignatius J. Reilly looked petrified. "I'll bet he's a spy, guys. Y'know, for the cops? We could be on camera right now! We should strip him down, look for a wire." This earned him a smack in the back of the head from Warren.

"I am *not* a spy, Cam," said Aubrey. "I have just gone momentarily astray is all."

"*Sheep* go astray, you liar, not the shepherd," said Susan/Scout Finch. "You're our leader. We look up to you. Can you understand how upsetting this is to us?"

"Oh, come on!" I said. That was a little much. "No one here was forced into this, Susan. We all do this because we want to."

"Easy for you to say, you've never been at risk," she said.

"Hey, I put my neck out same as you."

"I bet Aubrey's been covering for you."

"That's not —" I halted mid-thought. Aubrey grimaced as I looked over at him. "Aw, fucking hell, Aubrey!"

He bit his lip. "Sorry, bro, but you've never been very good at hiding it. I sometimes had to distract Page."

"Me too," Danae said. "Sorry, babe, but you really do suck at stealing."

"I never said I was adept at stealing," I objected. "And we're getting way off topic here."

Aubrey held his hands up. "Look, everyone. I can't expect you to understand what I've done. But nothing's changed between us, I'm the same person I was. All I can do is beg your forgiveness."

Something thumped to the ground. "You fired me," said Emily. The Britney had slipped out from her hands. She pointed a finger accusingly. "How could you fire me?"

"You didn't give me a choice," he said. "You were out of control."

"I loved that job," she whimpered.

"I'm sorry, Emily. You threw books at the customers, what choice did I have?"

"Oh, I don't know, not firing me? You're no better than I am."

"I know. I'm trying to make it up to you."

"You bastard." She walked away into the dark. "You bastard!" she screamed. Her cries wafted into the air.

"I'll go after her," Danae said. "She'll be all right." She ran after her, Susan and August/Raoul Duke loping behind.

Aubrey sat down in a heap. "I didn't want this."

"We know that," I said. I looked to the others. "Right, guys?"

"I'm going home," said Tracey. "I need to think this over."

"Yeah, I don't know," agreed Gavin/Ford Prefect. "This changes things. How can we trust you anymore, Aubrey?"

He nodded. "I wouldn't trust me, either, Ford. I understand."

"It's Gavin, not Ford," he said dejectedly.

"So, are we all over now?" William asked. "Don't we get a vote? I don't want to quit."

"No one's quitting," I said, alarmed. The thought of stopping our meetings pierced me deep inside. Out in the night, Emily's cries could still be heard, Danae's soothing noises underneath. "This is just a blip. We don't stop just because one of us has a crisis. Everyone just needs to clear his or her head. Right, brother?" I asked Aubrey.

He looked up at me, gratified. "Amen, brother."

"Next week, same time," I ordered the Monkeys. "Business as usual. Anyone who doesn't show up with a backpack full of 'tags better have a good reason."

I should have dropped it there. Let it die its natural death.

Thomas

DOCUMENT INSERT: Verbatim FBI telephone call transcript. Speaking: FBI Detective Amanda Daimler (primary), Unidentified Speaker.

Daimler: Yes?

Caller: Hello? Is Detective Daimler there?

Daimler: Yes, Detective Daimler speaking. Who is this?

Caller: I have information concerning Munroe Purvis.

Daimler: Yes, you told the switchboard that. Could I have your name, please, Miss?

Caller: What do you need that for?

Daimler: Your name, Miss, please?

Caller: I don't think I want to give you my name just right now.

Daimler: All right, then. Goodbye.

Caller: Wait. Don't you want to know what I have?

Daimler: Not without a name. You know who I am, don't you? I just want to know who I'm dealing with. Don't you think that would be fair?

Caller: I don't think I should. Maybe this was a mistake.

Daimler: Look, you got past the switchboard, so they obviously think you know something. Something that you couldn't just pick up from a newspaper clipping. They're trained to weed out the freaks, the idiots who think they'll get famous, or a reward. They think you might have something, or are you just some lonely idiot who craves the attention?

Caller: That's not me.

Daimler: So then. Give me something to go on. If not your name, something that proves to me that I'm not wasting my time here.

```
Caller:   What do you want to know?
Daimler:  You called us, remember? You have
          information we'd be interested in.
Caller:   I don't know.
Daimler:  Fine, you don't want to tell, fine. I
          thought you had something to get off
          your chest. Obviously, I was mistaken.
          Goodbye.
Caller:   Wait, don't hang up.
Daimler:  Give me a reason not to, it's been a
          long day, and I'm just about out of
          patience.
Caller:   I —
Daimler:  I have no desire to waste my time with
          some little Pollyanna who craves
          attention. Go home and cry to daddy,
          Miss, I'm going to get some sleep.
Caller:   Books.
Daimler:  What? What was that, books? What does
          that mean?
Caller:   Books. We'd burn books, out in a field.
          There were fourteen of us. We called
          ourselves Shelf Monkeys. You didn't
          mention that in your press release, did
          you?
Daimler:  All right. You have my attention. Go
          on.
Caller:   I'll want immunity. For everything.
Daimler:  Give me some names, and I'll see what I
          can do.
Caller:   Can we meet?
```

TO: ermccorm@yahoo.ca
FROM: iamashelfmonkey@gmail.com
SUBJECT: Reprieve!

Dear Eric,

My faith in humanity has been restored! Take that, pessimism, you bastard! Back to the cave from whence you came!

I can't tell you where I am, of course, but I have now free access to a computer and proper software, with no worry of police interruption.

I was travelling by bus, deliberating my next move. My head was down, hat brim pulled low, wide sunglasses hiding my eyes. Utterly suspicious in my attempt to look inconspicuous. A body sat down next to me. I didn't look up, feigning the indifference of the average traveller. I saw a lap clad in cotton slacks, a pair of hands opening a book. I cautiously craned my neck over to get a peek at the title. Phew, no MUNROE RECOMMENDS THIS! sticker. T.C. Boyle's *Drop City*. I let out a cautious murmur of appreciation. Nonchalantly, I brought out Irvine Welsh's *Filth* from my backpack, earning an approving grunt in return. I relaxed. The unspoken game of literary one-upmanship now complete, the Boyle-lover and I read to ourselves in companionable silence.

"I know who you are."

I stiffened, crinkling the pages in my fingers.

"I saw you get on, Mr. Friesen. It's okay, don't panic. I won't give you away."

I looked up. "I'm sorry, are you talking to me?" I asked innocently.

He grinned. "Aw, I knew it was you," he breathed. "I've been looking, ever since they said you might be nearby."

I fought to keep my voice steady. "I'm sorry, Sir, I think you must have me confused with someone else." I bent back down to my book. Behind my shades, my eyeballs distended themselves in panic.

The man snickered. "Okay, I get it. Travelling incognito. Good idea. No worries here, my friend. Lips are sealed." He went back to his book, taking a pen from his pocket and scribbling something inside the cover.

The bus was pulling up to a stop. "Have you ever read this?" the man asked, showing the book to me.

"No."

"You really should, it's a great book." The bus rumbled to a halt. He stood up to go, placing the novel down on his empty seat. "I'm done with it. You can have it if you like. Enjoy." He sauntered himself out the door, and walked away without looking back.

I picked up *Drop City*. Inside the cover was written a name, an address, and a short message: *I am a friend. I believe in your cause. This is a safe house, if you need it.*

I got off at the next stop. It was a risk, but I had nowhere else to go. If he wanted to collect the reward, so be it. I'm so tired of looking over my shoulder.

The man welcomed me at the door with a warmth I haven't felt in months.

So, as I write this, the gentleman is off preparing dinner for two. He's kind of a loner, I gather, and definitely an odd sort, being as he is the sort who will approach a fugitive from the law and offer him sanctuary. Like I said, odd. Could be a priest, could be a serial killer, could be both. No explanations needed, no gratitude on my part expected. I feel like I could stay here forever, just close my eyes and dream that I'm safe, but I know that's impossible. I'm putting him at tremendous risk.

Why would he help me? I tried to ask, but he just waved the question away. But, if you need a hint, here it is:

As I write this, the smell of chili con carne permeating the air, I am surrounded by books.

Aubrey was showing signs of imminent mental collapse. His new status as employer/co-emperor of **READ** resulted in exile from the ranks of his employees. Aubrey was now *persona non grata*, the ghost of Marley, haunting the miles of well-worn carpet, rattling his chains to the annoyance of others. Once-friendly chums became blank slates of indifference at his approach. They'd stiffen as he rounded the corner, guarded and suspicious of hidden motives in his hellos and how are yous. Yes, Sir. No, Sir. I'll get right on that, Sir. Hey, I'm the same guy I was before. You want to go grab a coffee and muffin? My treat? No answers, not verbal, anyway. Just looks of condemnation.

In desperation, he threw himself into his work, confronting customers at every opportunity with helpful suggestions. There was no challenge he didn't meet. Every thrust of an R.A. Salvatore was parried with a Louise Erditch. Every Don Pendleton clothes-line was matched with a Norman Mailer suplex. It was glorious to watch him fight, but it was always a losing battle. The forces against him were too strong, too numerous. With every "Where's the *Star Trek* section?" a little piece of himself went up in smoke. The hirsute feelers on his skull would sadly go limp, and he'd trudge forlornly, scif-fi geek in tow, toward the *Star Trek/Star Wars/Battlestar Galactica* aisle.

"I don't know if I can take it much longer, brother," he confided to me in Greeting Cards. He didn't look good. Battalions of acne commandeered his forehead, while dark bags of skin had taken up residence under his eyes. I thought his skin might clear up with a haircut, less follicle fallout to deal with, but I didn't have the heart to suggest it. "Every person, I try it, y'know? I say, 'Hey, put down that Compton, how about a McMurtry instead? Yes, it's huge, but it's a *western*, everyone loves westerns, right? It won the Pulitzer, it's better than you could ever deserve.' They look at me like I'm crazy, like anyone who would read a book that big must have no friends." Groaning, he buried his arms in his hair. "Fuck 'em, right?"

"Right," I agreed. "Fuck 'em all. Amen, brother." When I called him that, I thought he'd break down and cry on the spot. Not that I would ever judge him for it, but I'd never seen him so despondent.

The Shelf Monkeys were likewise lost, directionless, wandering the northern fields without a Nanook Moses to lead us to the Promised Land. Two abortive attempts at a burnalong had left Aubrey weak and fed up. He boycotted the next meeting, sitting inside while Warren laboured to lead the group in a limp-dick fizzle of a burning. My purloined copy of Peter Benchley's *White Shark* smothered the flames out. Danae cried all evening long. Gavin and Cameron got into a fist-fight over *Life of Pi*, Gavin adoring, Cameron loathing, the two eventually wrestling them-selves over the smouldering ruins, only stopping their hissy-fit when Warren hoisted them both into the air by their noses, forced them to shake hands, and then walloped each over the head with his offering, the Travolta-endorsed and Scientologist-approved edition of *Battlefield Earth*.

Without Aubrey as guru, it didn't feel complete. He started skipping work, to our consternation and Page's blatant happiness, citing the flu as cause. Page seized the moment to transfer both Warren and I to the Munroe Purvis display. It was our job to care for the head, clean up the area, and read every single book to ensure our customers were satisfied with our knowledge. Aubrey just shrugged and went back to his Robert Coover. Danae lost patience with my once-endearing, now-irritating attempts at wooing. "Give it a fucking rest, will you?" was how she put it.

We were dying, the last remnants of a once-proud race consigned to oblivion.

Footnotes to an era.

And then —

Well, you know what happened then, don't you, Eric? Detective Daimler, any guesses? No hints from me.

"Yes, Ma'am, this is, ah, the newest Munroe, it, oh, goddamn, this thing itches!"

"Well, excuse me!"

My Jerry Cornelius costume had me perspiring buckets. The wig, a golden curly haired five dollar investment from Ragpickers Emporium designed for a cranium two sizes larger than mine, constantly and arbitrarily shifted itself about my head. The prodigious amount of hairpins Danae had lent me jabbed and scratched my scalp as the wig slid about, converting my new mane into a tortuous toupee of nails fit for the members of Opus Dei. The frilly blouse, another Danae contribution, was a snug fit. She lent it on the strict condition that I not rip it, resulting in a near-constant state of light-headedness as I kept my stomach and lungs sucked inward. The violet pants I had bought at the Sally Ann fit perfectly and agreeably complemented the ensemble, but the leather boots were high-heeled, ideal for the Cornelius effect but hell on my balance. My homemade needle gun was too heavy, pulling my belt off-centre and causing me to list to the right. I was proud of the total effect, but all this effort for a Halloween costume all but those most bibliographically adventurous of booknerds would greet with confusion was a touch unnecessary. But the esoteric appeal was worth the blank stares of those unfamiliar with Moorcock's anti-hero, which, as it turned out, was pretty much everybody. I think a Klingon may have recognized my get-up, but she was apparently determined to speak only the language of her native tongue that day; she gave me an admiring glance, pointed her phaser at me, and grunted "Gut-*twawg!*" Take from that what you will. Maybe she needed the Heimlich.

No one thought Page would agree to it, dressing up for Hallowe'en as characters from fiction. It was a half-hearted proposal Aubrey presented at a morning meeting the week previous. Page, perhaps calling a momentary truce to their feud and wishing to engender goodwill, jumped at the suggestion. Or maybe she just saw an ideal marketing opportunity. The latter. She put up awards and gift certificates for the best costumes, making a theme day out of it to include the customers. Come as your favourite character, win a prize. All adults want to play make-believe, it was a great success. By the end of the day, I had counted twenty-three Gandalfs/ Dumbledores, fourteen Harry Potters (half of which were men well into their thirties), three wookies, two Sherlocks, and a parade of interchangeable Xenas, Buffys, Hermiones, and Arwens. The last weren't all women, either.

A massive two-headed space hipster approached me while I sorted and arranged my section. "Mr. Cornelius," the right head said in greeting. "A pleasure, as always." The left head nodded as if in agreement, then decapitated itself. "Shit," the right head muttered, "not again."

"Mr. Beeblebrox," I replied. "Long time, no see. Nice head, Warren, where'd you get it?"

"Bought a mannequin from Value Village, sawed it off." Warren picked the dummy head off the ground and dusted it off. "Damn thing won't stay in its harness, though. Have to stand completely at attention or it falls off."

"Ouch, what a headache."

"I'm used to it." While Warren affixed the head back onto his shoulder, I noticed a slight billowiness to his pants. Catching my look, he shoved his hands deep into his pockets, grabbing the fabric in his clenched fists to keep the slacks from crumpling around his heels.

"Before you ask, I'm fine," he said. "Really. Just a minor complication due to the myriad of chemicals currently in my bloodstream."

"This is why you weren't around last week?"

"Yeah, having Aubrey as a boss has allowed me some degree of freedom in scheduling. However, I still refuse to take a dime from him in charity. Still a bit ticked off, I guess."

"How much have you —"

"Twenty pounds lost this week. Apparently, my metabolism is functioning at one hundred forty percent efficiency." He gave me an anorexic smile, only accentuating the suddenness of his weight-loss, transforming his face into a beaming varicose skull. I could count the capillaries in his forehead. The real one, on the right. "This is the last time, Thomas, I promise. It should be a hell of a weight-loss pill, though. Look at me, Warren Krall, the medical marvel."

"What's a marvel is that you haven't died yet."

"Well, it's better than the last test."

"True." Three weeks previous, Warren had signed up for a testing cycle of a new protein bar. The ensuing flatulence kept Warren surrounded in his own self-perpetuating haze of noxious aroma for four days. I unthinkingly called him "Gaseous Clay" to his face one lunch hour, which earned me a merry chase throughout the store for my efforts. "Hey, I dig the boots, very groovy, very retro," he said. "I can almost look you in the eye now."

"Thanks. My bloodstream thoughtfully stopped its flow to the toes an hour ago, so they're quite comfortable now."

"Bonus."

"Omigod omigod omigod omigod omigod!"

"Was that you?" I asked.

"Omigod!" A flash of crimson ran across the end of the aisle.

"No."

"Omigod, you guys!" The frantic red blur reversed its direction, and now ran up the aisle toward us. "Omigod, omigod, omi-whoa-ouch-fuck!" Danae had tripped over her red handmaiden robe, smacking her forehead on the tiles at our feet. "Guys, guys, guys!" She hopped to her feet, grabbing our shirts and ripping my blouse. "Guys, guys, oh damn, that was my favourite shirt, oh hell, guys!"

She fell into me, laughing.

"What?" I asked, enjoying holding her up.

"Oh, man, sweetie, Warren, you guys are not going to believe it!"

"What?" asked Warren, bending forward in anticipation, catching his second head as it fell from his shoulder. "Man, I hate this freaking costume. What's the point, no one gets it anyway."

"Come on," Danae said. "We've got to find Aubrey. Oh, he'll be so excited."

She took off, running through the corridors, jostling past a Lara Croft, a Sulu, and two Neos, repeating it like a mantra, omi*god*omi*gad*omi*gawd*omi*god*. Warren and I struggled to keep pace, Warren's parachute pants vying with his extra head for the title of least convenient running accessory, while my boot heels took a sudden left when the rest of me took a right, sending me airborne into a well-dressed gentleman carrying an empty picture frame.

"Oh, hey, you okay, friend?" the frame carrier asked.

"Yeah, sorry 'bout that, it's these damn . . . Aubrey? Oh hey, we're looking for you, I . . . what are you supposed to be? Shouldn't you be in homemade armour, a colander on your head or something?"

"What, I can only dress as my alter ego? I don't see you in a flight uniform."

"Touché."

"Decided to go in a different vein, that's all. Think James Joyce."

"You're James Joyce?"

"Almost." Aubrey hoisted the frame, positioning himself in the centre. "I'm the portrait of the artist as a young man. You like?"

"Awesome. I don't think Joyce had dreadlocks though."

"You ever try gelling something like this down? I figured the frame was enough."

"How 'bout me?" I gave Aubrey a deep gentlemanly curtsey.

Aubrey appraised my outfit, puckered his brow, and snapped his fingers. "Moorcock?" I tapped my nose. "Ooh, a Jerry Cornelius, *very* slick, good choice. Visually dynamic, and just so obscure as to allow yourself a justified sense of superiority. I really like those boots."

"Thanks."

"You're welcome. Zaphod, you're looking well," Aubrey said, nodding to Warren who had finally caught up to us, bunching the extra fabric of his pants into one hand and holding his second head to his shoulder with the other.

"Mr. Gray. I never would have recognized you, you're looking younger by the day."

"He's not Dorian Gray, you idiot," I said. Warren threw a clumsy punch in my direction, and lost his head again.

"So, what's the hubbub?" Aubrey asked. "Does it have anything to do with the red-clothed nun who just ran by shrieking blasphemies?"

"That was Danae, she's —"

"Omigod, Aubrey, there you are!" Danae had spotted the three of us, and launched herself helter-skelter between the shelves. "Guess, you'll never guess!" she wheezed, pulling up alongside us and bending over to catch her breath. "Guess . . . you'll never . . . whew, ohmigod . . ." She went silent, swallowing great gulps of air, trying to compose herself.

"Guess what, Offred?" Aubrey asked.

"Sound it out, girl!" Warren said. "How many words?"

"Did Timmy fall down a well?" I asked.

"Big head," she hyperventilated between mouthfuls. "He's coming."

"Big head is coming?" I asked.

"BRLAT!" she belched in assent.

"Well, I'm confused," said Warren.

"Munroe!" Danae gasped. "Big head! Munroe!" She stood up, shaking herself. "Munroe! Is! Coming!"

"What?" I asked.

"What?" Aubrey asked.

"Holy shit," Warren said. "What?"

"Munroe is coming, oh man, he's coming *here*," Danae gushed. "Page just got the call, he's coming here!"

"Wait, what, Munroe?" Aubrey repeated. He shook his head in amazement, the tendrils befuddledly threading themselves through the air. "Here, he's coming *here?*"

"His people just called. **READ** is the only bookstore big enough in town to put up his show. You should see Page, she's, well, she's *happy*."

"Ew." Warren stuck his tongue out.

The picture frame clattered to the floor. A look of utter joy flooded Aubrey's face, followed by a concentrated frown. "Conference," he said, taking off toward the lounge. "The three of you! Now!" We followed, Warren abandoning his head behind him, Danae pulling on my arm before running ahead, gleefully shrieking. I tried to keep up, hobbling valiantly on my high heels for a few steps, and tripped over Warren's now-forgotten shoulder-mate. Grunting with pain, I squatted to remove my boots and redirect my blood flow in a screaming tingle toward the feet, effectively crippling me for a few minutes. Unfettered but still wobbly, I tottered toward the break room.

The trinity had their heads together over the table. Aubrey sprung to his feet as I entered and embraced me warmly. I returned the hug, a little discombobulated, but heartened that he had cheered up.

"Rejoice, my brother, rejoice!" he sang, gallivanting about the room. "The devil is coming to **READ**, and we are going to be ready for him." Warren and Danae tittered loudly. I joined in, smiling broadly to mask my slight discomfort. It was a zero to sixty reversal of Aubrey's depression. Did he have to be so, so manic?

"So, what's the plan, Stan?" I asked. "Protests? Sabotage? Water balloons above the stage?"

"Yeah, balloons!" said Warren, rising to join Aubrey who was now bouncing merrily on the sofa. "We'll soak him head to toe! Splash!" They bounced together, whooping effusively until the springs gave way with a loud crunch.

Aubrey sat back down and motioned to the chairs. "Sit. To business, brothers, sister, to business. We have much of importance to discuss." We sat down. Warren was transfixed by Aubrey, Danae seemed tickled by his enthusiasm. I withheld judgement, unsettled by his sudden overabundance of energy.

"So, what will we do?" Aubrey asked.

Stillness. Aubrey stared expectantly at the three of us. We returned the favour. I looked at Danae. She looked at me, then

Warren, who looked to me, then Aubrey, who looked to Danae, who looked back at me. "Um. What do you mean?" I ventured.

He jumped back up and began to pace. "What do I mean? WhatdoImeanwhatdoImeanwhatdoImean? What I mean, Thomas," he said, pointing at me. "What I mean *is*, the nemesis of our group, the antithesis of everything we hold dear, Munroe fuckin' Purvis himself is coming to our establishment to infect our hearts and souls with his goodwill blather and contempt for perceptions that lie beyond his narrow little curly headed world! He is coming here! Soon!"

"November 14," said Danae. "That's what Page said."

"November 14?" Aubrey clutched his hair. "Not enough time, not *nearly* enough. We need a plan, people!"

"We'll do whatever you say," said Warren, Danae nodding her head in agreement. "Whatever you want, we're in, you know that."

"We'll need the others," Danae said. "The other Monkeys, they'll want to know this."

"Good idea!" said Aubrey. "I'll start calling everyone. Emergency meeting at my place, tonight."

"Aw, man, this is gonna be great!" Warren said, pumping his fists in the air. "We are gonna nail the fucker!" He held up his palm to Danae, getting a high five slap from her, then showing it to me. "We'll make him sorry he ever even learned to read! Right, Tommy-gun?"

"Right-o, bro." I smacked his hand weakly.

"Hey, hey, hey, Thomas," said Danae. "Why the long face? Aren't you happy?"

"No, no, I'm great." Was I? "I'm fine, I just . . . well, I wonder, see, I hate to be the voice of reason here, play the devil's advocate, but what is it exactly that we're thinking of doing? I mean really?"

"We're living the dream, baby!" Warren cried. "Isn't that obvious?"

"Well, yeah, this is great, the dream and all, but, I mean, we had our fun with Agnes." I puckered my lips into a frown. "We got that out of our system, didn't we?"

Aubrey chucked me under the chin in amusement. "Hey, brotherman here has some qualms, I think." A great pool of annoyance welled up inside me. "Agnes was small potatoes, Thomas. This is the big time."

"Yeah, but, well, Page will never even let us near it, will she?"

"Hey, Page *likes* me," said Danae. "I'm not the one who caused Agnes's breakdown. As far as Page knows, I'm gold. It's you three who have to worry."

"Maybe we could use that," suggested Warren. "Page'll never expect something from Danae, Aubrey."

"You could lose your job," I reminded her. "Hell, we can all lose our jobs. I don't think Page would be quite so forgiving as last time, not in this instance."

"You leave Page to me," said Aubrey.

"God, man!" I sniped. Something in Aubrey's frenzied mania began to royally piss me off. "C'mon! Look at this! You've been moping around for weeks, you've shut out the rest of us, and now you're prancing around like Baryshnikov on crack!"

"Thomas, what?" Danae asked. She gave me a pout. "Honey, I thought you'd be happy."

"Oh, hey, I'm happy, I just think we're working ourselves up here for disappointment. Do you really think we'll be able to pull a stunt here? This isn't like Agnes, that wasn't televised or anything. All that got us was some bad local press and a nod in *USA Today*. It didn't even make Munroe's show. This is for television, American television. Believe me, Munroe and his people, they are going to make sure nothing goes wrong, that's their job."

"Dude, you're harshing our buzz," said Warren, put out at my opinion.

"I'm sorry, guys, but I think we should just lie back awhile. Just let this happen."

"Jerk-off."

"No, Thomas is right, we're jumping the gun a bit," Aubrey said. "Look, brother, just come tonight, all right? We're just having a get-together, pizza and beer among good friends. It'll be fun."

"What'll be fun?" I wasn't going to blindly play follow-the-leader. "What am I agreeing to here? Playing a prank? Sure, I'll go along with that."

His teeth stretched across his face. "A prank. Yes. That's exactly what we'll do."

"A prank, yes!" chortled Warren. "We'll give him the old what for, that's what we'll do!"

"Prank 'em," Danae said. "Prank the hell out of them!"

"Prank, prank, prank!" Warren began to chant, slamming his hands on the tabletop. "Prank! Prank! Prank!" Danae and Aubrey joined in, pounding their feet. "PRANK! PRANK! PRANK!"

I sat watching them quietly, stealing glances at the door now and then, fearful that Page might walk in. Aubrey was revving himself up to mythic proportions, leading Danae and Warren in a three-way whirling merry-go-round about the table and myself.

"PRANK! PRANK! PRANK!"

Gradually, they began to wind themselves down, noticing at last that I had declined to join in. "Well, that's that then," I said finally, standing up, stretching my body in an exaggerated yawn and straightening my wig. "A prank. Boy, this is going to be fun, huh? Can't wait. I guess I'll see you guys tonight."

"Yeah, tonight," Aubrey said hesitantly. I smiled at them as I walked out to the floor, ignoring the disappointment on Danae's face.

I was a pariah for the rest of the day. Warren became a chameleon, blending into the shadows whenever I approached. Danae pulled an H.G. Wells, disappearing completely from my radar. I didn't care. I told myself this as I pulled on my boots, ignoring the complaints my feet were busy filing with upper management. I don't care. No matter to me. Someone has to stay sane, might as well be the clinically depressed one.

Yes, I did care, I'm lying. It stung me that my friendship with them was of such a tenuous nature. What, I can't disagree without taking on the air of a Judas?

Aubrey approached me near closing time, while I was busying myself with shelf-checking Romance. "Brotherman, how goes the good fight?"

"Completely lost feelings in my lower extremities, but otherwise, fine."

He leaned against the stacks, crumpling the paperbacks. Ah, it *was* only the Romance section after all, and I was too tired to care. "I've called the others, it's all set," he said. "Ten o'clock tonight, all right?"

"Right, sure. Ten o'clock." I studied the Sandra Brown hedge for misfiles.

He cocked his head in sympathy. "You feeling okay, Thomas? You seem out of sorts."

"No, I'm fine. The boots are still too tight, that's all. And someone thought I was supposed to be Prince circa *Under the Cherry Moon*, which kind of got me down."

He looked around, saw no one but members of the browsing public, and leaned in conspiratorially. "Boy, Danae and Warren are really excited about this, huh?"

I shrugged in feigned nonchalance. "They seem to be, yeah."

"Yourself?"

"Oh, yeah, me too. Excited." Another shrug. Keep this up, I was going to get repetitive strain disorder.

"Oh yeah, you're real excited," he said quietly. "You're so excited, Danae broke down when you left."

"She did?"

"No, not really, but she looked displeased. I think you have a real chance with her, brother, and I'm not just saying that. She cares for you."

That stung, but I wouldn't let him know that. "Well, whatyagonna do? Women, huh?" I tossed in a half-hearted snort of derision *("Snuh!")* to display just how little I cared for her feelings. "She'll get over it."

"I sense hesitation, brother."

"I'm just not in a scheming mood right now."

"Listen, this isn't going to be easy. Munroe's going to be well guarded. We, uh, we could really use your help here."

"With what?" I said forcefully into his face, startling a nearby elderly woman into dropping her cargo of Jude Deveraux and Julie Garwood with a gasp. "Sorry, ma'am, sorry," I apologized, gathering up the refuse for her. "If you'll wait by the cash register, I'll see that you get a discount coupon for your next purchase." She left, sniffing haughtily. "Help with what, *friend?*" I persisted. "What do you plan on doing, what is the great scheme to end all schemes that will finally give our cause meaning?" Aubrey sulked. He actually pouted. His bottom lip stuck out and quivered. "Oh, come on! Don't do that!"

"What?"

"Make that face."

"What, this face?" His lip extended itself further. "Thith faith, you mean?" he lisped.

"Knock it off, I'm not in the mood."

The lip retracted. "No, I guess you're not." We stood there for a few moments as I busied myself with straightening up the shelves. "Look, friend," he started.

"There you are!" Page marched through the aisle. Surprisingly, she was also in costume, an obviously rented Princess Leia, cinnamon-bun hair and white robe, too perfect a costume to be homemade. Well, another childhood sexual fantasy bites the dust. I considered mentioning the tenuous connection Leia had to actual literature, but ultimately decided silence was indeed golden in this instance. She positioned herself before us, hands on hips. "I suppose you've both heard the news?"

"Why, whatever do you mean, Page?" Aubrey asked. "Thomas, any clue?"

"Nope. Oh, wait, unless she means —"

"— the second coming, is that what you're referring to, Page? Thomas and I were just discussing what we should wear to the Rapture, should we make the cut. I'm for togas and sandals myself, sort of a symbolic return to traditional values. How about yourself there, Thomas?"

"I'd go the other way," I said. "Black tie. You cannot go wrong with tux and tails." Aggravated as I was with Aubrey, I could never bring myself to see eye to eye with Page on anything. She could be a forceful opponent against the cannibalism of orphans, and I'd find some reason why wards of the state should be consumed.

"Hmm, interesting," Aubrey said. "Page, your thoughts? Will standard store attire suffice?"

"You assholes!" she fumed. "I can't believe you, Aubrey, this is our chance to take the store to the next level. We could use this to franchise ourselves, go national. Are you really so blind as to not see the potential here? We'd have more money than we'd ever need. But you, you'd ruin this chance for us, wouldn't you?"

Aubrey displayed his widest, toothiest grin. "In a second."

"You motherfu—" she spat, stopping before what looked to be a torrent of obscenities spewed forth. Her lips tightened themselves into a perfect horizontal white stripe of wrath. "You're on notice, both of you. That idiot giant, too. You even come close to the building when Munroe's here, and I will take you down. I don't care about the store, not for this. All I care about is seeing you destroyed. I will bring you to court, I will fucking kill you!"

"Anyone tell you you're ugly when you're angry?" Aubrey asked.

It was like someone edited ten seconds out of a film, Page's slap was so quick, jump-cutting from Aubrey's retort to Aubrey lying on the floor, the *crack!* of her palm off his face a sonic explosion that echoed through the store. Page pointed a finger at him, then at me. I flinched in anticipation of another attack, fearfully squeezing a drop of urine into my shorts. "You do anything, Aubrey, *anything*, and you can kiss everything you love goodbye," she hissed. "You too, lawyer-boy. I'll fucking kill both of you." She tidied up her robes and hair, smoothing herself back into control. "Goddamn you, Aubrey. We could have done wonderful things together." She sauntered away casually, already dismissing us. I helped Aubrey to his feet.

"Oh, that does it," he said, massaging his cheek. "That's it. It's on." His eyes goggled at me. "Did you see that? She hit me."

"I saw," I said.

"You're a witness, she actually struck me, Thomas."

"She's quite the heavyweight, that's going to bruise for sure."

"Oh, I am going to get her." He kicked the shelves petulantly. "That bitch! After all I've done! She'd still be a receptionist if I hadn't come along, you know that? She was so timid, so afraid to take a chance." I nodded slowly. The idea of Page as somehow ever being the shy and retiring type struck me as slight exaggeration, but I let it slide. Aubrey was in no mood for a discussion anyhow, this was a rant a long time in the brewing. "I gave her the idea, I convinced her to go in on this with me! And this is what I get out of it? This?" He was spinning now, looking around confusedly. "I gave her *this!* All this!" he yelled, waving his arms to the roof. "You believe that? How stupid was I, huh?"

"Yeah, it's a bitch, she's a bitch, no question," I said. I put my hands on his arms, forcing him to stand still. His head swivelled madly. "Aubrey, look at me. C'mon, boy, focus!" His eyes boggled themselves about the room. I snapped my fingers in his face. "Aubrey!" The pupils finally settled themselves on me. His hair, however, kept going, quivering with impending violence. "Aubrey, she has a point," I ventured. He began to shake again in refusal. I squeezed his arms tighter to hold him in place. "Just think for a minute, okay? If this goes well, you could get enough to leave the place. Franchise it, sell it, whatever. You could leave! Do what you want! Travel, write a book, anything!"

Aubrey shook himself free of my grasp. "Leave it?" he asked, astonished. "You fuck, this place is *mine*. When I leave, *if* I leave, it'll be on my terms, not hers. Not yours. Not Munroe's. Mine. You got that?"

I held my hands up in compliance. "Sure, brother, I got it. No problems."

"Tonight. Ten o'clock. You and me, Thomas, taking up arms against Great Cthulu and the Elder Gods. Are you coming?" It came out as a dare. Did I have the 'nads?

"Fine, ten," I said. "I'll be there."

"Good. See that you are, brother. This is going to be historic. You won't want to miss it." Aubrey turned and left. I stood there alone for a while, feeling a large object weave itself through my innards. It rolled up my colon, through the large intestine, finally making a home for itself in my stomach. It lolled about there for hours, coating itself in gastric juices. I felt ill the rest of the night.

"Boo him!"

"Pie him!"

"Rig the stage to collapse!"

"Let the air out of his tires!"

The couch and chairs of Aubrey's living room were full to capacity, and several Monkeys lay about on the rug, pushing aside the heaps of books to make elbowroom for themselves. Warren, thinking ahead, had fashioned himself a comfy ottoman from remaindered romance paperbacks Aubrey had liberated from the **READ** garbage bins, their covers ripped off and mailed away, proof for the publisher that they were given every chance to prove themselves at the cash register, but, well, things just hadn't worked out, you know? The crinkled pages bore Warren's weight with ease, but the sight of those poor lonely Harlequins and Silhouettes, dreadful though they all were, consigned to the fate of cushioning

Warren's now-bony ass, filled me with melancholy.

"Pie him!" William repeated. "Right on national television. Right in his smug face, a huge coconut cream!"

The Monkeys nodded general assent. "Yeah, Ralph Klein him!" said Muriel, three beers in and clearly enjoying herself. "Smoosh his nose in, yeah!"

"How about a smoke bomb?" suggested Andrew. "I looked it up online, not hard to make. Stinky, too." This garnered several stoned yelps of approval.

"We could hide in the audience with water balloons," offered Tracey. "Maybe fill them with paint, write something on them, Death to Munroe or something, maybe literary quotations? Aubrey, you could hide a few in your hat."

Aubrey waved off the suggestion. "Page isn't gonna let me even near the building that day, so forget about that. Kilgore and Yossarian neither, Munroe's security will see to that. No, you're not trying, brothers and sisters. I think we'll need to go . . ." He stretched his arms apart ". . . *bigger.*"

Aubrey had hung back in the corner for the first while, sitting cross-legged and idly scratching Margarita behind her ears, listening to the frankly inane ideas lob themselves about the room. It had been silly fun for the first hour or so, beer and plots flowing at equal measure, joints casually passed from mouth to mouth. Enough smoke had filled the room to qualify it as an environmental hazard. We started with the mundane yet rational approaches, the time-honoured highjinks of our forefathers: protesting outside the store barring him entrance, surreptitiously tripping him as he strode down the aisle to the stage, spitballs shot from various stealthy angles, having pizzas delivered to his hotel room, setting off the fire alarm. William had been pushing his pie idea ever since Aubrey opened the floor to suggestions. My own half-hearted idea, to cut the power in the building, plunging the production into darkness, was summarily dismissed as boring, an act of sabotage too easily rectified, not nearly flashy enough. Which it wasn't, of course, but I couldn't think of another act of any sufficient magnitude that wouldn't get us all into heaps of legal trouble. Dumping pig's blood on Munroe from the rafters was put up for a vote from Susan, but the idea was abandoned when Danae remarked that not only did **READ** *not* have any rafters from which to attach said bucket of porcine plasma, but were it to succeed, there might be some copyright infringement issues forthcoming by legal representatives of the Stephen King estate. It was all so goddamned silly, plotting our petty vengeances. Nerds living out their *Dungeons & Dragons* fantasies, planning the dreaded bully's demise through a six-sided die and level 12 charisma. I dared to hope Aubrey's previous madness had passed itself on, his mania the result of an undigested piece of Dickensian beef or glob of mustard.

"Ideas, everyone, ideas!" Aubrey said. He picked up a beer, his seventh or eighth of the evening judging by the bottles scattered about him, and chugged down a healthy amount. "You're not going far enough, people. This is not some simple-minded politician who deserves a pathetic comedic comeuppance. A laugh on the news. The act must not be allowed to overshadow its purpose. This is Munfreakinroe. When the antichrist comes to town to claim our souls, brothers and sisters, you had best believe spitballs, pies, and water balloons are not going to dissuade him from his agenda of destruction. We want our position to be loud and clear. *Vi et armis,* everyone. By force and arms we shall prevail. We don't want humiliation. It's not enough." He dragged the back of his hand across his mouth. "It's not nearly enough."

Cameron raised his hand. "Uh, Aubrey? If it's not too much trouble, what *do* we want?" He sniggered, sweet smoke drifting from his nostrils.

Aubrey twirled toward Cameron's voice. That is, his head twirled; his body followed a second later, in that drunken lurch that always signifies that this person may not yet be completely gone, but he's racing to leave. But as smashed as he was, Aubrey's dilated eyes were deserts of calm. "What do we want?" he asked quietly. He threw his head back, and yelled at the ceiling, "We! Want! *Justice!*" Aubrey tornadoed himself about the room, screaming *"Justice!"* in a high voice over and over, Warren and others egging him on until he drunkenly toppled over the back of the sofa, collapsing onto Burt's lap in a belching heap. He rolled off to the floor, tottered unsteadily on his knees, and crept toward Emily, sitting cross-legged by my feet. "Hagar," he said, something catching in his throat. "Oh,

Hagar, my dear. You've suffered so much."

Emily looked at the rest of us for help. "I don't know what you mean," she said, twisting her braids nervously.

"You've suffered for what you believe in," Aubrey said. He took one of her hands as he laid his head atop her legs. "You fought against such ignorance, and you paid for it, didn't you?"

"Well, yes, I guess I did," she said. "That is, I was fired, Page fired me for trying to help people." Aubrey caressed her cheek, his eyes moist. "I just wanted people to read other things is all. All I heard was Munroe, Munroe, and I couldn't stand it anymore! There's more to life than him, that's all I was doing, telling people to consider something else. Try looking beyond the walls he built. Would it have *killed* them to just try?"

"And Page fired you."

"Yes," said Emily, looking down at Aubrey accusingly and shoving his head off her lap. "But you could have stopped her! You own the place, too! You fired me! Why didn't you say anything?" *Yeah,* I almost piped up, but caught Danae throwing me a questioning look, and held myself back.

"I did, Hagar. I tried, but I can't win every battle. Page threatened to take me to court if I kept it up. I couldn't risk losing the store. It's all I have."

"Bitch," Warren said.

Aubrey stared at him for a second, and nodded. "Bitch. She, as much as Munroe, is to blame for our predicament." He struggled to his feet. "We've all got stories like this. We've all been victims, haven't we? Teased for reading books. Beaten up for being smart." The room took on the hushed tone of a cathedral as we took in his oration. "They were afraid of us, because they *knew* we had something they could never have, and they hated us for it. They still do. The world is run by grade 3 bullies, and we still cower near our lockers, hoping they won't see us."

"I never went to the washroom all through high school," said August. "Every time I went in, I'd be cornered by Mark Kilfoyle. Fuckin' asshole. Every day I tried, he was always there, the same thing, pushing me into the urinal from behind, soaking my pants." August began to hiccup as he relived the memory. "I'd have, hu, have wet myself ruh, rather than go in."

We all nodded in commiseration. Ben Monaghan was my school's particular tormentor in that area. He practically lived in the Boy's Room, the troll of the toilets, giving swirlies and worse to whoever dared enter his domain, before he was expelled for threatening a teacher with a knife. I saw him years later, driving through downtown Winnipeg in a rusted pickup held together with spit and hope, a bumper sticker proudly proclaiming, "Kill a Queer for Christ." Sometimes, Eric, you really can tell how a person's going to end up.

"Marshall Wiebe threw my books in the mud," said Susan, stuttering slightly at the memory.

"John French pants'd me in choir practice."

"Ashley Blake made my life hell!"

"Blair Wallace set fire to my locker!"

Once unlocked, it couldn't be stopped. It became a litany of our lurking demons, a communal release of the ogres who chased us down darkened hallways, destroyed our textbooks, gave us facewashes in urine-soaked snow. The fiends who found it obligatory to influence our formative years, transforming us into silent wraiths in school, and maladjusted individuals in adulthood.

"Chad Wilton!"

"Wesley Richardson!"

"Jason Gordon!"

"Vikram." That was mine. My personal Grendel, only I was too timid a Beowulf to fight back.

"Dylan Merchant!"

"Crystal Perry!"

Aubrey smiled. "Page Adler."

"Assholes! Kill 'em all!" yelled Warren, leaping to his feet and commencing the destruction of his bookish ottoman. "The entire fuckin' school. They all pissed on me 'cause I wouldn't play basketball or football. Excuse the fuck outta me for wanting to read a book, y'know? It's like my going to math class was a cardinal sin or something."

"That's right, they hated you," said Aubrey. "They still hate us. They see us reading on the bus, and they laugh. We don't know who won last night's game, and they pelt us with shit. They hate us because they know we're better than them.

"We have to strike back, and this is the time! Time to settle the score! We have the ringleader in our sights, and all we need to do is pull the trigger. It'll be the Mother of all Punishments, the decisive blow to all those who have lorded over us through brawn over brain."

"What do you want to do, Aubrey?" asked Danae. "We'll do it, I swear." I shifted uneasily as I watched her. I didn't care for the glimmer of madness her eyes had taken on.

"I say . . ." Aubrey said, then stopped and looked at us. The Monkeys were beaming in eagerness, teeth bared in a feral anticipation of blood. This was the true beginning of the end, right here. Whatever Aubrey said, it was hereby the word, and the word was good. And the word was —

". . . *fatwa*." He lengthened the word in a whisper of insanity. "The Shelf Monkeys declare a *fatwa* on Munroe Purvis."

That put a stop to things in a hurry. Aubrey might as well have pulled open his shirt to reveal a chest wired with explosives. Someone laughed after a moment, Tracey, I think, but the others and I just sat there, uncertain. I wanted to say something, crack a joke, good one Aub, now pull the other one. Aubrey just watched us, daring us to rebuke. No one doubted he was serious.

"Fuckin' awesome," said Warren.

"Are you insane?" I'd like to lay claim to this statement, by far the sanest thing said all evening, but Cameron had beat me to the punch. My tongue had taken leave for a few moments to gather itself together. My throat constricted in preparation for a panic attack. I patted my pockets for a pill, but hadn't brought any with me. I settled for a lengthy drag from my spliff instead.

"Yeah. *Fatwa*," Warren continued, rolling the word over his tongue like an exotic candy. "A price on his head, a reverse Rushdie. Harsh but fair. Maybe we could take out an ad in *Soldier of Fortune*. Anyone know someone with a gun?"

"Whoa, whoa, Aubrey," said Burt, flapping away a proffered joint from Warren. *"Fatwa?* Dude, I'm not *that* high."

"Yeah, Aubrey," said Andrew, putting down his beer, "I mean, fun is fun, but you're kidding, right? We want to show our outrage, sure, but I'm not about to hurt anyone over it."

"Outrage?" Aubrey asked. "You want to show outrage, go join

the Manitoba Writers' Guild, I hear they're planning to picket the store, for all the good it will do. Anyone can protest! That's what they expect us to do, because we're weak. Signs and placards, coffee and doughnuts afterward for a job well done. It makes our point, and no one gets hurt, right? Screw that! What are we? Are we those pathetic souls who believe putting a flag on their SUVs somehow makes them patriotic? A bumper sticker stops the war? Wearing a ribbon cures AIDS? A letter to the editor constitutes a viable form of protest, a point made? No!" Aubrey barged around the room, Monkeys scrambling to get out of his way. "I am so tired of people who *mean* well. I am tired of people who talk and talk and talk and don't *do* anything. This is our time! We have to strike! At his heart! He has offended our beliefs, down to the very core of our being." He reached toward Emily. "This is your chance, Hagar."

"For what?" she said, slapping his hands away. "Come on, Aubrey! I miss my job and everything, but fuck you, you think I'm doing something that stupid! Pulling a Rushdie? What, I look like a zealot to you?"

"Hagar —"

"Don't call me that!" she yelled up at him. "That's a name we use for fun, it's not who I am. Don't you know that? I'm not Hagar, you're not Quixote, we are all just who we are."

"Okay, everyone just calm down a little," I said. "Aubrey's just venting here, like the rest of us. No one is seriously considering this. This is just the alcohol talking, not you. Fun's fun, and it's nice to dream, but we're none of us killers." I raised my arms upward, exaggerating a stretch of exhaustion with a complimentary *rowlf* of a yawn. "Well, I've got to work in the morning. I guess I'll be motoring on. Anyone give me a ride? Danae?"

"Wait, we can't leave," Danae said. "Thomas, stay. We need to discuss this. Aubrey, how would we do it?"

A tiny voice piped up from near the kitchen. "Could we try poison?" asked Susan timidly. "Maybe slip something into his coffee before he goes on, something like that?"

"Now *that's* thinking big!" Aubrey enthused. Susan shone with pleasure.

"Poison, yeah!" Gavin said. A dismaying number of the Monkeys nodded their agreement. "A few drops, he goes down,

BOOM!" He mimed Munroe's crash to the floor with his arm.

"Do you know anything about poison?" I asked, not without sarcasm. Susan shrugged. "Anyone else here an expert on unidentifiable solutions that kill within seconds and leave no trace? No? Warren, you? Gavin? Muriel? No one watches *CSI* for pointers? Gosh, I guess we're all just whistling out our asses."

"Thomas, it's just an idea," Danae complained. "It doesn't *have* to be poison. We'll think of something to do."

"We're not doing it!" I shouted. "Christ, Danae, let's go already. This is just the marijuana smoke. We can all talk about this after Aubrey's slept it off." I grabbed our coats, flustered, tossing Danae's at her.

She batted it aside. "I'm not leaving. This is important to me, Thomas."

"No, this is important to *him*," I said, patting down my pockets. Come on, just one little pill, c'mon! A Paxil, a Xanax, a Niravam, anything! Why do I ever leave home without my meds? "What, Aubrey, you're serious? We're not terrorists! We don't start holy wars, we sell books! We're fucking *nerds*! We fight with words. *We* don't do things like this, because *we* are the ones who're supposed to know better!" Shit, here come the shakes. I pistoned my arms into my pockets, let the anxiety manifest itself in a steadily tapping foot. "Danae? Can we go now?"

"Aw, Tommy, man," said Warren. He had somehow gotten behind me, and placed me in a not-quite-affectionate bearhug, constraining me. "Don't be like this. We're just spitballin', y'know? Wishing upon stars, shits and giggles. Sit down, have a beer."

"Like this? What is *this* that I'm like? Sober? Rational?" I flailed my legs, knocking over several beer bottles and Cameron, but I might as well have been shackled to a wall. "I am rational, I am so freaking rational now, so let me go!" I shot a heel down, connecting with Warren's toes. He dropped me with a yelp. I darted across the room toward the doorway before he could regroup. "And don't fucking call me Tommy."

"I'll give you a ride, buddy," said William, standing. "I'm having fun, but it's getting a little too intense in here."

"Can I grab a ride, too?" asked Tracey.

"Me, too?" asked Muriel.

"No prob," William said, putting on his coat. He walked out to the foyer, calling out as he opened the door. "Anyone else coming? I got a van." The others began to rise.

"Hey, hold on, wait," said Danae. She stood next to Aubrey. "Now, let's not all get angry here, Emily, William, wait . . ."

"Oh, drop it, Danae," said Emily. "I'm not killing anyone. This is stupid. In fact, I quit!"

"Emily," Danae said, shocked. "You don't mean that, honey."

"Hell I don't, don't tell me what to do. My therapist told me to get —"

"Therapist?" Aubrey exclaimed.

"You mean you've *told* someone about us?" Warren groaned.

"Oh, calm down, it's cool." Emily huffed in annoyance. "Doctor-patient confidentiality, okay? She won't tell anyone. Anyway, she's been telling me for weeks to get out of this. I think she's right. This isn't healthy, it's sick. I need out."

"But, Haga — Emily, you're one of us," Aubrey insisted. He snatched her hands, pulling them to his heart. "How can you leave us, when we need you most?"

"Oh, Christ, will you listen to yourself?" Emily pulled away in distaste. "We need. We need. What about what *I* need? You *fired* me, asshole! Who needs *this?* It was fun, but Aubrey, you're going off the deep end. And you're pulling the rest of us in with you."

"Aw, Emily, it's not like that," Susan said.

"It is exactly like that. He's lost in his psychosis, and the rest of you are just begging at his heels. Lining up like the good little Svengali-ites you are." Emily grabbed her jacket, hurriedly putting it on. "I'm out, guys, sorry. This is way too fucked up for me. See you around, it's been fun." She walked out to the van.

"Emily," Aubrey said quietly after her.

"Fuck," said Muriel. "She always was a little flighty."

"Yeah," agreed William. "She can't even tell you're joking, Aubrey. Who needs her, right?"

"Right," said Aubrey.

"Yeah," said Cameron. "Forget her. We'll talk at the next burning, Aubrey, okay?" He shuffled past me toward the open door. "Aubrey, the next burning, right? Next week? I've got a perfect 'tag, you'll see."

"Right," Aubrey said again. He opened another beer. "Burning. Sure. Fun." He chugged it down. "See ya," he mumbled between gulps.

I waited until the others had filed past us, shyly saying goodbye as Aubrey waved them away. Danae and Warren stayed where they were. "Tell William I'll be out in a minute," I said to Susan. The four of us had the room to ourselves. Danae, I noted with an enormous surge of jealousy, had taken Aubrey's hand.

"Are you coming?" I asked her. She shook her head, no. "Fine. Warren, need a lift? I'm sorry about the foot, big guy, it was the grass, angries up the blood." Warren turned his head, engrossed in something on the far wall. Cold shoulder country again. Why was I even apologizing? I turned to Aubrey. "It'll be better tomorrow, brother. Promise."

"I thought you were one of us," he said. "I thought you, of all of them, you I could count on."

I shook my head, more in frustration than negation. "Look, Aubrey. Danae, Warren. I love being with you guys. But we're elitists, that's all, not fanatics. All we are is a club, like chess or curling or Latin. What we do is for ourselves, to make ourselves feel better. We're not out to hurt anyone, and you know it. What we do is, fuck, it's great, it's terrific, I haven't felt this good in years thanks to you. But there's nothing we can do. We aren't a political party. We have no clout. Think about it, we're weirdos, meeting in a field to burn books. No one would understand it, I don't understand it, and I love it! We do our best, we tell the world what it should read, we write angry reviews on Amazon and Chapters, we blog to our heart's content, that's our place. But we have no power here. None. We, the fourteen of us, we cannot compete with major syndicated television programs. It's hopeless." A horn honked from outside, my cue to leave. "We're all just drunk and miserable right now," I said, walking out the door. "We're not terrorists."

I was almost to the sliding door, the van packed with faces watching my approach. Aubrey called out behind me. "What's the difference?" I turned and faced the house, the three of them. Perfect strangers only four months previous. Aubrey, Warren, and Danae, the only real friends I felt I ever had, jammed in solidarity in the doorway. Danae had her hand on Aubrey's shoulder, and Warren loomed behind, his arms comfortingly around the both of them. Danae did not look sad to see me go. "Why can't we be terrorists, Thomas?" Aubrey asked. "What's the difference between us and them?"

I thought about this for a second. Given the benefit of hindsight, I should have pondered the question more seriously. But as it stood, my brain still moderately steeped in a syrupy haze of alcoholic fluids and misty intoxicants, I decided instead to be flippant, and uttered quite possibly the stupidest, most damaging thing I'd ever said:

"At least terrorists, they get the job done."

I might have well signed my own death warrant.

Dinner's over, and a warm bed now beckons me with the promise of uninterrupted slumber. The mysterious benefactor has laid out clean sheets, and has washed and dried my clothes.

Good night, Eric.

Thomas

From The Toronto Star

MUNROE MANIA COMES TO CANADA

TORONTO — A crowd of hundreds at Pearson International Airport greeted one of American television's most influential figures, as Munroe Purvis and his entourage arrived in Toronto to begin the much-ballyhooed Canadian tour of his popular syndicated talk show.

Mr. Purvis, jovial and approachable, set about shaking the hands of the throngs of fans that had camped out for hours to get a glimpse of their hero. "Hello, Canada, how's every little thing?" he asked the crowd, getting a huge laugh in response.

"This is just so incredible," gushed Martin Bleichart, a computer analyst who drove himself and his family up from Windsor for a chance to get a glimpse of Munroe. "I figured he'd be stuck up, or at least tired from the trip, but he took the time to shake all our hands and let us know that we matter to him."

"I have to tell you, I am over-whelmed by the passion of this greeting," a visibly moved Munroe told this reporter. "To be honest, I wasn't sure anyone would even come out to see us land. I mean, it must be only twenty above, or below, or whatever the metric system says it is up here. But I guess the promise of good literature is strong enough to get people away from the hockey courts."

TO: ermccorm@yahoo.ca
FROM: iamashelfmonkey@gmail.com
SUBJECT: Beginning of the end

Dear Eric,

I think I've made a terrible mistake. I mean, any port in a storm is fine in theory, but of all the ports to dock at, why did I opt for port Wacky McNutjob?

This morning, enjoying the first leisurely breakfast I've had in months, it suddenly occurred to me that my current sponsor might not be the most, how shall I put this, *stable* individual. This was at about the time when he asked if I'd be up to a public appearance at the bookstore where he works part-time as a cashier. Perhaps do a reading from the novel of my choice. Possibly lead the congregation in a burning. I tried to refuse gracefully, saying how, while pleased by the offer, it might not be in my best interests, what with my being sought after by the police and all.

He stared at me from across the breakfast table, digesting this. "So, that's the thanks I get," he said finally, rising and taking my unfinished plate of Eggs Benedict away. He slid the food into the garbage can beneath the sink, muttering about ungratefulness and risk and hospitality and table manners. I tried to apologize. He said no apology was necessary. He asked me what I wanted for dinner, I said anything would be fine. He said he had to leave, he had to go to the store for *supplies*, and would I be okay alone for ten minutes or so? I'm italicizing that word to demonstrate the subtle emphasis he put on it. Not supplies, *supplies*. Not food, not drink, but *supplies*. What supplies? Corn? Milk? Rope? Handcuffs? Oh my God, I'm in a John Fowles novel; I'm Miranda, and he's Freddy, keeping me like a butterfly. Or, worse, he's Annie Wilkes, off to get her axe to chop off my foot, hobbling poor celebrity Paul Sheldon so as to keep him as a personal keepsake. I watched through the window as he walked down the street, waited until he turned the corner, gathered my things, rifled through his bedroom for spare cash, grabbed this laptop, and ran for the nearest bus stop, don't care where, just take me away.

I'm holed up now, different city altogether. Maybe I overreacted; he was probably just lonely. Would have done the same for any fugitive. Probably has done it before. Might have the bones of D.B. Cooper in his basement. No way to be sure.

There sure is a lot of pornography on his hard drive, through, full to bursting with it. Nothing demented, no pre-teens or anything, just straight male-on-female cum shots. Nothing to brag about to mom, but nothing illegal. I'll try to pawn it soon, get myself some running around money. It doesn't have wi-fi. But I should complain?

But for now — where was I?

Fourteen days passed excruciatingly slowly. It could have been worse, I could have been on fire, but it hurt nonetheless. Aubrey was a no-show at work. "He's still sick," Page announced at morning group. "Something must be going around."

"Cowardice," snickered Waylon loudly, earning him some muffled guffaws from co-workers. I caught up to him later and warned him to watch his mouth. "Like I'm afraid of you," Waylon spat. "All you guys, with your little clique, think you're better, smarter. You got no power here anymore, Tommy. Page is just looking for an excuse." He was exactly right, but it was that one word, *Tommy*, that got to me. I pushed him back into the shelves, my fist raised. He never said anything, he just cowered and shook. Every bully who ever pushed my face into my lunch cheered me on from the sidelines. I managed to reach the restroom before I acquainted the toilet with the digested remains of my lunch.

Without Aubrey's behind-the-scenes influence, the store rapidly became a police state of intimidation and fear. Page was a potentate on top of the world, transforming her role as manager/owner into that of the Glengarry-esque closer, complete with hanging pair of brass balls. Quotas were set on certain books per section; don't sell enough, get a warning. Two warnings, earn a talking-to. Three, you're fired. Her nemesis was AWOL, her idol inching closer with each passing day. She would hand down new edicts every morning, Danae nodding along complacently.

If Aubrey's absence was worrisome, Danae's snubbing was anguish. Calls went unanswered. Pleas at work for her under-standing were shelved away and ignored. I became frantic, hounding her through the aisles. A quick word from Warren put a stop to my romantic pursuit. "She wants me to break your arms," he confided to me one day as his forearm held my neck in place against the lunchroom table. "I don't want to, Thomas. I'm not enjoying giving you the silent treatment. But you betrayed her trust. You've broken the group. So back off. It'll be better for everyone."

I squirmed my way out from under his pressure and hid under the table for protection. "I betrayed her trust? Hey, she lied to both of us, remember? She kept Aubrey's little secret from you for how long again? She's untrustworthy, Aubrey's untrustworthy, me, I'm the only one *not* jerking you around!"

Warren crouched down and looked at me, worry creasing his forehead. "You think I don't know? But Aubrey's my best friend, dude. Danae, she's his. You, you're the odd man out. If you want back in, you're welcome, but for now, sides must be chosen." He stood up, his knees cracking. His voice filtered down through the leaves of the table. "Make an effort, Thomas. Meet us halfway."

"I'll think about it," I said, trying to sound harsh. My position under the table diminished my tough-guy resolve somewhat.

What did I want, anyway? Did I really believe Aubrey was nuts? That Danae was, well, also nuts? It was all just Monkey-talk, wasn't it? The frustration of the ignored. Tough talk from the class nerd, vowing revenge in his diary, never to truly accomplish anything. Picking sides? That was just silly; there were no sides here, only hurt feelings and misunderstandings. Who was I to judge another person's sanity, anyway?

Truth was, I was lonely, miserable, and tired of fighting. I resolved to make it up to Aubrey, to Danae, to all the Monkeys. I craved Aubrey's warm companionship and Danae's smile; I couldn't tell you which I wanted more. I called around to see if interest was still there. "Sure, Thomas, no problem," Aubrey said on the phone. "I'll set it up. It'll be fun. Like old times." His voice sounded dead, but I chose to ignore its implications. A meeting was scheduled, one last-ditch effort to continue the fun. I showed up early, eager to make amends. A newly released copy of James Patterson's latest Alex Cross novel waited patiently in my backpack, *Four Blind Mice,* a peace offering I felt sure to please Aubrey.

He stood by the oil drum, Margarita at his heels barking

ferociously at me, as if such a thing could make any sound seem ferocious. Aubrey's eyes were fixed on the flames, searing his retinas, scrambling the rods and cones. Not a word was uttered as we waited for the rest of the company to slowly arrive. Danae and Warren arrived together, hand in hand. I wondered if they were sleeping together, then cursed myself for caring.

"Shall we begin?" Aubrey said, refusing to look up. He continued to study the fire.

"Yeah, I've got a perfect 'tag," said Gavin. "Look, Aubrey. Dee Henderson, see. You heard of her?" Aubrey nodded.

"Wait," said Susan. "Emily's not here, we can't start."

"She's not coming," Aubrey said. "Left a message on my machine. She's never coming back."

Cameron spoke up. "Aw, she was serious? No, man, that's not right, I'll call her." He held out a hand. "Who's got a cell?"

"She's out, Cam," Danae said. "I've been talking to her all week. She keeps saying her therapist says this is unhealthy."

"Fuckin' shrinks," said Warren.

"Amen, brother," Aubrey said. "Fucking shrinks."

"No, no, I can talk to her," said Cameron. "Tracey, lend me your phone?"

"Sure."

"HAGAR IS NOT COMING!" screamed Aubrey, still focused on the fire. Danae jumped in surprise. Tracey dropped her proffered phone into the snow. Cameron made no move to retrieve it.

"She has made her priorities abundantly clear, Ignatius!" Aubrey continued to rant. "She has chosen her side. Hagar is no longer welcome. She is a traitor to our cause! She is dead to us!" Margarita rolled herself about in the snow in confused excitement. "Ubf! Wif? Fub! Ubfubfubf!"

Cameron backed away slowly, hands up in supplication. "Sure, Aub, no problem."

"It's okay, Aubrey," said Andrew. "Really, right, guys?"

"Absolutely," Gavin said. "Emily. Screw her, right?"

"So, Emily's really not coming?" asked Burt. He pulled a paperback novel from his pocket. "Can I burn *Stone Angel* now? Can I finally torch this?"

"Aw, Burt, don't," said Danae. "She's not even here, don't do it."

"Let him do what he wants, Offred," said Aubrey. "If you wish to burn it, Gandalf, do so. No one here will stop you."

"Well, all right!" Burt beamed a smile at the rest of us. "She doesn't want to save her book, she should have shown up. Serves her right, right?" He strode triumphantly to the fire and held the Laurence in the air. No one moved to stop him. "Here she goes!" he yelled, cocking his arm into a throwing position. "I'm gonna do it!" He held his arm back, looking around anxiously.

"Well?" asked Aubrey. "We're waiting, Gandalf. Burn it."

Burt furrowed his brow. "Isn't anyone going to stop me?"

Danae turned away. "Just do it, Burt. Get it over with."

Burt pulled his arm back even further, and then let it drop slightly. "Aw, this is wrong."

"Burn the heretic, Gandalf," Aubrey said angrily. "This is your chance. You've been waiting months for this moment!"

"Yeah, but . . ." Burt took a step away from the fire. "I can't do it. I never wanted to burn it, really, I just liked getting Emily riled up. I mean, Aubrey —"

"My name is Don Quixote!" yelled Aubrey deliriously, startling Burt into dropping *Stone Angel*. It landed near the fire, stopping just outside of singeing range. Aubrey squished his face together in frustration. "Quixote!" he howled. Burt retreated away toward the group as Aubrey thrashed his arms about, battering his head in frustration. "This is what we have agreed! We are Shelf Monkeys! We cannot hold together if we cannot follow even this one simple little rule!" He halted his self-abuse and looked at us, blinking madly. He pointed a finger at Andrew. "What is your name?" he asked.

"It's Andrew, Aubrey, you —"

"Don Quixote!"

"Quixote, sorry."

"What's your name? Your secret name?"

"Aub, stop this, I **ow**!" Warren had rabbit-punched the back of Andrew's head. "What the hell, you big prick?"

"Answer him," Warren grunted.

"Okay, okay. Queequeg. My name is Queequeg."

"Queequeg," Aubrey repeated with satisfaction. He laid his hands on Andrew's shoulders. "Queequeg, my friend. You are Queequeg, I am Don Quixote." Aubrey pulled him closer. "What's your name?"

"Queequeg."

"And are you proud of that name, Queequeg? The name you chose for yourself? There was a time not long ago that name meant something to you."

"Yes." Andrew sniffed and pulled his shoulders back, standing at attention. "Yes, I am very proud of my name."

"And are you proud of what we do here, Queequeg?"

"Very proud, Don Quixote."

Aubrey patted Andrew's shoulders in admiration. "I'm proud of you, too, Queequeg." He turned and walked back to the fire. "I'm proud of all of you."

Danae joined him and stared into the blaze. "We are all happy to be here, Don Quixote. All of us."

"Thank you, Offred."

Warren walked up to Aubrey's other side, reaching into the fire and pulling out a small log from its cold end. He thrust the makeshift torch to the stars. "I am Kilgore Trout, Shelf Monkey," he announced with satisfaction.

Danae took the torch. "I am Offred, Shelf Monkey," she intoned.

August was next, taking the torch from Danae. "I am Raoul Duke, Shelf Monkey."

He passed the torch to Susan. "I am Scout Finch, Shelf Monkey."

Andrew. "I am Queequeg, Shelf Monkey."

Tracey. "I am Lyra Silvertongue, Shelf Monkey."

Burt. "I am Gandalf, Shelf Monkey."

Cameron. "Ignatius J. Reilly, Shelf Monkey."

Muriel. "Lady Fuchsia Groan, Shelf Monkey."

William. "Valentine Michael Smith, Shelf Monkey."

Gavin. "Ford Prefect, Shelf Monkey."

Gavin held the torch out to me. A small hand reached out from the darkness. "I'll take that," said Emily, snatching the flame from my grip. She shrugged to our gaping mouths. "I can't change my mind? Nothing good on TV tonight anyway."

"What did you hear?" asked Danae, welcoming her with a loving squeeze.

"All of it. I've been holding back, trying to make up my mind." She walked up to Andrew and gave him a clumsy hug, juggling the torch to avoid setting him ablaze. "Thanks for not burning me, Queequeg. I know that can't have been easy."

"Aw, shucks," Andrew said, blushing at the intimacy. "It was, you know, wrong. I'm sorry I never liked it."

"Never apologize, Queequeg," Emily said, giving him another hug, then stepping back. "You stick to your guns. I admire you for it."

"You've made a decision, then, Hagar?" Aubrey asked warily.

"For better or worse." Emily held the torch aloft. "Hagar Shipley, Shelf Monkey. I've always known it. Screw that shrink anyway, what does she know about what's healthy? This makes me happy." She offered the log to me. "Sorry to butt in, Thomas, here you go."

My head filled with the screams of a crowd. *Don't take it.* The wind had blown the flames out by Muriel's turn, and now it was only a blackened log dotted with embers, faintly smoking in the darkness.

Don't take it, Thomas, don't you dare.

I accepted it, held it up. An errant cinder broke off, blurring away into the sky.

Don't say a word, walk away.

"Yossarian. Shelf Monkey."

Oh you goddamn pussy.

Aubrey held out his hands. Slowly, we linked ourselves together around the bonfire. Aubrey sighed happily. "We are complete once again, brothers and sisters. Where once we had weakened, we are now strong and resolved. United we stand.

"I hereby call this meeting of the Shelf Monkeys to order." He removed his backpack. "I felt this evening might work out this way," he explained, digging into the pack. "I hoped it would, so I thought something special would be in order."

"Champagne?" suggested Burt.

"Better." He began leisurely pulling out copy after copy of Munroe selections, a MUNROE RECOMMENDS THIS! on each cover, flashing in the firelight. "A sacrifice worthy of the occasion." Agnes Coleman. "Something to reinvigorate ourselves." Gerry Ewes. "A reminder of just what it is we fight against." Nicholas Rapley. "Of just *who* it is we fight against." Another. Another. Another.

"Ahhh," the Monkeys sounded. August clapped happily. My heart beat faster.

"We are agreed then?"

"We are," we said.

"Is Montag right?" Aubrey held the books above the fire, its flames reaching hungrily for the offering.

"He is."

"Is it a pleasure to burn?"

"Yes."

Aubrey dropped the load as a whole into the drum, the pages at first smothering the flames in protest, and then surrendering with bursts of orange glory. Smoke arose into the air, filling our lungs. A single golden label detached and fled up into the breeze, taunting us. God, it felt so right. I was mainlining on Coleman's death. Freebasing on Munroe's funeral pyre until my head exploded in rapture. All was forgiven. There was only good on the Earth.

We lingered silently in our circle, basking in the heat as it fondled us.

"We are together again, then?" Aubrey asked, the blaze dying in strength.

"Yes, Quixote," said Muriel. "We are together."

"All for one, one for all," said Gavin.

Cameron shivered in ecstasy. "Man, I don't know about the rest of you, but I forgot how good this could feel! When that Rapley hit the heat, I was — wow." I nodded in tandem with the others. Was I the only one with a woody? I doubt it.

"Welcome back, brother," Aubrey said fondly.

"I was really scared there for while," Danae said. Her pupils were alive in the dark, crackling red sparks. "I thought we'd never be together again." She looked calmly at me across the flames as she said this. "I never want to feel like that again." My mouth went dry.

Aubrey clapped his hand, ruining the moment forever. "Now, brothers and sisters, back to business! A demon in human form approaches, and we must make preparations if we are to be ready for his arrival."

"Oh, Jesus!" I spat it out without thinking, dropping Muriel and Burt's hands in despair. "We're still on that?"

"The only true way for evil to triumph is for good men and women to do nothing," he preached at me.

I was livid, at my own stupidity for believing things could change more than anything else. "Guys, back me up here," I said to the others. "Burt, you're not going along with this, right?"

"My name is Gandalf," he said. "I ask you to respect the sanctity of the organization, Yossarian."

"Oh, come on!"

"Don Quixote's right," August said. "We have to do something, man. Anything. I haven't slept in days. I keep picturing Munroe's fat face, taunting me."

"Well, take a pill, then, that's what I do, don't plot assassination!" Thirteen pairs of eyes watched me with contempt. "Is no one here with me?" I pleaded weakly.

"If you could go back in time and stop Osama bin Laden from being born, wouldn't you do so?" asked Gavin. He looked to Aubrey. "Wouldn't we have a responsibility to stop him?"

Aubrey nodded. "We would, Ford."

"Munroe's not bin Laden, Aubrey," I said.

"Don Quixote."

"Aubrey!" There must be one ounce of sanity left *somewhere* in the group. "He's not even Jerry Falwell or Pat Robertson. He's a goddamned talk-show host, guys! That's all! In ten years, who's going to remember him, huh? Who remembers Morton Downey, Jr. anymore? No one. Ricki Lake? Gone! This too shall pass, Aubrey."

"Don Quixote."

"Oh, fuck this!" I spun in place, hysterical. "You know what, Emily was right, this is unhealthy. I quit!" I stopped my spin, gathered my bearings, and left the circle for home.

"Yossarian!" Danae yelled after me. "Please, sweetie, don't leave! We need you!"

I whirled to face them. *Stay, Yossarian, please,* an unfamiliar voice begged within my head. *Don't leave, this is where you belong.* I was losing my grip. *These are your friends, Yossarian.* "My name is Thomas!" I bellowed into the night, drowning the voice in my own. "Thomas Friesen! Thomas! Thomas! Thomas!" Danae buried her face in her hands as I continued my dramatic exit, now a frantic run to catch up with my sanity, wondering how I could collect on the thirty pieces of silver I was owed.

What do you do when you discover that your best friends are clinically insane?

Aubrey didn't show up for work the next day. Page announced Aubrey was taking a period of "indefinite leave" from the store. Her grin was so wide, she was one unhinged jaw away from swallowing a guinea pig whole. Danae continued her steadfast refusal of my reality, ignoring my clumsy attempts at reconciliation by pursuing every customer she saw, imploring them to please, read a Pérez-Reverte, won't you at least try a Thomas Keneally, have you considered Naipaul for your reading pleasure, no please, don't stop at the Danielle Steel, put down that Jackie Collins, not Sandra Brown, no, please! Affecting a migraine, she slunk to the back room, hissing at me, grimacing at the ever-present cameramen who were inspecting the erected stage area for Munroe's imminent arrival. Warren I opted to stay away from completely. I walked into the lunchroom one day, catching him alone. He was immersed in reading William Gass' *The Tunnel*, sipping from a coffee cup, when he looked up from the page and saw me standing there. We shared a moment of self-conscious silence. "You should probably leave, Thomas," he said. "It wouldn't do to have you in my eyesight right now." I backed out of the room, nonchalantly, as if I *always* left rooms back-end first. Warren was smiling, and someone who didn't know him would think Warren was kidding around. A more careful observer, however, would notice the knuckles of Warren's hands fading, pink to white, as he compressed the pages of the Gass together in anger.

My tenure at **READ** became a dour mixture of antagonism and paranoia. Page, now in full stormtrooper mode, enlisted me to help set up Munroe's stage. Her glee at my distaste for the task was approaching Wicked Witch of the West levels. I caught a peripheral glimpse of Danae, her flirtiness a distant memory. She watched as I set up the chairs, her eyes welling up. She turned away before compassion could get the better of her. I concentrated on the work, swallowing something bitter and sharp.

The day before Munroe's triumphant visit to Winnipeg, Aubrey broke the stalemate. I was mourning my isolation on my day off, eating tortilla chips, chewing pills, smoking piss-poor pot I had wheedled from the guy across the hall, and quaffing beer after beer as I squinted my eyes at the television. I had numbed my senses with Tarkovsky's *Solaris*, Kubrick's *2001: A Space Odyssey* on deck to pummel me into incoherence. Then, a double-bill, *Schindler's List* and *Shoah* to lighten the mood. I needed entertainment that matched my spirits, and I had tired of Leonard Cohen albums. Aubrey's phone call lowered my spirits further still.

"Brotherman, how goes the fight?"

"My friends treat me like I've got Ebola, but hey, who's complaining?"

"Yeah, sorry about that."

"Fuck you. I don't have any books tonight, Aubrey, or oh gosh I'm sorry, Don Quixote. I don't know who I'm talking to here. Tell you what, I'll stay home and broil a copy of *The National Review* in my oven."

"Hey, I'm trying to apologize here," Aubrey said. He sounded truly contrite. "I'm extending an olive branch. Least you could do is hear me out."

"So talk," I said, punching play on my DVD remote. Men in monkey suits began stroking a large rectangle on the screen. "Talk away, you have my undivided attention."

"I sense disbelief."

"No, no, I'm really interested in what you have to say." I fast-forwarded to a polished femur soaring into the sky, jump-cutting itself into a space station.

Aubrey sighed. "I guess I got a little intense there."

"No, Joe McCarthy was a little intense, Aubrey. You were in all-out Chucky Manson territory."

"I'd like to make it up to you."

"To what do I owe the honour?"

"We miss you." I paused the film, stopping a space shuttle's docking with two rotating rings in mid-penetration. "Danae is miserable without you."

Hah! I knew it! "She could tell me that herself," I said coldly. I should make this easy?

"Look, Thomas, the plan, Munroe, it's all over, all right? We were hyped up that night, but it didn't last. We met a few more times, and we all agreed you were right, it was a pointless exercise in futility."

"Really?"

"Really and truly. No plans, no revenge, nada. We'll just stay home."

"I think that's best." For the first time in forever, I relaxed and allowed myself a weak smile.

"Me too."

"So, we're good again?"

"We're good, brother," Aubrey said. I could hear the contentment in his voice. "I've done some soul-searching, rereading old favourites and such. There's nothing like a little Aldous Huxley to put things back into perspective. I'm going back to work next week. I'm asking you for another chance."

"Sounds good."

"But, Munroe is coming, and I can't pretend I'm not depressed by that. Warren and Danae are coming over tomorrow night to visit and ride out the media storm. We'll play some games or something. Would you like to come?"

"Well, I don't know."

"Did I mention how much Danae misses you?"

"Yeah. Did Warren mention how my mere presence drives him into psychotic rage?"

"Yeah, he did. But he promises to behave, and I've got a trank gun if he goes ballistic on you."

"Well —"

"Danae *really* misses you."

"Well, I guess that's that," I said. The glowing numerals of my watch said the time was almost midnight. We had passed a pleasant evening drinking beer, eating Chinese take-out, getting mildly stoned, resolutely *not* mentioning Munroe Purvis or how the taping of his show might have gone, and playing Risk, Warren and Aubrey teaming up again and again to wipe my pieces off the map while *Sketches of Spain* played in the background. I griped and moaned about fair play and UN regulations, but I didn't really mind. I was never very good at the game, somewhat lacking in the military acumen necessary to both defend one's terrain and mount a successful world conquest, invariably finding my pieces had dwindled to two or three armies of red on a continent of green or yellow. But maybe I had it coming from these two. They were taking pains to mend our relationship, but who could blame them for relishing a little dice-decided payback? The board was now an entire planet tragically devoid of all but three faltering armies of red, smoking their last cigarettes before facing the firing squads of the rebel insurgents of the greens and blues. Ah, well, such is life. At least in a world where Canada is divided into four provinces.

"What's that?" Warren asked, looking up as he shook the dice in his hands. "You giving up, Thomas?" He released the dice, howled in triumph, and finger-flicked the second-last of my troops from the board.

"I'd advise against quitting just now, brother," Aubrey said, peering over the bloody massacre. "I'd say you've got us just where you want us."

"Lured us into a false sense of security," Warren said, studying the pieces. "Very clever."

"No, I think you've now both got an indisputable sense of security, thank you very much," I said, stretching the kinks from my back. "I've done what I came to do, made you two feel better about yourselves."

"Hey, worked for me," said Warren. "Aubrey, you?"

"Why, I've never felt better."

"Then my work here is done," I said, plucking my last armies mercifully from the battlefields. "My men and I can suffer the humiliation of defeat no longer. I surrender. Just promise me you'll send flowers to the widows of all the brave soldiers you've slain in combat."

"Hey, brother, you can't leave yet," Aubrey said, commencing another dice war with Warren over the fate of Ontario. "You'll miss my coronation as undisputed master of the known world."

"Hah! You wish!" Warren chortled. "Your defences are weak in Africa and Europe. You lack the will of the warrior, my young friend. The world is mine!"

"But I control Australia, Warren. The stronghold of the southern hemisphere. I'll sic the wallabies on you. Armies of platypuses are at my disposal. The koalas are readying arms as we speak."

"Ooh."

"Hey, in a minute I will control all of North America. It'll be only a matter of time now until I get the antiballistic missile defence system up and running."

"I really don't think the Parker Brothers have prepared for that eventuality in their rules."

"Besides, Thomas," Aubrey said in a teasing voice, "leaving would be a bad idea. Danae is coming, if you'll remember."

I stopped in mid-rise. I had honestly forgotten. Danae's absence that evening had gone unmentioned by the three of us, her presence at Munroe's program a sore spot for Aubrey, I believed. When I had asked where she was after I arrived, trying unsuccessfully to control my shameful hope of reconciliation, Aubrey fluttered a hand dismissively. "She's with *Munroe* tonight." The name came out in a long, sarcastic drawl.

"Danae decided to go to the taping with Page," Warren added, "as a show of solidarity or something. She didn't want to go, really, but Page insisted. She'll drop by afterward, she said, maybe."

"Maybe," Aubrey repeated. "*Maybe* she'll pop by. If it's not too late." I braced myself for another tirade, sighing inwardly. Aubrey held it together, however, taking a deep breath, holding it, then clapping his hands and saying, "Who's up for a game or two?"

"Twister?" I asked.

"I said, Danae's not here," Warren joked, prodding my ribs in jest.

No more was mentioned of Danae that evening, and I put her grudgingly out of mind, happy just to be with friends who seemed to have forgiven and forgotten my trespasses.

Now, I rechecked my watch. "The taping's been over for hours now, Aubrey. I don't think she's —"

"Wow, Risk," a lovely voice said from behind me. "You guys really know how to set the night on fire." Danae traipsed happily into the room, snowflakes melting in her hair. My heart jumped at the sight of her, but I decided to play it cool and merely pant silently to myself. "Next thing you know, you might get crazy, break out the Pictionary." She dropped her coat to the floor, revealing a stunning red dress that expertly highlighted every body part I yearned for (hello, sisters Brontë, how've you been?), and flopped herself lengthwise on the couch in feigned exhaustion, cuddling her head into Margarita's living canine cushion.

"Long night, sister?" Aubrey asked with a smirk.

She rolled her eyes. "Oh, honey, you have no idea." She fixed her beautiful orbs on me. "Hello, Thomas, glad you stayed. You okay with all this?"

"Oh, can't complain," I replied, heroically averting my eyes from the ample décolletage her dress had on display. "Wingus and Dingus here have repeatedly committed non-UN-sanctioned genocide on my people, but otherwise, I'm cool."

"Harsh, dude," Warren protested. "It's just a game."

"So," I said, "at the risk of starting a conversation I'm sure I don't want to be a part of, how was the show?"

"Well." Danae made herself more comfortable on Margarita's back, getting an irritated *Ubf* for her troubles. "Munroe, in person, is even more repulsive than you can imagine."

"Do tell," said Aubrey.

"I do tell. It's not just the rampant fawning, which comes off him in waves. He has this sweatiness that must be covered with lighting or something. You can smell it on him." She shuddered. "He leaned in toward me for a quick look-see when Page introduced us. Didn't even try to disguise it. You'd need a crowbar to pry him out, he was that far into my cleavage."

"Classy," I said. *Why are you wearing such a revealing dress, anyway?* is what I wanted to ask.

"How was Page?" Warren asked.

"Oh, wow, you've never seen the like. She was like a schoolgirl being asked to a dance for the first time, all giggling and blushing. I knew she was a fan of his show, I didn't realize she was such a fan of *him*."

"She just smelled the money," said Aubrey. "It's an aphrodisiac for Page. She was the same way when we talked to the bankers about loan options to get the store off the ground."

"Whatever it was, she was all over him. It was like a car accident, you couldn't help but watch. The fact that he had no interest in her, that made it just that much sadder. She just couldn't see it."

"Sorry I missed it," I said. "Sounds like quite the party." I stood up and brushed the wrinkles from my pants. "Well, time to mosey on home. Page'll want me to help tear down the chairs in the morning. I'll see you guys later."

"Honey, you're leaving?" Danae asked. "But the party's just starting."

Honey? I bit down on my tongue, holding back a bitter rejoinder. "Well, you know, we all need our beauty sleep."

"He doesn't know?" she asked Aubrey. "You haven't told him?"

"I was waiting for the best time, but it never came up." Aubrey looked me up and down. The crunch of tires on the new snow in the driveway filtered into the room. Aubrey perked up. "Warren, is that a car I hear outside?"

"Oh fuck!" Warren jumped to his feet, knocking the game pieces off the board. "Get ready, guys!" He ran through the kitchen toward the back of the house, tearing through the rear entrance and running outside. The screen door banged itself shut behind him.

"Tell me what?" I asked. Faintly from outside, I heard the slam of a car door being shut. "What's going on?" I looked at Danae for help. She had sat up, tensing herself into readiness. Muffled footsteps sounded from the porch. The doorbell rang.

"What's going on?" I asked again. "Where'd Warren go, Aubrey?" Aubrey remained sprawled on the floor.

"Why don't you answer the door, Thomas?" he asked, looking bored.

"It's your house, you do it," I snapped. The doorbell sounded again.

"You never told him," Danae said tersely. "Oh, Aubrey, you should have told him, I begged you. Oh, God." She brought her hands to her face.

"Thomas is a big boy, Danae," said Aubrey. "He can make up his own mind, can't you, Thomas?"

"Make up my mind about what?" Panic tickled at my spine. "Danae, please, what's happening?"

"I think you should answer the door, brother," Aubrey said, still so maddeningly composed.

"Well, it's your house, *brother*." I stood still, blood hammering my eardrums.

"Answer the door, Thomas."

"Answer your own fucking door."

"Answer the door."

"Fuck you!"

"Thomas, please," Danae said. "Just answer the door. Please." I ground my teeth. "If you ever cared for me —"

"Christ, cared?" I spat. "Cared? You haven't talked to me in weeks, Danae!" I loomed over her on the couch. "You ignore me, now you talk like everything's okay?" Doorbell again, a longer tone this time, its ringer holding down the button impatiently. "Who's outside, Danae? What's going on here? I thought we were past all this secret bullshit." Everything blurred as tears rimmed my eyelids.

"Please answer the door," she said. She hadn't moved when I approached, still sat rigid, staring me down. "I'm begging you, Thomas. If I ever meant anything to you, answer the door. Now."

Aubrey flapped his lips with irritation. "Get the door, Thomas."

"It's important, Thomas," Danae said. She put a hand on my leg. "Please."

I shoved her hand away. "Oh, it's important?" I yelled, taking a step away toward Aubrey. She groaned dejectedly. "It's important to Danae, Aubrey, did you hear that?" He nodded. "Is it important to you as well?"

"You have no idea how much," he said. So fucking cool.

"Shall I get the door then?" I kicked the game board away.

"Please."

"Well, sure, then." I stomped furiously to the front door. "Why not? Danae wants me to answer the door, Aubrey wants me to answer the door, well then, I'll just answer the door then! I mean, as long as it's so goddamned important to you two!" I put my hand on the doorknob and yanked the door open, screaming "WHAT?" at the top of my voice.

"Oh, I'm sorry, I must have the wrong house," the ringer said, taken aback. He looked to the house numbers on the outside wall in confusion.

"Uh," I gulped. "Uh . . . er . . . what . . ."

"BANZAI!" Warren hollered, tackling him low from behind, driving the two of them into me, sending the three of us hurtling inside. I lost my balance, tripped and fell, suddenly finding myself the base of a weighty, ungainly, sweaty pile of thrashing limbs. Warren spun himself off, pulling the screaming man along in a barrel roll until Warren was atop him, pressing his knees into the man's chest. A fist went up, came down. Knuckles collided with skin, a head bounced off the hardwood floor, and all went silent.

"Fucking awesome!" Warren yelled. Somewhere far away, Danae was laughing. Underneath Warren's knees, Munroe Purvis lay unconscious and bleeding.

I'll finish this up later, Eric. One or two more. Then I'll pull my D.B. Cooper routine. Promise.

Yours truly,
Thomas

DOCUMENT INSERT: Note found in inside left suit jacket pocket of Munroe Purvis (exhibit #139).

Dear Munroe;

Oh, gosh, I'm so embarrassed. I've never done anything like this before, really. But I may never have this chance again, so, here goes. I'm going to write quickly, before I lose my nerve.

I have wanted you ever since I first laid eyes on you. You are so kind, a generous, sympathetic person. I watch your show religiously, and, oh, hell with it, Munroe, you make me damp.

Watching you pour your heart out, so open, so giving, I practically come at the sound of your voice.

I don't want commitment. I know you'd never be interested in someone so ordinary. But, to be crude, I want to fuck you so badly.

If you feel the same, come to 728 Martel Bay after the show.

Please.

Eric:

Got to finish the story. All eyes on the bus follow me as I fumble my way down the aisle. The grocery clerk asks too many innocuous questions as to my plans for the weekend. I'm running out of places to type, FBI agents are lurking on every corner. Pictures of Munroe in the hospital still adorn the magazine racks. It's my fault, I know, drawing attention to myself instead of just withdrawing into obscurity. If I had disappeared, I could have passed into the stuff of myth. Legend has it, if you so much as crack open a Barbara Delinsky, you can hear the tortured screams of Thomas "Mad Monkey" Friesen echoing through the air.

You've seen the program, of course. It was never shown on television in its unedited entirety, but even if portions of Munroe's Winnipeg appearance hadn't already been broadcast on *60 Minutes* and *20/20*, bootleg copies are not hard to find. Try eBay. It's a big seller.

It was vintage Munroe. Page kept her promise to the producers; the program was a closed set, and no ne'er-do-wells would be crashing the festivities. Learning from the ruinous example of Agnes's appearance, attendance was permitted by pre-approved voucher only. A select group of Winnipeg business people and politicians known to be Munroe aficionados were comped in, with the rest of the three hundred seats going to a mix of radio contest winners and individuals wealthy enough to afford the two hundred dollar entry fee. Even at that price, tickets were snapped up as soon as they went on sale. The mayor was in attendance; fan or not, I can't say, but politically savvy enough to realize that being seen even peripherally in Munroe's presence could help him in future elections. There was a rumour, only a rumour, thank Christ, that he'd be renaming a street or a bridge in Munroe's honour, but I guess Queen Elizabeth's earlier visit to the city exhausted all available landmarks. An aging rock star or two made the list. Representatives from all major political parties. A few Blue Bombers and their wives. A disgraced former member of the city council. A local radio talk-show host. From a Winnipegger perspective, it was quite the show.

Munroe was in rare form, waddling to and fro, a bionic host bestowing upon his audience the sweat, saliva, and sycophantia of ten normal men. Everybody was a target for his patented blend of hugging and sharing. He forgave the former city counsellor for his sexual harrassment conviction, tears flowing on both sides of the embrace. Norman Lawton, local boy and Munroe's newest "authorial discovery," gave a spectacular, gut-wrenchingly awful reading from his novel *Picking Up the Peaces*. Fitness expert Reverend Donald McAdams led the audience in a vigorous set of jumping jacks to promote his new manual *The Holy Body and Spirit: Putting the Fundamentals BACK into Fundamentalism*. Watching Munroe, Lawton, and the mayor perform rigorous squat thrusts as the reverend shouted inspirational Psalms at them is entertaining for all the wrong reasons. In sum, it was an excruciating test of one's tolerance for saccharine, an assault on good taste, and an event everyone involved could be proud of.

Now, what was *not* picked up by the cameras; that was the important stuff. Protesters from the Manitoba Writers' Guild, picketing outside with signs proclaiming WE RECOMMEND MUNROE LEARN HOW TO READ! and DOWN WITH THE PURV! Meh. Barely worth a mention in the next day's papers. Lawton's book signing afterward rated a five-second clip on the late news, completely innocuous. And yet, in the background, just behind and to the left of Lawton as he chatted up the mayor, isn't that Munroe standing there, and doesn't he look a tad distracted? Flushed, even? Did he lick his lips? He was crumpling a slip of paper into his suit pocket, what could that have been, do you think? And that momentary flash of red on the periphery of the screen; could that have been the briefest glimpse of a dress, its wearer just beyond the camera's range? And wasn't Munroe tracking it with his eyes?

It was perfect in its simplicity. How do you kidnap someone? Make him come to you. Lure him with an offer so tempting he'd be bound to come. Promise him an ever-so-discreet round of Olympic-calibre rutting, topped by numerous eye-popping orgasms. Shroud the offer inside a wrapping so luscious and delectable that refusal would be tantamount to insanity.

And so, fairly unsurprisingly given all that, Munroe Purvis lay unconscious on the floor. At our mercy.

"WHAT THE FUCK HAVE YOU DONE?"

That was me. I was screaming at my fellow kidnappers.

"OH, CHRIST!"

I had begun to scream the moment Warren took Munroe down from behind, the *clunk!* of Munroe's head impacting the floor still ringing in my ears.

"OH, SHIT!"

I kept screaming as Aubrey quickly bound Munroe's hands and feet with duct tape.

"SON OF A BITCH!"

I maintained my screams as Warren and Danae dragged Munroe into the living room and Aubrey closed the blinds.

"AAHHH!"

And then Danae slapped me, and kept slapping me, and made it abundantly clear that the slapping would continue for as long as the screaming did. I finally succumbed to her persuasive pain dispersal. My face burned. "What have you done? What have you done, *what have you done,* WHAT HAVE —"

SLAP!

"Ow, stop that! Jesus!" I rubbed my cheeks.

"We need calm here, Thomas," Danae said. She held up her hand, its reddened palm toward me, prepared for another go-round. I flinched. "Are you calm?"

"Calm," I said. "Calm, I'm calm, stop hitting me."

"Warren, if he freaks out again, could you shut him up?"

"No worries, babe." Warren took a place next to Danae.

"I am *calm,*" I said, watching Warren's meathooks warily. "I am an oasis of calm, I'm placid, I'm the freaking Dalai Lama, all right? Calm. I am calm. Calm I am."

"How's our boy doing over there, Danae?" asked Aubrey, busy propping Munroe into a sitting position on the couch. Margarita, irked at having to share her space on its cushions, began nudging Munroe with her nose.

"He's fine," Danae answered. The soothing massage of her hands on my cheeks kept me quiet. "Thomas is going to be just fine."

"Good." He stood up, wiping his hands on his jeans, leaving a dark swatch of something thick and wet on the fabric. Munroe's blood, I realized with queasy horror, which was still flowing from his mouth, two teeth having shattered upon impact with the floor. Hysteria began to rise inside again, but the sight of Warren flexing his fists, anticipating another freak-out, quelled the attack. I settled for simple outrage.

I pointed at Munroe. "What is this?"

"This," said Warren proudly, plopping himself down aside Munroe's body and putting an arm companionably about his shoulders, "this, dude, is a blow for freedom."

"No no no, this, this is nuts," I said. Danae began lovingly stroking my arm, cooing tenderly. I shook her off, furious. "Stop treating me like a freakin' child! You knew about this? And you didn't tell me?"

"Thomas, honey, you've been a little too aloof lately. The three of us agreed that you couldn't be trusted."

"But you can trust me now, is that it?"

"They wanted to leave you out completely, but I convinced them you would come around."

"Don't blame Danae," Aubrey said. "If you had known ahead of time, well, I didn't think you'd take to this too willingly."

The enormity of what had just happened slugged me in the plexus, knocking the breath out of me. Black dots popped and zoomed before my eyes. "Oh . . . Christ, oh . . . the police —" The dots were swiftly congealing into one very large, very black, very inviting, all-encompassing hole in the middle of the room.

"Whoops," Danae said. "Guys, he's fading, make room!" She grabbed my arm before my legs could collapse beneath me. Aubrey grasped my other arm, halting my slide to the ground, and together they arranged me on the couch next to Munroe, shoving him over to the side so that his face was buried in Margarita's fur. She didn't seem to mind.

"Here, drink this," said Warren, holding a beer bottle to my lips. I inhaled the liquid into my lungs, reflexively spewing it back in their faces. "Sorry, dude."

I coughed, holding myself in a protective self-hug for a few minutes until reality decided to refocus itself. "The police," I finally said. "They'll be looking for him. We've got to get out of here."

"No one's looking, sweetie," Danae said, wiping the beer drool from my chin. "They won't even know he's gone until tomorrow, and even then, they won't know where he's gone. We're clear." Munroe snorted weakly beside me as Margarita shifted herself. "Warren, get his face out of her fur before he chokes on us."

Warren righted Munroe, still unconscious, his face now a painting of blood and wisps of dog hair. I began to assess what had happened. "What's he doing here, how —?"

Aubrey sat himself down across from us. "Thank Danae for that. She's the genius."

"Now, Aubrey, you laid the groundwork," she said.

"But you provided the masterstroke."

"Stop congratulating yourselves!" I snarled, grabbing the beer from Warren's hand. I pulled a long swig, concentrating on the bitter taste to help clear my head. They watched impassively as I kept drinking, draining it with a gasp. "Just tell me how he's here," I sputtered.

Danae twirled herself around, the red dress rising fetchingly about her thighs. "You think you're the only one who can't resist this?" she teased. "Munroe, at heart, is a skirthound, like I thought. It wasn't hard to catch his attention. An arch of the eye," and here she wiggled her eyebrows comically, "a shimmy of the hips," she bada-boomed her hips back and forth, "and he was putty."

"But *how* is he here?" I asked, impatient with Danae's cutesy act.

"She slipped him a mash note," Warren said. "We cooked up a real juicy one, made it sexy, promised Munroe to take him to the moon if he showed up here after his show. If it didn't work, no harm done."

"Oh, Munroe, I'm such a *huge* fan of yours!" said Danae, putting on a sweetie-pie voice. "Gosh, I know it's forward, but, I'll never have this chance again!"

"We made sure to promise anonymity, to sweeten the proposition," Aubrey said. "A night of mind-blowing sex in a guilt-free environment. All he had to do was get away from his people. Who could resist?"

"But," I sputtered, "what if he told someone?" I strained my ears, trying to hear the wail of approaching sirens. Nothing. "He would have told *someone*. He had to."

"Well, there's always an X-factor," said Danae, dismissing the problem with a perfunctory flick of her wrist.

I pulled my hair in anguish. "That's one fucking huge X! He could have left a note, or told his handlers, or . . ." I struggled to get to my feet. "Jesus, the cops are probably already on their way!" Aubrey shoved me back down.

"Everyone," Munroe moaned, coming around. "I told everyone, please, everyone knows I'm here." He opened his eyes and took us all in. "He's right, the police will be coming."

"Ubf!" Margarita struggled herself onto Munroe's lap.

Munroe licked his lips nervously, gagging slightly on the blood. "Please, I don't know who you are, but they expect me back any minute."

Warren crouched down, staring into Munroe's eyes for a good minute, until Munroe looked down. "Nope," he decided. "No, he didn't tell anyone." He grabbed hold of Munroe's chin and pulled his face up. "Did you, Purvis? Who did you tell, big boy?"

"Everyone knows, they expect me back soon, I swear it, please!"

"He's lying," Danae said. "He couldn't risk the scandal if they found out. Munroe Purvis out trolling for tail? Think of the headlines."

"They forgave Oral Roberts," I reminded her.

"Please, I . . . I don't know you, I never saw you, not clearly," Munroe pleaded. "I'll never tell. I don't know where I am, not really, I could never find you, even if I wanted to, please, please!"

Aubrey seemed to consider it for a moment. "Warren, gag the pig," he said finally.

Munroe began to squeal, "No, no, please, I, HELP! HELP! SOMEBODY HE—" before Warren mercifully cut him short, applying a liberal swatch of duct tape to Munroe's mouth. He moaned and kicked for a good minute before giving up. Margarita, undisturbed by his movements, set about falling asleep atop his legs.

"So, brother, shall we begin?" Aubrey asked me. "Warren, call the others, tell them to meet us by the pyre in an hour or so."

Warren made for the kitchen, then stopped and looked back. "Should I tell them why?"

"No. Judging from Thomas' reaction here, surprise might be a better choice. I trust their judgement, but this is something that they'll have to see to understand. It's too dangerous to give them a choice. They might not come otherwise." Warren left the room to begin phoning the Monkeys.

"What are you planning?" I asked. "Are you holding him for ransom?" I stood up cautiously. With the threat of Warren's size and violence momentarily gone, I got down to calculating the odds on a safe escape. I couldn't run far, they'd catch me. "What's the score, Aubrey? What do we do now?"

"You disappoint me, Thomas," Aubrey said. "You know what needs to be done." He began to pace. Munroe tracked him with large eyes. "This man is scum. Retribution is the only option."

"Meaning?" I took a step closer to him, standing next to Danae. She played her fingers lightly along my shoulder.

"This is our *fatwa*, Thomas," she said. She kissed me, a passionate slamming of lips that I did my best to avoid being aroused by. Fuck. "Think, honey. What is the inevitable outcome of such a command? What should a man such as this receive for his crimes?" She left my side and grabbed Munroe by the hair. He yelled in pain beneath the tape. "Do you feel pity, Thomas? For *this?*" Munroe's head rocked back and forth as she yanked. I imagined I could hear his scalp ripping from the strain. "Aw, does Munwoe not wike dat?" she asked him, pretend baby-voiced, as he whimpered with each pull. "Doesn't he deserve everything he gets?" she whispered in delight.

And as shocked as I was by Danae, completely astonished by her capacity for cruelty, down in my belly, a part of me was turned on by the inner savagery of her nature. I wanted to join her, kiss her all over, and beat the bejesus out of Munroe. Sitting there, mewling, at our mercy. Every tormenter I had ever suffered at the hands of, they were slumped in front of me, sobbing. Every bully. My rage at who he was, what he represented, began to rise. He was the antithesis of what I believed humanity at its best should be, a lumpy mix of gross opportunism and wilfully blind fundamentalism, holding everyone back for believing they ever had a choice in how they lived their lives. I watched Danae, slithering herself over Munroe's body in a parody of copulation. She was shining, a goddess of malice and spite in a blood-red uniform. At that moment, I would have joined her, willingly. I would have dropped down on my knees and begged forgiveness for my weakness.

"Look at him, Thomas," Aubrey hissed in my ear. I hadn't realized he was so close. "Isn't he pitiful?"

I nodded yes.

"You can't wait to tear into him, can you?"

I shook my head no.

"You can taste it, same as us."

Yes.

"You're one of us."

Yes.

"You know what needs to be done, to complete the *fatwa*. The only solution, brother. Death."

The word sliced itself through the haze.

"Death to the infidel."

I spun, raising a fist, and launched the first honest-to-God punch I had ever thrown in anger. Caught unawares, Aubrey instinctively took a step back as I turned, subsequently moving the target I had hoped for, causing my fist to collide solidly with his chin. He staggered back, falling over as he slipped on a tattered paperback. "ow!" we both yelled, his yell in surprise as he fell, mine from the shooting pain that shot through my hand. I cradled it over my left forearm. "I think I broke it," I whined.

"Thomas, what are you doing?" Danae berated. She helped Aubrey up to his feet. "Aubrey, are you okay, hon?"

"Yeah, I'm okay. Good punch, brother."

"My hand is broken over here!"

"Warren, could you get some ice from my freezer?" Aubrey yelled. "Thomas has hurt himself!"

"No prob!" Warren hollered back. "I've almost got everyone."

"Broken hand, hello?" I complained. I didn't think it was broken, actually; the fingers moved without too much difficulty. But the knuckles were already beginning to swell with bruising.

Warren walked back in. "Everything okay, boss?"

"Fine, Warren," said Aubrey. "Thomas just had a momentary crisis of faith. He's okay now. Right, Thomas?"

I shrugged. Warren tossed me a plastic bag loaded with ice cubes. "Hold that on the knuckles, it'll cut the swelling." I did as he told me, sighing as the cold numbed my hand.

"I think we'd better get started, now that Thomas has that out of his system," Danae said. "Warren, you get everyone?"

"Almost, five more to go. Everyone's coming so far."

"Good," said Aubrey. "You finish calling. Danae and I will go move Munroe's car around back, keep it hidden." Danae fished the key from Munroe's pockets, slapping him when he began to moan again. "When we're done, we'll head out back, get the fire nice and hot. Thomas, you get to work."

"Work?" I asked.

"Work, counsellor, work." Aubrey clapped a hand on my shoulder. "We're not animals, Thomas, no matter what you think. You're in this now, all the way. Munroe will get due process, like all our 'tags. If he's innocent, we'll let him go. Promise."

"Innocent? Of what?" Bile formed in my throat.

"That's for you to figure out, if you haven't already." Aubrey gathered up Margarita under his arm, giving me a wink as he followed Danae from the room. "You're his lawyer, after all." My mouth remained gaping for a good long time after he exited.

Cue the bombastic John William score for emphasis. Bum, bum, BUM! Narrator's voice: "Tune in for tomorrow's exciting conclusion, *Death Reads a Book!*"

Yours,
Thomas

FILE # 09978

DOCUMENT INSERT: Journal entry of Thomas Friesen.
From patient files of Dr. Lyle Newhire

It all comes down to this, doesn't it? All the talk, the group therapy, the crying, the denial, the meds (ah, the blessed meds!). Still need to cover the day that cracked this nut. Otherwise, how will you ever achieve closure? Why did Thomas try to cross the road? What was on the other side? Was it candy? You know, if all attempted suicides knew that homework would be the ultimate outcome of their cries for help, they'd try a little harder to finish the job.

Three months, doc. That's how long I articled. Not even a year, couldn't even manage one simple year. Some folks last for decades, their mental illness out for all to see. Me, I go minutes. Couldn't last long enough to qualify as a failure. Three months of bail hearings, harried public prosecutors, judges who couldn't care a whit for your clients, and clients who cared for themselves even less. Rapists. Assaults. Eleven-year-old car thieves. Fetal alcohol syndromes by the dozens. Two or three people who couldn't remember their own names. It's not that they didn't deserve representation; competent and committed representation by trained individuals. People said this to me all through law school. "It's important work. Everyone has the right to legal counsel. It's in the Charter of Rights and Freedoms. It's what makes our society so gol-dang wonderful. But, really, why would a nice young man such as you ever choose to defend such people? I mean, do the crime, do the time."

They needed someone, that's why. And I cared for them all.

Lawyers are cold fish, that's what people complain. Never listened to our feelings. Treated us like a job, not a person. There's a reason. Lawyers go nuts otherwise. Getting emotionally involved in the life of someone too dense to realize that breaking into someone's house to steal a clock radio will probably get them into trouble, that will drive you over the edge, guaranteed. But it's just a radio, man!

You cannot allow yourself to care, cannot worry about their well-being, must treat them like the work product they are. Crash and burn is the only alternative.

Case in point.

I can't tell you her name. Can't describe her face. Was she blonde? I wouldn't let myself see her, had to keep calm. Had to maintain a professional distance. She was eighteen, still had that new-adult smell. No more youth centres in her future. Remand or worse from here on in.

"Why am I here, I don't understand."

Keep head down. Focus on page. "According to the report, they picked you up at three this morning?"

"Yeh, needed cigarettes. That a crime now? Fuckin' Winnipeg."

"You've been living at Manatonkwa House?"

"Yeah, they make me stay there."

"You left the centre at three in the morning for cigarettes."

"Yeah."

Maintain. "You're not allowed out after ten."

"Yeah, but I'd be right back. I needed a smoke, man."

"You knew you weren't allowed out. You sneaked out. This violates your agreement with the court."

"Man, I needed a fuckin' smoke." Harder now. Trying to get me to see the reasonableness of her actions.

"You couldn't wait?"

"Why'd they pick me up, I wasn't doing nothin'? I was just walking."

"One of your keepers called the police. You weren't supposed to leave. You knew this. That's why they picked you up. They were out looking for you."

"Yeah, so, get me out. I hate it here." A quiver in her voice. Don't look up. Play with my tie instead, study the pattern.

"Honestly, I don't think I can. You broke the rules of your release."

"They aren't hard enough."

Shit, I looked up. "What?"

"The rules aren't hard enough, they're too easy to break." Thick liquid in her eyes. "I need harder rules, that way I'd follow them."

Staring at her. She's serious. "So. You can't follow the rules they gave you, but *harder* rules now, that would help, that's what you're telling me."

Open tears. "Yeah. These ones are too easy, too easy, more rules would help, I'd follow them then, tell them that."

"These were the harshest rules of release outside of prison. There are no more."

"I want out."

"I can't get you out. You've shown the court no ability to follow the judgements they've given you. You've had every chance. This is your fifth violation in two months. I have nothing to show the court that you are in any way willing to help yourself." Start packing up the files, business as usual. Go home, have a beer, watch TV, *Law & Order* maybe, zone out.

"I want to see my kids, c'mon, they'll never let me see them if I go to jail."

"Kids? You have kids?"

"Yeah, two. My mom's got 'em. They're never gonna let me see them, you gotta get me out."

"Kids." Kids. Plural of kid. She's eighteen. Barely.

"I woulda had more, but I got a couple abortions." There's no stopping the crying now. Big, snotty tears gush out. "The last one was a septic abortion, where the womb gets infected, y'know? Really fucked up. So that one hadda go."

"Septic."

"Yeah, so you gotta tell the judge, I need to see my kids, so I'll be better now, I've figured it all out see, I'll be good for my kids. Tell the judge that."

"But you haven't been good."

"But I will now."

"But you haven't."

"But I will now."

"You tell me then. What can I tell the judge that will prove you'll follow the rules? What makes this time so different from last time?"

"   . . .   "

"And the time before?"

"   . . .   "

Close the briefcase, stand up. Keep voice steady. Look her in the eyes. "I'll see what I can do, but it doesn't look good." Grab the doorknob. "I'll talk to you tomorrow. Goodbye."

"No, don't!" She's leaned across the table, she's grabbed my hand. "C'mon, don't be like that, c'mon, don't leave, I'll be good. Promise."

"I'm sorry, I don't know what else we have to say."

"We don't have to talk, just . . . don't leave, okay? Stay?" Her fingers stroke mine, play melodies on my knuckles. "We don't have to talk, you don't wanna. We could do, y'know, somethin' else."

I'm dense beyond imagination. All I can picture is myself getting out of this room, out of this building, breathing clean, wonderful, automobile-polluted air. "What?" I ask, barely registering her hands now creeping up my arm, pulling me down, closer to the tabletop.

"We could, y'know, I dunno, y'know, fuck?" Her left hand crawls away from me, down her shirt, begins to unzip her jeans. "Wouldn't you like to fuck me? Hey? Touch me here?" She massages herself, moans in pleasure. I glance up, try to find a guard, anyone, someone to barge in and stop this. No one in sight. Either they don't care, or this is a common happening. "C'mon," she says, pulling my hand toward her, rubbing it against her crotch. "C'mon, do this for me, huh? Lawyer-man? Sir? Get me out, we're gonna have good times. Promise." She's let go of my hand, it's moving on its own now, kneading her, I'm not paying attention, I'm watching her face, her breasts, her eyes, she fumbles at my belt. I can't breathe. "Promise. Just . . . get me out."

I wrench myself away. Grab my briefcase, tuck myself back in, pull up my zipper. Try to apologize, say something, can't talk, nothing to say. Open the door. Walk down the hall. Buzz for the exit.

"Hey."

Don't look back.

"Hey, come back."

Don't listen. You don't hear her. You don't hear anything. You don't feel anything.

"Fuck you, faggot!"

She's a case file. A client. Words on a page. Not your fault she's here. Nope. She's not even real. You made her up. You just walk away, out the doors, down the front stairs to the sidewalk. You take it all in, the premature darkness of winter, the tinted highbeams, the sound sound sound sound of horns bleating as you stride into traffic. When the car hits you, you don't even care. You can't feel the pain when your head bounces off the curb. When they bundle you up tight on the stretcher and load you into the soothing bay of the ambulance, all you think is, thank Christ, I don't have to go in to work tomorrow morning.

TO: ermccorm@yahoo.ca
FROM: iamashelfmonkey@gmail.com
SUBJECT: climax

Dear Eric,

So tired. Pawned the laptop, didn't even try to haggle. I should have just enough to pay the café for this e-mail. It's a big one, but I'm finishing this now. Enough fucking foreplay. Chug the coffee, head down, type.

I took a moment to gather my thoughts.

What the fuck what the hell fuck fuck what the fuck?

My thoughts were in more disarray than the room I stood in, scattered around the floor of my mind like so much useless trash. Munroe's groans brought me back into focus. I waved my hands to clear away the imagined miasma. The tide ebbed away slightly, slowing its current, creating an eddy around my navel. Satisfied, I waded over to Munroe. A bubble of bloody snot expanded and relaxed from his nostril with every frenzied breath, refusing to burst. I studied it, mesmerized. The sphere's rhythmic dance cleaned my head. The lake evaporated, leaving me, Munroe, and the reflective surface of the globule alone to make small talk.

"Are you all right?" I asked.

"Mmmph!" Munroe replied. His response broke the bubble's surface tension with a tiny *plip!*

"I'm going to take the tape off your mouth, all right?" I grabbed an edge of the tape, then stopped. I took his face in my hands, staring him down, smearing blood over my palms. "You've got to trust me. If you yell or scream, I'll put it right back. There's no one even remotely within hearing, so it'd be a useless gesture anyway. You understand?" He nodded. I reached for the tape again, then had an idea. "Hey, you have a cell phone?" Head shake, no. Shit. Could I not catch one break? Did I even have a choice anymore? I considered that perhaps this was all pre-ordained; I was a character on a page, trapped in the alcohol-energized writings of a failed writer. I strained to hear the typing of a keyboard. Fuck was I losing it.

A rattling in my front pocket roused me. Pills! I struggled the breathmint tin out and popped the lid, threw my head back and poured the contents out, more capsules missing my mouth than hitting, probably saving me from an overdose. Gagging as the dry pebbles bounced down my trachea, I closed my eyes and lay still. Surprisingly, the stereo was still on, Miles Davis still birthing cool. I concentrated on a solo, picturing the notes pushing the cartoon obscenities out my ear. Munroe was still there, watching my crackup with a scowl. Sighing, I leaned over and tenderly peeled the duct tape away from Munroe's mouth. A thick blood and saliva slurry poured out as he gasped for breath. I wiped my hands off on his jacket, taking care not to jar my knuckles. Now what? Go with what you know, I thought. Grabbing a pad of paper and a pen from a nearby shelf, I sat down on the couch next to him. "Now, first thing. I have been appointed counsel in this matter. I'll need some background. What's your full name?"

"Counsel? What's going on?" Munroe said. The blood coated his chin in a slimy red goatee. "Please, you've got to help me. Please. You obviously aren't a part of this. Let me go, I won't tell anyone. We could go together."

"You must really be out of it, you think I'm that stupid," I said. Munroe sobbed a response, pushing his head back into the couch in despair. Despite myself, I felt sorry for him. "You want some water or something?" I asked. He shook his head. "Beer?" He nodded. "You want a glass, or you okay to drink from the bottle?"

"Bottle'd be fine. Thank you." I fetched a Two Rivers from the fridge, Warren watching me warily from the phone. I smiled, hoping he'd take it as proof that I was part of the team. Warren just scowled, turning back to his calling.

Munroe slurped greedily at the bottle's mouth as I held it to his lips. Presently, he sat back with a burp, the bottle almost empty. "Thank you."

"Don't mention it."

"Please let me go."

"You start that, the tape goes back. You want that?" He shook his head. I picked up the paper. "All right then. Name?"

"Munroe Frederick Purvis."

"Age?"

"Fifty-three."

"That young? Huh. Place of residence?"

"What does that . . . Berry, Wisconsin."

"Nice place?"

"If you like Wisconsin."

"Do you understand the charges against you?"

"Absolutely not." I stopped writing. He looked at me expectantly. The beer had calmed his nerves somewhat, and he regarded me levelly. "I'm sorry," he said, "if you expect me to understand what I'm doing here, I really don't have a clue. Is it money?"

"You haven't figured it out yet?" I asked.

Something happened. Something dark and terrifying shifted deep within Munroe. He took a deep breath. "Figured it out?" he shouted at me. I recoiled instinctively. "Figured it out, you cock-sucker?" His face changed, hardened itself. The pudginess of his cheeks deflated somehow as his lips curled themselves into a sneer. I sat stock-still, terrified. I felt like those bystanders who happen to be nearby when Bruce Banner gets upset. Munroe Purvis the television host left the building. Munroe Purvis the businessman had just walked in. He fluttered his lips as he exhaled. "Look, all I know is I just wanted to get laid, buddy. Didn't expect the reception I got. What is this about? What, is she your girlfriend, is that it? You slamming her? You jealous? She is a fine piece of ass, no question."

I slapped him. Solid. Satisfying. Munroe's head bounced back into the couch. Blood shot from his mouth with the force, spraying the wall. I yelped as my hand reminded me that it was not in the best of shape at the moment. Munroe waited a moment to see if I'd continue, then he smiled. "No, you haven't tapped it. You want to, though."

"It's all an act, isn't it?" I asked. "All of it. The toadying, the, the bootlicking, the love. The whole image." I was genuinely shocked.

"Duh. What, you think someone could be that wishy-washy and still stay number one in his time slot? Of course it's an act, dickhead. Jesus Mary Mother of God." He leaned forward and spit onto the floor. "Now," he said, "what the fuck you cunts want?"

"Do you understand the charges?" When faced with the inexplicable, stay the course.

"Why don't you explain them to me, chief, as you're so touchy." I wiped his blood off the bottle's lip and drained the remaining beer down my throat. I was beginning to sweat, the room more humid than it had been a moment ago. Munroe leaned himself back, reclining comfortably. My hand shook as I drained the bottle. "You getting nervous there, champ?"

"Don't talk to me," I said, throwing the bottle away. It bounced off the wall and hit the floor, where it rolled itself away under the couch, unbroken. I stood up and began to pace. "You don't know what trouble you're in. This is serious shit going on here, I'm trying my best to help."

Munroe snorted. "Trouble, you think? This is trouble?" he asked. He leaned even further back, his eyes boring into me. Perspiration ran down my armpits. "You don't know trouble. 'Nam, now, *that* was trouble. Squatting in a foxhole, praying that you're faster on the draw than the other guy. Trouble. I'm sitting on a couch, getting slapped by a little girl. Why don't you tell me what trouble this is, that I'm in? Seeing as you're the one who's sweating and all."

Oh God, Munroe was giving me a Vietnam remembrance speech. I was in Hell. I coughed into my hand, trying to compose myself. "You are on trial for crimes against humanity."

He laughed politely. "I admit the show bites, but a war crime, that's a little severe."

"You admit the show sucks?"

"Hey, c'mon, I'm just trying to make a buck, same as everyone else," he said. "Yeah, the show sucks, of course. Pandering to fat, stupid *hausfraus* about how goshdarn wonderful their goddamn insignificant lives are? Christ, of course it fucking sucks. That's a crime, I'm guilty. But that's not what this is about, is it?" I shook my head. "No, your pals Fuzzy and Monstro out there don't strike me as the TV couch potato critic types. You neither. Is it money? Because that I got. You say the amount, I write a cheque, get it certified for you no sweat. Promise I won't press charges. Honest Injun. Scout's honour. We can sweep it all under the rug. Can't have Mrs. American Fat Ass Housewife knowing that I've got weakness for screwing, can I?" His face rearranged itself back into harmless host mode. "I've got my fans to think about, after all,

God bless them, every one."

"This isn't about money."

"Then what? Ask, and ye shall receive."

"This is about the books." Jeez, even as I said it it sounded lame.

"The books?" he asked. I nodded dejectedly. He looked scared. "My profits, you mean? My accounts?" I shook my head. His eyes searched me over in confusion. Then his smirk returned, widening into a full grin, the teeth stained cherry red. I felt sick. "The books? Books? *My* books? I've been kidnapped over fucking BOOKS?"

I ran my good hand through my hair. "Yeah," I said, "something like that."

He roared. Blood-specked saliva flew as his laughter echoed off the walls "BOOKS!" he hollered. "Oh my God, and I was worried!" His laughter seared my eardrums. "Books! I've been booknapped by librarians! Oh, help, help, help!" he screeched in a mincing falsetto. "Dewey Decimal has me in his clutches! Help!"

"Shut up!"

"Oh, fuck you, bookworm!" he yelled back. A contented, contemptuous sneer settled itself on his mouth. "Books. Fuck, do you have any idea who I am? The minute I'm noticed gone, the *minute*, the FBI is going to be all over you like lice. Get prepped for twenty years of getting rammed up the ass, buddy! And I'm gonna get a front-row seat. Hey, maybe I'll keep the slut out of it, hey? Do her a favour. Keep her on the side, like. Fuck her while cellmate Bubba fucks you." I punched him in the nose, my good hand this time. I was getting good at this. He shrieked with pain, but his sneer remained. "You're gonna freaking die, asshole, and I'm gonna pull the switch!"

I pulled away from him. We stared at each other, wheezing. "That's no way to talk to your legal counsel," I said.

"I don't know what's funnier: you losers, or the fact that I fell for it." He rocked his head. "Tail. Always tail. Thought I'd know better by now."

"So you really didn't tell anyone. Why would you be that stupid?" I was gobsmacked. It had at last sunk in that if Munroe hadn't shown up, I'd be sitting down with my friends, commiserating over beers and a mutually shared toke. We'd laugh and giggle, and maybe cry a few nerdy tears over the Purvisization of the world. They would keep their plans to themselves, and I'd be none the wiser. Or maybe they'd confess when it became apparent Munroe wasn't coming. We'd laugh uproariously over our failed attempt at a criminal act. Everything would have been *right* again. Friends to the end, one for all, all for one, huzzah. And now this? All because Purvis wanted to get laid? I yelled in his face, "Why the *fuck* couldn't you control yourself?"

"Huh," he said softly. "Look at me, will you? Look at this." He shoved his belly forward toward me. "Look at *these.*" He puffed out his cheeks. "I have gone through my entire life looking like this. Smarter than everyone else, should have been admired for my intellect, really a natural born leader, but stuck in this thing? Not fair. Didn't even get laid until I got up the gumption to pay for it.

"Thought the army would help, be all I could be, work off the fat. Stupid idea. Ended up getting dropped into jungles with assholes with guns who treated me worse than the gooks. And still, nothing changed. This fucking *thing,*" he poked his chin down at his fat, "it made me less than nothing to them. I survive, get home, think maybe now things'll be different. I'm a man at last. And still, *this.* A hopeless fat fuck everyone feels sorry for. A loser, like you.

"But now, *now,* all of the sudden, people listen to me. They want to hear what I say. Why'd it happen, I don't know. Had a cable access show in North Dakota, for fun, making the most of my communications degree. Had to do something after the army, I wasn't staying there. People started watching, they liked it, started talking. I built up a fan base. Thing is, they didn't get it. I was making fun of them. I hated them. I was showing what I thought was satire on their pathetic lives, the things they thought were important, because they were good, honest, white people who couldn't see anything outside their homes, and couldn't understand why they should care about anything but themselves. I was making fun of them, and the people didn't see it, they thought I was serious!

"God, they were so pea-brained stupid, so fucking stupid, all of them. Every day, I coddled them, smiled and capered, told them they actually mattered, the rest of the world was evil and corrupt and vile but they, *they* somehow had got it right. I got on my knees and sucked them long, hard, and raw, and they loved it. So I thought, hey, you want, you got. People have treated me like shit for so long, it's about time I took them for all they're worth. And it is bottomless, this pit. There is no problem that can't be blamed on someone else. Democrats, immigrants, faggots; *anyone,* just so long as I don't have to account for my pitiful little existence as the end product of anyone's fault but my own. After all, *I* love God. *I* love America. How could anything be my fault?

"But still, there was always this face, this body. Everyone loves me, no one wants me. I spend my whole life now, making them feel better about how utterly hopeless they are, they're right and everyone else is wrong, but still, who'll fuck me? Front page of *People.* My own publishing company. A media empire is forming, buddy-boy, this is only the beginning. I'm rich, I'm powerful, and I'm alone. Who'd want this? Freaks, that's who. Sexual losers and deviants. I get so many invites from these people, ugh, they make me sick. These people, because I look like them, I should be with them, right? I should take what I can get, I know, I tell myself this, but I could never bring myself to . . . that. And believe it or not, paying for it gets old really fast. Too risky now, anyway.

"Now and then, though, you get that one woman, somehow, who wants you and who you want back. It's not love; most of these women are so stupid I feel guilty afterward. But I'm only human. And her, well . . . *look* at her. She's the complete package. Could you refuse? And should I be punished for it?"

I sat on the floor. Cognitive dissonance burrowed itself into my brain. The Munroe I knew from television, the energetic dancing prancing suck-up, replaced by this? An angry, bitter man bent on revenge, using those who tormented him all his life to placate his loathing. I didn't want to know this; I'm not so deluded as to not see the similarities.

"You have some serious problems," I croaked. "Have you ever sought therapy?"

"Advises the kidnapper."

"Touché."

"Besides, this is better than therapy. I can say whatever I want, and you'll tell no one. Besides, even if you did, who'd believe you? You just kidnapped a universally beloved television personality.

They'll stone you before you get one word out." He tested his nose, wriggling it up and down, wincing as he flared the nostrils.

"You want some ice for that?" I asked, feeling stupid.

"No, it's fine," said Munroe. "You're not that strong. I don't think it's broken anyway, just sore." He awkwardly moved his head, wiping his face against the couch.

I pushed myself up, making myself comfortable on the couch next to him. "But couldn't you just stop?" I asked, trying to sound calm. "You've made enough, you've made whatever point it is you wanted to, why not just walk away, if you hate it so much?"

"It'll never be enough," he said. "No matter how much, there's always more to have. I'll never stop."

"How about just stopping the book club?" I asked. I was grasping at everything I could. "These people are serious, and I can't stop them. I don't even know if I *want* to stop them. Drop it, maybe they'll let you go then. That's all Aubrey cares about. Maybe we could make this all go away."

"You believe that? You think he'll let me go? You really think I'd just let all this go?"

"No."

"Fucking right I won't. I never let the fuckers win, not them, not you. I'll play along. More evidence for when they fry you."

"We don't have the death penalty in Canada," I said. It didn't seem to faze him. Didn't make me feel any better either. "You understand how serious these people are? I am the only thing standing between you and an angry mob."

"A mob of bookworms. Excuse me if I don't defecate in terror."

"You admit, the books are shit."

"Doy." Munroe spit another bloody stream to the floor. "Of course it's shit. It's all shit. I tell them it's gold, they rush out and buy it. Gives the mouth-breathers the feeling like they're intellectuals. Ooh, look at me, reading a book, if the boys at NAMBLA could see me know. Everyone watches Oprah, suddenly they all think they can write a book. Course, no goddamn way she'll publish them, that bitch can read, she has a reputation. No way. So they come to me. I had manuscripts up the ass, so many everywhere. Fuck, I didn't even read them, just had the idea. You get someone who doesn't have a clue, pisses all over themselves when you notice them, and have them sign their life away.

"Agnes, boy." He made a face of mock shame. "She is so trusting, right? Sitting there at her kitchen table, pouring her heart into this shitpile of a book. She would have kneeled down and blown me in public when I agreed to help, and smiled when she swallowed. Sure, she's comfortable. She's a star now, she meets the people she sees in *People*, she's ecstatic. Too stupid to even consider getting an agent of her own. She needs an agent, I suggest Kura. He's my agent too, so I figure what the hell. Talk about no scruples, he'd push his mother down the stairs, there was a dollar in it for him. And the others? Same thing. Not one of them smart enough to realize they're getting screwed. Do you know what I make in residuals from these things? Shit, I'd quit now, I wasn't having so much fun!"

"Man, you are *ice*," Warren said. He'd walked in sometime during the last few minutes of Munroe's diatribe, hanging back by the kitchen. "I cannot *wait* to fry your righteous ass!"

"Ah, Gigantor, you're just in time. I think I'd almost convinced the retard here to let me go." Munroe winked at me. "Isn't that right, sport? I feed you some sob story, and you get all weepy-eyed."

"You really don't know when to quit, do you?"

"Let me tell you something, the both of you assholes." Munroe yawned in boredom. "I'm holding all the cards here, boys. You two, the others, you are all now officially fucked. Only question is, how bad are you going to get it?"

"Okay, everything's set," Aubrey announced as he walked in. He tossed a snow-coated Margarita onto Munroe's lap. "Car's hidden, Danae's getting the fire a-blazing. Warren, the calls're made?"

"Check," Warren replied. "Man, you should listen to this guy talk, brother. He is all kinds of seriously fucked up."

"Said another kidnapper," Munroe murmured.

"No doubt," said Aubrey. He looked to me. "You get everything you need, Thomas?"

"No, uh, yeah," I said. My tongue was the Sahara. "Yeah, all set." I gave him a sarcastic thumbs-up.

"Well then, let's get a move on and fry this fucker!" Warren hooted.

Aubrey shushed him with a look. "Please, brother, a little

restraint. This is a solemn occasion, after all. A grave injustice is about to be righted tonight." He hunched down before Munroe. "And what about you, Mr. Purvis? Any words before we begin?" Munroe sighed something, an inaudible response. "I'm sorry, I didn't catch that," Aubrey said, leaning in close. Munroe hawked and shot. A bloody glob of spit landed on Aubrey's face.

"Did you catch that, asswipe?" Munroe said. "Clear enough for you?"

"Clear enough," Aubrey agreed, and forced a tennis ball into Munroe's mouth, reapplying the duct tape over it. "The festivities are about to commence, brothers," he said to Warren and me. "I suggest you get ready. Warren, if you would be so kind as to haul Mr. Purvis outside when you are ready?" Warren left to look for his jacket. "Thomas, have you prepared Mr. Purvis's rebuttal?"

"Rebuttal? Aubrey, have you any idea, has it even crossed your fucking mind how fucking screwed up this all is?"

Aubrey heaved his shoulders in a sigh. "Fine. If you want to leave, Thomas, then leave. We won't stop you." He stood to the side, motioning me to go. "Go to the police, tell them everything. I'm sure they'll get here in time. They'll take us in, arrest us and lock us away. You'll be a hero. Munroe here will make a star of you, I'm sure. Warren and I will rot in prison. Danae will rot. But you, you will be a hero. Maybe Munroe'll publish your story. Is that what you want? Will that make you feel better?"

"This is madness, Aubrey," I whispered. "Please don't make me choose."

"You've already chosen, brother," he said, drawing close to me. "When Vikram teased you, so many years ago, you chose. It's us and them now. No middle ground exists, not now, not anymore. You're either with us or them now." He pointed to Munroe, busy bouncing his lap up and down to rid it of its furry inhabitant. "You want to side with that, brother, you go ahead. You let that go, and you think of this world in five years. In ten. Where is it going to be? Where will you be?" This last sentence in an urgent whisper. *"Where will you be, brother?"* he hissed.

I couldn't help it, Eric. I loved Aubrey. I loved Danae, I think. I hated Munroe. Nothing made sense anymore except this. What I thought I loved versus what I was unquestionably sure I loathed.

The choice was clear.

"I'll do it."

Munroe grunted noisily behind the tape as Warren squatted and tried to position Munroe's body for a fireman's carry. After fussing with him for a good minute, it was clear Warren was not in the best of shape to hoist Munroe's ample frame with ease. Shamefaced, Warren grabbed Munroe by the feet. "Let's go, guys, time's a-wasting," he said, dragging Munroe out the door like a squirming sack of apples. Aubrey clapped my shoulder to follow.

"Could I have a minute alone, Aub?" I asked. "I need to clear my head, get my arguments together." I held up two fingers in the classic salute. "Scout's honour, I'll be good."

"I know you will. You're one of us, brother. You always have been." He stepped out into the cold. "Take your time, brother. The rest of us will be outside." He trod off into the snow.

And now is the point in the story where everyone reading this will scream, "Go for the phone! Call the cops!" Because that would be the sensible thing to do, wouldn't it? Why would someone stay in such a situation when they had a way out? I could give you the abused woman syndrome explanation: I thought they'd change their minds, I thought they'd never go though with it, I thought I could change them if I tried harder, I loved them and they loved me and everything can be fixed if I only show a little patience and understanding. It's all true; every justification for staying rushed through my thoughts. But in the end, I stayed because I wanted to. I wanted to see exactly what I was made of. I wanted to see how the evening would unfold (it had been a doozie so far), and I didn't want a contingent of police officers breaking up the party before the fireworks display. So I raided Aubrey's fridge for a beer, sat on the couch, drank it down, and weighed the pros and cons of the evening thus far. The wind rattled, and the walls of books groaned as the house shifted itself slightly. I stared at the bloodstains on the rug, considered the empty bottle in my hand, and couldn't come up with one good reason not to see this thing through.

I sullenly trudged my way out to the field. The congregation was there, vibrating in the cold. Danae and Warren huddled their heads together for warmth. Whatever fire Danae had managed to light had blown out, the coals glowing bright red as the wind blew past. Aubrey sat leisurely atop a lumpy, strangely shaped blanket, keeping what lay beneath it from the others. Margarita sat next to him, salivating and *ubf*ing contentedly.

"Yossarian!" Aubrey shouted as I approached. "The circle is complete!"

I nodded my hellos to the others, who looked more or less equally miserable. "Let's just get this over with, Aubrey," I said. Danae held back, holding Warren's hand. I guess I had to prove myself to her. Fuck, I can't believe I still cared. "Start the damn thing, let's do this."

"Calm yourself, friend," Aubrey said between chattering teeth. He spread his arms wide to the group, held them there as the wind buffeted his open jacket, ruffling his shirt. A black-red fire rose above him, his hair twisting angrily. "Brothers, sisters, I call to order this historic gathering of the Shelf Monkeys!"

"Aubrey, my 'nads are fuckin' cold," Gavin/Ford Prefect piped up. "What's the emergency, anyway? I thought we all agreed to just stay home tonight, try to forget Munroe's show." Hoots of agreement from the other Monkeys.

"In good time, Ford, in good time." Aubrey's continued insistence on pseudonyms wearied me. "First, let me put forth a question for you all. Exactly why do you think we were put here on the Earth?"

"Oh, Christ, it's too cold for this, I'm going home," Tracey/Lyra Silvertongue said. "I don't even have a 'tag for tonight."

"I've got one, something by Bertrice Small," said August/Raoul Duke, "a real stinker, let's toss it on, get some warmth."

"Yeah, Small blows," Cameron/Ignatius said. "Throw a Bertrice onto the barbie, what do you say, Aubrey, let's —" Cameron abruptly stopped, looking afraid. I guessed the hard look Warren zapped him with had something to do with it.

"We were placed here," Aubrey continued, "to right the wrongs of literature. To incinerate the infidels. To remind the world that books still matter. To bring to an end the tyranny of those who would foist their inferior prose upon us, who would feed us shit and have us call it ice cream!" This was getting tiresome fast. "And so, my Shelf Monkeys, in the spirit of the cleansing fire, I present to you, the ultimate montag!" He whipped the blanket off with a flourish. What lay beneath spilled out into the snow.

"Oh, my God!" someone yelled. Munroe writhed at their feet,

snuffling breaths through his bloody nose. Warren had blindfolded him with tape, bands of grey wrapped again and again around his head. Small, terrified grunts escaped from underneath the ball and tape.

"What have you done?" a tiny voice said, almost inaudible. "What is this?" It may have been Muriel/Lady Fuschia, I'm not sure. William/Valentine Michael Smith fell to his knees. Someone retched in the dark.

"I've struck a blow for our cause!" Aubrey was now dancing excitedly about, Margarita in his arms. "I'm bringing an end to the despotic rule of Munroe!"

"Ubf!"

"Oh, dude, this rocks!" That was Warren, joining in the celebration. He clasped Aubrey to his sunken chest, an enormous skeleton waltzing with Moses. Danae clapped her hands in happiness, the smile on her face more chilling than the wind. "Oh man, this rocks, this is gonna be awesome!"

"Stoke up the fire, Kilgore," ordered Aubrey. *"Hora fugit,* brother. The hour flies, and we have much to do tonight." Warren began throwing wood onto the embers.

"Much to do?" William/Valentine bellowed. "You fuck, what have you done?"

"We're going to jail, aren't we?" a hushed Burt/Gandalf asked.

"All will be explained, my friends," Aubrey said. He sounded so sensible, like a professor lecturing an exceptionally dense group of pupils. It was killing me.

"Yeah, let him explain," Danae said. "Let's hear him out, guys. Please?"

"How'd you get him?" asked Gavin/Ford. He had walked over to Munroe, still flopping about in the snow, and now stood over him in what looked like amusement. "I'm dreaming this, right? There's no way this is real." He nudged Munroe with his foot. "You real? Huh?" he asked, getting moans that were most assuredly ball gag-muffled obscenities in response.

"It's real," I assured him, lightly pushing Gavin away. "God help us, this is real."

"I like reality," said Aubrey. "It tastes of bread. Who said that? Proust? Anouilh? Anyway, this is reality at its tastiest, brothers and

219

sisters." He began to stride around the group, stroking Margarita affectionately in his arms. "We have been afforded an opportunity many of our ilk have wished for for eons. Thanks to the tireless efforts of myself, your muscular brother Kilgore, and comely sister Offred, we now have our chance for revenge. Here on this chilly night, where this dish is served to us most definitely cold."

"And now what?" Tracey/Lyra asked. "What, we kill him, is that it? How far are we prepared to go with this?" There was an aroused edge to her voice that caught me off guard. Munroe lay inert on the ground, gradually succumbing to hypothermia. "How can we get away with this? No one's looking for him? No one's gonna ask where he is?"

"Of course people will ask, let them," Aubrey replied, very sure of himself. Why shouldn't he be? He knew we were in the clear. "No one saw him drive up here, he was alone. He never told anyone he was coming. They won't know he's missing for hours!"

The world spun around me.

"Here's what we propose," he said, addressing the others. To my horror, they didn't all look equally terrified as I was. Not nearly. They were altogether too composed. Cameron/Ignatius, to his credit, looked vaguely ill. Gavin/Ford's face was beaming, smiling a wretchedly happy grin. There was a lunatic gleam in Valentine Michael Smith's eye that I did not care for. If Emily had ever once shown an unwillingness to participate, it had long since departed. In its place, unmitigated merriment. This, from the woman who threatened to leave our group if we so much as pranked Munroe.

"We must treat Mr. Purvis here with the respect and courtesy we give any proposed montag," Aubrey said. "Both sides of the issue must have their say. I will serve as the prosecution, while brother Yossarian has bravely offered to act as counsel for the defendant. The devil's own advocate, if you will. We will present our cases, leaving it for you to judge. The 'tag's ultimate fate lies in the hands of yon impartial jury."

"Solid plan," said Burt/Gandalf. "I can't believe this, but I'm in, all the way. But, what if we find him innocent? Do we let him go? Aren't we all, well, fucked?"

"Not at all, brother Gandalf, I assure you. As you see, the 'tag, like justice herself, is blindfolded. Your identities are assured to remain anonymous. Should the defendant be found not guilty, only myself, Kilgore, Offred, and Yossarian will take the fall for our actions. We are prepared to accept this eventuality. Isn't that right?" Danae and Warren nodded keenly. I shrugged noncommittally. "And, should the 'tag be found guilty for his crimes —" Aubrey reached into his pocket, drawing out two books and displaying the jackets aloft for our perusal. My heart sank as I read the titles. *Oh shit.* A faded copy of *Word Made Flesh* by Jack O'Connell, and Clive Barker's *The Books of Blood Vols. 1–3.* "His punishment shall fit the crime. We will turn him into something he hates more than anything else. We will carve him up into literature."

"Oh, that's perfect," Queequeg squealed. "We'll slice him up like bacon!"

"A book of blood, yeah," Scout Finch squeaked. "Wherever he'll be opened, he'll be red."

"That's goddamned poetic," Lady Fuchsia snorted in jubilation.

The Monkeys were nodding, capering, clapping their paws in agreement. Danae's eyes were alight with joy and bloodlust. Warren managed to re-ignite the pyre, and the Monkeys whooped with glee. On the ground, Munroe returned to life again, emitting a muted keen that could have been a scream of terror.

Watching him lie there, supplicant to our whims, oh, Eric, wasn't there a part of me that was gladdened by his situation? Seeing him squirm in terror, at the mercy of our cabal; could I admit to myself that a not very small portion of my conscience was rejoicing, singing hosannas, ecstatic at the vision of the mighty destroyer of all things good cowering at my feet? You bet I could. I wanted payback. Revenge. Ralph Emerson's recoil of nature, that's what I yearned for. I wanted Munroe dead. I wanted to slice him, dice him, burn his remnants, and piss on the ashes.

"Yossarian?" Aubrey asked, startling me from my bloodlust fantasy. "Shall we begin the trial, counsellor?"

I mentally sliced Munroe's throat one last time for good measure, then brought myself to look at Aubrey. The wind had picked up, angrily slamming itself into his side. His locks fought nonsensically amongst themselves. *Let's just butcher the pig,* I thought, *drink his blood and dance in his gore.*

Law school, however, was equally present in my soul. A respect for due process, even under conditions such as these. You don't sucker student loans for thirty thousand without picking up a few bad habits along the way. "You bet," I said. Aubrey smiled a full-wattage grin of love across to me. I smiled back, imagining Aubrey's trachea exposed by my bare hands as I ripped out his throat.

"Brothers and sisters," Aubrey began. He crouched beside Munroe, pulling him up into a sitting position. He put a comradely arm around his shoulders. "I present to you, the defendant, Munroe Purvis. I ask that you not let your emotions be unduly swayed by the more pitiful aspects of his current condition. A man is determined by his actions, not his image. Let us instead examine those deeds, a list so heinous to the beliefs of anyone with a lick of common sense that you will have no choice but to find Munroe Purvis guilty. Mr. Purvis has, through direct action and with malice of forethought, single-handedly lowered the expectations and quality of life for untold millions of his viewers." The Monkeys whispered excitedly. "He is scum of the highest order!" A snowball flew past me, striking Munroe dead centre of his face, knocking him flat.

"Objection!" I yelled out. Worried looks passed through the group. "Drawing conclusions without facts placed in evidence! Unfair characterization of the defendant!"

"Sustained," Danae said. "Stick to the facts, Don Quixote. And Hagar, dear, let's hold off on the snowballs?"

"Sorry," Hagar said. "Couldn't help myself." A few snickers escaped from the group.

"My apologies, your honours," Aubrey said, lobbing an evil look my way. What, I was supposed to go easy on him? I suspected the judges of bias, but held off on that accusation. "Let us examine the evidence. I am sure the facts will speak for themselves.

"Mr. Purvis has, in addition to his monthly club picks, released thirty-two works of fiction in the last year, all published by his vanity company MuPu Incorporated. Due entirely to his constant and tireless promotion of these works through his television program, these novels have each vaulted themselves to the top of every major bestseller list there is.

"Fact. Agnes Coleman's *My Baby, My Love* has sold more copies than the last novels of Philip Roth, Thomas Keneally, and Carol

Shields combined." Smart, that, using a local hero to engender feelings of resentment toward the accused. Not that much was needed anyway, but I thought it was a nice touch.

"Fact," he continued. "Mr. Purvis's recommendations are routinely challenged and condemned for their utter lack of even the basic tenets of quality storytelling. 'Utter trash, unredeemed even by choice of font,' says Harold Bloom in his review of Patricia Yellow's *A Dime or Two for Your Thoughts.* 'Indescribably awful, a wellspring of gagging bile that chokes you into unconsciousness,' Russell Banks designates Douglas MacDonald's *Jesus Rides Shotgun.* Margaret Atwood denounces Ian Falk's *Shame on All of You* as 'a failure on every level, even if charitably viewed as intentional parody.'

"Fact. Not only has the accused failed in every conceivable way to recognize and promote anyone with even the merest hint of talent, Mr. Purvis has gone so far as to denounce not only those who oppose him, but also to dismiss any book that he feels may strike the general population as challenging or incisive, and thereby of no value to his followers. He calls John Irving a hack. *Of Mice and Men* is too long by half. *To Kill a Mockingbird* made him sad and uncomfortable. He has labelled anyone not on his approved reading list as the product of overrated liberal agenda filth.

"Fact. Mr. Purvis is not only responsible for the publication of some of the most appalling shit —"

"Objection!"

"Overruled!" said Hagar Shipley, squawking with laughter. They were enjoying themselves immensely.

"— the most appalling shit to ever be printed, he has of late begun threatening to reissue novels whose copyrights have long since expired, rewriting them through careful study of the reactions of test audiences so as to appeal to today's less discerning, shorter attention span viewer. *Bleak House* updated into a less bleak pamphlet! *Gulliver's Travels,* minus the satire and the Lilliputians, to save time! *Moby Dick* in one hundred and fifty pages, fourteen point font, double-spaced, 're-imagined and set right' through the pen of the author of *The House I Done Built!* And the whale loses! Ahab gets his revenge, and sails away to further adventures. Test readers found the original ending depressing. The possibility of a sequel was deemed an uplifting and therefore more appropriate replacement." Queequeg wailed in protest. "Of all his crimes, this is perhaps the most heinous of all, the equivalent of dance remixes by those incapable of writing something new!"

He launched a well-placed kick into Munroe's mid-section, sinking his foot painfully into Munroe's layers of protective fat. Judge Lyra overruled my objection. "Ladies and gentlemen, brothers and sisters, I present to you Munroe Purvis. Millionaire. Talk-show host. Spokesman. Vanity publisher. Fraud. Criminal. I put it to you, there can only be one possible decision when faced with the magnitude of his sins.

"I call now for a decision of guilty. The world must be cleansed of the cancer that is Munroe. Do not let his crimes go unpunished."

I never had much opportunity to hone my skills at reading juries, but a blind man would have seen the venom Munroe's captors were spitting. Were they real monkeys, they would have thrown their feces at him. Shrieking, grunting, they pointed fingers and pulled hair in torment. They swung from the trees in anger. The tribe wanted blood, they craved a feast of skin and sinew. They would suck the marrow from Munroe's bones, play the xylophone on his ribcage.

Aubrey looked to me, delighted. "Your move, counsellor."

I rubbed my eyes with my palms, compressing the orbs to bounce fantastic colours off the insides of my eyelids, trying to settle my thoughts.

I could throw in the towel. Take a dive. Dine on roast pig, go home, throw up, and get on with my life. Maybe take out another loan, go for my Masters in Library and Information Sciences. Yeah, that'd be a piece of all right.

But he was a montag. The game had to play itself out. I thrust my chest out, threw on an intimidating cloak of Atticus Finch righteousness, faced the Supreme Court, and commenced oration on my client's behalf.

"Is Munroe Purvis guilty? Yes." Munroe moaned on the ground in disapproval. *Sorry, asswipe,* I thought, *you should always work with your lawyer, not against them. You get out what you put in.* "Munroe Purvis is clearly, unequivocally, unmistakably guilty of the crimes my esteemed colleague has presented you. He must be held responsible for some of the worst crimes put to paper since the hallowed days of Bulwer-Lytton himself. You don't like him? Fair enough. *I* don't like him. I look at him, and I see embodied in blubber every daily outrage in our newspapers. I see religious intolerance. I see bigotry. I see fear of the other. I see xenophobia, and warmongering, and deaths in the name of nebulous higher powers. I look at Munroe, and I see cultural terrorism yet to come on a scale I cannot comprehend. He has swiftly hijacked, subverted, and reduced our civilization to the lowest common denominator. I hate Munroe Purvis, and everything he has come to stand for."

What was my point, again?

"Yet, let us not condemn him outright. Munroe, for all his faults, is only a symbol of something far, far worse. A rallying point for the marauding hordes. A flag, nothing more. It is easy to revile that which we do not understand. This is what he and others want. If we condemn without comprehension, we might as well subscribe to FOX News and get it over with. We must fight those instincts that advise us to kill without reason. If we arbitrarily punish this man without introspection, we prove ourselves to be no better than those we criticize for narrow-mindedness and intolerance. I ask you, I beg you, we must not fall victim to this mindset. The question therefore is not *did* he commit these crimes, but *why*.

"I put it to you, brothers and sisters, to dare yourselves to ask, why? Is Munroe really that superficial and thoughtless a person? Or does there exist deeper meaning to his actions? Though this be madness, yet there is method in 't.

"I ask you to look at the accused. Study him. And ask yourself, why? I submit there exists a profound significance to his actions. Like him or not, Munroe Purvis serves an important purpose. He has shown to us, has revealed to the world, that the forces of ignorance are far stronger than we care to realize. Each week, Munroe pulls aside the curtain to expose modes of thought and belief that until now we have been content to ignore as a tiny quotient of the whole. Munroe has performed a public service. He has become more than a person, he is now a symbol, and if we bring the symbol down, we risk lending credence to his beliefs. He has given face and voice to the enemy. He has provided tangible targets for our rage. Remove him, and you risk the removal of the most accessible avenue that exists to this shadowy subworld of bigotry and fear.

"If Munroe Purvis did not exist, we would have to invent him."

I let the wind and snow assail my face for a minute. Munroe lay quiet, his whimpering long forgotten. The Monkeys crowded together, watching me.

"Don Quixote!" I yelled above the bluster. "Quixote! Offred! Kilgore! The rest of you! I submit that Munroe Purvis must be released! His crimes may be numerous and indefensible, but his value to our cause cannot be estimated!"

I bowed my head, exhausted. Rearranging deck chairs on the Titanic as it sinks takes a lot out of a man. It was a lost cause, but some of the Monkeys looked uncertain. Valentine Michael Smith bit his lip apprehensively. Lady Fuchsia and Gandalf clasped hands in misery. I didn't dare hope for a win, however. Lyra bared her teeth at me. Queequeg and Ignatius stared at Munroe's body like it was beef on a spit. At best, the confusion might allow for a mistrial, but I didn't think a hung jury was in the cards for me. Under the circumstances, such an outcome was pretty fucking unlikely. Perhaps a Hail Mary might be in order.

"Shelf Monkeys," I began again. "Some of you may have heeded my words. Some may have already made up your minds. But my client stands, sorry, *lies* before you now at your mercy. He is powerless. Will you not allow him the opportunity to speak in his own defence?"

Aubrey considered this, while Raoul Duke and Ford loudly derided me. "Very well, Yossarian," he said.

"Aw, fuck this shit!" yelled Scout.

"It does seem only fair, brothers and sisters. After all, we've never before had a montag that could speak for itself. Remove the gag."

I helped Munroe up to a sitting position, tenderly working the tape from his mouth and scooping the ball out, loosening another flood of saliva and bile. Munroe panted heavily and began to blubber. "Why are you doing this? Who are you people?" Munroe the ineffectual wimp was looking for leniency.

I flicked my finger against his forehead, getting a satisfying whimper out of him for my troubles. "Knock it off, you're not fooling anyone." I put my hands on the sides of his head. "I don't know if you have any hope here, but you just might," I said softly in his ear. "This is your only chance, Munroe, don't blow it."

"Please," he begged, "please don't hurt me, please. I'll pay you whatever you want, I won't go to the police, I swear I do whatever you want, please!"

"Munroe Purvis," Aubrey proclaimed, pulling his hood tight over his head. The Monkeys were crouched together behind him, swaying. "You sit before us charged with crimes against the humanities. Do you have anything to say in your own defence before we pass sentence?"

"What?" His head whipped around blindly, snot running down his chin, freezing to his moustache. "I don't understand, what do they mean?" His wandering hands found my pants leg and tugged me to him. "Please, don't hurt me, I'll do anything you want."

I yanked my leg away, leaving Munroe to sob into the ground. I wish I could lie and say I had been merciful. Make myself more sympathetic for the movie version. But I had no pity to offer. Munroe's dog and pony show was all a sham, and knowing it only made him more pathetic. I looked down at him, and all I felt was an itchy disgust. I wanted him buried in a pit of lime.

He stilled himself, slowly comprehending his position. "All right," he said. Again, the transformation was instantaneous. The snivelling little coward was gone. He pulled himself up to his knees. "All right, you fuckers, that is it." The Monkeys shrank back in confusion. Even blindfolded, Munroe stared directly at us. "I don't know what's going on, really, but you all need to understand a few things. You're nothing but a pack of losers. You sit at home and read, and pretend you're better than everyone else, you're so . . . *special.*" He spat a wad of blood, spraying my boots with a Pollock print. "You can all kiss my ass. You're no better than me. You fuckers better run, now, because when I'm done with you, you'll wish your fathers had never gotten drunk and raped your mothers. I am Munroe Purvis! I am worth sixty-five million dollars this year alone! Net! You pussies are going to rot in Hell, and I am going to laugh from Heaven above as you fry. Do your worst, you pissant little bookreading faggots. Assholes."

I've got to hand it to him. Munroe has balls. Little sense, but big balls. Any hope he had for clemency, however, went swiftly down the toilet.

"Have you anything further to submit, Yossarian?" Aubrey asked.

"No, that should do it."

"Shelf Monkeys, the montag has made its case." Aubrey turned to face us each in turn. "We have heard the evidence. Have you reached a verdict?"

"Guilty!" Danae yelled. But it wasn't Danae who spoke — it was Atwood's Offred, taking her sweet revenge on the religious patriarchy that condemned her to a life of forced fertility.

"Guilty!" agreed Warren, now completely Kilgore Trout, unwashed and misunderstood, pissing out obscure near-genius science-fiction stories.

Guilty, guilty, guilty, spreading like a virus through the group.

"Guilty." Lyra, saving the many worlds from the tyranny of an oppressive religious state.

"Guilty." Valentine Michael Smith, frothing at the mouth, clearly finding nothing in Munroe worth grokking about.

"Guilty." Scout Finch, all grown up and conveniently ignoring the lessons of Atticus.

"Guilty." Hagar Shipley, old and crotchety and unapologetic.

Aubrey laid his gaze on me. "How say you, Yossarian?"

"Yossarian?" laughed Munroe. "That's your name? What kind of stupid pansy pseudonym is that? One of the biggest wimps in post-war fiction, that's who you choose? Might as well be Holden Caulfield, biggest pussy of the twentieth century."

Well, that made it easier. "Guilty."

Aubrey pushed Munroe over with his foot. "Munroe Purvis, you have been tried and found guilty by a jury of your betters. You are hereby designated *hostis humani generis*, an enemy of the human race."

"Fuck you."

"You will now bear the punishment for your evil deeds."

"Fuck your mother."

Aubrey slapped the tape back over Munroe's protesting mouth.

"May God have mercy on your soul, Munroe Purvis." He strode to the far side of the fire, bending down to retrieve an object from its coals. The point of the large awl glowed a scorching red as he removed it from the flames. "Hold him down, everyone."

Kilgore grabbed Munroe's shoulders and pushed down, crushing him into the frozen ground. Offred sat atop his legs, Queequeg and Scout pinned his arms. Munroe bucked and tossed his bulk about to no avail.

Wielding the smoking tool, Aubrey straddled Munroe's torso and tore open the front of Munroe's shirt. Spongy pallid skin was exposed to the elements. Aubrey raised his arms to the stars, aimed the awl's point skyward, then dropped his gaze down to the sacrifice. "I do this for Shelf Monkeys everywhere." Aubrey dropped to his knees, settled himself on Munroe's mid-section, held the smoking awl like a pencil, and began to compose.

The aroma of seared pork arose from Munroe's chest. A sound like nothing I've ever heard escaped from the sides of the gag. An abattoir squeal. I fell back and vomited into the snow. Aubrey focused his attention on the lettering, stopping twice to reheat the tip, coughing to free his lungs from the odour. When he had finished, he fell back, sweating from the effort.

We hunkered over the raised letters, slowly making out what he had inscribed. *La Mancha,* and the rough outline of a windmill, teased from Munroe's skin in steaming welts.

Shakily, spastic tremors running up his arm, Don Quixote offered the awl to Queequeg. "You next."

Ten minutes later: *Moby Dick,* along with an uneven Maori facial tattoo dotting Munroe's cheeks and forehead.

The night went on, each monkey autographing Munroe in a butchered parody of English composition. Munroe had thankfully passed out halfway through Aubrey's labours. We were crazed, we were wrath. Scout threw up twice engraving *Mockingbird*, each time wiping her mouth and determinedly soldiering on. Lyra Silvertongue completed *Golden Compass* with relish, adding swoops and curlicues to her cursives. Laughing, Ford Prefect impressed a charred *Don't panic!* above Munroe's right nipple.

The body slowly became artistic attestation of our mania, a living library card.

Middle Earth, wrote Gandalf.

Breakfast of Champions, wrote Kilgore Trout.

Lady Fuchsia Groan flipped the canvas over and inscribed *Gormenghast* on Munroe's back, cackling like a madwoman.

Offred wrote *Handmaiden* across the chest.

Raoul Duke penned *Fear Loathing Las Vegas,* skipping the conjunctions.

Ignatius J. Reilly combined literature and personal feelings on Munroe's stomach: *Dunce.*

Valentine Michael Smith: *Grok,* perverting Heinlein's intentions.

Hagar Shipley: *Stone Angel.*

And I?

There was no question I would brand him.

It was wrong; I knew it then, I know it now. I was no longer Thomas Friesen. I was a force of nature. I was Hell, and my forces were legion.

I became unspeakable in my fury.

I pressed steel to skin. *Catch-22.* Followed by *Joseph Heller.* Followed by ©*1961.* I was damned if I did, and damned if I didn't.

Our manuscript complete, we gathered around it for a final proofread. Blood stained the snow. Munroe's harsh breaths were the only noise, save the occasional *pop!* of a pocket of air from the fire.

Danae took my hand. Her cheeks were red with excitement and frostbite. "Let's go," she whispered. "I need you. Now."

"What do we do now?" I asked in the silence, provoking a squeak from Gandalf. "We can't leave him here."

"I'll handle it," Aubrey said. He had lurked in the background while we mutilated Munroe, a feral dingo waiting for scraps while the monkeys, now a family of enraged silverback gorillas, sated themselves. Now, he had taken charge again. "Kilgore and I. The rest of you leave now. Go on, it's over."

Lady Fuchsia started to sob. "What did we do?" She wasn't Fuchsia Groan any longer, if she ever existed. There was no point in pretending. She was Muriel again, an assistant librarian in emotional distress.

Aubrey snapped at her. "We did what was necessary, Fuchsia. Go home. We have done a good thing tonight." Ignatius, the rage finally passed and fully Cameron again, put his arm about her shoulders, letting her cry into his chest.

We dispersed into the night. Danae pulled me along, leading me to her apartment. I had no thoughts in my head. What we did might never have happened. A peace settled itself over my heart. I had never felt so alive. Free. Invincible. We never made it to the bedroom. Danae pushed me to the floor, I decided not to resist, what we were doing was by far the sanest act I had performed in months. We wrestled for hours, hands locked, our bodies sleek and delicious.

Afterward, somehow having reached the bedroom and collapsed in exhaustion, I began to dream.

The shelves stretch out to the horizon, each a kilometre high, crammed full to overflowing with books. There's no rational order to the mess, no alphabetization, no connection as to size, no corresponding hues of book jackets. They're squashed together, horizontally, vertically, diagonally, facing back, upside-down. Mashed against one another, spines bent and torn, pages ripped and dog-eared. I leap from one shelf to the next. I have an incredible sense of balance, my toes are longer, more flexible, fur covers my arms and legs, I have a prehensile tail. Springing from monolith to monolith, screaming "No order! No order at all!" as I grab books left and right, reshelving them, trying to manufacture a semblance of order, but the shelves are now conveyor belts and elevators, they move constantly, I no sooner find a place for *A Tale of Two Cities* next to *David Copperfield* than it has shifted down and I've inserted a Dickens next to a Mack Bolan. I curse, my teeth gnashing, saliva bolting from my mouth, coating a first edition *Cat's Cradle* with salty glaze. I jump away, landing on Gutenberg's Bible, horrified at the blasphemy as my ink-soaked fingertips soil the fragile parchment. On top of each shelf is a monkey, a million monkeys smashing a million typewriters, while Ray Bradbury sits next to me, vomiting onto his typewriter again and again. "Get down from there, fucker," a voice snarls from below, it's Ernest Hemingway, balancing an elephant gun on his shoulder, "you don't deserve the privileges this life has afforded you," and he fires, the Bible exploding underneath me, I'm falling, forever, imploring him, "But I always thought Mariel was underrated as an actress!" Grasping at the works of Pete Dexter and Emily Brontë, latching onto a precariously balanced edition of *The Life of Pi* with my tail, until hitting the ground. I hit the ground! I didn't wake up! Virginia Woolf plants her feet around me, "Why don't you kill yourself, best thing I ever did, look at my career now!" but it's not Virginia Woolf, it's Nicole Kidman with a big nose, and she's thrashing me with her Oscar, joined by Fred Ward as Henry Miller, and I run, scurrying back up the shelves, they can't possibly reach me up here. Strong, warm arms embrace me, smother me, it's Oprah Winfrey, squeezing my innards out through my nose in a bear hug, screeching "What do you mean, you've never read Maya Angelou?" and I slide out, down, vaulting and sprinting, swinging through trees, each leaf a page from a timeless novel, I'm tearing off *Jacob Two-Two Meets the Hooded Fang* with one hand while the other mangles passages from *Gunga Din*, they aren't holding me, the pages are shredding under my nails, and I'm sliding down the vine, smacking the bottom, and it's a grave, my grave, Aubrey looms above me, shovelling books, they rain down, their edges striking me, I'm bleeding, and Danae! Danae is there! "Help, please!" I shout, but she's shaking her head, "The books are all that matters, Thomas, you know that," and she's shovelling too, I'm buried alive, my sepulchre lined with *Flowers in the Attic*, that's the last thing I'll ever see, it's not fair, I didn't want this, Warren drops a match, I ignite, flapping my hands uselessly against the flames, and Munroe's giant head swoops down from its perch and blows on the fire, the flames leap and prance on my face, I hear bacon crisping in the pan, I wake up next to Danae, and I'm screaming, she's holding me, I can't stop crying, she holds me until I pass out from exhaustion.

I opened my eyes, fully alert. Danae was draped across me, snoring loudly. How she made even that sexy I'll never understand. I wormed my body out of bed without waking her. My throat was grated raw from crying. Pulling on my pants, I wandered through the apartment, looking at her shelves, lightly stroking the books as I read their spines. *Red Earth and Pouring Rain. The Black Dahlia. The Long Dark Tea-Time of the Soul. American Gods. The Love of a*

*Good Woman. Tripmaster Monkey. The Grapes of Wrath. Crash. The
Shipping News. In the Skin of a Lion. Junky. The Snapper. The Music
of Chance. Eats, Shoots & Leaves.*

I could have loved her, no question.

The sky was lightening in colour, black to a sooty grey. Soon,
people would be waking up around the city. Page would be
opening the store, cleaning up after Munroe's performance. She'd
hear about it on the radio, perhaps, or maybe she'll get a phone
call, Munroe is missing, is he there? The police would be called.
Questions would be asked. Someone had to know. They'll trace his
steps. Employees will be separated, grilled under lights. Hotel staff
will be quizzed. Surveillance tapes will be checked, APBs will be put
out, a state of emergency will be declared.

The walls of the apartment warped and shrank, cocooning me.
I needed space.

Snow fell as I walked, disguising my footprints, erasing the
evidence of our act. Street lamps became ominous spotlights.
Headlights lit me up from behind. I tucked my head down,
pretended to be fascinated by my shoelaces, catching the first bus
I could, giving the driver a surly early-morning grunt in response
to her overly cheerful, "Late night, huh?"

I kept small in my seat until I reached Aubrey's house. The
curtains were drawn. The nose of Munroe's car poked out from the
backyard.

I knocked quietly at the door. Faint shuffling noises could be
heard behind it. "Aubrey," I said in a low voice. "C'mon, brother,
it's me."

"Ubf!"

The door opened a crack, allowing Aubrey's eye to peer out. It
regarded me with displeasure. "What do you want, Thomas?"

"Let me in, brother. We need to talk."

The eye withdrew silently into the dark. Hearing no movement
inside, I pushed the door open and slipped in.

Aubrey had been busy with his houseguest. Munroe was
drooped over the sofa. His neck lay at a painful angle. Short,
bubbling breaths came out of his nose. Cigarette burns on his face.
His legs bent in too many places. Margarita sloped herself over his
lap, snuffling into his crotch.

Aubrey sat next to Munroe, lighting himself a cigarette, offering the pack to me. I politely declined.

He drew a long, deep puff. "I guess I went too far, didn't I," he said. It wasn't a question.

"We both did. We all did."

"Oh, that's right, you did, too." He winked at me, inhaling smoke. "You remember that, brother. *You* did it too."

"I know, Aubrey. I'm as culpable as the rest of them. *Factum fieri infectum non potest* and all that."

"How's that, friend?"

"What is done cannot be undone."

He nodded. "Precisely, very good. I didn't know that one."

"What do we do now?"

Exhaling, he grinned, smoke filtering through his teeth. "What do you think we should do?" he asked, plucking the cigarette from his mouth. Serenely, his face neutral, he blew upon the embers until they glowed, and placed his cigarette against Munroe's cheek. That odour of baked meat arose again as he ground the smouldering ashes in. "What should we do, Thomas?"

"We have to take him to a hospital."

"That's one option." He didn't seem inclined to follow my lead. "Hospital, yes. They'll fix him up. That's what we'll do. Then we'll go to jail. Get gang-raped." He put his head on Munroe's shoulder. A hushed moan escaped from Munroe's mouth. "It's what we deserve, after all."

"Fuck that," Warren said from behind me, emerging from the bedroom. "I ain't goin' to jail, not for this sack of shit." He walked unsteadily to the couch, kicked Munroe's leg. "He deserves all we gave him."

"That's one vote for, two votes against the hospital," said Aubrey. "Democracy in action, Thomas." He hopped to his feet, staggered his way toward me, putting his hands on my shoulders. Alcohol fumes burned my eyes. "Any more bright ideas, counsellor?"

"He'll die," I said.

Warren barked. "I thought that was the point."

Aubrey looked at him. "Kilgore? You enjoyed it, I gather?" he asked.

"Fuck yeah!" Warren exclaimed. "I haven't had that much fun

in a long time."

"I'm glad, Warren," said Aubrey. "Are *you* glad, Thomas? Has any of this made you happy?"

"No," I managed to say, a muffled noise. "Yes. This has all made me happy. No. I am not happy."

"I know exactly how you feel, brother."

"I have to make this right, Aubrey."

"I knew you would, somehow."

"Fucking pussy," Warren spat. "Never a surprise from Thomas. No balls." He made a slow, cock-eyed lunge at me, catching his foot on a beer bottle and crashing to the floor. "Slippery little fucker."

"Warren?" Aubrey asked.

"What?" Warren made no move to rise.

"Go to bed."

"Good idea. Big day today. Gotta trash the evidence." Warren squirmed his way past me toward the bedroom. "G'night, Aub."

"Good night, brother."

"Good night, Warren," I said to Warren's retreating form. An eventual door slam was my response.

"He used to drink a lot more," Aubrey commented. "Lucky for you he's no longer that man. He was a mean drunk."

I looked over at Munroe. "Lucky for all of us."

"Oh, don't blame Warren for all that. He got in his shots, but he's too sloshed to cause any real damage. Most of that is my own handiwork. We all contributed to the piece, but as editor, I felt I had final say. Publisher's privilege." He blew a fogbank of smoke into Munroe's face.

"We went too far, Aubrey."

"You think?"

"We lost our minds."

"That we surely did. I did. Where did I put it? I don't care to know. Overrated organ never caused anything but trouble and misery to me."

"I'm going to take him, Aubrey. He'll die."

"I know."

"Are you going to stop me?"

"I guess we'll see." He sat there, hunched over his knees, daring me to move.

I started to walk forward. I walked to Munroe. I shoved Margarita rudely from his legs. I gathered Munroe up in my arms as best I could, grunting with the effort. I walked backward to the door, dragging Munroe slowly out.

I looked over at Aubrey. He hadn't moved.

"Take care, Yossarian."

I began to cry again. "You too, brother."

I dragged Munroe down the stairs, his mouth drooling blood onto his shirt, his feet thumping loudly at every step. I manoeuvred him into the passenger seat of his car, praying that Aubrey had left the keys in the ignition. Luck was with me. I drove Munroe to the nearest hospital, leaving him lumped on the sidewalk in front of Emergency. I went home, put some clothes in a bag, grabbed what money and pills I could, and ran.

I imagine how my life could have ended differently. I stay a lawyer. I meet a nice lawyerette, settle down and litigate each other to our hearts' content. Raise a litter of solicitors to carry on the gene pool, take some big cases, pervert the intent of the Law for my own personal success, raise a mint of a nest egg. I retire early, open my own second-hand bookshop, name it DOG EARS. People stop by to browse and chat, no pressure to make a purchase, I recommend whatever I feel like, and if I never make a profit, who the hell'd even care? Weekends, I hold screenings of movie classics in the back storeroom, discussing the thematic differences between the novel and its cinematic interpretation with anyone who cares to attend. Aubrey visits the store, and Warren, and Danae, we become fast friends, they tell me about a bizarre little book club they belonged to when they were young and foolish and honestly believed they could ever hope to make a difference in this world. We laugh over the whims of our youth, and rearrange the bookstore shelves according to date and publisher, giggling like schoolgirls.

We all know the rest.

Aubrey, Warren, and Danae. Gone. Together? I don't know, but I'd put money on it. Aubrey's house burned to the ground, I suppose a distraction manoeuvre. Aubrey splashed the entire house with gasoline, and in that house, what wasn't covered with fuel was likely made of paper. The most indiscriminate burning of 'tags the Monkeys ever had. Firefighters didn't have a chance at putting out this blaze. They sifted the ashes for days before they concluded that the house was empty.

Munroe slipped in and out of a coma for two weeks. Our disappearance was suspicious, but no one firmly placed us and him together until he awoke. Once he described Aubrey to the police, mentioning his hair, all the pieces fell into place, and the manhunt began in earnest.

The other Shelf Monkeys? Fortunately, Munroe couldn't describe any of them in enough detail to conduct an effective search. They might have gotten away clean. But Emily, damn her therapist-encouraged soul, turned traitor in exchange for immunity. Claimed to find religion. Munroe has already professed to have forgiven her. Big of him. She'll get a book deal out of this, I'm sure. Published by MuPu Incorporated. The brazen story of one woman's fight to escape the clutches of a diabolical cabal of biblioclasts. I hope she appreciates the irony. Know this: that as she carved her entry into the book of Munroe, the look on her face was that of a child riding the teacups at Disney World, wanting the ride to go on forever.

Most of the Monkeys went willingly enough. I think they were happy to be caught; it saved them the trouble of atoning for their actions on their own. I rather liked Tracey/Lyra Silvertongue's high-speed chase down the Trans-Canada. Good television. They all quickly received major sentences. At the time I thought it was very decent of Dr. Newhire to speak on their behalf. A mass delusion of omnipotence brought about by a combination of work-related stress disorder and a charismatic yet insane leader with ideas of godhood. They were helpless, held in thrall to his charms and promises. We would have swallowed the phenobarbitol and begged for seconds. Nonsense, but it sounded good for the cameras.

In my daydreams, the Monkeys still meet in prison, gathering new recruits among the convicts, sacrificing the unworthy. Starting an underground network of Shelf Monkey Clubs. Perhaps a sanctioned franchise one day. The first rule of Shelf Monkey Club? You do not talk about Shelf Monkey Club.

Of course, I didn't help my case by fleeing into the wild. Maybe

I should have stayed, taken my chances. Maybe the four of us could have fled together. It wouldn't have been so bad then. Just as well. I wouldn't even have tried to protest my innocence. As a lawyer, I blew, but I understand the law well enough to know when someone is well and truly fucked.

Goddamn, I am tired of all this. I've said all I have to say, and I'm no better off than when I started. I hoped for some closure, but I'm still on the run. Only difference, I'm even more desolate now. I ran out of anti-depressants two months ago, and the edges of tall buildings are beginning to tempt me. I can't remember if I even had a point. It's all so stupid now.

I'm going to stop running, Eric. I won't turn myself in, I won't willingly stick my head in the lion's mouth, but I will step into the cage to see if he's hungry. Start eating in restaurants again. Going to movies. Joining a book club. Going to bookstores. Reading in libraries, in plain sight. That's what I'm going to do.

If I have to go out, I'll go out on my terms.

Goodbye, Eric. I wish I could say I'll see you around, but we both know that won't happen. Unless you visit me in prison. Or the morgue.

Goodbye, Detective Daimler. I'm sure I'll see you soon.

If someone could apologize to my parents, I'd be most grateful. They neither asked for nor deserved all the attention.

On second thought, just leave them alone.

All I ever wanted was to read a good book.

Yours truly,

Yossarian

MANHUNT COMES TO VIOLENT END

NEW YORK CITY — One of the largest manhunts in American history came to a violent conclusion yesterday as Thomas Friesen, suspect-at-large in the Munroe Purvis kidnapping, was wounded and captured by police.

Agnes Coleman, friend of Munroe Purvis and author of the bestselling novel *My Baby, My Love*, contacted police when she glimpsed Friesen browsing the stacks at a Barnes & Noble bookstore.

"I was there for a book signing of my latest novel, *Baby Madeleine, What Happened*, when I thought I saw him in my audience. Then, that horrible man appeared in the customer line, asking for my autograph," Ms. Coleman told reporters. "I immediately notified store security, who called the police."

According to eyewitnesses, once officials had cordoned off the area, Friesen began throwing copies of *Catcher in the Rye* at police before running throughout the store.

"He led us on quite a chase," Sergeant Luis Rizzuto related at a press conference later that afternoon. "He evaded us for quite a time by ducking into the Travel section, but we finally cornered him between Women's Studies and Gay Issues."

Despite attempts to calm him down, Sergeant Rizzuto said the former lawyer's actions left police little option but to open fire.

"He nailed our negotiator in the head with a copy of Elmore Leonard's *Stick*, leaving us no choice," said Rizzuto. "Despite our best efforts at calming him down, Mr. Friesen was determined to die."

Sharpshooters were called to the scene, finally managing to bring Friesen down near the music department.

"He had armoured himself by placing several large novels under his jacket, which proved difficult to shoot through. Our bullets were unable to penetrate the leather-bound edition of *The Collected Works of Herman Melville* that he used to protect his heart.

"They got through *Billy Budd* all right, but the bullets stopped about halfway through *Moby Dick*. We finally had to bring in armour-piercing shells. That is one hard book to get through."

FILE # 09978
DOCUMENT INSERT: Personal letter from Thomas Friesen.
From patient files of Dr. Lyle Newhire

Dear Doc,
Before I begin, allow me a little literary license.

Epilogue

How many people get a second chance to discuss the end of
their life? The only example I can think of is *A Clockwork
Orange*; bloodthirsty Alex finally maturing beyond his nightly
visits to the milk bars with his droogs and the intoxicating rush
of a touch of the ol' ultraviolence afterward. I hadn't planned on
it, certainly. I thought I was finished there, all over but the
shouting. When the bullet pierced the Melville, driving seventy-
two pages of dense maritime symbolism deep within my chest
cavity, well, that was it as far as I was concerned. I felt Ishmael's
journal carve itself through what turned out to be the lining of
my right lung, the leaves neatly perforating the tissue with their
gilded edges, and an extraordinary fragrance filled my nose as I
collapsed, a spicy mingling of blood and ink. If one gets to
choose their final sensation on this plane of existence, it was the
most appropriate scent I could ever have hoped for.

I wish I could say there was a bright light and a chorus of
seraphim, or the jab of a pitchfork in my ass, or *some* trick of
the light that I had crossed theological dimensions and pierced
Bowles' sheltering sky to take repose, some concluding almighty
brown-out of my fuses giving me the full *Altered States/2001*
experience of complete corporeal shutdown, *something*, but all
there was, was pain. Then nothing. No thoughts, no dreams, no
cries of the damned or choir invisible. Nada. But I guess that
can't *quite* be all there was; when I opened my eyes after the
weeks of dark, going from black to sterile white at the speed of
thought, it was not the point A to point B route that I had
always anticipated a near-death coma to be. It wasn't bookstore–
bullet–pain–hospital bed. It was bookstore–bullet–pain–. . .
–hospital bed. I had nothing to fill the blank but time, and
while I have no empirical evidence, I swear to you, I knew that

three weeks had passed. Three weeks as dead weight on a mattress, and when I awoke, I was strapped down to the bed so tightly you'd think I had just been placed there, twisting and screaming at the orderlies to let me go while I came down from crystal meth–induced hysteria.

So, after all that's happened, this is what I get, more psycho-intensive homework? Back where I started? Now *that's* irony. After all our sessions together, you medical hack, you insult to the medical profession, you piece of shit, all I wanted was to be away from you. Maybe you're just one of those people I'm fated to run into again and again. No, let's add a medical analogy to it, as befits your profession. You're herpes. I thought the medication would help, but here you are again, reddening my rim. I suppose I thought I'd be grateful to you, after your pleas to the judge for leniency on my behalf, but you'll forgive me for taking said pleas with several grains of salt. You have your book deal, your fame, your shot at a nationally syndicated talk show of your own; I have at least the next twenty-five years of my time left on this planet to spend in the grey-walled concrete splendour of Stony Mountain Penitentiary, with the ever-present promise of prison love to keep it interesting.

Boy, you thought I was bitter before? I suppose the trial may have something to do with it. Quick doesn't begin to describe it. Considering the ratings the re-enactment garnered Court TV, I'd have thought they'd want to keep it going a while longer. Even Michael Jackson didn't get these numbers. But my lawyers and I decided that silence on my part was the only chance I had of clemency, and that shortened the proceedings considerably. To no avail. Once Munroe took the stand, unsteadily pointing his cane at me across the courtroom, the ending was a foregone conclusion. Life imprisonment. The rest of my natural life behind walls of endless grey. It could have been worse, I know; some U.S. senators went apoplectic trying to keep me in the States to stand trial. The concept of a government that doesn't support the death penalty really stuck in their craw. I mean, sure, I tortured a man, almost killed him, certainly scarred him physically as well as psychologically, but it's not like I'm a bishop buggering a busload of boys here. I'm not making excuses, but come on, in the grand scheme of things, what's one hateful little man? And I did have my supporters, muted they may have been. No one condones torture, but many people didn't care for Munroe either, and in many editorials on Munroe's collapse, there's often the hint of a "good riddance." Or maybe I'm reading between the lines a little too carefully.

But the whole debacle was strictly a Canadian affair, legally speaking, and so it was back to Winnipeg to stand trial. Even then, some back-benchers in Parliament suggested that the hangman's noose be brought back for one more go-round, so I suppose I got off lucky.

So, why the response to your request? Why the candour? As you might be able to glean from this letter so far, my opinion of you is far from complimentary. But the story needs an ending, and I'm going to give it one more shot. You may be writing the textbook on the subject, but I am the subject. This could be the next *In Cold Blood* or *Executioner's Song*, if you've got any talent. I'm sure you've contacted the other Monkeys, and maybe some of them see cooperation as a way to reduce their sentences. But unless the Big Three are ever captured, I'm still the main event, the big Canadian cheddar cheese in this sandwich. So I've got your little list of questions propped up in front on me as I lie, stomach-down, on my surprisingly firm prison-issue mattress, and I'll give them a shot. After this, however, you'll never hear from me again, so don't bother trying.

Why did I get in line to see Agnes?

That's your first question? You really are earning that one point two million dollar advance on the book, aren't you? Surprised I knew that? We get *Us* magazine in here, and *People*, plus the occasional *InStyle*, so I've managed to keep up with popular culture. I notice you've slimmed down, very nice. I think my bunkmate Vincent has a crush on you. Yet another reason not to visit me; I may decide to introduce you.

Why did I do it? Wish I knew. I don't even know how I ended up in New York City, it's just where I happened to roll off the train, I suppose. I had completely run out of anti-depressants by then, and whaddaya know, you may just have been right after all, I have suicidal tendencies when under pressure. Then again, maybe I just wanted out. I hadn't eaten a meal in days, and was hungrily scrounging a half-eaten bagel out of a garbage can when I saw a flyer for Agnes's reading. I had no plans to harm her, as she has continually surmised to anyone who'll listen. I really wasn't thinking at all by that point. I was nearing the end point, I knew. All I wanted was to feel human again, to be part of an excited line-up of people clamouring for a worthless signature on a piece-of-trash novel that nonetheless would become the highlight of my life. Or maybe I wanted to spit in her face just once before I died. The matte black bumpers of passing sedans and SUVs were beginning to whisper to me again. *Jump in front of me,* they breathed as they drove by. *You're dead anyway.*

But there was no surprise in that end, was there? Thomas Friesen, the great Canadian fugitive, committing anonymous suicide. How banal. How weak. How so very much expected. Couldn't even bring himself to stop the massacre of Munroe. Content to let himself become so much road pulp.

No, I needed to die in a symbolic act of defiance fraught with significance. Fuck the naysayers who say Mennonites don't know how to dance. I knew what the public wanted; they wanted comeuppance and copious amounts of gore. They wanted an ending that would sell magazines and become the topic of late-night Letterman monologues. A bloody finale guaranteed to win whoever played me in the movie version an Oscar nomination.

And by the way, Luke Perry? You gotta be fucking kidding me. All this trouble I went through and I get *90210*'d? Couldn't even get Jason Priestley, at least he's Canadian. I admit Jude Law was a long shot, but come on, you're telling me David Arquette wasn't available? But ABC had to get the movie done on the quick, get ratings for the advertisers because I Can't Believe it's Not Butter had a poor showing in the last quarter, and so Munroe gets the big weird-looking guy from *Spin City* and I get a leatherface who couldn't out-emote furnishings, in a performance *USA Today* described as "brave." The less said about Freddie Prinze Jr. as Aubrey the better. And I did not shout "Shelf Monkeys unite!" as the bullets took me down. Do you know the ribbing I took from the guys around here for that? For weeks, all I heard was "Shelf Monkeys unite!" whenever I entered the cafeteria. I had lobbied for movie night to be cancelled that Thursday, but apparently the prisoner population of Cell Block F *really* wanted to see what all the fuss about my incarceration was about.

It was all worth it, though, to see Agnes's face when I challenged her that day. Again, I did not threaten her, I pulled no knife, I made no theatrical leap for her throat (although that did get me some newfound respect here — I've been invited to accept membership in several gangs impressed at my mettle). What I did was very simple. I laid the book in front of her, open to the title page. I said very calmly, "Could you make this out to Thomas, please?" She looked up at me, and there was nothing, no hint of recognition. A sniff of distaste escaped her nose, and I suddenly realized how different I must look. I hadn't even washed myself in the bay that morning. She quickly scribbled something and shoved the book across the table to me. I took the book back and read the inscription, not relinquishing my place in line. "To Thomas, my number one fan. Love, Agnes." I reread it a few more times to be sure I wasn't missing any hidden subtext, hearing the people behind me begin to grumble complaints as I stood there.

"Is there a problem?" Agnes asked. She looked a trifle nervous at my continued presence in front of her.

"No, no problem," I said, and gave her the widest, most honest smile I could muster. "I'm just wondering how you knew, that's all."

"What's that?"

"That I was your number one fan. You've met a lot of people, I'm sure, and I guess I'm just a little overwhelmed at this kind of recognition. I mean, wow, Agnes. I'm number one? Really and for true?"

"Hey, buddy." The store security guard was suddenly standing next to me. "You're holding up the line, why don't you just take your book and go, okay?"

"Excuse me?" I asked incredulously. "Miss Coleman here has just designated me her number one fan, and that is number one out of everyone in the world. I should think I could have just a little extra time to converse with her, seeing as I am her number one and all."

"Sir, that's just a phrase I use," Agnes piped up. "It doesn't mean anything."

"Maybe not to *you,*" I said, shaking off the guard's hand that had somehow found its way to my shoulder. "Maybe to *you* it's a phrase, something you toss off without thinking, I love you, cheque's in the mail, of course I'm concerned about global warming, I promise I won't come in your mouth, but to *me,*" I poked myself in the chest where I could feel my lungs begin to tighten with anxiety, "to *me* words are important. They mean things, and you'd have to be a real thoughtless bitch to label someone your number one fan and not mean it. Are we all your number ones, is that it? We're all interchangeable?" I spun to face the now quite agitated line behind me. "Everyone! We can go home, it's all a sham! She cares nothing for us!"

"Now that's not true!" Agnes protested. The guard had reattached his hand to my shoulder and began pulling me aside. "I care about all of you!"

"It's a crock of shit!" I screamed, wrenching myself away from the guard. I ran back to the table where Agnes sat and grabbed an armful of novels. "IT'S FUCKING CRAP!" I threw a book at the onrushing guard, and my aim was true, the spine crushed itself into his forehead. "SHE HATES YOU ALL!" I threw another book at the guard, this time on a downward slant as the first book had driven him to his knees. This copy drove itself straight into his groin. "AGNES COLEMAN MUST BE STOPPED!" I tossed a novel her way, causing Agnes to dunk herself under the table. I pummelled the table with books. "YOU DESTROYED MY LIFE!" I leapt atop the table and began jumping, hoping to break its legs and crush the now-shrieking Agnes underneath. "YOU CUNT!" Why was no one stopping me? Aside from the guard, still on the floor and grasping at his genitalia in pain, the audience had not moved since I started. I halted my jumps, and the only sound was Agnes, whimpering. I stopped breathing. I closed my eyes. I willed the pressure behind my eyeballs to ease up. The world stopped its rotation. My boots rose from the surface of the table. I floated up to the ceiling. I opened my eyes and began counting the stucco mountain ranges. I saw a lovely valley between two white plaster K2s, and set about plans to one day build a cottage there. In a short while the police arrived, gravity resumed, my legs ran, my torso followed, and the bullets began embedding themselves in whatever was handy. I may have screamed more things; maybe I did yell something monkey-related. I can't be exact in my recollection. I lined my clothes with books. I hid next to J.D. Salinger and squealed in fear. A sizzle of heat removed a chunk of muscle from my left arm. I scrambled away from an eager policeman who had snuck up behind me, leaving him slipping in the red trail I left. There was the metallic *snuk!* of a bolt-action rifle being primed. An explosion in my chest tossed me into a wall. That smell of ink and blood and bullet and lung and bone and sweat became my universe.

But I'm feeling much better now. If there's something the Canadian prison system is fabulous at, it's supplying its forced inhabitants with as many *legal* drugs as possible. I couldn't even pretend to be nuts in here. They want me nice and sane so that I may fully appreciate the enormity of my actions and their consequences. No fair going nuts to relieve the tedium.

Do I regret my actions?

Do you think even a minute passes as I stare at the bars of my cell where I don't wish I'd never even heard of **READ**? Hell, I regret my parents ever read to me as a child. I regret the A pluses I got in elementary English. I regret Miss White indulging my penchant for hiding in the stacks. I regret Gutenberg's invention of the printing press. I regret the invention of written language itself, and wish we'd all stuck to cave drawings. I don't suppose I would have gotten nearly as ensnarled in this plight if Munroe were advocating a lesser variety of charcoal renderings of bison on the walls of caverns. Again, you are really earning your advance here, Doc. On the whole, I'd rather not be in prison, but I suppose that's not what you're getting at.

I do regret it, of course. You find out quickly that in prison, life is all about regret. I regret it in the way a junkie regrets shooting up, even as he prepares another dose. That is to say, I regret the end result, but the route I took getting here, well, that was a hell of a ride, and I don't regret it one bit.

After all, I've become quite the celebrity here. I'm respected and admired within these walls to a degree I never could have anticipated. I'd like to impose a bit of irony to the story here, take some literary license with my memoirs, make up some sad paradoxical *Outer Limits* ending that would please my detractors, maybe being placed in charge of the prison library, a library that consists exclusively of Munroe Purvis Book Club releases. Picture the scene: the camera pulls back slowly, a crane shot, revealing your hero surrounded by boxes and boxes of the very thing he despises. He raises his arms to the sky and screams, "Noooooooooooooo! Why, God, why?" He collapses to the floor. Music swells. Fade to black. Credits roll. Please deposit your empty popcorn bags in the nearest trash receptacle on your way out. Now *that's* a scene that cries out for an actor of Luke Perry's calibre.

But other than working in the library — how could the warden *not* put me in charge of that? — none of this is true. It turns out the inmate population here has just as much animosity toward Munroe as I have. Not for the same reasons, of course; some years ago, Munroe did a week-long exposé on the woeful inadequacies of the prison system, concluding that all criminals should be lined up and shot (his words) rather than continue to drain valuable tax dollars from the pockets of honest citizens. It was a very popular program, and as an indirect result, all prisoners have a fond daydream of one day being released, tracking down Munroe, and shanking him, sticking a shiv between his ribs and hearing him squeal. I've heard what that sounds like, and I understand the appeal.

Predictably, I am treated with the sort of deference and awe usually bequeathed upon deposed godfathers and made men. Prisoners seek my opinion on matters. I have attained folk hero status. The Man Who Would Kill Munroe. I have started up a temporary book club — in here everything is temporary, and our meetings are always one unruly pedophile away from being shut down — and somehow I have managed to sensibly discuss the merits of Jonathan Lethem and Barbara Gowdy with murderers and rapists within a climate that usually precludes such endeavours, instead preferring fight nights and the occasional riot to relieve tension. I won't claim that prison life is a breeze, but I can sleep at night now, secure in the knowledge that my cellmate and new Michael Chabon fan Vincent will kill anyone who tries to do me harm. Little old me, with a bodyguard. I don't think even Munroe himself is so well protected.

Actually, speaking of Munroe, I do have one chief regret; we honestly should have killed him. We had the chance to stop Osama, but chickened out and left him with a stern warning instead. Well, I chickened out. Sure, we made an impact on his sensibilities: how could we not? But sad as it is, the new Munroe, all twisted and scarred, is infinitely worse. Becoming mentally unhinged may have cost Munroe his day job, but he is making a killing on the lecture circuit. He's still spewing the safe righteous indignant ignorant crap, but it's not an act anymore. He honestly believes it. Watching clips on the evening news of his speech at Bob Jones University, propped up by Jerry Falwell and blathering on about "secular humanist sodomites" and "intellectual Osama bin Liberals" and "the Democrat plague," it's clear we took a bad thing and made it even more reprehensible. Before he was an irritant; now he has the ear of the President.

But again, all is not bleak. I expect no reprieve, these walls are my home, but as I'm sure you're aware, I have become the *cause célèbre du jour,* the new poster boy for celebrities needing a cause to fuel their days. Small c celebrities, but still. Boy, you know you've made a difference when your fellow yardbirds are envious that E. Annie Proulx has come to visit. I've had quite the number of bookish luminaries visit me in the last few months. Douglas Coupland came in just to shake my hand. Tim Winton, Roddy Doyle, and Ha Jin called to wish me well. Thomas Pynchon brought me a signed copy of *The Crying of Lot 49*: at least, he said he was Pynchon. James Ellroy interviewed me for a *Vanity Fair* piece, but I'm afraid I came off looking rather insane; it was too soon after my capture, and the daily triple-doses of Paxil had not yet taken effect. I don't recollect half the conversation, and the half I do remember is a three-hour bi-polar mishmash of ranting, sobbing, and seething against the injustice that Ellroy has not yet won a Pulitzer. Apparently I also discussed the Shelf Monkey trial, but it's all a blur. I do recall being dragged from the interview in restraints and sentenced to two days of "quiet time." Norman Mailer and I had a good long chat; he offered to smuggle me in a cake with a file in it, and looked somewhat crestfallen when I told him I didn't wish him to publish my life story. I've said all I've need to say, and I should not suffer the great Mailer the indignity of telling my tale. I'm no Gary Gilmore, and the man who wrote *Tough Guys Don't Dance* deserves much better than that. It hasn't all been accolades; Tim LaHaye condemned me to Hell, but that was pretty much a given anyway. Sadly, Eric hasn't dropped by, but I can't blame him. I did damage his career, what with the uproar from certain quarters that his novels were somehow the instigators of my deeds. It all blew over, but the harm may be irreversible. Lynn Coady said she'd pass on my apologies, but I don't expect he'll be too eager to renew our acquaintanceship. His novels have been selling quite briskly, though, so perhaps some reconciliation is possible. Down the road.

No doubt you've read my book reviews in *The New York Times*. I thought it was weird, but authors evidently consider it a badge of honour to have their book critiqued by a Shelf Monkey. Much as a painting by John Wayne Gacy is highly sought out by art collectors, I suppose. I try to be kind, but I don't pull punches. Either way, the books sell very well. People want to read the books I like, and even more people want to read the books I dislike, all Munroe supporters of course. They think that to purchase books on my "hit list" (the editor's idea, not mine) somehow allows them to get back at the man who mangled Munroe. Like buying these books teaches me some valuable lesson about not torturing celebrities. Here's the truth: I've been stringing them along. I'd never hate a novel by W.P. Kinsella or David Bergen or Greg Hollingshead or Eden

Robinson or Yann Martel; I have nothing but capital A Admiration for them. Didn't anyone even get the joke when I called Joseph Heller "an over-praised relic who coasted on the goodwill created by *Catch-22* for far too long"? What, too subtle?

But if there is one way that all Munroers are alike, it is in their uniformity of response, and if my foolish trash-talking of Messrs. Updike, Vanderhaeghe, Vonnegut et al. allowed those authors to get a little extra pocket money, then I take it as a victory. The idea that an Agnes Coleman admirer should be so incensed at my acts that they should willingly purchase and read a James Morrow to get back at me makes me feel all giddy.

As much as I've enjoyed this little fling with fame, the best is still to come. Rex Murphy has invited me participate in his *Cross-Country Checkup* review of the season in books. It's by phone of course, and I expect a full grilling from Mr. Murphy, but how could I say no? He's a Canadian institution, and I expect that to be verbally crucified by him, live and on-air for the amusement of millions of Canadian listeners, will be the highlight of a very busy life.

Where are the others?

Well, that's an easy one. I have no fucking clue. If I knew, do you honestly think I'd tell? I am the Judas in this little tale, but I think I've done my part for law and order. Let the cops figure it out for themselves. Or maybe Emily's the Judas. She's certainly received more than her share of silver for her troubles, and got Leelee Sobieski to portray her in the bargain. All I got was the guilt.

I initially scoured the hate mail I've gotten for some code as to their whereabouts — you'd think with all the trouble they're going through to keep me chemically upbeat the prison officials would withhold such potentially unnerving correspondence from me, but no, I get hundreds of death threats a week — but I never found any hidden messages there. After a time, all the "hope you die" and "burn in Hell fucker" and "I believe in Christ but you don't deserve to live you horrible horrible man" comments just become one big blur, leavened slightly by the occasional offer of marriage. Munroe was right about that at least: there are some very sad and lonely people out there. If the other Monkeys have tried to write me from their cells, their mail has not gotten through.

But there are other ways to get a message. I guess this is the true reason why I've decided to confide in you, Doc. I *have* received word from the outside. Certain channels have been established, and a plump, damning little note has fallen right into my lap. Literally. I was inspecting the new arrivals for the library, and I happened upon a new edition of *Catch-22*. As I never ordered it, the title kind of leaped out at me. What, I'm not going to open it? I flipped through the pages, and there it was.

```
Dear Thomas:
    I guess an apology at this point won't
cut it?
    Danae and Warren have warned me against
writing you a note, saying it's too risky,
but you deserve the truth. You were always
there for me, in the end, and you never
acted less than a true friend should. When
I called you brother all those times, it
was meant in the truest sense. We are
brothers in pain, and the fact that your
pain is ongoing causes me no end of grief.
I don't at all expect this letter to bring
a halt to your sufferings, but every story
needs an ending, of sorts.
    We were all prepared to take you with
us. Yes, the three of us always planned to
run; there was no way we could hope to get
away with our Purvis-cide. At most, we'd
have a few days' grace to put some distance
between the police and ourselves. But I
have (or had, rather) a tidy nest egg put
away. I was a far better businessman than I
let on, and between investments and
savings, I guess you could call me rich. Or
rich enough to comfortably hide ourselves
```

away. I managed to sell my share of the store before the shit went down (yes, I did think that far ahead). My guess is there's a very silent, very upset city councillor looking at the store's plummeting finances right about now. He couldn't believe the price I quoted him. Munroe's appearance was primed to make READ a national force in bookselling, and here I was jumping ship in calm waters. In receivership, I hear. Aye, she was a cursed vessel from the start, and woe be those hands who went down with her. Page, where are you now?

So, thanks to business acumen, I can now take the risk of sending out this missive. Hearing of your current position as librarian out at Stony, it was fairly simple to get a letter to you. A bribe here, an inserted note there, and voilá. The only real problem was ensuring that you get the note before anyone else; what book would you peruse? If you're reading this, then I guess the obvious choice was the correct one. If someone else is reading this, well, shit happens. Could you get this to Thomas Friesen when you're done?

You were the X-factor, Thomas — the one truly unpredictable element. The others, they were sheep, and sadly, I hold no real affection for any of them. They drifted into our circle over time, but they were acquaintances, not friends. Book club friends, if anything. Emily was the only one I ever cared about, and you know how that turned out. Do you ever hear from her? I suppose not. They were all only bit players in my life story, only existing to keep the narrative flowing until a new plot twist came along. They all have their own stories, but I was never all that interested in reading them, if that makes any sense.

I should have guessed how you'd react to everything. I did guess, actually; I just hoped I would turn out to be mistaken, that you would surprise me. But true to form, you just couldn't follow through. Yes, you were there, you participated, you extracted your pound of flesh, but in the end, your heart just wasn't in it.

Yossarian suited you, I thought: the lone voice of sanity in the wilderness of madness, the calm in the middle of the storm, that sort of thing. A fine complement to my admitted habit of tilting at windmills. From the start, you were special. Raw, unfocused, slightly manic and bi-polar, highly suggestible, but special. Danae, Warren, they're special as well, but I somehow felt a stronger kinship with you. Maybe you were the stabilizing element I needed; I probably would have gone ballistic far earlier without your companionship. Strange that your character was what I admired, and yet in the end was what disappointed me. Irony?

Like you, Yossarian was never a doer, he was a follower. He was a commenter on humanity, never an active participant. You performed the tasks asked of you, Thomas, but like Yossarian before you, you're a reactor, not an actor. You've never been in control of anything. Yet in the end, Yossarian triumphed through acceptance of the madness that assailed him. He fought madness with madness. You never embraced the madness. You sought conformity. You could have done anything that evening: called me out, shot us, pushed Warren into the fire, led the others in armed uprising against me, anything, and I would have admired you for your passion. You're not a Yossarian. You don't deserve such an admirable appellation.

You're not a lead character, Thomas. You're secondary. The best friend. The shoulder to cry on. You're not even the main protagonist in your own story. You're the one who watches, the one who almost but not quite understands what's going on, the one who is always just one step behind the reader.

You're the sidekick, Thomas.

You're the Watson.

Jimmy Olson.

Sancho Panza.

Rosencrantz and/or Guildenstern, grasping vainly for clues as to their existence.

You know who you really are? Nick Carraway. There's poor Nick, watching, commenting, narrating the actions of others, and never once comprehending what is going on. Sure, he's the first person narrator, the survivor, the filter through which events are processed, but in the end, who remembers him? No one. They remember Gatsby, that enigmatic playboy. And well they should: Nick is boring. And so are you, although you were so close to being interesting. If you'd just taken that final step. But you took the side of traditionalist values.

Danae was so proud of you, Thomas. She honestly believed you to have joined us. She cried for days afterward. Danae has her own demons, which I cannot pretend to understand. An abusive father? A child of divorce? There is something missing in Danae, something she fills with books, with the lives of others. As we all do. You got closer than anyone, and I don't know if she'll ever fully trust anyone again. She talks very little these days, while Warren, frankly, won't shut up. We are not the close-knit trio I'd hoped we'd be, but we are all we have, and it holds us together.

That, and books. For now, anyway.

I could go on in this vein, but like poor Nick, I'm going to leave you with the mystery. What was the driving force behind my obsession? Perhaps you were never meant to know, but you never even thought to ask. Gatsby never wrote his own book, why should I? All I can say is, I never regretted for a moment what I did. My only regret is you, and you know what?

I'll get over it.

Goodbye, Yossarian. I very much doubt you will hear from me again. But keep reading the newspapers, I might pop up somewhere. I'll burn a 'tag for you, when Dan Brown shits out another bestseller. Do the same for me, for old time's sake?

Yours,
Don Quixote

Now is it just me, or is this just a tad hurtful? How could I win? If I follow Aubrey, then I'm not a follower. If I don't follow him, I'm a follower. Yossarian never had this kind of conundrum to think out.

Maybe it's not real. Maybe the note is a plant, a ploy to enrage me enough that I give up my friends. Possible, but unlikely. I choose to accept it as truth, if only for closure's sake.

Is it all true? Am I simply a follower? I've had ample opportunity for self-reflection lately and I think Aubrey has a point. But are you a follower when you've done what you truly wanted to do anyway? So what if Aubrey was in charge; I chose to participate. No one forced me. Maybe part of it was to get close to Danae, but even if love is not a choice, my actions always were. I could have walked away. Could have quit anytime I wanted to. Just didn't want to. Doesn't mean I was addicted or anything. Who gets addicted to burning novels?

Still, I did get Danae if only for a moment. Give me that, at least.

I'm glad they're still free, though, together or not. In my daydreams, the Americans got their way, and I'm strapped to a metal cot with a needle brimming with death inserted into my arm. Aubrey, Danae, and Warren have somehow sneaked in, and watch from the bleachers as the poison is pumped into my system. Danae smiles, but I don't know why. Does she miss me? Does she wish it were her finger on the plunger? But my last conscious image is of her smile, and whatever its intent, it is a glorious thing.

And there you have it. The summary of the rest of my life. There's no point in writing any more about it. Every day is so similar to the last as to make no discernible difference. A pleasing routine is now the norm for the rest of my life. I don't lack for companionship, I get regular exercise, and as for women, I can't claim to miss them, as the drugs they've got me on are so powerful that sex would be an impossibility were it to ever cross my mind, which it rarely does, due in large part to the aforementioned drugs. Every day is waking up, getting dressed, having breakfast, working in the library, writing reviews, and reading for three or four hours before slumber claims me. Bliss.

When I do feel an itch for something beyond the routine, I answer fan mail. There were only a few at first, but every week the pile grows a little larger. People asking for advice on what to read, and more and more often, what to burn. I don't want to frighten you, but there's something happening out there. I can feel it in my bones. Mark my words, people are gathering. In basements and apartments and public parks. They finally feel an itch they didn't know they had, so long have they ignored it. But it itches now, worse than ever. It's in a place they cannot scratch. On the advice of co-workers, they buy the latest bestseller, and they are overcome with hives. There's only one cure for this allergy. It's tentative at first, a tearing of a corner. Many will laugh at themselves, and shrug at their silliness. It's only a book. Not worth getting upset over. But some will do more than tear. They will rend. They will shred. They will mince. Grind. Crumple. Split.

And in the end, they will burn. They will remember us, and think we were on to something. They will seek out others of their ilk, and congregate, and prepare lists of members, and start newsletters and blogs and zines. It will grow beyond the ability to control itself. It will spread. It's the new flu. Monkey flu. People will be helpless once infected.

And I will stay here, in the pen, and read, because it is what I was born to do. On sunny days in the spring, I will choose a novel from my personal stash, and go for a walk in the yard. My neck will ache from looking down at the book in my hands, but it's a pain I enjoy. The wind will pick up, and a familiar scent will take me back to happier times. Somewhere, out on the far side of the mortar and grout of walls now so familiar to me I cannot easily recall the world that exists beyond, someone is setting fire to a Barbara Cartland.

And I will envy them their freedom, and wish them well.

From The Associated Press

BOOKSELLERS REPORT RECORD THEFTS

In what is becoming a disturbing trend for the big box bookstores, American large-chain bookstores have reported a huge surge in incidents of shoplifting for the third quarter in a row.

"Frankly, we're stumped, and the higher-ups are very worried," said a middle manager of a Washington Borders who spoke on assurance on anonymity. "Books are flying off the shelves lately. For every person we catch, we must lose at least twenty hardcover novels. They're very brazen. One woman we caught had six paperbacks hidden in her pantyhose. It's almost an epidemic.

"We know why it's happening, but we are forbidden to talk about it. It's almost a police state, it's gotten so bad.

If we so much as utter the words 'Shelf Monkey,' even as a joke, we are given a verbal reprimand."

In one extreme instance, an Oakland Borders store was the scene of a bizarre flash mob as over fifty people swarmed the store and managed to make off with every copy of the works of authors Dan Brown and Robert James Waller in the space of four minutes. The books were then doused with lighter fluid and set ablaze in the store parking lot.

When reached for comment, Thomas Friesen, currently incarcerated as one of the ringleaders behind the now-infamous Shelf Monkey gang, was overcome with laughter and had to be sedated.